DRYAD-BORN

BY JEFF WHEELER

WHISPERS FROM MIRROWEN

Fireblood

Dryad-Born

Poisonwell (To Publish 2015)

LEGENDS OF MUIRWOOD

The Wretched of Muirwood

The Blight of Muirwood

The Scourge of Muirwood

LANDMOOR SERIES

Landmoor

Silverkin

DRYAD-BORN

WHISPERS FROM MIRROWEN
BOOK II

JEFF WHEELER

47N●RTH

Published by 47North, Seattle

www.apub.com

ISBN-13: 9781477849316
ISBN-10: 1477849319

Cover illustration by Magali Villeneuve
Cover design by becker&mayer! Book Producers

Library of Congress Control Number: 2013944441

Printed in the United States of America.

To Gina

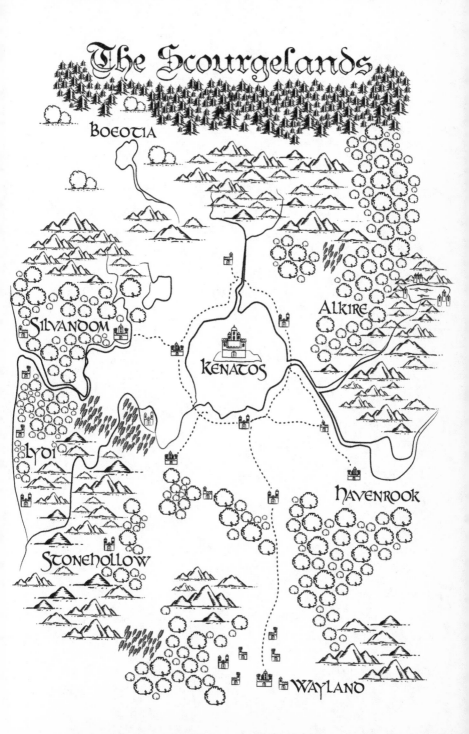

I

"Another story, Phae. Please!"

"Yes, please! Please!"

The children's eyes were so full of anticipation that Phae almost relented. She folded her arms and shook her head. "If I tell you too many, there will not be any stories left. One is enough for tonight. It was a long one. To bed . . . all of you."

And they did. The trample of little feet made her smile, and then they climbed into the beds filling the loft. There were twelve who slept there, the youngest of the orphans. Little Kriss planted a wet kiss on her cheek before wriggling up the edge of the bed, too proud to ask for help. Phae rubbed her arms and stood, watching them poke and jab at each other as they fussed to get comfortable. It would take a while before they completely settled down, but they would eventually. She retreated to the ladder, waving goodnight to little Owen who smiled shyly at her and waved back.

Phae stepped down the ladder swiftly, giving a last smile before clearing the final rung. There was Brielle, curled up beneath the ladder with a book, half-hidden in the shadows.

"To bed, Brielle," Phae said.

The little girl never spoke. Her big eyes found Phae's and she nodded, folding the book shut and clutching it tightly.

"Can you read?" Phae asked her.

Brielle shook her head no. She had never spoken. Not once since she had come to live at the vineyard. She was seven or eight years old. No one knew anything about her except that someone had brought her to the Winemillers to care for. But then again, Phae thought wryly, most of the orphans had ended up here that way.

Clinging to the book, Brielle navigated the ladder and disappeared into the loft.

Children younger than ten stayed in the loft. The older ones shared rooms on the main floor, small cupboard-like rooms, each with a small bed and little else. Phae crossed the hall toward the kitchen, she heard Dame Winemiller's voice as she sat gabbing with others. She was a talkative woman and rarely let you pass without engaging in a lengthy conversation.

Phae tried to slip by unnoticed, but when Rachael waved to her, it gave her away.

"Phae! Are the children down yet? Good, you are so patient with them. Just the other day, I thought little Owen was going to burn his fingers on the stove as he tried snitching some honey cakes. I think we should name him Owen Carnotha. He is always snitching treats."

Phae stared at Dame Winemiller a moment, gazing into her eyes. She had her attention fully, eyes locked together. Phae blinked, snatching Dame Winemiller's memory of seeing her in the kitchen. Before another word could be spoken, Phae slipped away from the kitchen and left through the rear doors of the main house, clutching the memory like a fragile leaf in her mind. She let it drift away into the twilight.

Phae possessed a strange gift. She could make people forget.

It was a form of magic, she believed, some innate ability that no one had ever explained to her. It had happened randomly at first, but eventually she caught on to the pattern and began to understand it. The first time she remembered doing it was when she was a child, perhaps five. They were playing the seeking game and she had hidden herself in a large empty wine barrel. An older boy had found her and was about to call out her name. She remembered how desperately she had wanted to remain hidden, to not let her part in the game end. She had been staring up at him, crouched in the barrel, willing him not to see her. As soon as their eyes met, a strange look came over his face. She wished he would forget he had seen her. She had blinked at him. And then he walked away. When she had asked him why he hadn't revealed her, he scolded her for telling stories.

The gift made her special. She realized that.

When there were difficult chores to be done, she could make herself escape notice. She did that for several years, actually, until she realized that by stealing memories, she was becoming invisible to the family. No one called her for supper. Her room was given over to others. It frightened her how subtly it developed. The gift transformed into a curse. When she was twelve, she stopped using her power for a full year and things began to change and all for the better. She used it occasionally now, and only for trifling things, like escaping an unwanted conversation when she'd rather use her free time to roam outside. She wanted to be remembered, and more importantly, loved.

The air smelled like summer and she savored it. She was sixteen, full of life and energy and happier than an orphan should be. She could not imagine a better place to live than the Winemiller vineyard. As she walked away from the main house, staring back at the glow coming from lamps in the windows, Phae shuddered with pleasure and tramped briskly toward the rows of grapevines. She delighted in roaming the grounds and being outside and now that her chore of putting the little ones to bed was finished, she wanted to savor the final moments of sunlight.

The sun was nearly down, but she could see well in the dusky sky. They lived in the foothills, west of Stonehollow, leagues away from the city. Their nearest neighbors were not close and she relished the privacy and the feeling of family they had. There were seventeen children in all, some teens like herself, and many younger than Brielle. The Winemillers could not have children of their own, and she considered herself fortunate to have been adopted by them.

Dame Winemiller was short and squat, quick to laugh and tease and tell a story. She was generous and fun-loving, and unfortunately rarely able to keep a conversation brief. Her husband, Master Winemiller, was taciturn and hardworking. He had a temper sometimes, which cowed everyone at the house, but he worked hard and demanded others did as well. He was strong, though not big, and he labored from sunrise to well past sunset, making sure all the chores were done to his standards and threatening dawdlers with a hand gesture that promised a thrashing, regardless of their age.

Phae tousled the grape leaves as she roamed the vineyard, enjoying the give of the sandy earth beneath her work boots and relishing the thought of another fall harvest when the grapes were finished and it was time to make wine. She loved climbing into the vats and pressing the grapes by foot. The small children relished doing that too.

She loved her life. The Winemillers had taught her how to run a homestead, how to make wine, how to bake and sew, how to chop wood and sharpen an axe, how to swim in ice-cold water and dry fruit into raisins. Summer was fun, but her favorite time of year was the fall. Harvest was amazing. And then there was the fortnight when Master Winemiller and the oldest boys took the wagons into Stonehollow and sold the barrels to Preachán traders bound for Havenrook and the auctions. Without his strict hand, it was the most carefree time of the year. Phae longed for it.

There was someone coming up the road.

In the dusk, it was difficult to see. Rarely did a traveler arrive at the end of a day without intending to stay the night. She slowed her walk, continuing to glide through the green leaves. Buds of grapes were just starting to arrive on the stems. They would probably start culling soon. She stared at the approaching figure, feeling a prick of apprehension. There was something familiar about the gait.

"Trasen!" she yelled, breaking into a run.

She had not expected to see him, and when he waved to acknowledge her shout, she ran even faster until she was breathless. He had left the homestead a year before to train to be a Finder. His visits were typically short, but she looked forward to them most of all. They were close in age, closer even more in spirit, and she was more than thrilled to see him.

He met her halfway and scooped her up into a big hug. He was not tall—in fact, he was a little shorter than her, a fact she knew irked him. He had curly black hair and a narrow face, but he had the stamina of a thoroughbred and could outrun her, outdistance her, or outwrestle her any day.

"Look at you," he said with a grin, pushing her back. "You are still growing? This isn't fair, Phae. Where's the axe? I should chop off your feet to even it out again."

"What are you doing here, Trasen?" she said, nearly gasping with surprise. "Where is your master? Is Holt coming too?" She looked over his shoulder, but there was no one else coming up the road.

"He gave me a fortnight leave and so I thought I would come home. I could stay in Stonehollow a few days, but the inns are expensive and . . ."

"And you thought you'd save your ducats by staying here?" She linked arms with him and they both started back to the house together. She brushed hair from her eyes.

Trasen beamed and started a strong stride back to the house. "I miss everyone, of course. I tell you though, Phae, there are so many stories. So much is happening in the world."

She squeezed his arm. "The Plague?"

"Rumor says it has already struck the east. Havenrook. The road is blocked. I even heard that someone set fire to the woods to prevent cargo from coming or going."

"Really!"

"I know. It is difficult to believe. So many rumors. But if there is a Plague, we will all be safe because of you." He tousled her red hair and she elbowed him in the ribs. She was the only child in the vineyard who possessed the fireblood. The family knew and had trained her how to keep it under control. Because of it, she was never allowed to go to Stonehollow, where they persecuted those with it.

"What else!" she begged. "I am running out of stories and you know how the children get. What else have you heard?"

He pursed his lips. They were approaching the house quickly. "Trouble in Kenatos as well. One of their conjurers went mad. You know—I can never remember what they are called. Paracletes or something? I heard one betrayed the Arch-Rike. In punishment, he ordered their towers demolished. They are selling bricks from the towers in Stonehollow. Several mason families have been commissioned already to reconstruct it. It's caused quite a stir."

Phae nodded hungrily. "What a story. The Paracelsus Towers. Really? What else?"

"The Queen of Wayland is having an affair with one of the dukes."

"Rumor, Trasen. An old one too. What else?"

"Boeotia is at war with Silvandom."

She grinned. "Those people are always fighting. I am glad we live here in the mountains. No army would ever want to invade us. It's not like you could steal the stone anyway."

"Not to forget that the roads to enter Stonehollow were carved through enormous boulders. You have never left the valley, Phae, but the tunnels through the rock are narrow and long." He used his arms to gesture the size. "It would require very few men to hold off an army. There is no way to pass those stony hills except through the road."

"Enough of tunnels and rumors and armies. Tell me how you are doing, Trasen. How goes your training? Is Holt as harsh as Master Winemiller? Does he work you hard?"

Trasen smiled ruefully. "No man works as hard as Winemiller. Not even the stonemasons. I think Holt was surprised that I already knew how to cook, make rope, and repair a bow. I enjoy the work, Phae. Truly, I do. I'm quite good at it."

She gave him a probing look. They shared each other's heart. He was eighteen, and they had been friends for most of their lives, and she knew by the sound in his voice that there was something he hadn't told her yet.

"What is it?" he asked her, seeing her probing look.

"You are hiding something. Out with it." She gave him a coaxing smile.

"I don't know how you do that," Trasen muttered, his forehead wrinkling, his mouth pursed with unease. "I feel as if all of my secrets are laid bare."

"Are there secrets between us?" she reminded him, glancing ahead. "We are almost to the house. Tell me now before I wrestle you to the ground and force you." She knew all of his vulnerable spots too, especially the ticklish ones.

He hugged her with one arm, giving her a smile that faded into a frown. "You did not ask why I have a fortnight leave. Holt enlisted us to join the Wayland army. There is talk of a new treaty.

I do not know much about it, but I've heard there may be some problems with the trade routes. The King of Wayland is paying handsomely for able men to protect and warn. They say skill with a bow is worth something."

She stopped, her heart lurching with dread. "Is it dangerous? I thought the Romani govern the trade routes?"

"They still do. But there are rumors that if Havenrook has the Plague, someone else will need to guard the shipments. I can earn more in one year than what a mason can earn in three. It's good money."

"Your life is worth more than ducats," Phae reminded him in a serious tone.

He nudged her playfully. "I'm not afraid of hard work. And I will not be protecting a caravan all alone. If you send enough men, no one will want to attack it. Holt taught me how to fight. How to read signs in the land. I know more than just making wine now, Phae."

She was devastated but tried not to show it on her face. The thought of him being hurt was unbearable. They closed the gap to the porch steps. "Go on ahead," Phae suggested. "I have to stack a few empty barrels. They will all want to see you and hear the news. Go."

He looked at her expression, and she knew they would be talking about it later. She gave him a little shove to move him along and stood in the shadows off the porch, hugging herself for warmth from the sudden chill of the night air. She had a bad feeling about his new job. It disturbed her. The thought of losing him in a war—she did not even want to think about it.

Phae walked to the barns where the new barrels had been unloaded earlier that week. The barn door was open and she strolled in, seeing the stacked barrels just inside. The job was already done, and Winemiller had probably done it. She smiled fondly. The barrels were made of oak, imported from the north and constructed by Winemiller's brother-in-law in Stonehollow. Uncle Carlsruhe was a carpenter and gifted at making sturdy barrels. The smell of oak was one of her favorite scents. She ran her hands across the rounded slats, enjoying the feel of the grain against her palms. It was in the barn where she had hid in just such a barrel and first used her magic. Being there reminded her of it.

Slowly, she walked down the row of barrels, feeling each one, pausing to approach one, now and then, and to smell it. The smell of oak flavored the wine. It was a family secret.

A body detached from the shadows in front of her. Her first thought was that Master Winemiller was finishing his day late and starting to come back to the house. She nearly thanked him for stacking the barrels. She hesitated, realizing it was not his shape. It was no one from the orphanage at all.

Terror froze her in place.

"I have traveled to every kingdom within these lands. I have seen the Vaettir of Silvandom fly amidst their tall trees. I have visited the forges of the Cruithne and witnessed their experiments with chemicals and gemcraft. I abhorred my visit to Havenrook and the gambling Preachán who risk everything on a shake of the dice. I have supped with the King of Wayland and his many dukes and thought how the Aeduan race multiplies faster than the others. But I encountered no hospitality whatsoever in Stonehollow. They are a suspicious bunch and keep to themselves. I hardly learned anything during my first visit. With those in Stonehollow, you must earn their trust before you earn their hospitality."

—Possidius Adeodat, Archivist of Kenatos

11

I startled you," the man said in a firm voice and with an accent she did not recognize. As he stepped away from the shadows, Phae saw the black tunic and white collar marking him as a Rike of Seithrall. There were no Rikes in Stonehollow. His very presence startled her. She wanted to flee, but her muscles wouldn't move.

As the light from the nearest window exposed his face, her shock increased. Not only was he a Rike, he was also Vaettir-born, meaning he had to be from Kenatos. He had dusky skin with slightly slanted eyes. A healthy crop of hair covered his head, though not long. His face was earnest and serious, his expression slightly disapproving. Was she required to kneel in front of him? How was she supposed to know what customs were proper in Kenatos?

She barely found her voice. "I . . . I must go," she whispered, edging away from him.

"No," he said, holding up a warning hand. He studied her shrewdly. "Yes, it is you. Even the hair marks you. Child, you are in grave danger. The Arch-Rike of Kenatos is hunting you. I found you first and must lead you to safety. There will be Finders set loose to track you down. He may even send someone to kill you. The Quiet Kishion. You must pack your things and go with me to a safe haven. Take me to Master Winemiller. I will explain this all to him."

If his presence had not already terrified her out of her wits, the warning nearly turned her legs to water. Her stomach did a spasm of dread and she took a distancing step backward, ready to flee. Who was this man, and what sort of greeting was this?

"Are you not a servant of the Arch-Rike yourself?" She backed away from him but he followed her, his face vanishing in the shadows. Her power would not work with him in darkness. They needed to be able to lock eyes for her magic to work.

"I am Prince Aransetis of Silvandom," he said, his voice growing more dreadful. "I was sent here on an urgent matter to save your life. To protect you from harm. What is your name, child?"

She was dumbfounded. "You came all this way, and you do not even know my name?" Distrust swelled inside her.

She glanced at the opening of the barn, trying to judge if there was enough room to sprint for it. Anger began to replace the fear, and her fingers started to tingle with pricks of heat. She was not totally defenseless, but she had never summoned the flames to harm anyone before. She was not certain she could do that.

"You do not understand the danger," he said, reaching out and grasping her wrist, preventing her from bolting.

She struggled against his grip, but it was like iron.

"*Pyricanthas. Sericanthas. Thas*," he said out loud. They were Vaettir words, words she had been taught as a child to control her anger and the fireblood. He put his other hand on her shoulder. "I know what you are. I know who you are. Your father sent me to find you. What we do not know is the name the Winemillers gave you. That was done deliberately to protect you. Your name, child."

He was outmaneuvering her in every possible way. His approach was deliberate. He had purposefully sought to meet her alone.

Everything he did was in reaction to her, anticipating what she would do next. She wondered if she should surprise him, stomp on his foot or something. His grip was hard, but not painful.

"My name is Phae," she answered, not knowing that she had a choice.

He seemed to breathe it in. He was quiet for a moment. "You may call me Aran. I would like you to go back inside the house. Tell Master Winemiller to meet me here in the barn. I will explain to him the danger that will befall this place when the Arch-Rike discovers it. While he and I speak, you must prepare for a journey. We will travel far, to the woods of Silvandom."

"I won't go with you," she answered firmly. "This is my home, this is . . ."

His voice hardened. "For your own protection and the protection of this family, you must come with me. Now do as I say. Send Master Winemiller to speak to me. Pack your things. We leave by moonlight."

He released her suddenly and she nearly fell over. Phae chafed her arm and hurried away from him. As soon as she was free from the barn, she sprinted to the main house and slammed and locked the door behind her. She was shaking violently with fear and unspent anger. Her heart raced, making her dizzy.

Rachael saw her from the kitchen and her eyes crinkled with worry. They shared a room together and had become friends. "Phae?"

The commotion in the kitchen surrounding Trasen's return quieted. All of the older children were there, the teens such as herself, gathered around to hear Trasen's stories from his wanderings with Holt.

Dame Winemiller looked concerned. "She's pale. Are you sick, Phae? Come into the light."

Trasen sat on the edge of the table, the center of attention, and he quickly leaned off and approached her, his eyes suddenly serious. "Phae?"

The door handle jiggled and then a heavy fist began pounding against the door. Phae stifled an involuntary scream, her eyes burning with tears.

The pounding increased and Phae backed away from the door, staring at it in horror, as if a legion of soldiers were battering it down. Trasen opened the handle and Master Winemiller entered with a scowl of annoyance for being locked out of his home.

"Will someone tell me what is going on?" he said, gazing from Phae to Trasen to his wife, completely bewildered at everything happening at the moment.

She struggled to control her feelings, but seeing him brought a semblance of sanity back into her mind. Master Winemiller could fix anything. He was not an educated man, not like the Archivists of Kenatos, but he knew the ways of the world and he was wise and fair. He was very slow to trust anyone.

Phae pulled Trasen with her and dropped her voice low so that only the two men could hear. "There is a man in the barn. A stranger."

Winemiller scowled. His wrinkled forehead furrowed even more. His skin was so weathered by the sun, he almost seemed he could be part-Vaettir. There was a liberal amount of gray in his goatee and hair. "A stranger?"

She nodded, out of breath from the shifting emotions. She felt like shaking her hands, but she was afraid fire might start gushing from her fingertips if she did. "He's a Vaettir lord, but he's dressed like the Rikes of Seithrall. He said his name is Aransetis. That the Arch-Rike wants me dead. He said many things. I'm frightened."

Dame Winemiller's voice came from the kitchen. "What is happening? Is she sick? I can bring a towel. What is wrong with Phae?"

Phae gazed at her adopted father's eyes. He did not look surprised. In fact, he looked as if part of him had always been expecting news of this kind. He patted her shoulder. "He is in the barn?"

Phae nodded. "He bid me find you. He wants to speak with you."

Master Winemiller nodded as well and turned back to the half-open door, but Phae caught his sleeve. "I don't want to go," she pleaded. "Don't make me leave. I . . . I . . ."

Winemiller rested his hand on her shoulder. His eyes were smoldering with buried fury. "You will not go anywhere, Phae. You will not do anything until I come back." He looked at Trasen. "Bolt the door while I am gone. Stay with her."

The mood in the house was somber. The older children thronged the kitchen table, around Dame Winemiller, who was surprised and shocked to learn a stranger had come to the vineyard and no one had bothered to tell her. When she learned it was about Phae, she frowned and shook her head, stroking Phae's hand repeatedly and trying to assure her that all would be well. The words were said with a tremor in her voice that belied the assurance she was trying to bestow.

Phae rose from the table and paced the kitchen, clutching her stomach, looking at every face as if it might be her last chance. There were so many memories imbued in the home. She saw all the cobwebs in the nooks and the crumbs scattered beneath the table as well as the good times, the laughter, and the teasing. Trasen beckoned her over to the hearth. She joined him gratefully.

"Sit a moment," he said, offering her a seat on the stone next to him. His eyes never strayed for long from the front door. He had been watching it like a cat since Winemiller had left.

She eased down, feeling her emotions close to the surface. She hated it when her feelings ran away with her. She was always the one that others came and confided in, always able to soothe a hurt or mend rifts between the children.

"I wasn't expecting my fortnight leave to be so interesting," he said in a conspiratorial voice. "Guarding caravans of peaches will seem downright boring compared with this."

She tried to smile, but her mouth felt all wrong.

"How did the last harvest go?" he prodded, trying again to distract her.

"I know what you are doing," she said, trying not to whine. "Let's go back to our first conversation." She gave him a level look. "I don't like the thought of you being a soldier, Trasen. The Romani are dangerous."

"So are the Wayland Outriders," he countered. "I'm not going as a soldier. Finders are paid much better."

"Why are you so suddenly interested in earning ducats?" she asked, butting his knee with hers. "Is there a fancy bow you are craving? A new blade?"

He smiled wanly, looking down at the floor suddenly. "It takes ducats to start a homestead, Phae. Of course, there are all those abandoned ones in Wayland from the last Plague. But I've heard they are haunted."

"You would go to Wayland to start a homestead? Why not here?"

"Is this where you want to spend the rest of your life, Phae?"

"Not in the city. But yes, I love this country. I thought you did too."

He nodded. There was something in his eyes again. Something he wasn't telling her.

"Why do ducats mean so much to you now, Trasen?" she pushed again, unrelenting. "If anything were to happen to you . . ."

His eyebrow twitched up, waiting for her to finish.

She did not. There was a knock on the door and Trasen was on his feet. The others deferred to him, since he was the oldest and he opened the door cautiously, hand resting on his dagger hilt.

Winemiller entered, followed by the Vaettir prince. Phae's heart fell to the bottom of her boots. The other children hushed at once, and even Dame Winemiller stopped her chatter when he appeared.

"Children, we have a guest tonight," Winemiller said. Phae stared at his face in suspense, wondering what he would say. "This is Prince Aran of Silvandom. He will be spending the night with us. Devin and Tate—you will give up your room tonight and sleep in the kitchen. The Prince needs some privacy and he refused to take our room. All right, boys? Good. Everyone needs to go to bed. We have extra chores in the morning. Go on, now. No stories. You can hear more from Trasen in the morning. Sorry, lad, but you will sleep in the barn tonight. We don't have any extra beds at the moment."

Trasen waved it away. He was used to sleeping out of doors.

Phae bit her lip, meeting the Prince's eyes as he looked at her, almost scowling. His expression was grave and disapproving. He bowed thankfully and declined Dame Winemiller's offer of wine to drink. He stood aloof as the children began crossing paths, unused to heading to bed so early.

Winemiller approached Phae at the hearth and Trasen joined him.

"I must leave?" Phae asked, devastated.

He nodded brusquely. His voice was low, almost a whisper. "But not as this man wishes. I do not know who he is. I do not trust him. I am not letting you leave with him tonight."

Her heart surged with joy.

"He says he knows your father, claiming he is a Paracelsus at Kenatos who is out of favor with the Arch-Rike. Some bad debt, probably. You never know with these things. He told me quite a tale. I don't know how much of it is true." He glanced back at the Vaettir a moment, saw the man in conversation with his wife. Winemiller half-smiled and dropped his voice even lower. "Mother will keep him distracted a while. You have a necklace, Phae. Made with a blue stone. The one that was left in the basket with you."

She reached for it around her throat, but a subtle jerk from his head made her stop. "No, he can see you from there. When you go to bed tonight, leave it under your pillow. Apparently, that is how he found you. Then I want you to crawl out your window and go straight to the barn. Trasen, take Phae to the cabin in the mountains. Also take some bows, a few braces of arrows, knives, and short axes. Rope. It's always good to have enough rope. A change of clothes too, but travel light. If you leave tonight, you might get there by nightfall tomorrow."

Phae had not even thought of that. She wanted to hug and kiss him, but knew that it would attract the Prince's attention. She needed to look forlorn and rejected. She put on her best pout.

Trasen folded his arms, nodding warily. "Will you send word for us?"

"I will come myself," he promised. "If what Prince Aran told me tonight is true, the whole family is in danger. We might all need to go live in the cabin for a while. But it gives me some time to verify what I can from his story. I don't care how many people the Arch-Rike can pay. This is Stonehollow. Our neighbors mind their own business. We won't be as easy to find as Aran thinks."

"Thank you," Phae mouthed to him. She gave Trasen a hopeful look.

"No one threatens my family," Winemiller said angrily. "We look after our own. We always have. We always will. You are a Winemiller, Phae."

The other children had slipped away to their rooms. Dame Winemiller was still engaging Prince Aran in conversation, prattling on with her wealth of stories. Phae slipped past them into the corridor, looking downcast but secretly eager. She passed the ladder leading up to the loft and debated within herself if she should climb it one last time and peek in on the little ones. She chose not to, but opened the door and found Rachael nearly ready for bed.

When she started pulling together another shirt and pants and stuffed them into a pack, she heard Rachael gasp. "You're leaving, aren't you?"

Phae nodded and then the two orphans hugged each other fiercely. Rachael kissed her cheek. "I don't like sleeping alone. What will I do without you?"

Phae smiled. "Will you do my chores for me? Until I get back? The little ones need stories. Can you do that for me?"

Rachael nodded, wiping a tear from her eye. "Are you leaving soon?"

She sighed, nodding silently, and continued stuffing clothes in the pack. Fetching her cloak from a peg on the wall, she fastened it around her neck. The action reminded her of what she needed to do. Around her neck, she wore a simple chain necklace with a blue stone set in a gold band. The stone was light blue with a white cat's-eye streak in it. Dame Winemiller had said she had been delivered to them with the necklace, that it was the only thing she had arrived in, save a blanket. There was no name and so the family had chosen one for her. Phae.

Phae unclasped the necklace and stared at the curious thing. She was reluctant to leave it behind. It was the only physical part of her past that was left as the blanket and the basket had fallen apart years before. It was heartbreaking to part with it.

Phae knelt by the bedside and rumpled the covers. She slipped the necklace underneath her pillow. Then, rising, she hugged Rachael one last time and unbolted the window. With a hard push, it opened outward on the hinges. The sky was black, dotted with shimmering stars. The smell wafting in was the one she had smelled earlier coming from the vineyard. Planting her boot on the edge of the bed rail, she gracefully climbed up and swung herself out the window. She dropped to the ground outside with only a little puff of dirt. Rachael handed her the pack and shut the window behind. Pressing her face against the glass, she waved goodbye.

Fear and anguish were Phae's companions. She did not want to leave the homestead. But the cabin was not so very far. Perhaps this would all be nothing. Perhaps the danger wasn't real.

Perhaps it was.

Head down, Phae walked to the barn. She was so grateful that Trasen was going with her. It would make everything so much easier. What an adventure they would have together. Hopefully, by the time his fortnight of leave was over, it would all be resolved.

Trasen saw her approach and met her from the shadows of the barn. He was equipped with the items Winemiller had suggested and handed her another bow to carry. She saw the dagger in his belt.

She bit her lip, glancing back at the house. "Can I borrow your knife?" she asked.

He looked at her curiously. "Why?"

Her heart was suddenly very heavy. "You said there were rumors the Plague was coming. If it is, I want to do what I can for the family. I'd like to leave a little blood on the lintel. Just in case."

He stared at her for a long time, weighing her words. In other parts of Stonehollow, a girl like Phae would have been publicly executed at the outbreak of another Plague. Her blood was the property of all and it was no crime to kill someone with the fire-blood. She had no idea why that was, but it was commonly believed that their blood, spread on the lintel, protected a household from the Plague.

Trasen nodded and handed the knife to her.

"A great poet from ancient times put it this way:

Love is the beauty of the soul."

—Possidius Adeodat, Archivist of Kenatos

III

It was a small cabin, pockmarked from woodpecker drill-
ing and dusty from lack of use. The sun was just beginning to set behind the massive range of mountains,
causing a shadow to fall over the dwelling hidden in a copse
of evergreens. There was always snow in the winter, and so
the cabin had a steeply slanted roof to prevent too much from
accumulating. Phae and Trasen were both exhausted from the
arduous hike into the mountains and since neither had slept
the night before, they reached the door grim-faced and weary.

Trasen hefted a short axe and motioned for her to stay back.
"I'll go on ahead. Wait here."

The windows were covered in dust and the curtains drawn.
He opened the door—there was no lock—and warily pushed it. A
lizard scuttled out near his boot, and a plume of dust came as well.
He paused in the doorway, listening intently, letting the fading light
from outside reveal the small interior. Trasen gave her a warning
look and then ventured inside.

A few moments later, he returned and beckoned to her.

The cabin was deserted. Winemiller stocked no provisions

because of the bears that roamed the mountains. They had to eat what they brought. The meal was silent, for both were exhausted, and then Trasen used some wooden wedges to seal the door shut.

"No fire tonight," he said. "Even though someone can't see the smoke, they can smell it. I'm so tired I can barely stand. But I will keep first watch tonight and wake you later." He yawned.

Phae nodded greedily, thanking him with a grateful smile, and then nestled in a blanket on the floor on the far side of the room.

"Trasen?"

"Yes, Phae."

"Why do you want to buy a homestead in Wayland?" She stared at him, her eyes growing heavy.

"I would be content to get one in Stonehollow. With all the abandoned ones, you would think the Council would give them away."

Phae smiled. She admired Trasen for his work ethic, his sense of humor, and his friendship. He was growing up, though. The responsibilities of being an adult were starting to weigh on him.

She lifted her head and rested her cheek on her palm. "Have you ever thought about coming back to the vineyard? You could work there. Perhaps Master Winemiller would give you part of the land someday."

Trasen lowered himself sluggishly and leaned back against the door. "I want my own place. My own family."

"Are you going to collect orphans too? You need help running a homestead, Trasen. One person cannot do all the work alone."

"I know." He looked down at his boots and then used his dagger to pry loose a pebble. "Maybe you could help me." He glanced at her.

A warm feeling shivered in her skin. She blinked at him, trying to stay awake. What did he mean by that? The thought was delicious. Working side by side with him. Having their own homestead. Being with him day after day. It sounded wonderful. Did he mean something more, though? Did he look at her as more than a friend or a sister?

"Look at you," he chuckled. "You can hardly keep your eyes open. Don't answer me tonight, Phae. Just think about it. Get some sleep."

When her head rested on her forearm, she fell asleep instantly.

The sound of jackdaws awoke her in the morning, just before sunrise. Grayish light filtered through the dusty windows. She heard the birds flittering along the roofline and slowly shook her head. She sat up and saw Trasen leaning against the front door, his jaw slightly open, deeply asleep. Part of her wanted to laugh at the expression on his face, but her stomach was raw with hunger and her feelings were all tangled with anxiety. There was little to laugh at in their circumstance, fleeing from the homestead and hunted by the Arch-Rike of Kenatos. But Trasen's presence did make her feel safe—even though he had fallen asleep himself and forgotten to wake her.

Rising quietly, she rubbed her arms for warmth and went to the window facing the slope of the hill they had ascended when climbing the mountain. She parted the curtain and rubbed a small square panel in the corner with the back of her fist to clear the glass.

Dawn was just beginning to peek through the tangle of bristlecone pine and cedar. She waited patiently, watching the horizon light up. It was a clear view to the foothills below. There was a speck on the horizon, a blot of black against the pale long grass mingled with boulders. Her heart started to pound feverishly. The blot was moving.

"Trasen," she whispered, staring in shock. "Trasen!"

He was awake instantly, cursing himself for falling asleep. He rubbed his hand over his face and scratched the curly tangle of hair on his head. "I'm sorry."

"Look!" She pointed, her mouth suddenly dry.

Trasen rushed to the window and squinted into the dawn. His countenance fell. "So quickly? That must be Winemiller."

"If he's come already, it must be worse than he thought." She rubbed her hands together, a growing dread in her heart.

Trasen kicked the wedges away from the door and opened it, welcoming the morning air with its chill. Puffs of mist came from their mouths as they emerged on the porch. Squirrels chased one another into the trees nearby, chattering at each other playfully.

The person was still a ways off and it took time to draw near. Phae studied the shape, watching the relentless way he walked. It gnawed at her suddenly. She had expected Winemiller to go to Stonehollow first and learn what he could. That would have taken time to go there and return before venturing west into the mountains. Two days. That trip should have taken two days. How could he have come so soon?

Trasen shielded his eyes from the rising sun. "It's difficult to see him," he said.

A pang of nervousness slid inside of Phae. A butterfly danced on the morning air, coming in front of her. Strange to see such a creature so early in the morning. The feeling of dread intensified.

"Something doesn't feel right," Phae murmured.

Trasen nodded. "I agree. It feels wrong. Grab your things."

Phae went inside and collected her blanket and gear. She saw Trasen stringing his bow and did the same herself. She tested the pull and then put an axe in a hoop on her belt. After securing her pack, she joined him on the porch.

Trasen shook his head and muttered softly to himself. "Doesn't have Winemiller's gait. I don't know how the Vaettir did it, but I think he followed us. Let's go into the woods a bit where we can watch the house. Might have to put an arrow in his leg to slow him down. I hope not, though, if he's a prince. Come."

They shut the door firmly and fled into the trees surrounding the small cabin, moving to higher ground. Many giant boulders had tumbled down the mountainside and finally crashed through enough trees to slow down and stop. The boulders were oddly shaped and varied in size. They were interspersed with a variety of trees—mostly stunted bur oak and bristlecone.

Trasen pointed to a cluster of granite boulders and motioned her to join him where they could observe the cabin and remain hidden.

The smaller stones allowed footholds to mount the rest and soon the two sat amidst the stones, above the ground and with a clear vantage. The stone was freezing against her palms and Phae started shivering. The feeling of dread that had eased somewhat as they walked intensified again. She was not prone to irrational bursts of emotions, but the fear and dread she experienced was quite real. She leaned close to Trasen, trying to share his warmth a little and hoping it would calm her.

It didn't.

Phae watched the stranger approach the cabin, a man with a hood and cloak. He was dressed in browns and grays, a woodsman's garb and not the black vestments the Vaettir had worn. This man was not a Rike of Seithrall. Looking at him caused a shiver to go down her back. He approached the cabin straightaway and tugged at the door, not bothering to conceal his approach.

Trasen shook his head worriedly. "Looks like a Finder," he muttered.

Phae knew somehow he was wrong. She knew it by instinct. Every part of her body warned her to flee that man. "I don't think so."

He nodded with certainty. "They wear garb like that. Strange that he doesn't have a bow. Lucky for us. Wait, he's come out already."

As soon as she saw him, Phae's stomach turned to jelly. She began shaking uncontrollably.

"Cold?" he ventured, then looked at her face. "What's wrong?"

"We should go. Now."

"We've both got bows, Phae. He has none. If he follows our trail, I'll give him a fair warning. I could hit him in the leg easily before he reaches us. He's ill-equipped to be hunting us."

"I don't like it, Trasen. We should go."

"We'll be all right, Phae. It might be helpful to get some information out of him."

"No!" She clutched his arm tightly. Her breathing was short, gasping. Every part of her screamed to run.

He saw the look on her face and sobered. "Remember the trail we found years ago, leading up the mountain? Dragon Pass, we named it. There was that stump that we fancied was a dragon's skull. You go up there and I'll wait here. I'm a good shot, Phae. I can handle this."

She shook her head adamantly. "We need to go, Trasen. Now. Come on." Phae scrambled down off the rocks.

Trasen waited a moment longer, staring at the cabin. "He's coming after us. He's not even pausing to look at tracks."

"Come on!"

The two began winding their way up the mountainside. It was steep, the trail overgrown with thick green vegetation and mossy boulders. The trees were thicker now, crowding together to block the vision of their pursuer. Phae's heart started to calm once they began moving again. She felt slightly better, though still panic-stricken. The path ran up and back, winding sinuously along the steep edge. Sweat came easily now and she was no longer chilled by the morning air. Phae had assumed they would have several days together before Winemiller showed up. Something was terribly wrong.

The trees whipped by as they hurried up the hillside. It rounded and leveled off slightly, exposing a small grove of trees. She recognized the place immediately as it was always a favorite haunt during the family trips to the cabin. She could not recall which of them had discovered it first, but part of her was comforted when she saw the large misshapen tree stump, whose gnarled roots were shaped like a dragon's head.

They paused there, resting a bit, trying to catch their breath.

Trasen's neck was gleaming with sweat. He bent over, huffing, and stared back down the trail.

Phae began pacing. The feelings were coming back again, stronger than ever. Every moment resting was a danger. "We can't stay here."

"You're right," he said, staring. "I hear him."

Phae jerked around and then she too heard the trod of boots coming up the trail after them. A moment later, the figure appeared around the bend, cloaked, veiled, and relentless.

Fear nearly made her scream.

"Go," Trasen said, dropping to one knee next to the stump. He turned the quiver over and spilled the shafts on the ground next to him. In a fluid motion, he fit one to the string and raised the bow. "I will find you. Just start running. Change directions often. Try to throw him off. Cross water when you can. Go!"

"I can't leave you . . ."

"Don't be a fool," he said. "He's after you, not me. Now, go!"

Phae's conflicted feelings made her nearly refuse. But the presence of the stranger struck terror in her soul. She kissed Trasen's hair and then rushed away from the grove and plunged into the woods.

Moments later, she heard the bow twang and a shaft thud into a tree, then Trasen's voice. "That was a warning, friend. Keep following us, and the next one won't miss."

Her legs burned with the effort. Her chest heaved for air. There was another thrum from Trasen's bowstring.

The sound of the arrow thumped as it struck something solid. Not a tree.

"I got him," Trasen shouted. "He's down."

Part of her feelings surged with relief, but the black cloud of fear had not left her. She noticed several insects buzzing around her. Birds were chirping at her as well. It felt as if the entire forest was alive and heckling her to run.

"You got him?" she called back, stopping. Instead of relief, she still felt intense worry.

"I was aiming for his leg, but I hit him in the chest. He walked right into it. Collapsed. I'm going to search the body."

Phae stopped, leaning back against a tree, trying to calm her heart but unable to. The conflict inside her raged on. She could not leave Trasen behind. He was her best friend. She should not have doubted his aim. Yet why did she feel such irrational terror? Why were her feelings screaming at her that the danger had not passed? She pushed away from the tree, head spinning with confusion. She started back down the trail to him.

She watched Trasen approach the body, another arrow nocked and ready. He was being careful. His boots were nearly soundless despite the brush and needles carpeting the area. Their pursuer was crumpled nearby. Where was the arrow? She could not see the arrow sticking out of him. At that close range, the tip should have been poking out his back.

As she was about to call out in warning, Trasen reached the body.

The stranger moved like a serpent striking a mouse. He was lying still for a moment and then suddenly Trasen's bow and arrow were jerked from his hands and tossed aside. The stranger was on his feet again, unharmed. It had been a trap.

"Trasen!" she screamed.

"Run!" he yelled back, yanking the short axe from his belt. He swung it expertly, defensively, driving toward the cloaked man with every intent to kill him.

Phae stared in horror.

The stranger watched the stroke of the axe, stepped inside it, and suddenly Trasen was on his back, slamming so hard the axe flew out of his hand. Before Trasen could do anything else, the stranger hauled him up and encircled his neck with his arm. The cowl raised as he looked up toward her. She could see the stranger's scarred face, the quill-tipped dark hair, and ice blue eyes. The eyes stared right up at her menacingly.

Phae looked in his eyes and tried to connect with him to steal his memories away, but she sensed he was too far away. She had never attempted doing so with someone at that distance. She blinked but nothing happened.

Trasen's eyes were panicked. He could not breathe. Then his whole body went slack.

Phae ran. She did not bother to hide her trail or attempt any trickery. She was running for her life, and she knew it. There was no mercy in those eyes. There was only determination. She was his prey. He was hunting her, not for any fault of her own that she could understand, but for some debt owed to someone else. What did it matter?

She ran, dodging trees and boulders. The trailhead split two ways and both were steep. One went higher into the mountains. She knew it would reach a ridgeline and then descend on the other side and there would be a river. A river could possibly help hide her tracks. She chose it instantly, her legs throbbing with pain as she continued up the mountainside. Tree limbs swatted at her as she clawed past them, trying to put distance between them. Was he torturing Trasen? Was he already dead? Her stomach threatened to heave with the thought. Guilt at abandoning him threatened to choke her. If he died, she would never forgive herself.

She did not dare to look back, even once. The feelings swirled inside her, bidding her to flee. She trusted the feelings. She should have trusted them earlier. Her legs strained with the pace, but she knew she would reach the summit soon, then it would be downhill to the river. That river was the farthest she had ever traveled in her life. They had camped at the river's edge on a summer's eve three years ago. Winemiller had warned them not to cross the river and enter the mountains on the other side. He said that it was dangerous on the other side. She would follow the river down the mountain then.

When she reached the summit, the sun was blazing with promise. The light blinded her momentarily and she stumbled and sagged to her knees, coughing so violently she vomited. Her legs trembled with the punishing pace. Her stomach was lurching again, and again she felt the fear. He was behind her. He was hunting her. The man with ice blue eyes. The eyes of someone without a soul.

"There are many things in this world that cannot be explained. There are an equal number of foolish theories that persist despite the evidence to the contrary. To kill a mistruth or an error is as good a service as, and sometimes even better than, the establishing of a new truth or fact."

—Possidius Adeodat, Archivist of Kenatos

IV

Phae tripped and plunged into the stream, soaking her pants and cloak. As she struggled to her feet, a branch raked her cheek. She nearly tripped again, but managed to catch herself in time. Ahead there were few boulders to hide behind.

The steepness of the brook challenged her differently and the stones and boulders were treacherous enough. It slowed her to stay in the water, and so she decided to scrabble up the other bank and enter the dense woods for concealment. The sounds of nature around her were terrifying. Blue jays flapped and squawked and even the insects formed a cacophony of sound. Moths and butterflies flitted in the sunlight all around her. She swatted at them and tried to squeeze water from her drenched cloak as she walked. She followed the sound of the brook, knowing it would bring her back to the low country.

Her stomach was twisted and worried about Trasen. She knew going back would be foolhardy, but it was agony not knowing what had happened to him. Her ears strained for the sound of her pursuer. Her legs felt swollen and aching from the punishing pace. She was grateful to Master Winemiller for all the years of hard work. A weaker girl would have collapsed.

The sun was deceptive beyond the branches of bristlecone. She did not know how much time had passed. Her stomach began raving with hunger and so she sat on a small boulder by the creek to rest and eat. Immediately the feelings of dread and worry exploded inside of her. She had to keep going. She pushed away from the boulder and ignored the hunger as best she could.

Her mind was a jumble. It took concentration to avoid the pitfalls that would twist an ankle, but the pace did give her some time to think. Somehow her father was involved in all of this. That her father was even alive was a complete revelation to her. She had assumed that he was dead, killed during the last bout of Plague because he had the fireblood. Winemiller had never even mentioned the possibility of him being alive. Why had her father sent the Vaettir prince and not come himself?

She wished now that she had gone with Prince Aran and not put Trasen's life in danger. She did not know the Prince's abilities, but he was obviously someone her father had trusted with her safety. It was the nature of those from Stonehollow to be wary of strangers. Master Winemiller had not trusted him either, but she knew he was even more wary than most. Her feelings were conflicted. If she could just make it back to the homestead, perhaps she would find them both there and determine what to do next.

A loud crack of a branch sounded behind her. She glanced over her shoulder but could not see anyone, but the sound was nearby. The feelings inside her fanned even more, driving her faster. She started to run. Her throat was parched, but she dared not scoop up some water from the creek. Her head buzzed with fatigue. There was no path through the woods and she found herself slogging through thick brush and maneuvering around twisted bristlecone somehow growing from cracks in enormous boulders.

The creek continued to snake its way down, her alongside it, until at last she reached a pond, choked with scum and moss. The water there would be undrinkable, so she knelt by the brook's edge before it spilled there and gulped down some water quickly. It made her dizzy but the water was delicious.

Stopping even that short amount of time caused a wave of panic inside her. She splashed through the pond and crossed it. If her bearings were right, she was heading back toward the valley of Stonehollow. Her leg muscles burned. Relentlessly, she continued. After crossing a small meadow, she saw that there were fewer bristlecone now and more bur oak trees offering shade and more cover. Phae left the meadow behind and entered the shady woods. It felt better. Her heart began to calm. The green of the oddly-shaped leaves was inviting, causing dappled patterns on the forest floor.

She ran her hands along the rough, ridged bark of the oak trees, noticing the strange acorns with their furry caps. Ahead, a dazzlingly big blue jay squawked at her from a branch of an enormous tree. The noise caught her attention. It was as if the bird was speaking to her. She glanced backward and felt a surge of terror. Looking back at the tree, she felt safe. Phae approached it cautiously but quickly. The trunk was huge and wide enough to conceal her entire body. She gazed up at the gnarled branches and velvety green leaves. A butterfly zoomed by her ear, fluttering its wings. It was too beautiful to swat.

She was drawn to the tree in an inexplicable way. Its very presence was a comfort and that puzzled her. Staring up at the branches, she noticed thick bunches of mistletoe crowding around some leaves. She finished circling the trunk and then gazed back at the direction she had come.

The stranger was in the grove with her.

Phae froze instantly, clutching the bark with shock. He was not staring at her but at the tree. She saw him rooted in place, an enemy. She began to shiver with dread, knowing he was too close. He had not seen her yet. Slowly, she pulled back and slid down the trunk until she sat. She tried to make herself as tiny as she could. Even her breath was barely a whisper, despite the hard journey.

Twigs snapped and crunched. He was moving closer.

One thought came to her. If she could look into his eyes, those soulless eyes, she could steal his memory of her. It had not worked before because he was too far away. She hoped that was the reason it had not worked. If she held perfectly still and waited until he found her, she could stare into his eyes and blink, just as she had as a child in the wine barrel. She was not totally sure it would work, but it was the only thing she could try, knowing that even Trasen's aim with a bow had not stopped him.

Drawing in little breaths, Phae listened to the sound of him approaching from the far side. She twisted some strands of hair away from her face and tried to calm the trembling. There were dead leaves all around the tree, creating a crackling carpet as he approached. She heard silence as he paused.

He appeared around the corner of the oak, so close she could see the scars on his face. He had a rugged look, sun-browned skin from a life out of doors, and scars across his face as if some terrible beast had clawed him savagely. Up close, he seemed a little younger than he had from afar. He stared at the tree, not down at her, his gloved fingers touching each ripple of bark. There were twin daggers sheathed in his belt. She could not believe he had not noticed her cowering in front of him. His lips pursed and he paused again, sniffing the air. He came closer, his boots nearly striking her. Phae tugged her legs against her body. Was he blind? How could he not see her?

An expression came over his face, a clouded look. He shook his head, as if he smelled something bad. Then he proceeded to circumnavigate the trunk. His boot collided with the tip of hers.

He was right over her. She stared up at his scarred face, willing him to look at her. But he did not glance down.

Phae let out a slow breath of relief when he finished his circuit of the tree and then tromped off into the woods, never looking back. She did not understand it, but she was grateful. Hugging her knees with both arms, she pressed her face against the bark and felt tears of relief well up in her eyes. Perhaps, he would not find her after all. After resting, she could retrace her way back to the cabin and see what had become of Trasen. Exhausted, she dozed, pressed against the oak.

A hand shook Phae's shoulder to wake her. She started. Kneeling by the oak tree she encountered a man with a gray beard and snowy white hair. He had a stern look on his face. She saw a Druidecht talisman hanging from his neck and a surge of relief immediately quelled the panic.

His beard was cropped and she noticed he was short. He glanced back at the woods the direction her pursuer had gone. "You are safe for now," he said in a whisper. "But your pursuer is nearby."

Phae nodded vigorously. "He may have killed my friend up on the ridge. How did you find me?"

He gave her a curt smile. "My wife led me to you. She saw you running from that man. How she called me is a Druidecht secret. But you are safe as long as you stay near this tree."

"I can't stay here," Phae said, shaking her head. "I need to go back up the mountain and search for my friend. Can you guide me?"

He shook his head angrily. "You do not understand who is chasing you. It is one of the Arch-Rike's minions. Who are you, child, and why does he hunt you?"

"I don't know you," she answered, immediately distrustful.

"I am a Druidecht, girl. You can trust me."

She said nothing.

"For pity's sake," he grumbled.

"Where is your wife?" Phae asked, looking around.

His grizzled beard quivered with frustration. "You are a troublesome girl."

"I'm not trying to be difficult. I don't understand how that man passed by me without even seeing me. It was as if he could not see me."

"Well, he couldn't!" the old man said, annoyed.

"How could that be?" Phae said desperately.

He ground his teeth. "Wonderful," he mumbled. He turned to the tree. "Well? Am I supposed to explain it to her all by myself?"

Phae suddenly had the feeling the old man might very well be insane. "You are talking to . . . the tree?"

He put his face in his hand and shook his head in frustration. "You know I don't like talking to people. Maybe *you* should tell her."

Phae swallowed. "Who should tell me? Who are you talking to?"

"To my wife," he answered. "She's here with us." He looked up at Phae. "You don't know what you are, do you?"

He was talking about her fireblood. He saw a girl with red hair. A man was hunting her in the woods. The Plague had been reported in Havenrook. The protection her blood provided would be valuable. She understood now.

"Yes," Phae said at last. "I know what I am." She slowly stood. "Not even the Druidecht intervene when we are taken. You are like the rest of them."

His eyebrows crinkled. "No, I don't think you understand. Do you know how rare you are? Who . . . who was your mother? Where is your mother? Haven't you been taught about Mirrowen? Do you know . . . ?" He ground his teeth in frustration again. "I shouldn't be the one telling her!"

Phae backed away from him slowly. "I don't have the fireblood," she lied. "Not everyone with red hair does have it. I'm Aeduan, just like you. The man hunting me thinks I have it. He'll murder me. If you are a Druidecht, then use your magic to stop him."

The Druidecht shook his head. "Druidecht magic won't help against him. Come back to the tree, girl. Now."

Phae shook her head. "No."

He turned to the tree with an expression of helplessness and aggravation. "Show her! She thinks I am crazy. Please!"

Phae was ready to run when a girl stepped around the side of the tree. She was no older than herself, young and pretty, wearing a fine gown from a dressmaker in Stonehollow. The designs on the sleeve and the ruff at the trim marked it as such. Her eyes were as green as the oak leaves. Phae stared at the old man and then at the much younger girl. The girl was barefoot and had a bracelet fashioned into the shape of a twisting serpent around one ankle.

"Hello," the girl said timidly. "This must be very strange to you. But I can sense what you are. You are not bound yet."

Phae stared down at the ground. She had felt a strange feeling of intimacy after glancing at the girl's eyes. Phae knew that the other girl could steal her memories, that they shared the same power.

"Tell her!" the old Druidecht implored. "She doesn't know!"

"This is your wife?" Phae said, still looking at the ground. Her stomach filled with revulsion. An old man and a young girl. It was disgusting.

"Well . . . yes, but you don't understand. Are you going to tell her?"

"Listen to me," said the girl. "Listen to my words if you will not look into my eyes. You must know the truth. You have great power. And there is great danger. You must listen."

Phae shook her head and backed away. "Stay away from me."

"You are Dryad-born," the girl said. "And you have the fireblood. There has never been such a combination of powers. You must stay here and learn. You must let me teach you about your heritage. I have never heard of another like you. You are powerful. And dangerous. To yourself as well as to others of our kind. You must stay and let me teach you. I can guard you from the man chasing you. You are part of Mirrowen, child. It is in your blood. If you do not choose it soon, you will forever lose your magic. Please, child. Look at me. Let me share my memories with you. Let me help you understand."

Phae did not look at her, only at the bracelet around her ankle. Why a serpent? Was there significance to the tail and how it forked? She was so confused and afraid.

"I am a Dryad?" Phae asked. She had never heard that word before. "Is that a race? What is it?"

"Look into my eyes."

"No," Phae insisted. "You can steal my memories if I look at you."

"True. But I can share mine with you as well," she answered. "I can teach you how to control the magic. You must go soon to Mirrowen, child. You must visit the garden and eat of the fruit. I need someone who can care for this tree. I need *you*, child."

Phae continued to back away. "I don't want any of that."

"He's coming!" the Druidecht warned, his eyes tracking the erratic flight of a moth nearby. "He's coming back this way!"

Phae whirled and ran, fear pounding in her heart. She heard the Druidecht calling after her. She did not care. That forest glen was a trap. The luring words were meant to harm her.

She ran as hard as she could, sprinting through the dead leaves that crackled and split as she passed over them. She ran farther, passing mammoth boulders and dwarf bristlecone. She ran hard until her legs and hips finally revolted and she collapsed in the woods, lost and sobbing.

Exhaustion robbed her completely. Her lungs burned with fire. Her chest heaved and she choked. There was no strength left. She had pushed herself too far. The forest floor seemed to pinwheel beneath her. Dizziness. Somehow, it felt as if she were flying, even though she knew she was not. Spots danced in front of her vision. Her fingers clenched around twigs and leaves.

She wept softly, hearing the crunch of boots approach from behind. Her muscles throbbed and ached. She could not move.

Phae waited, her ears ringing and legs twitching. She heard him stop nearby and waited in anguish to die. The fear, hunger, and fatigue stole away the last of her strength and she fainted.

When she revived, it was dark. The moon had just risen, bathing the world in silver light.

The scar-faced stranger sat by a boulder, staring at her.

"*In Silvandom, there is a form of magic, though they do not use that word to describe it. In that kingdom, it is called* keramat—*a Vaettir word that can be translated into our tongue as 'miracle.' They are more open in discussing their beliefs than the Druidecht are. I have come to learn that there are various powers of* keramat. *Some can heal by touch. Others are known to travel great distances in a short time. One might even say that the Vaettir's ability to float in the air is* keramat. *But the greatest gift they possess is the power to revive the dead. It is an awesome power but it comes at a dreadful cost.*"

—*Possidius Adeodat, Archivist of Kenatos*

V

Annon of Wayland was only eighteen. He stared out the smooth glass window into the sculpted gardens. He was despairing, wondering how it would ever be possible that he, a young Druidecht, would be able to outthink and outmaneuver the Arch-Rike of Kenatos. His uncle, Tyrus of Kenatos, had vanished with the man the Arch-Rike sent to kill him. Logic insisted that he consider Tyrus dead.

In a bizarre twist in his life, the man who had pretended for years to be his uncle, who had abandoned him as a baby to be raised by Druidecht, had endowed Annon with a quest to destroy the Plagues that threatened the kingdoms. It was a quest Tyrus had failed to fulfill. How could Annon be expected to succeed?

He sighed deeply, trying to contain his conflicted feelings. In the days since Tyrus's disappearance with the Kishion, his confidence had begun to wane. The task he had been given felt beyond daunting. Yet he was not alone in the struggle. He had powerful allies now. He thought about them, one by one.

Prince Aransetis was the greatest ally. He was a Vaettir prince from Silvandom. He had the wealth and connections to assist. He was like no prince that Annon could imagine. He wore the black cassock of a Rike of Seithrall in order to better understand the thinking of his enemy. Annon glanced down at his own clothing, taken from a dead Rike of Seithrall just days ago. It was a peculiar feeling, but Aransetis was wise. Just wearing the robes and the ring made him feel different. It changed, however subtly, his way of thinking. Clothing was a symbol and a powerful one.

Another ally was the Prince's cousin, a girl named Khiara Shaliah. In Silvandom she was a healer with a notable reputation. She was a meek girl, with long black hair and fine Vaettir features, sloping eyes and dark skin. There was some unspoken angst between her and her cousin. Annon felt it in the way she looked at him. It had never been spoken of, though, and Annon knew too little about customs in Silvandom to risk prying.

Then there was Erasmus. Annon glanced at the Preachán and nearly chuckled. He was the smartest man Annon had ever met, his memory and ability to calculate were freakish. He was from Havenrook, a detestable land that Annon hoped he would never need to trespass again. Erasmus looked like a common man of his race, except his eyes were not exactly aligned and it was not easy to determine what he was looking at. He also had the annoying habit of pronouncing predictions. Still, his skills would be invaluable.

Annon turned back to the window, thinking next of others who were far away. His sister Hettie, for example. He missed her already. They were twins at birth, she the firstborn. The midwife was a Romani and had stolen her. Hettie had been raised by the Romani and had been sold at the age of eight to a Finder with a single earring to mark her. Ten years had passed and it was time for her to be sold again. But an elaborate ploy had been used by the Romani to bargain her freedom for a weapon of deadly magic that Tyrus had cleverly hidden. In the end, Tyrus had offered her freedom to live in Silvandom, the only Romani to be granted that privilege. Annon did not doubt for a moment that her freedom would be contested.

His thoughts turned darkly to Kiranrao. If a black widow spider could also be a man, he would exist as Kiranrao. Both were deadly and silent. Kiranrao was a little of everything. He was Vaettir-born, like Khiara and Aransetis. But he was the secret master of Havenrook and controlled the caravans and goods transferring between kingdoms. It was said his wealth rivaled the Arch-Rike's. Years before, Tyrus had tricked him into stealing the blade Iddawc from the Arch-Rike, a deadly weapon that caged an evil spirit for a thousand years. Tyrus had finally given Kiranrao the blade in the final encounter with the Arch-Rike's minions and the man had simply vanished away with it, a gleeful look in his eye, realizing that the rest would probably die without him. Had Tyrus done it deliberately? Had he set loose a monster to distract the Arch-Rike? Or had the panic of the moment caused him to misjudge Kiranrao's motives? Annon did not know.

While Annon did not trust Kiranrao, he knew that Paedrin hated the Romani. Paedrin was an orphan from Kenatos who had been raised at the Bhikhu temple. He could fight with a staff, a piece of rope, or with his own hands and feet. Annon was more than impressed with his abilities and grateful to have someone like him as an ally. Even better, his sense of humor made him pleasant to travel with. He and Hettie had battled constantly during their travels together, and Annon secretly felt the two were growing in favor with one another, until it was revealed that Hettie had betrayed them. Annon hoped they would learn to trust each other again. They were both very stubborn, though, and he did not know whether it would even be possible.

He sighed, shaking his head slowly. What a mismatch of loyalties. How was he ever going to unite them into a common purpose? Tyrus's goal had been straightforward from the start. The land was troubled by devastating Plagues that happened every generation. Eighteen years earlier, Tyrus had led a group into the Scourgelands, which he believed contained the secrets of the Plagues' origins. The group had been massacred. Only Tyrus had survived because of the Druidecht woman who was Annon and Hettie's mother. She had explained the lore of the Dryads to him, how they could steal memories and were guarding the Scourgelands. Tyrus had also deduced that the Arch-Rike had surreptitiously foiled the expedition. From that ultimate betrayal came the seeds of his latest plan.

The secrets of the Scourgelands could only be learned by someone who was Dryad-born.

Tyrus himself had sired the one chance they had to uncover the secrets. Prince Aransetis had been sent to find the girl in Stonehollow and bring her to learn her destiny. Paedrin and Hettie were sent to uncover a weapon of power to help them survive the dangers of the Scourgelands. Kiranrao had been tasked with causing mischief with the Arch-Rike's plans. And himself? Tyrus had given Annon the most difficult challenge of all. At the conclusion, they had agreed to meet at the Dryad tree that Annon had protected from an attack by Boeotians. Annon had charged and dispatched several spirits to watch for the arrival of the others and to lead them to the Dryad tree.

He felt Nizeera nuzzle against his leg.

They are ready.

Annon glanced down at the sinuous cat, part mountain lion, part spirit creature. Her eyes were a beautiful shade of silver. Through the talisman he wore beneath his clothes, he could hear her thoughts. She had made an oath to protect him. Her claws and teeth would savage anyone who tried to harm him.

"Thank you," he murmured, stroking the fur near her ears. He walked back to the table where the dead Rike from Kenatos lay prostrate. Khiara spoke in low tones, in her tongue, to a wizened old man who had been summoned to perform the ceremony. He did not have many years left to live, but the gift they were asking of him was enormous. Part of his life would be required to revive the dead man. It had taken all of Khiara's persuasion and the Prince's reputation to secure his cooperation in the end.

Annon stared at the body. The man on the table was fair-haired with streaks of silver. Erasmus had used his great abilities of observation to conclude that he was the one most likely to know the information they needed. It was a risk though. There was a great chance he might not know anything useful.

The skin was pasty and white and he was lying as a man on a bier, hands clasped over his heart. They had not removed his black cassock or his possessions, though nearly all had been rendered useless by Tyrus during the battle. Only the black rings still worked, the infamous black rings that allowed a Rike of Seithrall to know the truth.

"Are you ready, Annon?" Erasmus asked, rubbing his mouth. He shook his head slowly. "He will not be easily deceived. He may even know he died. He will be disoriented and wary. I think you have a one in five chance of being able to convince him you are from the Rikehood."

"Is that really all the chance I have?" Annon asked wryly.

"I was feeling generous. You're a stripling. At least with the rings we've taken, we'll know if he is lying to us."

Khiara nodded to the old man, patting his shoulder affectionately, and looked over at them. She nodded that all was ready.

Erasmus retreated to the shadows of the room. He wore the black cassock as well, but his eyes were peculiar enough that he felt it unwise to be too near, lest they give him away. Annon sent Nizeera to join Erasmus in the alcove. She enjoyed tormenting Erasmus and licked his hand as if preparing to take a bite.

Annon rested his palms on the table, breathing deeply to calm himself. He was the only Waylander among the group, an Aeduan, and they all felt that provided him the best chance to deceive the Rike. The task that Tyrus had given him was to learn the location of the Arch-Rike's secret temple, the oracle of Basilides. It would be heavily guarded and possibly contain information on when the next Plague would strike.

The old man smiled at Annon and then raised a trembling hand over the dead man's chest. He began murmuring softly in the Vaettir tongue. It had a lilting quality to it, almost a melody. Annon stared at the face of the Rike. He waited, knowing that even Druidecht magic took time to manifest.

The body convulsed. It jerked once, then again, spasms rocking through it. Then slowly the chest swelled with an intake of breath. Annon glanced at the old man, who was breathing in deeply. The two bodies were in rhythm together. The old man winced and his hand trembled even more. Khiara clutched him, holding him upright as he continued the ceremony. Another deep breath. Then another. Annon watched the throat of the dead man swallow.

His eyes fluttered open.

Suddenly, he was gasping and choking, sitting up quickly, hand clutching his chest as if in great pain. Annon grabbed his shoulders.

"You made it back," Annon said. "You've been dead for two days. Another day and we'd have lost you forever."

The Rike coughed ferociously against his own forearm. He shook and trembled, his body twitching and convulsing. "I was dead," he said hoarsely. "The light. The pain. I still remember it."

"You have information the Arch-Rike needs," Annon said, swallowing his nervousness. He needed to be sure he phrased his words so that the ring would not alert the Rike of a lie. "What happened in Silvandom?"

The Rike shook his head, as if his neck muscles were suddenly twitching. "Where am I?"

"You're still in Silvandom. We arranged for a healer to revive you. How do you feel?"

"How do you think it feels to be dead?" the man snapped impatiently. "My muscles are tingling. The blood is sluggish. I'm lightheaded." He lay back down quickly. He stared up at Annon, his eyes suddenly confused. "Nausea. A bitter taste in my mouth. Are you writing this down? This is important to record for the Archives. Blasted fool. I cannot move my legs yet. Ugh, the pain of blood circulating. I have no memory of what happened after my death. I cannot recall anything about the afterworld. I probably was not there yet. Two days, you say? Interesting. Did any of the Paracelsus survive?"

"None of them," Annon answered. "All were killed."

"Even the Kishion?" the other asked doubtfully. "That cannot be." He held up his hand with the ring.

"No, of course *he* wasn't killed," Annon replied. He stared down at him. "Do you know of the place called Basilides?"

The man swung his head around sideways, staring at Annon, aghast. "How do you know of Basilides? You are no more than twenty, if that. How could you know of it?"

"I don't know exactly what it is," Annon replied carefully. "Only that it is spoken of in hushed tones. A Paracelsus told me it's an oracle."

"You dare to even speak of it?" the man said warily.

"I see," Annon said, nodding apologetically. "Then you do not know where it is. We were ordered to go there, but lack the information to carry out the request."

"Why would you be ordered to go there?" he demanded. He twisted slightly, easing himself up on his arm. His eyes began darting throughout the room, gazing at Khiara and the old Shaliah healer and then at Erasmus in the corner.

He looked at Annon suddenly, his gaze intense. "Who are you?"

"You wouldn't know my name. I'm from Wayland originally," he answered, his stomach twisting uncomfortably. He was losing the man's trust by the mere mention of Basilides. He cursed himself for asking about it so soon.

"Where did you say you were from?" he asked, his expression suddenly perplexed. His eyebrows twisted with confusion and his face grimaced as if he were experiencing great pain. He tried to lean closer to Annon.

"Are you sick?" Annon asked. "If you need to rest a moment . . ."

"Help me," he said, shaking his head. "My legs still don't work." He reached down and tried to pull his leg up a little. Annon was not sure what to do.

Then the Rike grabbed a fistful of Annon's shirt and dragged him on the table. He stumbled, losing his footing, and planted his hands on the table. A silver knife swung around and pressed against his throat.

"Your carotid artery is right here, alongside the slope of your neck. If you or any of your friends attempt anything foolish, I swear I will cut it open and you will bleed to death in moments. Your ring confirms I speak the truth. Now you will answer *my* questions, boy!"

"The very essence of instinct is that it's followed independently of reason. Sometimes it is those instincts that serve us best."

—*Possidius Adeodat, Archivist of Kenatos*

VI

The edge of the table cut into Annon's stomach. He reflexively grabbed the Rike's wrist, to pull away the dagger, but the man's strength was increasing and he felt the blade nick his throat.

"Struggle and I'll kill you," he seethed. "Now answer my questions. What is your name? Say it!"

"Annon of Wayland," he answered, his heart hammering.

"The Druidecht. Tyrus's nephew. Visited the city very recently and was foolish enough to tell the Rike at the gate who you were. Lad, I pity you. The Arch-Rike will not excuse your treason easily, but if you surrender to me . . ."

Pyricanthas. Sericanthas. Thas.

Blue flames appeared at Annon's fingertips, still clenched around the Rike's wrist. The sudden sting of scorching heat made the man start with pain and jerk his hand away, dropping the blade. He scooted away from Annon, his eyes wide with fear but his legs were still not working.

Annon struggled to control his fury. "You were dead for two days," he said in a low, threatening voice. "You were only brought back because I thought you might have useful information. Whether you live or die makes little difference to me."

The Rike stroked his burned wrist, which was bright red from the burn and blisters were already appearing on the skin. "I can be useful to you, Druidecht."

"I doubt it," Annon replied. It was a battle controlling his anger. "I seek the location of Basilides. As you just said, you are forbidden to speak of it."

"I did not say that," the man replied with a calculating grin. "What were my words? You bear the ring. I could not lie to you."

Annon's memory was perfect. He could remember every word that anyone had ever spoken to him in his life. A Dryad's kiss had unlocked his mind completely. "Clever. Few dare to even speak of it."

"You remembered. Well done. I've heard the Druidecht have good memories. I know the location of Basilides. If that knowledge will save my life, then we can discuss terms. I cannot tell you where it is—that is forbidden—but I will take you there if you spare my life."

Annon glanced at Khiara. She stared at the Rike with disgust and wariness, her hands clenching the tapered oak staff. She was ready to use it against him. Erasmus moved from the shadows, approaching.

"It costs a great deal to revive someone from the dead," the Rike said. "I can also guarantee you that no other man who came with our force has the information you seek. You chose wisely to seek me out."

Erasmus rubbed his mouth thoughtfully. "You would only give us the information we seek if it would benefit you in some way. You would benefit most from our capture. Leading us into a trap."

The Rike turned around to look at him. "Ah, Erasmus of Haven-rook. Well met. You bet foolishly throwing in your lot with Tyrus."

"Not if we succeed," he answered blandly.

"Even you cannot tally the odds of that happening," the Rike replied with disdain. "This is Prince Aransetis's manor still? I promise you, whatever resources this prince of Silvandom has, it will be paltry compared with what the Arch-Rike brings to bear against you. For my life, I will give you the information you seek. But may I attempt to persuade you to surrender yourselves to my custody? If you return with me to Kenatos, I swear to you that I'll plead your cause with the Arch-Rike personally. He may be lenient."

"How comforting," Khiara said, her expression void of compassion.

"What's your name?" Annon asked.

"I am Lukias, a Provost-Rike of Kenatos." He closed his eyes, squinting against pain, and started to move his legs. He grunted as they began to twitch and buck. "Amazing powers the Shaliah have. I have seen someone dead a few hours brought back to life through our arcane methods, but I have never . . ." He paused, overwhelmed by pain, and straightened his legs until they dangled off the table edge. "I need camphor leaves. The pain is excruciating. I see why, after three days, one cannot be revived. This knowledge would be useful to have in the city. There are no Shaliah there."

"Nor will there be," Khiara responded. He nodded for the old man who had revived Lukias to leave. His expression was quizzical and Annon believed he could not understand the nature of the conversation, but that he was disturbed by what he had seen.

"Before we agree to terms, we must ask you a few questions to judge the risk," Annon said.

Lukias smiled brazenly. "The risk? You have no chance of success. The Arch-Rike is aware of you, he is aware of your quest, and he managed to subvert one of your group beneath your notice. You have no chance. None."

"Then you risk nothing giving us the information we need. Is the oracle inside the city of Kenatos?"

Erasmus held up his hand. "We must be more precise, Annon. Words are too slippery. Is Basilides in the city of Kenatos?"

"No," Lukias answered. "Its location is a carefully guarded secret. But it is not in the city."

"Why would you bring us there then? What motive do you have?"

Again, Erasmus held up his hand. "Let me ask the questions, Annon. A man has many motives. Any of which would not break the ring's prohibitions for lying." He studied the Rike for a moment. "Tell us what you can of Basilides."

Lukias's mouth twitched into a frown. "A good question."

Erasmus smiled at the compliment.

"Basilides is often referred to as an oracle. Do you know the concept of the mastermind?"

Annon nodded. "My uncle spoke of it, yes. He learned it from the Arch-Rike himself."

Lukias smiled shrewdly. "Good. It is a group of individuals united together in a common purpose. They embrace a common goal. Basilides is the Arch-Rike's mastermind. You approach it at your peril."

"My uncle said it's a pool or a grove," Annon said.

"He was well informed, but never given the full information. It's located near a pool. You must understand that the Arch-Rike's mastermind are the dead. They are the rulers of the past. His predecessors in rank. Centuries of wisdom preserved from destruction. It is considered the highest of honors to be granted permission to visit Basilides. It is a mark of the Arch-Rike's favor. That is why I know of it. As you can already discern, he trusts me."

"And yet you tell us these things?"

"Only in a sincere effort to persuade you that it is madness trying to go against him. Tyrus of Kenatos is a brilliant and calculating man. He is a Paracelsus without peer and wiser than most. He was once the Arch-Rike's ally. But he turned against him and provoked the Arch-Rike's wrath. I have seen what happens to those who incur such displeasure. I can only imagine what lies you have been told."

Erasmus held up his hand subtly to forestall Annon. "What have you been told about Tyrus's intentions?"

"His stated intentions or his true goals?" Lukias sneered.

"Both, if you please."

"Overtly, Tyrus of Kenatos has pursued a single-minded goal. His research into the Archives has been monitored and evaluated. His accomplishments are legendary. He says that he seeks to end the Plague. This is probably how he persuaded you to join him."

"It is so," Erasmus replied. "But you say that he has another agenda?"

"It is equally obvious. He seeks to hide and control the learning of the Paracelsus order. He has deliberately falsified Archive records and obscured references, even forging addendums in the texts to mislead his peers. He destroyed his own tower in order to prevent his knowledge from being studied by others. It was not the Arch-Rike that destroyed the tower, it was Tyrus's own doing! A heap of rubble. Millions of ducats worth of magic shattered and devalued. He is on a quest to abolish his own order!"

Erasmus pursed his lips. "And so you have been told."

"More than told!" Lukias said defiantly. "I have helped lead the investigation into his crimes. I have known Tyrus of Kenatos for many years. I have seen these records myself. I know Tyrus's handwriting. I am an expert on the Paracelsus order and their rituals. Do you know how many books were in his tower before it exploded? How much knowledge was disintegrated in an instant due to his pride and reckless ambition?"

Annon's temper flared white-hot. The flames in his fingers began to swell. "The entire Paracelsus order was formed around the slavery of spirit beings," he said angrily. "The lights that power your great city shine because they are beings trapped into servitude!"

"Spare me these Druidecht sensibilities," Lukias answered patronizingly. "There is no servitude or bondage. It is only because you do not understand the principles of matter involved that you scorn it. In the past, the Druidecht developed superstitions to explain forces of nature. You are jealous because you do not understand the truth. Wayland is a backward kingdom in every sense. You know nothing about it."

Annon stepped forward. Khiara shot him warning look. "I have been to Kenatos, as you well know. I have seen this imprisonment with my own eyes. I visited my uncle's tower. I took a blade from a Preachán in Havenrook, one that had been constructed by a Paracelsus, and released the spirit trapped inside. Does your ring tell you that I am lying?"

The Rike looked at him with a preposterous expression. "You believe what you want to believe. What you have been trained to believe. Mirrowen does not exist. It is a fool's legend to bind a fool's mind."

"You condemn yourself with your own logic," Erasmus said. "What do you know but what you have been told and trained to believe?"

Annon nodded firmly. "My mentor was a wise Druidecht. He said that there are many men who wished to deceive, but not one who wished to *be* deceived. Since they are unwilling to be deceived, they are unwilling to be convinced that they have been deceived."

"I know that precept," Lukias responded flatly. "I tell you, boy, that *you* have been deceived. I can feel the passion in your words and can discern that you have not knowingly told me any falsehood. Your attempt to stop the Plague is misguided."

"Why is that?" Annon challenged. "What does the Arch-Rike say causes the Plague?"

Lukias looked at him with disdain. "It is obvious to anyone with a mind for research that the Plagues are caused by bad air. And it does not require an oracle to predict that Havenrook will be the next kingdom to succumb to it. You have traveled there yourself and can vouch that it reeks of corruption and insufficient means to drain away its own excrement. The Arch-Rike knows this and has begun making preparations to replace the trade routes. The Romani are part of the corruption and have long violated even the most basic laws of commerce. Yet I am certain you would say that the Arch-Rike is overseeing the fall of Havenrook. Wisdom often appears as evil to those who do not have it."

Annon shook his head. "I see how powerful he is in persuading his own followers. Truly, your mind is imprisoned as much as the spirits."

Lukias chuckled. "There are no spirits, boy. What you have been taught is a tradition, nothing more. Even your power over fire, in the end, will be understood after sufficient research is complete."

Nizeera, Annon thought forcefully. *You must help me persuade him.*

With pleasure, came a soft, purring reply.

"You say that Mirrowen is a hoax," Annon said. "You are convinced that there are no spirits being imprisoned by the Paracelsus of Kenatos. Not only did I learn this from my uncle, but I learned it from another Paracelsus who quit the order and became a Druidecht. I learned it from Drosta."

Lukias's eyes widened with concern. "He is dead."

Annon approached him. "He and my uncle were friends. They were like-minded. Drosta forged a weapon for the Arch-Rike, a blade known as Iddawc. I have held it in my hand. I have heard its whispers through the talisman I wear. Believe me, Lukias, that the spirits of Mirrowen are real. There's one in this very room with us."

Lukias smiled sickly. His expression exuded doubt. "I will not fall for your superstitious tricks, Druidecht. I must have evidence. No one but the Druidecht can see these beings. That is the very nature of deception, is it not?"

"Not all spirits are invisible," Annon replied. "Some take the form of birds or insects. Some are as tiny as pollen. But there are others more powerful. Nizeera, welcome our new companion. He travels with us to Basilides."

The growl from Nizeera's mouth caused Lukias to turn in fear. She padded up to the table, leapt on it in a single bound, and pressed her whiskered nose directly up to his forehead.

"It . . . is . . . a . . . cat. A trained . . . cat. You gave it a signal . . . I could not see."

"Stubborn," Annon said. "You require more proof. Whisper a name into Nizeera's ear and I will hear it. Choose whatever word you wish. And to assure you that I cannot read lips, I will turn around."

"It cannot . . . be . . ."

"Choose your word wisely. Choose a phrase. I can hear her thoughts and she can hear mine. Only a Druidecht can do this, Lukias. Say what you will, and I'll hear it."

Annon turned around, but not before noticing the subtle nod of approval from Erasmus and Khiara. He waited a moment before he heard the whisper.

I believe you. The ring on Annon's finger confirmed it.

"A Rike once told me a wonderful proverb. A thing is not necessarily true because badly uttered, nor false because spoken magnificently. Men deceive and are often deceived in turn. I do not fully know the tradition of when the Rikes of Seithrall began wearing rings that divine the truth, but I do know that doing so made it possible for the city to complete its construction and to become a prosperous kingdom in its own right. I do not know if the rings actually work. What I do know is that just the thought of them working make men more honest. For once trust is broken within a group or amongst individuals, you can be sure that only evil will result."

—Possidius Adeodat, Archivist of Kenatos

VII

When Hettie and Paedrin emerged from the Dryad tree in the midst of the Paracelsus Towers in Kenatos, it was crowded with workers intent on rebuilding the broken edifice. The transfer from the Prince's garden in Silvandom had been instantaneous and it was early in the day still, though crowded and full of dust. Scaffolding had been erected throughout the inner courtyard and workers of all types carted wheelbarrows, baskets of chisels, and fragments of stone. Dung from cart animals littered the way, bringing with them the buzzing of flies and the smell of manure.

Paedrin stood gawking at the commotion in the inner courtyard and Hettie grabbed his sleeve and tugged at him impatiently. He had no idea how to blend in with a crowd or make himself unseen.

"Stop staring," Hettie whispered. "It makes us conspicuous. We need to get out of this courtyard. The gate is over there. Haven't you been here before?"

He jerked his arm away from her, but he did follow her to the gate leaving the tower courtyard. There were individuals up on the scaffold already, hammering fragments of stone and rubble away to prepare neat flat surfaces for the replacement stones. As they passed outside the gateway, Hettie saw the Cruithne soldier look at her and Paedrin, his eyes narrowing. So many people passed the gates day after day. Would he recognize her as Tyrus's niece? She had to assume so.

"Faster," Hettie murmured, increasing her pace. Her ears were frantic for the sound of pursuit. Her heart raced with panic. It was a bold move coming to Kenatos after what had just happened in Silvandom. However, it would be the last place the Arch-Rike would suspect them to go.

Outside the gate, an enormous wooden structure had been erected, with long beams fastened to it and rigged with counterweights. The structure was as tall as the outer wall and reminded her of the equipment used at the docks to unload ships. There were numerous workers around it, mostly burly Cruithne who were managing the chains and ropes and counterweights. It was impressive how quickly the repair was underway. The city was truly a hive of activity.

"I did not know there was a Dryad tree in the midst of Tyrus's tower," Paedrin said. "It did not even seem alive. Few if any leaves."

"Are we speaking to each other again?" Hettie asked with an edge of anger in her voice, but she kept it low. "I was under the impression you wanted nothing to do with me."

"You understand correctly," he answered. The look in his eye was full of venom. "I was making an observation."

"You are too simple, Paedrin," she said. "For all your talk of the Uddhava and anticipating motives, it stings that you were outwitted. Your pride is injured. Pain is a teacher. But Tyrus thought we would be more successful working together." They were both walking at a very fast pace, heading down from the tower heights toward the Bhikhu temple.

"Working together would require trust, which is something we lack between us right now. At least I lack it. Perhaps in your culture, it is acceptable to betray someone and then continue on as if nothing happened. Maybe you feel you deserve praise for doing such a wonderful job?"

"Am I the only one who betrayed us, Paedrin? You led the Arch-Rike and his men into Silvandom to destroy us."

The look he gave her in a short glance showed the depth of his humiliation and pain. It was too raw a wound still. She should not have pecked at it.

"You are such a fool, Bhikhu," she muttered angrily. "Why do I even bother trying?"

It took several long, furious strides before he had mastered himself enough to speak again. "My will was not my own," he said tautly. "That ring he tricked me into wearing made it impossible for me to tell you the truth. I think you saw it in my eyes. I wanted to tell you, but I could not."

"In many ways I felt the same. I betrayed you deliberately. I lied to you—"

"Here, this way. The alley is shorter."

The shade from the alley brought a relief from the sun for a moment. It was narrow and full of rubbish and garbage, but no one was there except for pigeons examining the refuse. They fluttered and hopped to keep away from them as they walked. Wet clothes hung from poles extending from the upper windows, causing an almost rain-like pattering to descend, bringing with it the smell of laundry.

When they were far enough in, Hettie stopped and stared at him, hands on her hips. He looked wary of her, his eyes tight. She wanted him to say something humorous again, a quip or an insult. Something that showed the spark of who he truly was. This sulking, hurt creature was not her Paedrin.

"I did those things," she said in a low voice. "I admit it. You were being forced by the Arch-Rike's ring on your finger. I have a ring piercing my ear. It was forced on me when I was little. I am due another ring because of my age, but the debt has been paid. Kiranrao has what he wanted. He sent me to Kenatos to trick Tyrus. He promised me my freedom if I succeeded, which is more than Tyrus ever offered. But now I have been given my freedom, a chance to live in Silvandom." She looked him straight in the eyes. "I want you to break this earring off. I am no longer a Romani."

Her emotions were swelling inside of her, almost uncontrollably. All her life, she had wanted to be free. Only a Romani man could break the ring off of her. She knew she was violating the customs. She knew it could cost her her life. But if their quest was successful, they would remake their world, and it would be a world without the Romani curse. If what Tyrus had said was true, many Romani would be removing their earrings.

He looked at her sternly. "You said you did not know what would happen to you if you removed the earring. Was that a lie?"

"Of course it was a lie," she answered impatiently, wanting to choke him. "You do not fully understand how good I am at lying. But this is the truth. This is the truth now. I wanted to tell you, Paedrin. I wanted to confide in you. I was not sure if I could trust you. I was not sure I could trust Tyrus. I knew I could trust Annon because he is my brother, but he's not strong enough to save me from a man like Kiranrao."

Paedrin nodded slowly. "What you are saying is the girl I thought I knew is a lie."

She let out a pent-up breath and then stared him hard in the eyes. "The best of me was real. The rest was a lie. I was playing a role, Paedrin. He who pays the piper calls the tune. Kiranrao called the tune. I was dancing for my freedom. But I have been offered an opportunity to spend the rest of my life living in Silvandom. Freedom, at long last. I will snatch it! That's the one place where the Romani cannot find me. Now break this earring. I don't want to wear it a moment longer."

She stared into his eyes, willing him to obey her. Words would not persuade him to trust her again, only actions would. And this act, something he had admonished her to do when they first met was one she hoped would begin to soften his heart to her.

Hettie turned her cheek toward him and smoothed the dark hair away from her neck. She thought she saw him swallow, but she kept her eyes locked on his.

"What will Kiranrao do to you for this? I need to know the consequence."

"I don't know what he will do for sure. He may do nothing."

"I doubt it."

She sighed. "The punishment for disobedience among the Romani is poison. There is a cruel poison called monkshood. Only Romani men and only a few of them are taught the antidote. When I was a child, I saw one of my sisters poisoned for disobedience. They let her suffer a long time before administering the cure. The symptoms are horrible and painful. Break this earring, Paedrin. The Romani will be the Arch-Rike's next victims."

Paedrin touched the earring as if it were a slug or a disgusting insect. His finger brushed her earlobe. He used both hands to find the spot where the ring had been welded together. Looking her in the eye, he snapped it.

"You are free," he whispered.

Hettie bent the hoop wider and unattached it from her ear. She studied it in her hand, noticing the dull gleam from the tarnished gold. The feeling of nakedness on her ear was startling. She touched her skin gingerly.

Then she stared Paedrin in the eye. "I will never lie to you again," she promised, crushing the hoop in her hand and throwing it down on the ground.

His gaze narrowed. "Someone just entered the alley behind us."

Hettie turned and saw the Preachán immediately. He saw them, turned, and ran.

Paedrin started to go after him, but Hettie grabbed the front of his tunic. "We don't have enough time. You said you needed to see Master Shivu to learn where the Shatalin temple is. This may be our only chance."

His look turned to anger and he shook his head with frustration. "How I despise it when you are right."

Paedrin had been raised in the city of Kenatos and he knew the streets and byways. He wore the traditional tunic and sandals of a Bhikhu that made him an ordinary sight in the city. Even escorting Hettie would not seem that odd, since the Bhikhu were known for their charity and integrity and she looked more like someone raised in the woods than a Romani girl. He glanced back at her for a fraction of a moment, unable to stop the pain in his heart every time he saw her.

He had been fighting his growing affection for her for some time. He had buried it beneath the layers of his duty, but still felt it squirming to break free. It was her betrayal that had finally forced him to come to terms with how he truly felt about her. When she was Tyrus's abandoned niece, struggling against the odds to find a treasure to buy her freedom, she had been nearly irresistible to his sensibilities. That she was Aeduan by race had caused him some concern, but having grown up amidst all the races in Kenatos, it was not that unusual. She was beautiful in a natural way, not as the painted faces in the city in their expensive gowns. And her Romani accent had grown on him, along with all its witty sayings. Now that she was unmasked as Kiranrao's tool, the entire facade crumbled. The basis of his feelings was as shattered as the Paracelsus Towers they had just left.

But Paedrin was not as hasty as the city to begin rebuilding it straightaway.

Despite his anger and resentment, her apology rang true and she did genuinely seem interested in mending the breach. It would take time to regain her standing. What troubled him was the kind of character she had developed. They were truly as different as chalk and cheese.

But there was one thing he knew they could agree on. Tyrus's quest to banish the Plague was an effort they could unite on. That needed to be the top focus and they could sort out the nuances of their relationship afterward. Tyrus had charged him to find a lost relic—the Sword of Winds. Master Shivu had mentioned it to him while he languished in the Arch-Rike's dungeon. Now he understood that Tyrus had made a pact with Shivu to help restore the lost Shatalin temple and that his master had been training him all along to face the dangers of the Scourgelands. It had been subtle training, but always his master had hinted at greater things beyond the walls of the city. As a child he had been encouraged to float up to the roof of the temple and gaze at the lake waters surrounding the city.

Defeating the Arch-Rike. Ending the Plague. Traveling the world. It was everything that appealed to Paedrin. When it was over, he was certain he would be allowed to live anywhere he chose. A hero among his own people, the Vaettir.

He stopped the thought, remembering Master Shivu's training. He could almost hear the old man's words in his mind, so often he had heard them repeated. *A desire to be observed, considered, esteemed, praised, beloved, and admired by his fellows is one of the earliest as well as the keenest dispositions discovered in the heart of man. Beware of those desires.*

Paedrin had always been ambitious. He had felt destined to do great things, being one of the few Vaettir orphans in the city.

It was important to check that ambition, to be sure he was doing it for the right reason, lest he become a true renegade like Cruw Reon who had stolen the blade and brought on the downfall of the Shatalin temple.

"There it is," Hettie said. "How should we do this? Should we go in together?"

"The temple has so few visitors that the bell ringing brings an inordinate amount of attention. Let me float over the walls and see if I can find Master Shivu alone. You watch for trouble and ring the bell if any comes."

"What information do you need from him?" she asked.

"Where to start looking," he answered. "The Shatalin temple could be anywhere. I did not even know it existed."

"Agreed. I will stay hidden near the front gate and ring the bell if trouble comes. But I will meet you outside the wall at the back of the temple, not the gate, when I ring the bell."

He nodded and they parted ways. As he approached from the east, Paedrin's heart filled with warmth when he saw the moldering walls, the broken tiles on the roof. In his mind's eye, he could imagine himself as a boy, perched up there and overlooking the city. He increased his pace, feeling a sense of restlessness. It was nearly midday and he could not hear the clack of staves or shouts from the students training. That was odd and made him wary.

Paedrin reached the edge of the outer wall, examining the tender vines that snaked the surface and made curving patterns on the stone. The training yard should be on the other side. Where were the students? Where were his friends?

He inhaled and scurried up the side of the wall, ascending rapidly. When he reached the top, he crouched at the edge, staring down at an empty yard below. A few tufts of weeds had sprung from some of the flagstones. There was not a soul to be seen.

Alarm. Worry. Dread.

Paedrin battled his feelings down, studying the training yard for any sign of movement. There was none. He exhaled and lowered to the ground inside, dropping low and watching for clues. Finding none, he rose and quickly went to the sheltered walkway that led to the main building of the complex. As he passed the columns, he could imagine seeing himself in the yard, trying to impress Hettie with his abilities as she walked where he did. He pursed his lips. Something was wrong. Was the temple abandoned?

Paedrin reached the doors and pushed and they opened. There was a smell of death in the air. He felt the skin on the back of his neck prick and gooseflesh went down his arms. It smelled like a sewer. He could hear the sound of buzzing flies. Paedrin began to tremble, his stomach coiling into knots, his face beginning to twitch with raw anger and horrible fear.

He started across the tile toward Master Shivu's chamber and nearly collided with another Bhikhu, his friend Sanchein.

"Paedrin!" he gasped. Sanchein was Aeduan and nearly his own height. His face was pocked and his eyes were swollen with fatigue. He stared at Paedrin in confusion. "They said you were dead. They said the Arch-Rike executed you!" He touched Paedrin's arm, shaking his head with disbelief.

"Where is Master Shivu?" Paedrin asked forcefully. "I must see him."

Sanchein's look of surprise was stricken with grief. "He is dying. Everyone is sick. The Rikes say it is the Plague. None of us are allowed to leave the temple. There are only four of us left alive."

Paedrin stared at his friend in horror.

Just then, the gate bell began to ring.

"*I have always been impressed by the Bhikhu. They do not rely on ducats or influence for power. Their integrity is their power. The master of the Bhikhu temple, in my opinion, is the epitome of the virtue of humility, which is the foundation of all the other virtues. In the soul in which this virtue does not exist there cannot be any other virtue except in mere appearance.*"

—*Possidius Adeodat, Archivist of Kenatos*

VIII

The sadness and shock nearly overwhelmed Paedrin. The look in Sanchein's eyes showed that he was not lying. He had no reason to. The grief in his expression was clear as the dawn. The truth of his words shredded into Paedrin's heart with full misery. He did not believe it was the Plague. It was the ruthlessness of the Arch-Rike that was to blame. It was revenge, cold and hard. For a moment, he was too stunned to speak. But the tolling of the bell meant that Hettie was warning him to flee. He could not do so yet.

"Take me to Master Shivu," Paedrin whispered hoarsely. "Quickly, I must see him!"

"But how did you . . . ?"

"I swear I will crush your other toe if you do not take me to him right now!"

A little smile wavered on Sanchein's mouth as he remembered. "Come."

The two hastened through the darkened temple. The smell of sickness was everywhere. As their sandals clacked on the tiles, Paedrin stared at the empty corridors. The sound of flies swarming filled the air. He gritted his teeth, preparing himself for what he would see.

Sanchein wavered at the doorstep. "He is in great pain, Paedrin. I've never seen a man suffer so. Pain is a teacher, but what lesson this pain teaches is beyond me. His agony weakens him. I can't believe he's dying, Paedrin." Tears glittered on his lashes.

Paedrin pushed his way through the fragile doorway and saw Master Shivu. Or what remained of him. He had shrunken with the sickness, making his body appear like a skeleton. His skin was flushed and he wore no shirt, so that his bones protruded like some reptilian thing. The stubble on his head was growing and he had not shaved in several days, allowing white whiskers to grow on his face. His eyes burned with fever and he sat erect, sweat glistening on his body. A bowl of vomit sat between his legs.

The skin and eyes were sallow. The stench in the room was overpowering. Dried lips parted, trembling with clenched pain. "Paedrin," he croaked.

Seeing the agony in his master's eyes shook him to his core. Shivu was Vaettir-born. Paedrin could not remember a single time he had ever been ill. Now he looked like a desiccated leaf, trembling under a breeze, waiting for the stem to snap off.

"Master," Paedrin sighed, rushing to him. He reached to take the bony hand, but a subtle nod bid him stop.

"I . . . I . . . hoped you . . . would come. Grieve not for . . . me." His breath was shallow, full of pain. "I will . . . rest . . . soon."

"Master," Paedrin said, shaking his head. Tears stung his eyes. How could he not grieve for the man? "I need your help. But I cannot leave you like this. There are Druidecht who can heal you. If I can take you away from here . . ."

A clicking sound came from Master Shivu's throat. "Too . . . late. No *keramat* in the city. Only the Arch-Rike's magic. He will not . . . heal me. Or the students. He is . . . angry for my refusal. Seek

. . . the Shatalin temple, Paedrin. Seek . . . the sword. You will need it . . . to survive." His eyes closed. "Scourgelands. To survive . . ."

"But where is the Shatalin temple?" Paedrin pleaded. He wiped his eyes furiously, unable to prevent the pain of his breaking heart. "Where do I look, Master?"

"The Vaettir . . . arrived . . . by sea. Shatalin. The ocean . . . west. Fog and mists. Rocks and mountains. Beyond Stonehollow. Seek Lydi. Shipyards. They will know where . . . in the mountains. When the ships came . . . they founded Shatalin for training Bhikhu. Separate from . . . Silvandom."

Shivu grimaced, eyes blazing. His whole body trembled and shook from his legs to his neck muscles. He moaned and reeled, struck by another fierce wave of pain. The bed started to rattle with his convulsions. Paedrin stared at him helplessly. He wished Khiara had been there, who with a touch could have calmed the pain. He was furious with the Arch-Rike for allowing his master to suffer.

A bony hand grabbed his wrist. Master Shivu's face was contorted. "Forgive them, Paedrin. Forgive."

"Who?" he said, staring with grief. His heart was nearly bursting. "Who?"

"This is not the Plague. Romani poison."

Paedrin stared at him in horror. "This is poison?" he gasped.

"Sanchein," Shivu gasped. "Tell him. The Preachán."

Sanchein hovered at the doorway. He entered meekly, wiping tears from his eyes. He looked beaten down by a great secret. "He arrived not many days ago, Paedrin. He was looking for you."

"Who was?" Paedrin stammered. "This doesn't make sense. Who are you talking about?"

"A Preachán fellow, claiming to be from Havenrook. He said you had stolen some magic from him and he wanted it back. A blade. You had taken it during a fight. He said the Bhikhu cannot have treasure and he wanted it back or ten thousand ducats. Master

Shivu sent him away. He said that you had been executed by the Arch-Rike and that the temple did not have any ducats at all. The man was angry but he left with a surly expression. That night is when the first signs of sickness came. It happened after mealtime."

Paedrin gripped Sanchein's arms so tightly the man winced with pain.

Oh no, he thought in despair, his heart shuddering at the realization. He remembered the night in Havenrook when the mob had come after them at Erasmus's home. With his Bhikhu training, he had dispersed the crowd, but one man—one of the men at Kiranrao's table—had challenged him with a dagger imbued with power. Paedrin had broken both of the man's arms and had assumed it would take months for him to heal.

Not so. Not in Havenrook, where everything was for sale.

The realization struck him like thunder. The man had sought revenge. He knew Paedrin was from Kenatos. He had come there seeking retribution. He had probably observed the temple for a day or two, learned about their mealtimes. And then he had poisoned the food or the well with monkshood, the poison Hettie had told him about. Only the Romani knew the cure.

What have I done? he shouted at himself. He stared at Master Shivu, whose eyes burned with agony and stared into his.

"Forgive," Shivu whispered. "Uddhava will not save me. Revenge will not . . . raise the dead. Restore the Shatalin temple, Paedrin." His chest began to heave. "Restore the Shatalin temple. Bring back the Shatalin." His eyes began to bulge. "Stop the Arch-Rike!"

Paedrin felt pain from his master's grip, but he welcomed it. It was nothing compared to the searing agony in his heart.

"I will," Paedrin vowed.

The wave of pain passed and Master Shivu let out a long, relieved sigh. His expression softened. His shoulders sunk. It was only when he did not breathe in again that Paedrin realized he had died.

"Master!" he said, choking, gripping the frail hand that was now slack.

The body slumped back down on the bed, sloshing the bowl of bile. Paedrin stared at him as the brittle cracks splintered inside his soul, gripping the hand and trying to comprehend what had happened. The Romani had destroyed the Bhikhu temple. He did not know if Kiranrao had authorized it, but it did not matter much to him if he had or had not.

Forgive them, Paedrin. Forgive.

How could he do that? How could he absolve them of destroying all that he held dear? He wept bitterly, kneeling by Master Shivu's bedside.

A shudder came from the darkness of the corridor. The sound of thick heavy boots and a long stride.

"Someone is coming," Sanchein warned, dabbing his nose.

Restore the Shatalin temple. It was a charge and a commitment. He was free from the Arch-Rike's ring. He was free to fulfill Tyrus's quest. But he knew deep in his heart that he would never be free from hating the Romani. Rage could not describe how he felt and hatred was too soft a word.

"I brought this on us," Paedrin whispered darkly. The other orphans who had been raised at the temple. Dead, because of him. Only four had survived and the Arch-Rike refused to lift a finger. He turned his head, hearing the boot steps draw nearer.

Sanchein turned and went into the hallway. "What is your business here, Cruithne? Who let you in?"

The voice was deep and accented. "A Bhikhu just arrived. The Vaettir. Where is he?"

Paedrin touched Master Shivu's eyelids, closing them. He walked around the bed. A Cruithne? The one from the Paracelsus Towers?

"The only Vaettir living here was Master Shivu," Sanchein said stiffly. "He is dead."

"A good answer, for it is the truth. I will ask more directly. The Bhikhu known as Paedrin. Is he here now?"

Sanchein said nothing.

"Keeping silent cannot help them," the Cruithne murmured. There was a grunt of pain and then a choking sound.

Paedrin stepped into the doorway, advancing as he saw the Cruithne holding Sanchein on the ground with one arm bulging around his throat. Sanchein kicked him solidly, trying to wrench the grasp away, but the Cruithne was a giant of a man and it was like kicking an immovable boulder. It was the one from the towers. He saw Paedrin and stood, releasing Sanchein.

"There you are," he muttered. He opened his arms expansively, bowing slightly, as if inviting the Bhikhu to attack him.

"You are a big man," Paedrin said. "You stink like sour mouse droppings though. I hope you do not catch the Plague here. For you will certainly *not* catch me."

"There is no Plague here," the Cruithne said in a low, deep voice. "I've heard you were the best Vaettir in the temple. Is that true?"

"There are no longer any Vaettir here," Paedrin taunted. "While I enjoy a good conversation and a good fight, now would not be the right time for either. Give my flatulent regards to the Arch-Rike and tell him I am no longer in his employ." He sucked in his breath sharply and rose to the ceiling rafters.

"Wait!" the Cruithne shouted.

Paedrin ran along the edge of one of the ceiling rafters, breathed in again, and soared up to one of the windows embedded in the upper heights. He could hear the stomping of the Cruithne's boots, but it was laughable to think that such a man could ever catch a fleeing Vaettir.

Surely, he knew he could defeat the bulky man. He was sorely tempted to. But he knew, at that moment of weakness, he would probably kill him. Deliberately. Painfully. Or break every major bone in his body as a warning to the Arch-Rike and those who would hunt them. He used the Uddhava against himself. The bell had been Hettie's warning to flee. It was now time to flee the city as well as the temple. Gripping the edge of the roof, Paedrin leapt, breathing in and rising as he twirled, landing on the edge. He raced up the shingles, pulling in just enough air to keep his steps light and not reveal which direction he ran.

At the pinnacle of the sloping roof, he stood for a moment, gazing out at the city as he had done so many times as a boy. Bitter feelings swirled inside his heart. He had unwittingly unleashed the Romani wrath on his family. His actions in Havenrook had caused their deaths. The pain of that thought sent more cracks through his heart. There was only one way to atone for it. Destroy the Plague. Destroy the Arch-Rike's influence. And restore the Shatalin temple.

Hettie would be waiting for him at the back of the temple. He rushed down the opposite slope of the tiles and then kicked off the edge, leaping high into the air, breathing in deeply to add to his flight. He soared like a raven over the wall, swooping down, his lungs aching to release the breath. Down he glided, coming over the lip of the wall where he saw Hettie crouching behind a shed nearby.

He dropped down next to her, startling her with his sudden appearance. He loved doing that.

"The Cruithne from the towers," Hettie whispered. "He must have hired the Preachán to follow us here."

"Little doubt of that," Paedrin said, squatting. His emotions were jumbled together. He wanted so much to go back there and fight. He wanted to hurt someone. Anyone would do.

"What is it?" she asked, looking at him in concern.

She was Romani herself. He stared at her face, unable to quell the wave of nausea and antipathy for her people. "Master Shivu is dead. He was poisoned." He let the word hang in the air between them. "Because I took that Romani man's knife. The man who stabbed me with it."

Her expression darkened, her face hardening with suppressed feelings. "I am so . . ."

He held up his hand curtly. "Please. Spare me your sympathy."

She looked at him coldly a moment, then nodded. "I will. But perhaps you gain a little better understanding of why all your little sayings were hard for me to accept."

Paedrin frowned, anger throbbing in his heart. "Do not mock the virtues of my upbringing. They may be of little worth to you, but they are still a better way to live."

"It is a hard task to comfort the proud."

"Another Romani saying. You have not run out of them yet?" He glared at her.

"No. But at least you know where to start looking for the temple now, yes? A good beginning is half the work."

Paedrin's heart was anguished, and he dipped his head, trying to master his emotions. "I do." He sighed heavily. "Part of me thinks I should float off and leave you here. I can get out of this city easier. I can travel faster without you. I'm not fully convinced I can trust you."

"The problem with you, Paedrin, is that you have always talked *too* much. I don't need to hear every thought in your head to know they are there." She held up her hand and pointed at her finger. "Yes, you can leave me here all alone. You won't because you'd worry about me getting captured." She flicked one finger down. "You can get out of the city easier. But can you do so without escaping notice? There are Finders who will be tracking us. I can help there." She flicked another finger down. "You can travel faster without me. Very true. Any man can hasten to his own death. It may require both of us to claim the sword. One to distract and the other to steal it. That is how the best thieves do it." She lowered the third finger.

"You cannot trust me. Trust must be built and earned. I told you I would ring the bell if trouble came. I did. I told you I would be waiting for you here. I was."

It left a final finger in the air. She looked at him pointedly, her eyes burning into his. "The last thing, you did not mention. I have magic that will be needed in the Scourgelands. But I think that it would be wise to not have to rely on it alone. If I use it too much, I will go mad, you see. If I don't use it, I may be defenseless. I was hoping, along our journey, that you might start teaching me the Bhikhu ways." The final finger came down and then she opened her palm to him, an offer of almost submission.

He blinked at her in surprise. "Teach you?"

Her expression was carefully guarded. "If you would."

He rubbed his mouth thoughtfully. "You are serious."

"There is much I can learn from you, though it pains me to admit it."

Paedrin was uncertain how he felt about it. It gratified his pride that she asked him. He would enjoy teaching her the Bhikhu ways and to school her in pain. Was she trying to manipulate him? He would have to test it.

"Bhikhu don't eat meat," he said simply. "The philosophy comes with the training, not just the fighting. I won't train a mercenary."

"Agreed," she answered, looking in his eyes firmly. "I will eat what you eat. I will do what you bid me to do. Will you teach me, Paedrin?"

Restore the Shatalin temple. Forgive.

He stared into her face, amazed at how familiar it was to him. They had not known each other very long, but the shared experiences had given them a tight bond. "Not even a rabbit."

"Not even a bird," she agreed.

He sighed. "Very well. I will teach you. But there is something we must do first. We must shear off all of your hair."

He could tell by her expression she was not certain if he was joking or not.

Before either could speak they heard the ominous sound of boot steps approaching and promptly fled their hiding place.

"There is a saying among the Romani, or so I am told. 'It is folly to cross a bridge until you come to it, or to bid a hungry bear good morning until you meet him—perfect folly. All is well until the stroke falls, and even then nine times out of ten it is not so bad as anticipated.' It means that we should not dwell on our troubles until they materialize for they are often not as desperate as we fear. Of course, this may be complete rubbish."

—Possidius Adeodat, Archivist of Kenatos

I X

She was caught.

Phae realized it immediately, knowing that there was no chance she could run. The night was dark and chill. Her ankles and knees were throbbing, her face itching from tiny cuts. Small twigs and crushed leaves had been her pallet as the stars had swirled above. Lifting her head, she gazed at the one who had hunted her relentlessly. She tried to speak, but her throat was thick and she nearly choked. It took some coughing and swallowing to master it again. There was something she had to know. She dreaded his answer.

"Did you kill him?" she whispered hoarsely.

He was shrouded with the darkness, staring down at the ground in silence, his expression void of emotion in the pale light. He plunged the nub of a stick into the dead leaves, stirring them lazily.

"Did you?" she demanded, slowly sitting up. Her body groaned with the effort. "Did you kill my friend?"

He tossed the stick away and shrugged. "He wasn't a threat. I let him live."

She let out a breath of relief. Leaves clung to the tangled net of her hair. She was dirt stained, filthy, and looked like a shambling mess.

But her heart surged with gratitude. "Thank you," she said softly.

The man said nothing. He seemed to be waiting for something.

"Who are you?" she pressed, rubbing her arms, which were very cold in the night air. She was trembling and felt her voice quaver. She tried to subdue it.

He brushed some leaves from his pants and then rose, adjusting the cowl so that it covered most of his face. She took a moment to study him. Woodsman garb, a heavy tunic and sturdy pants and boots. He had leather bracers across his arms and gloves. The cloak was travel-worn and fraying at the edges. She saw his chin in the moonlight, but it was too dark to see the scars or his eyes. As he moved, the cloak ruffled and she saw the hilts of two daggers at his belt. Both had sculpted hilts with hawk-like heads for the pommels and tight leather wrappings along the handles. Oddly, he carried no knapsack or bedroll but he did carry a leather flask for drinking. Where was his food?

He approached her deliberately. "I know what you are. I know what you can do. Do not attempt to run from me. It will end badly for you. I have no qualms hurting you." He paused, folding his arms across his chest. "For now, you are of worth to my master, the Arch-Rike of Kenatos. I intend to take you to the city and you *will* come with me. If you prove difficult, my master has instructed me to kill you. I will do that. Believe me. Do we understand one another?"

Phae nodded solemnly, her heart constricting with terror. She could tell he was used to killing people. The dispassionate voice chilled her more than the night breezes. "Who are you?"

"I have no name."

"What shall I call you then?" she asked.

She thought she saw a twist in his mouth, a sardonic expression. "I am a Kishion. Call me that, if you wish. But I do not wish to speak to you. It would be best if this were enough. We go to Kenatos now."

She bit her lip. "Can I see my friend? Where did you leave him? I want to see him so that he can tell my family that I did not come to harm."

"I will obey my master by bringing you to Kenatos as swiftly as possible." He turned and began to walk. After a few steps, he paused, tilting his head slightly. She recognized it as a signal that she should follow him.

Folding her arms tightly, she started after him, wincing at the pain in her joints and the ravening hunger in her belly. Her pack thumped softly against the small of her back as she walked. The night made ominous sounds. The distant call of a night animal. Snapping sticks somewhere hidden in the gloom. Her mind whirled with dread and her insides thrummed with fear. She had thought he would use rope on her and drag her after him like a pup on a leash. His threat of death worked just as effectively as a bond.

Her body responded to the walking, bringing a flush of heat to her cheeks that helped ward off the chill. She was tempted to run for it again. She was young and quick. She tried slowing deliberately, to see if he would outpace her. When she did, he would pause, cocking his head slightly as a warning. He expected her to match him stride for stride.

What should she do? The dilemma forced her to consider the situation from a hundred different ways. Should she try to escape? Should she refuse to walk and force him to drag her? Would he kill her for disobedience outright? She knew she had to try something, but preferably something not too risky. He had let her sleep and rest. There was any number of reasons he had done so. She imaged it was because he knew she needed it and that it would be difficult for her to go on if she were too fatigued. Carrying her back to Kenatos would not be enjoyable either. Perhaps he would bring her to a Preachán caravan and she'd be bundled up like cargo?

Phae wanted to try something, to test him even a little bit. Would he be reasonable?

"I am thirsty," she said. It was true. Even if he wore a black ring beneath his glove, it would only confirm it.

The Kishion hardly broke stride. He slowed his pace slightly, pulling the leather flask from his belt and handed it to her. It was nearly full and she twisted it open and took a long drink from it. The water was warm and leathery. It tasted awful but it served its purpose. She wiped the moisture from her mouth on the back of her hand and gave it back to him.

The quiet and solitude tormented her. She had never been outside of Stonehollow. The thought of leaving the valley was excruciating. The Kishion's stride never faltered. He was tireless. He was terrifying. She struggled to think what she could do to get away from him.

The next day passed in strange quiet. Phae noticed that they often attracted the attention of robins or blue jays, and an astonishing number of butterflies and other winged insects. They fluttered and hovered nearby, and she thought it curious. Several times during the day she had seen a doe or a fox peering at her, as if trying to win her gaze. Their luminous eyes were almost pleading. She did not understand this. Never before had nature tried to commune with her in such a way. Was this what it meant to be Dryad-born? Or were the old man and the young girl both mad?

The Kishion stopped to let her rest several times during the day, for which she was grateful. His pace was punishing but not impossible. He would pause by streams to let her drink and foraged berries and roots from the surrounding woods for her to eat. She noticed that he rarely ate—a few berries, if that. He'd suck on a root for a good while before eating it. He also knew the differences in edible mushrooms, which he promptly gave to her. She thanked him, but he did not answer.

Who was this man who had caught her? Why had he not seen her by the oak tree? He was strange and enigmatic and rarely glanced at her face for more than an instant. It was as if the Arch-Rike had warned him about her gaze. She wished she knew more about her race, whatever she was. Dryad-born, the Druidecht had called her. What did that mean? Twice she tried engaging him in conversation. He refused to speak or answer her. On they plodded, crossing meadows along the fringe of the valley, near the rim of mountains. If they were journeying to Stonehollow, they would have been going east, but instead, she discerned a northerly bend to their journey. They were crossing the lowlands along the northern edge. Each step took them farther away from the Winemiller's vineyard. Her heart yearned to see it again.

In the late afternoon, they encountered an abandoned homestead. That it was abandoned was plain to see because the roof had caved in, the fence was rotting and dilapidated and the grasses had grown as high as their waists. It was a large stone cottage and the walls were intact, though the windows were missing, and Phae could see a hive of bees in the roofline, the swarm buzzing in the late afternoon.

The stone cottage was sullen and lonely and Phae pitied it immediately. There was an unkempt fruit orchard beyond the broken fence and she could see the branches laden with wild fruit.

"Can we stop a moment?" Phae implored, gazing hungrily at the trees. He glanced back at her, saw where she was looking and shrugged his indifference.

She walked through the high grass, enjoying the new smells on the breeze. The house looked so lonely and forlorn. How long had it sat empty of life? How long had nature laid claim to its seams and mortar? Trasen wanted ducats to buy a farmstead in Wayland. This one could be taken and rebuilt. A new roof could be put on, the grasses cut with a thresher. It was a sturdy-looking place and it seemed to weep in the light, begging her to stay. What if Trasen and she could fix it together? The thought of it sent a subtle thrill through her bones. Just the two of them, starting a homestead together.

When she reached the orchard, she discovered it was laden with dark, leather-skinned pears. They did not look very inviting, but she plucked one and sank her teeth into it. The flesh beneath the peel was as sweet as treacle and the flavor surged into her mouth. They were delicious! The skin was dark and rough, but the flesh was white and sugary. She devoured three quickly, appeasing her ravenous hunger. She quickly plucked several more and began stuffing them into her pack.

Turning, she spied the Kishion climbing the roof toward the beehive and gawked. He maneuvered up the corner of the cottage, his gloves tucked in his belt, and moved up the surface like a spider. The small seams in the stone and mortar were very small, but his fingertips and boots seemed to have no problem tracing their lines and finding suitable handholds. She stared at him as he reached the edge of the roof and slung himself up on the edge. He walked a few paces to where the beehive was fastened to the eaves.

Phae stared at him, chewing and swallowing. Was he mad? Brushing some hair from her face, she watched in shock as he crouched near the edge of the roof and then plunged his hand into the hive.

The bees reacted in a chorus of angry buzzing and darted at the Kishion's face and arm in response to the invasion. She watched the stinging creatures and nearly cried out to him, but the little stabs apparently meant nothing to him. He did not flinch or swat them away. He let them sting him. His hand withdrew a dripping gob of honeycomb. Then he leaned over the edge of the roof and plummeted to the ground.

Phae started in surprise, nearly rushing to help him, and saw him straighten from the impact. He had landed on his feet and looked as hale as ever. He strode toward her, breaking off pieces of the honeycomb and eating them. There were no welts on his face or hands, only the strange scars that had always been there. It was impossible. He should have broken his legs falling from that height.

He nibbled on another cluster of honeycomb and then offered the rest to her. She was almost too afraid to take it.

"What *are* you?" she whispered, staring at him in confusion. "Bees cannot harm you. Neither did the fall."

He offered the honeycomb again with a gesture and she took it, careful of its dripping. He wore a ring on his right hand.

"I am in the Arch-Rike's service," he responded, the first time she had heard his voice that day. "I am protected by powerful magic."

She nodded in respect, realizing the display of his power had been deliberate. He was showing her that nothing she could do would hurt him. The small axe tucked in her belt would be of no use against him.

"So the arrow Trasen shot did not even harm you," she said.

He nodded at her astuteness and said nothing. He looked back at the hollowed-out house. That was why he did not conceal his approach when he tracked them into the mountains. He knew he could not be killed. A stone of fear sank into her stomach. How was she, a poor homestead girl, supposed to escape him? She realized that it may not even be possible. The sense of dread was paralyzing.

"Can we rest here tonight?" she asked, trying to hide the pleading in her voice. "It will be dusk soon." She stared back at the house. She would love to fall asleep in the house, dreaming of what it would be like to live in Stonehollow forever. She had a feeling their journey to Kenatos would not take very long. Anything to drag it out longer would be a treasure.

He frowned, as if dubious of her motives.

"I will walk faster tomorrow," she promised. "We can make up the time. Please? I am so weary."

She did not want to beg. Biting her lip, she gazed down at the dripping honeycomb in her hand.

He nodded once and turned away from her.

"Thank you," she offered softly.

Phae ate part of the delicious chunk of honeycomb and then had the idea to combine it with a pear. The sweetness was almost too much, but she enjoyed it and licked her fingers when it was gone. She wandered the orchard a bit, counting about a dozen trees producing fruit and another dozen that were so wild they were barren. The Kishion entered the house to examine it and she had the sudden impulse to flee. She continued her deliberate walk, letting her hands brush the tips of the grasses. Glancing back at the house, she wondered if he was watching her from inside, waiting to see if she would run.

She wanted to. Though she was tired from the day's walk, she was more rested than she had been the previous day, and more alert. Her body felt firmer and her joints did not ache like they had. In the tall grass, she could almost disappear if she dropped low. Was he watching her? Was he testing her? It would be night soon. Did he need to sleep as well?

Phae decided it would be foolish to flee. She did not imagine that her endurance could outlast his. If she ran, he would chase her and he would catch her. Would he punish her? Or simply plunge one of his knives in her heart? She could not risk it. The best thing to do was to earn his trust by proving herself trustworthy. She decided to stay awake as long as she could and see if he fell asleep. She needed to learn everything she could about him, his strengths and—hopefully—his weakness. That was what she needed to learn more than anything else.

After exploring the perimeter of the house, she entered it from the main doorway. The door was missing completely. The inner hall was made of stone tiles and weeds grew in the mortar cracks where the sunlight touched it. There was a crumbling stone hearth with what looked to be the abandoned bed of a wolf or a fox. Dried droppings from mice and other small creatures showed it was used occasionally. Their presence would frighten off any creatures returning that night.

The remains of a loft were smashed on the floor, covered with rotted shingles. The Kishion had cleared away a space by the hearth, the farthest from the windows.

"No fire, I suppose?" she asked tiredly but she did not believe he would answer. She gazed about the innards of the cottage. It would take some work, but the place could be fixed. The walls had been constructed by a master mason. They were thick and solid and had not yielded to the elements or time. They were stones set to last five hundred years. A new roof was needed. The loft could be rebuilt. The orchard could be tamed once more. Horses and goats and oxen fixed in the pen. The cottage was lonely, all it needed was a family to care for it. The owners had likely died of the Plague. So many people gathered in cities that there was truly more land than available people to work it. She wished for it more than anything else.

"How old are you?" she asked, gazing at him covertly. He seemed younger than thirty by his looks.

Ignoring her, he rubbed his hands together, gazing at the dust motes twirling in the fading light. The sun was descending quickly.

"Did you have a name before you became a Kishion?"

He tapped some old rotting wood with the tip of his boot, staring down at it curiously.

Realizing that he would not engage in conversation, she slumped down near the hearth and imagined living in the cottage. In her mind, she began listing all the things she needed to do to make it inhabitable. She would need saws and hammers. Barrels for collecting rainwater. A broom for certain. Her eyes searched the room in the fading light, growing heavier and heavier. She tried to keep her eyes open, missing Trasen with a piercing pang that surprised her. He was alive. She could thank Kishion for that at least.

The darkness brought fatigue and bleary eyes. The Kishion watched her from the shadows. She could sense his presence as well as see him. Did he never tire? What sort of man was this? What sort of protection did the Arch-Rike's service give him?

She recalled the ring on his finger. She had seen it when he handed her the honeycomb. It was a black ring, probably made of iron. Was that ring the source of his power? Was that why he wore gloves, to conceal it? Her eyelids drooped. She pinched herself, struggling to stay awake. He stared at her. She could sense his eyes but could not see them in the shadows.

She stared back, wishing there was light, wishing there was a way she could steal his memory of her. A look and a blink. That was all it would take. Somehow he had missed seeing her at the Dryad tree. Was that his vulnerability? The beginnings of a plan began to form in her mind. She could not quite make out the edges, but she felt it brushing against her thoughts. It would have to be during the day. She would have to be very near him, to be sure their gazes met. She wished she had the power to force him to look at her.

The thought caused a tingling feeling inside her. She did not understand the feeling, but she sensed it. Something was missing. Some part of her was missing. Weariness stole quietly over her and she felt her chin bobbing down. Unable to fight it any longer, she stretched out on the tile floor and drifted asleep.

Phae awoke in the dark of night to the sound of a hauntingly beautiful melody.

"It is amazing the trinkets that are devised by the Paracelsus order. Some glimmer with iridescent light. Others can create dazzling smells. Some offer glimpses of hidden treasures to torment the mind. I do not pretend to understand how these devices work or by what principles they operate. Some of the most popular, I have learned, are those that weave melodies out of nothingness."

—Possidius Adeodat, Archivist of Kenatos

X

The melody was low and plaintive, and the sound invoked a hundred feelings of sadness. It was not made by a voice or any instrument she had ever heard. The sound curled into her ears, lilting and thick with sorrow. It was the sound of a breaking heart.

Phae opened her eyes to blackness, save for thin veils of moonlight seeping in from the shattered windows. The sound was very near and she thought she saw a glint of metal. She blinked rapidly, trying to understand what was happening. What was making such mournful music? Why did its presence threaten her with tears? The Kishion was cloaked and bent over something, but she saw his gloves on the floor, his fingers holding a delicately small locket. The locket was open and she perceived the music coming from it.

She studied him silently, not daring to move. He was fascinated by it. His fingers turned the locket over, examining the edges around the seam and then trailing the thread of a broken gold chain. He wrapped one end of the chain around his finger, twirling it in loops absently. Then he brought it up to his ear, as if straining to hear something deeper than the music. She expected him to jiggle it next, but he did not. He unwound the chain and set the charm in the palm of his hand, studying it more. She saw his head cock to one side, then he turned and gazed at her.

The sudden look startled her. She could almost see his eyes, but the shadow of his cowl prevented it. He did not look chagrined at being found out by her. He seemed not to care the least about her feelings. He studied it again.

"What is that?" Phae asked, almost afraid to ruin the spell the music was casting.

"A trinket," he replied softly, holding it between two fingers and examining it again. "They sell these in Kenatos."

Phae was amazed. "How does it work? The song is . . . haunting."

He nodded. "These have been around for centuries. Only a Paracelsus knows how they are made. The music stops after a while. It intrigues me."

He was talking to her. That was something.

"What is the melody? Do you know it?"

The Kishion shook his head. "I don't. But I should. It is . . . familiar to me somehow."

She waited several long moments before speaking. "You've heard it before then?" she asked, keeping her voice low and timid. She did not want to push him back into silence.

"I can't remember. I believe I have."

She licked her lips and carefully pushed herself up. "It sounds like autumn. Like the first rain after the death of a friend. It is powerful music."

She saw him nod in agreement. "It is the sound of mourning. I have heard it before."

Phae slowly stroked her arm, listening to the melody—drawing it into her heart. It made her think of her plight, of never seeing the Winemiller vineyard or Trasen again. It made her heart quail with sadness and longing. It made her want to cry. What creature had created such a thing? The sound of it would haunt her forever, yet its suffering was somehow soothing.

"Where did you get it?" she asked after another lengthy pause. She was very near to tears and felt her throat tighten. Its sadness permeated her bones and marrow.

The locket clicked shut. Her heart lurched when the music ceased. It almost made her plead to hear it again. She was desperate to hear it. Wincing with emotion, she stared at him and saw the expression on his mouth—full of bitterness and almost a sneer at her question.

"From a man that I killed," he said flatly. "No more questions. You would not like knowing more than that."

In that moment, there was a snuffling growl at the main door and the light was eclipsed by an even darker shadow—a bear with a shiny black pelt. It yawned with a bellowing cough, dropped to all fours, and charged the Kishion, all muscle and bulk and slathering teeth. A dust-like glitter shook from its pelt as it charged, bringing a strange phosphorescent light with it.

Phae screamed.

The beast was unlike any bear she had seen roaming the mountains of Stonehollow. It was bigger, hunchbacked, and both of its eyes glowed silver. With a roar and snarl it charged, its claws scraping the floor as it hurtled at them.

The Kishion was on his feet instantly, blocking its charge with his own body. The beast smashed into him with a shoulder, sending him back with crushing force into the stone wall. She watched the Kishion's head snap back, jolted. It started on him without a pause, roaring with fury and raking him with claws and teeth.

She was frozen in terror for only a moment before her legs commanded her to run. She went straight to the nearest window and vaulted out of it, hearing the beast shift and lunge after her. She landed in the tall grass at an odd angle and went down. Its head protruded from the window and slaver splattered against her cheek. It roared in fury and Phae quickly rolled through the grass, struggling to her feet, and sprinted toward the orchard. She knew that bears were faster and that they could run up hills or down hills equally well. Maneuvering through trees might slow it a little, but she did not care. She was fleeing from two enemies at once. The bear's frightening arrival was the luck she needed.

The limbs of the pear trees whipped at her, but she kept on going, ducking and dodging around them. A roar sounded in the night sky behind her. She heard huffing and then a bark of pain. A battle was raging inside the skull of a home. Phae stumbled over a tree root and went down. The impact bruised her arms, but she shoved herself up and hurried, praying that both of the beasts would kill each other.

Phae made it through the grove and reached the edge of a dilapidated fence. The moon provided fragile light, and she slowed to gauge the distance. She planted her hands on the edge of the fence and jagged slivers bit into her palms. They stung, but she managed to cross the fence wall and start running into the overgrown meadow beyond. There was a steep hill ahead of her and she ran toward the base of it where she found a copse of trees that would help provide some cover.

An owl hooted and flew overhead, nearly making her shriek in fright. The sounds of the battle were intensifying behind her, carried by the breeze. Growls and snarls brought images of violence to her mind. Then a death cry sounded, a shriek of pain followed by silence. The sound came from the bear. She knew it instinctively. The Kishion had killed it.

Fear.

He had warned her not to run from him. He had threatened her. Panic lengthened her stride. She was huffing to breathe, desperate for wings to carry her away. What would he do when he caught her?

Her stomach coiled with dread. Of course he would catch her. How could she run from a man who did not sleep? Who did not even tire? Who could not be killed, even by a beast three times his size?

Why had she run? What was she thinking? What could she possibly hope to accomplish against the Arch-Rike's most fearsome minion? She was nothing but a young woman. She had the fireblood, but she already supposed that fire would not harm him if bee stings did not. There was only her small axe to fight him off and she remembered how Trasen had fared against him. She had nothing. Nothing!

Phae's mind was scrambled with horror and desperation. Maybe he wouldn't bother taking her back to Kenatos now. She was too much trouble. He would just slit her throat and apologize to the Arch-Rike that she had been too difficult. Her legs thrashed in the long grasses, her stride increasing even more.

What could she do?

Should she go back? Should she apologize? Should she continue to try to escape and hope the battle with the creature had wounded him somehow? Perhaps it had. Perhaps it was a spirit creature that could damage him. Too many thoughts jabbed and poked inside her head, she could not decide which one to heed. Flee or stay? Submit or defy? Grovel or scorn? She hated the helpless feeling, the crack that drained her courage like a punctured cask. Trasen would know what to do. Master Winemiller would know what to do. Phae was only terrified and confused. She stole a look behind.

An uneven bit of earth and the tangle of scrub caught her foot and she went down hard again, landing in a patch of sharp brambles. The fall stole her breath and she lay gasping in the meadow grass, close to a copse of trees but still too far from it to hide. Her ear and cheek were cut on the brambles, causing sharp pain. She pressed her hand there and it came away wet with blood. It hurt, but she would not cry out and sucked in her breath to keep from sobbing.

The distance to the hills was surprisingly great still, despite her run. It had seemed near on first glance. The rim of the hill slope was closer. Phae crawled, moving forward through the scrub, desperate. She gasped for air and risked a look back across the meadow.

A black smudge in the moonlight, parting the grass at a dead run. He was following her.

A fresh spasm of dread fueled her to run again. Phae rose and sprinted, willing herself to reach the edge of trees, ignoring the pain of her ear. Perhaps she would find another oak there. Perhaps. Her stomach roiled with the jostling contents, bringing nausea to supplement the bile. Sweat streaked down her skin, but on she ran, pushing herself faster. She had to get away. She had to run to be safe.

The sound of his boots thumping on the ground behind her alerted Phae that she would not make the edge of the woods in time. The hill loomed above and then it seemed to split into two, as if next to a giant mirror of itself. Were there two hills instead of one? The false light of the moon was tricking her. The copse of trees was almost there before she realized it wasn't a copse at all. It was a wall covered with vines and foliage. There was a gate in the middle of the wall. A stone archway rose above the tattered fragments of leaves and branches. The archway was derelict, with gaps of stone missing from it. There was an iron gate in the archway and the gate was closed.

Phae realized she had been running toward the safety of the woods only to find a barred door in her path. Defeat struck her heart like an anvil hammer. She slowed in despair, dropping to her knees in exhaustion, and fell down on her arms, gasping for breath and waiting with dread for the Kishion to reach her.

There was nothing else she could do but beg for her life.

Trying to squelch her panic, she pushed up and turned to face the Kishion. Her chest was heaving.

"I'm . . . sorry!" she pleaded, holding her hands in front of her wardingly. "Please! Please! Don't kill me!"

He had slowed his run as he approached but there was a look of fury in his eyes that made her quail. His shirt was in tatters as was his cloak. Both hardly looked like garments made by men. The muscles beneath his shirt were bulging with the effort of his pursuit, but he did not look winded. Not at all.

"Please!" she begged, trying to look him in the eye. The moonlight was not enough. She knew it would not be.

The Kishion drew his blade, his mouth twisting with fury.

She was going to die. He was going to kill her.

"I warned you not to run from me," he said in a seething voice. "There is nowhere you can run that I cannot find you. Nowhere!" The pent-up rage in his voice exploded.

Phae quailed. "I'm sorry!"

He was standing over her, dagger poised in his grip. Every part of him felt dangerous and threatening. His tattered clothes rippled in the night breeze. "I should kill you now. Do you know how easy it would be? I could stop this chase and return back alone. I kill. That is what I do. I know a hundred ways. And you, a foolish girl from Stonehollow, thought you could just run away from me." His voice throbbed with menace.

"Please don't," she whispered hoarsely.

She saw the muscles in his arm tighten so hard they started to tremble. Then he crouched in front of her, the cowl shadowing his face. "Why not? You are a threat to the Arch-Rike. I could end it now. Do you understand me? I do not have to bring you back alive."

Her heart filled with pure dread. He was trained to kill. She knelt silently, wishing for a stray bit of moonlight to expose his eyes.

Suddenly, he jerked her wrist and spun her face first to the ground, pushing her bloody cheek to the hissing grass. His knee fixed on her side, and she felt the dagger tip press against her back. His breath brushed her ear.

"I warned you once. I won't do it again. Do not run from me. Do not stray from my side unless I bid you to. Do you understand me, girl?"

Sobbing in pain and terror, Phae nodded emphatically. She clutched her wounded ear, feeling the blood dribble through her fingers. The fear and suspense were horrible. "I'm sorry. I'm so sorry," she whimpered. "I won't leave . . . I won't ever leave your side. I promise."

When she said those words, something flickered inside her. A premonition of dread.

"*The ancients were truly wise. I have read on a fraying leather parchment with faded ink what was undoubtedly a copy itself the following line: People are swayed more by fear than by reverence. It led me to ask myself—what is fear? It takes many forms. It holds sway in all of us. Fear is pain arising from the anticipation of evil. That is my opinion.*"

—*Possidius Adeodat, Archivist of Kenatos*

X I

Trasen walked all night long, reaching the Winemiller vineyard before dawn. His eyes were puffy and dry and his left arm and wrist still throbbed from the violent way the stranger had subdued him. He had tracked Phae and her pursuer into the woods quite a distance before realizing it was utter foolishness to continue with that plan. The man had taken an arrow shaft in the chest and it had not even penetrated him. It would require cunning and speed to rescue Phae. Even better—a horse.

As he marched through the aisles of grapevines, he approached the barn from the rear and pushed open the door. He hesitated waking the family, but realized he should lest they worry about a missing stallion. Leaving his dusty pack on the dirt by the barn door, he crossed to the main door and tested it. The bolt was drawn.

Each moment of delay made his heart race with dread and worry. Phae was out in the wilderness alone, hunted by a servant of the Arch-Rike of Kenatos. He did not believe she could avoid capture permanently and so he assumed she was already apprehended and bound for the island city with a dangerous man. A spasm of pain went through his heart, wondering how she was being treated. He would have given his own life to separate her from that man. Clenching his jaw, he pounded his fist on the door and then sagged against it, resting his forehead on his arm and swallowing tears. Phae—where was she at that moment? Was she terrified? Was she injured? Was she even alive? The thought of losing her was pure torment.

Footsteps tread cautiously beyond the door. "Master Winemiller?" It was Tate's voice.

"It's Trasen," he answered. "Open the door, Tate."

The bolt jostled and he saw the youth's flushed—and relieved—face. "You are back too soon." He looked out at the darkened porch. "Where is Phae?"

Trasen couldn't bring himself to reveal it yet. The loss was too painful. "Where is Master Winemiller?"

"He went to Stonehollow to get help from Uncle Carlsruhe. We're expecting them both back today. I thought you were . . ."

"I know," Trasen said, anxious to depart. He saw Devin poke his head around the door. The two of them were always together. Devin rubbed his eyes blearily. "Listen, both of you. I need to take one of the horses. Fast, but sturdy. I'll take Paden."

"Master took her already," Devin said.

Trasen cursed under his breath. "Willow then. I assume he didn't take the wagon and the team?" They nodded in agreement. "Good. Fetch me some bread and another waterskin. Some food for the road. There is one way out of this valley and one road to Kenatos. I'm going after Phae."

Tate looks horrified. "You lost her!"

Trasen nearly boxed him. "I shot a man at twenty spans in the chest and it didn't hurt him so much as a bee sting." He grunted and shook his head. "I . . . I did what I could, but he was better than a soldier."

"Is that a bruise on your cheek?" Devin asked.

"Fetch the food, Devin. I'll saddle Willow. We don't have time to stand here and talk. Phae is in danger. Tell Master Winemiller I'm going after her. Tell him . . . I won't come back without her."

 ☘

Phae awoke just before dawn. Her muscles were cramped, and her ear throbbed with soreness. As she blinked, she tried to remember where she was and realized she had cried herself asleep on the grass. Her eyes were swollen, her throat parched. She sat up slowly, shivering uncontrollably at the memories of the night. The sky was turning violet in the horizon and the stars were beginning to vanish, one by one. Pale dawn was coming.

"Are you cold?"

His voice came from behind her and she flinched. She nodded meekly, but what made her shiver wasn't the bite of the morning air. She was terrified and wary of anything that might upset the Kishion now.

He shifted in the grass, rising, and then settled his tattered cloak over her shoulders. She could see his arms through the rips in his sleeves, all knotted muscles and dark hair. The smell of his cloak was musty and it did not provide any comfort.

"Thank you," Phae whispered hoarsely.

He came around and squatted in front of her, offering her leather pack that she had left behind in the abandoned cottage. She touched it, stroking the edge with her fingers, and another shiver ran through her.

"Let me see your ear," he said.

She shook her head and eased away from him. "It doesn't hurt much," she lied.

"Let me see it," he insisted. The light was slowly improving, but it was not bright enough for her to fully see his eyes. She would not have dared to try stealing his memories, though.

Gingerly, she combed her fingers through her knotted strands and brushed the hair back from her ear, exposing the wound to him. She looked at her left hand and saw dried blood on her fingers. He saw it as well, his expression hardening subtly.

The Kishion pulled out his leather flask and unstoppered it. He motioned the lip of it toward her hands and she cupped them. He poured water there and then took her wrists and began rubbing her palms together, letting the water spill through her fingers. He ripped a torn segment of his cloak from off her shoulders and dabbed her hands dry. Afterward, he examined her hands, appraising them at different angles, and then folded up the fabric. He poured more water onto it and moved closer to her, so close she could feel his breath. It was frightening having him so close. The scars on his face were becoming more pronounced as the sunlight began to swell across the horizon.

He pressed the sodden fabric against her cheek and she flinched with the sting. The Kishion set down the wad and turned, picking up a sprig with green leaves that was near where he had been sitting. He snapped off one of the leaves and offered it to her.

"Chew this. It will ease the pain."

She stared at the leaf curiously and smelled it first. The aroma was unfamiliar, and it tasted bitter but not disgusting. She worked it with her teeth as he took up the rag again and started cleaning the blood from her neck. In a few moments, he had cleaned up the stains and then blotted around the tender areas of her ear where it had torn. It stung fiercely, but she clenched her fists and was determined to brave it. He studied her closely, examining the wound, and then nodded with satisfaction.

"Thank you," she murmured, uncertain as to his motives.

He snorted, looking away from her at the first blush of dawn. They watched the sky together in silence as it began to turn green, then yellow.

He turned back and looked at her, his eyes wary. "I'm sorry I frightened you so badly." The words came out hesitantly. "I lost control of myself last night. That doesn't happen very often. I regret it."

Phae stared at him in surprise. An apology was not what she had been expecting. He could have rebuked her for running away despite his warning. He could have justified himself in countless ways. For a moment, she wondered if her damaged ear had heard it wrong.

She looked down at her hands in her lap, struggling with her dread. "Why do you even care?" she asked.

"Because you are harmless. Innocent. A frown would have been enough to prove my displeasure," he answered. "I acted last night out of . . . fear. I lost control. That has been happening to me . . . more and more." He sighed, rubbing his mouth. His breathing started to quicken. He shook his head.

"Fear?" Phae asked, perplexed. "Nothing can harm you. You were stung by a hundred bees and then jumped off the roof. Trasen shot an arrow at you and it didn't even pierce you. Look at you now. Your clothes are torn, but the bear didn't harm you. You were afraid? Of what?"

The Kishion stared down at the matted grass. He plucked one and twirled the stalk between his fingers. "When I am near the Arch-Rike, my thoughts are always calm and orderly. I understand what is happening and how to interpret my feelings and the emotions of others. But I am far beyond the influence of his power right now, and I have found those thoughts and feelings less certain and—" He paused, thinking how to stay it. "This will not make sense to you. Never mind."

"Please," she said, almost reaching out to touch his arm, but she did not dare. "Try. You frighten me for certain. You are not . . . afraid of *me* are you?"

He met her eyes for a moment then looked down. "I'm afraid of my past. Of what I cannot remember."

Phae swallowed. He was starting to open up to her. She had always had a natural gift for making people trust her with confidences. Even though she was terrified of the Kishion, her natural empathy had caused her to respond to his words, his confusion. The more she understood him, the better chance she had of escaping him. She did not ask him to elaborate. She just gave an encouraging nod for him to continue.

"A Kishion does not have a name. We do not have a past. I do not know where I was born. I cannot remember my childhood or anything beyond a few weeks ago when I was summoned . . . to serve the Arch-Rike again."

She stared at him, keeping her expression neutral. "Were you an orphan?"

"I assume so. Part of the magic that binds me to the Kishion steals my memories." He looked at her pointedly. "I think it is Dryad magic, in some way." He shook his head. "Every kingdom requires men to fulfill its justice. The King of Wayland has several heads-men, paid to execute those who violate his laws. That is what we are. That is what I am. But the toll is heavy for men in my role. The Arch-Rike relieves us of the guilt of our actions by stripping away the memory of the deeds. He takes it upon himself." The Kishion sighed deeply. "It helps, to be sure. But there is something awful in not being able to remember how vicious you truly must be. To know you have done horrible things that you would not wish to remember. The fact that I can't means that I must suspect or wonder at what I have done."

Phae's stomach revolted at the thought. "You have no past," she said with a frown. "With the bad memories, you lose the good as well."

"If there were any," he replied mockingly.

She could not imagine such an existence. Her entire life was a series of shared memories that had bound her to the Winemillers and all of her adopted brothers and sisters. What would it be like to not remember Trasen? To not savor the memory of trampling the grapes at harvest time? Memories sustained Phae when she was sad or discouraged. Stripping them all away would be a terrible punishment. It was why she had decided to stop stealing memories for the most part, even though she had the power to.

The sun peeked over the mountains at last, sending stabbing rays into her eyes. She saw the tattered shirt hanging over the Kishion's body. She fumbled with the straps of her pack and dug around inside for a moment, finding a spare shirt she had packed. It would not fit him, so she dared not suggest it. But at the bottom was a spool of black thread and sewing needle set inside. Master Winemiller had always taught her to prepare for things.

"Let me repair your shirt," she offered, showing him the spool. "I work quickly. It will not take me long."

"I can get a new shirt in the city."

"How far it is to Kenatos? I think it will take a week to get there, if I remember correctly. By horse it is faster."

The Kishion's mouth twitched. "We will be there in two days at the most."

She stared at him. "How can that be? It takes two days just to reach . . . Fowlrox—" She stopped, her insides shriveling.

He nodded. "Fowlrox is the gateway city to Stonehollow. When we reach it, we will be within range of the Arch-Rike's power. He employs certain devices that enable him to summon people back to his presence. With these devices, we will travel much faster. There are minions in the air that watch for us to approach."

"I see," Phae said, swallowing despondently. "Well, let me fix your shirt anyway. We can start walking soon if you wish."

The Kishion stripped off his shredded tunic. He was in the prime of health, but she saw that the scars that had ravaged his face also inflicted his chest as well, as if some great beast had savaged him years before and he had healed from it.

She pulled out the needle and started on the first gash in the torn garment. She worked quickly and deftly now that there was plenty of light. "You do not remember how you got the scars on your face?"

"No." His lip curled almost into a snarl. "But I have the suspicion, after last night, that it was inflicted by a bear. Or some other creature with long claws."

"There are bears in Stonehollow," Phae said. "We were warned as children not to stray too far and to make noise as we walk after they have finished their winter sleep. Their meat is delicious. Maybe this is your country. Maybe this is why your memories are starting to return?"

The Kishion shrugged. "When the creature attacked me last night, I feared it. I knew it could not hurt me." He rubbed his forehead angrily. "Yet I feared it. It must have something to do with my past. Something to do with these scars. I had them before becoming a Kishion. That must be true. But I cannot remember anything about it."

Phae secured the end of the line with heavy stitching and then bit the remaining thread loose before continuing her work on a ripped seam. "Are there other feelings you have had that were also from your past? Places that you recognize visiting? People that you have met?" She tried to make it look as if she was merely seeking conversation. She hoped to learn more about him and hoped it might provide an idea to escape. The looming threat of Kenatos spurred her on.

"The locket," he answered, fishing it from a pocket. "I think it was the music that attracted the bear last night. My own fault, not yours. Something about the sound haunts me. As if I should know it." He rested his chin on his muscled forearm. "It is maddening."

"You said you took it from a man?" Phae asked after a long pause. "You said it was made by a Paracelsus." She looked him in the eye but he would not meet her gaze.

He rubbed his chin back and forth across his forearm, his expression cloudy with turmoil.

She finished another tattered line and worked on another, letting the sunlight warm her face and hands. She bit off the thread. "It was my father."

He nodded mutely, refusing to look at her.

"You said last night that I wouldn't want to know more," she said softly, working the needle and thread effortlessly. "I can see why now." She sighed. "He is dead?"

The Kishion sighed deeply. "Yes."

She was not sure how she should feel. Her father had abandoned her at an orphanage. Granted, he had made sure it was one that would not fear her heritage and magic, but he had done nothing to reveal himself to her and his own actions had violated the Arch-Rike's trust. Now she was condemned because of him. The emotions were twisting and twining around each other, layer after layer. She resented her father. She craved to know more, even if it would wound her. What betrayal had he done to earn the Arch-Rike's contempt?

"I never knew him," Phae said, trying to keep control of her voice, to keep the conversation going. "I wish that I did. You do not remember your past, but what can you tell me of his?"

"You despise me," he said flatly. "Don't pretend otherwise. I do not begrudge you that emotion. I despise myself right now."

"For killing him?" she asked, leaning forward.

"It was my duty," he answered stiffly. "I am not entrusted with the reasons for my assignments, only to carry them out. I was first sent to arrest your father and bring him to the Arch-Rike for questioning. When I arrived at his tower, he used his magic to cause the tower to explode. I was left under a pile of rubble. Whether he knew the blast would kill me or not, I do not know, but it slowed me down. I began hunting him. His own actions labeled him guilty of treason. I fulfilled my assignment when I stabbed him and left his dead body crumpled near the edge of a pond. I don't regret killing him. But I do regret that *I* am the one telling you about it."

Phae nodded, tears welling in her eyes. It was so hard to listen to him speak of her father's murder with so little emotion. Part of her hated him for it. Another part of her hated her father for betraying the Arch-Rike.

She swallowed and found her throat very dry. "What was—" She swallowed again. "What was his name please?" She brushed away the tears.

"Tyrus of Kenatos. Tyrus Paracelsus. You look . . . like him. I see the resemblance."

Phae blotted the tears on her sleeve. "When we are back in Kenatos, you will give me over to the Arch-Rike. Then he will take away your memories again. You won't remember . . . me. Or this."

He stared at the grass and nodded solemnly.

She struggled to master her own emotions. She wanted to start sobbing, but she fought against the despair. "I don't think I could live without my memories. Even the painful ones. Even last night." She swallowed, looking down at her hands. "I think you should stop being a Kishion. You have a name. Someone out there must know it." She nodded forcefully. "When you are done with this assignment, you should seek it."

He looked at her in silence, staring at her thoughtfully. "You do not ask me to free you."

Phae shook her head, working quickly on the remaining tear. "I know you will not. Your duty binds you. But I do ask you to free yourself."

"What if I cannot live with myself?" he asked. "What if the memories kill me?"

She bit the last thread. "That is probably what the Arch-Rike wants you to think."

There was enough light now. He stared in her eyes, as if her words were sinking deep into his heart. She could blink and snatch it away. She could snatch away his memory of meeting her. She almost did. But Phae could not bring herself to do it, not after giving her promise.

There was the sound of groaning iron. The gate opened ponderously. Phae looked up and realized men had gathered on the battlement walls and were pointing in their direction. She saw the flash of metal in the sunlight as riders emerged from the gate, coming at them from a trot to a full gallop.

The Kishion snatched the shirt from her hands and pulled it on quickly. Rising to a crouch, he tensed with recognition. "Romani," he said venomously.

"Every civilization has a history, typically an oral tradition, that defines how it came into being. Many of these traditions are remarkably similar and require the belief in an unseen realm ruled over by an entity that is good. There is another similarity amongst these many stories. That is the part of evil and how it came to be. The stories all say that pride is what introduced evil into the world. It is good beings that turn into evil ones. If this is so, and pride makes a good man evil, then it requires humility to make men good. So often man wishes to be happy even when he so lives as to make happiness impossible."

—Possidius Adeodat, Archivist of Kenatos

XII

Even in Stonehollow, the Romani were recognized and feared. Of all the races or people, they were distrusted the most. Phae's insides writhed with apprehension as she saw the horsemen emerge from the gate.

"What do we do?" she asked in fear.

"They already see us," he answered, rising to his full height and brushing his hands together before fitting on his gloves. "They expect us to run. They expect us to be afraid and to barter for our lives." He gave her a sidelong look. "If it frightens you to be taken to the Arch-Rike of Kenatos, consider yourself fortunate not to be abducted by the Romani. You are young enough. They would pierce your ear and train you in their ways before selling you at eighteen. If you disobey, they poison you."

Phae gasped with dread and touched his arm. "What will we do then?"

The riders closed the distance quickly and the thundering of the hooves made Phae cringe and tremble. The Kishion faced the approaching Romani and stepped in front of her, blocking her with his body.

"The horses will not trample us," he said. "If one of the men tries to grab you, drop low. They won't be able to reach down that far. Stay near me. I will deal with them."

"How?" she demanded, for at least twenty approached. She pulled her pack and slung it around her shoulders.

"Just stay near me," he said as the first rider drew up to them. "Do not run."

"I bid you good day!" a Romani said, leaning forward in his saddle to regard the pair. He had dark hair, a charming smile, but his eyes were ruthless. Other riders slowed to a canter and filled in around them, blocking them in on all sides.

The Kishion said nothing.

"Our people have a saying that you should never bid the evil one good day until you meet him. Again, I bid you good day."

He was met with silence. One of the horses nickered softly and others began stamping.

"He's a rude one," said another man, one behind them.

"It's the quiet pigs that eat all the draff," said another.

The first one, whom Phae presumed to be the leader, looked askance at the Kishion. "Too proud to speak, are you?"

"Everyone is wise till he speaks," chuckled someone else.

The leader puffed out his chest, folding his arms. "He thinks that he's the very stone that was hurled at the castle. Look at him. He says nothing. Still no words for us? No begging?"

"She has red hair," said another Romani. His stallion came close to Phae, its dripping nose nearly grazing her arm. "Worth something this season, I think. Let me see you closer, lass."

Phae shrank as he reached for her, pressing her back against the Kishion's, ready to drop low. The man suddenly lunged, trying to get a fistful of her cloak. The Kishion moved like a blur, grabbing the outstretched arm and yanking him clear from the saddle. He fell so fast and hard he could not cry out before smashing on the ground. The Kishion snapped several of his fingers before whirling to face the leader again.

The Kishion's attack stunned them momentarily and then all was in commotion. With a bark of rage, the leader shouted for the Romani to kill the Kishion and drew a tapered long sword from his scabbard.

"Stay low," the Kishion whispered to her and disappeared. He sidestepped between two horses, his dagger whipping around and stabbing their flanks, startling them with pain and causing them to rear violently and pitch off their riders. Phae watched in awe as he moved, each step precise and measured, swaying with the rhythm of battle to avoid the clashing beasts and the sword thrusts coming down at him from all sides. He was never in one place for more than a moment, moving quickly and soundlessly, his tattered cloak fanning behind him as he stalked another victim, grabbing the reins from a man's grasp and jerking the bridle around savagely so that the horse would react in pain.

Phae remembered in time to drop low, just as another hand reached for her hair. The man tried in vain to snatch at her, and Phae scuttled away from him, only to hear another horse coming up behind her. Her heart raced with fear and excitement. Twenty against one. Somehow, she knew the Kishion would win. He did not bluster or threaten. He did not need to.

A man suddenly grabbed her around the waist from behind and hoisted her off her feet. She had not heard him slip off his saddle and she started thrashing, trying to squirm free from his grasp. He clutched her tightly, swinging her around.

"Oy!" he called to another Romani, dragging her to the man's horse. The rider reached for her and grabbed her by the arm. She struck him again and again, beating against his arm, trying to hit his face. The horse shied, but the rider was expert and controlled it. Fresh terror rose inside. The Kishion was boxed in by other riders. He could not see her.

"Lift her higher!" the Romani snarled. "This one is a wildcat!"

"It's for her own good that the cat purrs!" the one holding her said. "We'll tame you, lass. Cinder-headed or no, we will."

Phae struggled, her fear turning into anger. He had called her cinder-haired. Cinder—a word about fire. Her fingers began to tingle. The words came to her mind. *Pyricanthas. Sericanthas. Thas.*

The man grabbing her arms yelped when those very arms burst into flame. His cloak caught fire and the horse screamed in terror and bolted. All animals dreaded flame. Phae reached down and grabbed the man's arms that were crushing her middle. Though protected by leather bracers, the leather blackened and hissed and the man's skin blistered. With a howl of pain, he released her, scrambling to get back from her.

Phae turned and faced him, her hands wreathed in blue-violet swirls. Her anger seared her heart, fanning the power that flooded into her. Gone were the feelings of helplessness. Gone was the timidity and flinching. The power inside her surged like a fountain and she held up her hands, unleashing a storm of flames at the man who was tripping over his ankles trying to get away from her. He vanished into a plume of ash. It felt frighteningly delicious.

Horses shrieked in terror and bolted. In the distance, she could hear the groan of the gate as the Romani inside desperately pulled it closed. Phae stood in a half-crouch, staring at the fire licking the grass where the man had stood. Yellow tongues rippled with heat and charred the grass, spreading with the wind and causing billowy black smoke to rise in the air.

One of the horses was not running. The leader's mount was caught by the reins, the Kishion gripping it with iron, forcing it to remain.

"Over here!" the Kishion barked at her. He beckoned for her to come to him and swung up on the saddle. She noticed the Romani leader sprawled on the grass, his neck at a crooked angle. The feelings swelled inside of her. Part of her wanted to unleash the magic in her blood against the Kishion. Another part of her cringed at the thought. Surely if a hundred bee-stings could not harm him, neither would fire. But it was not just the logic of the thought. She cringed at the thought of harming him, of betraying him again.

Phae ran to him and let the flames die down inside her. He reached down for her and she reached up to him, grabbing his arm. He pulled her effortlessly up and she swung her leg around the saddle behind him.

"Hold tight to me," he said to her. The flames began to roar inside the grassland, licking through the dried grasses and blazing into the sky. Stamping the flanks, the Kishion jerked the reins the other way and started the beast at a gallop. Phae pressed against his back, holding around his middle as tightly as she could. They raced against the flames spreading out through the meadow. The ride was thrilling. She found herself smiling, even when she remembered the man she had just killed. It frightened her how easily she had done it, how powerful it had made her feel.

The euphoria did not last long.

Phae knelt by the stream and cupped water in both hands, gulping it down. Her stomach was in knots with anguish. She had killed a man. Yes, he was a Romani. Yes, he probably deserved to die. But she was sixteen years old and it horrified her. She had summoned flames with her hands as a child and had been taught to control her emotions and to control the flames with the Vaettir words of power. She had never desired nor even thought to turn them against a living person before. She swallowed the water and bowed her head, grief-stricken with how easily she had done it and how giddy it had made her feel. Phae loathed herself.

The horse drank deeply from the stream, resting its lathered body for some time. The Kishion crouched by the stream and filled his leather flask. He glanced at her and she tried to look away from him so that he wouldn't see the tears on her lashes.

"The first death is always the hardest," he said. "It will fade."

She wiped her lips. "Coming from you, that is not very comforting," she answered, glowering at him. "I do not want to *be* like you."

He snorted. "No one would wish it." He straightened, adjusting the saddle straps and patting down the beast. "The Romani have a saying. If you don't know the way, walk slowly. They should have heeded their own wisdom this morning."

Phae stared down at her reflection in the stream. She wiped her nose, feeling miserable. They had covered quite a bit of ground so far. The day was not all spent yet, but she could see the hills looming ahead of them, jagged with clefts of rock and stunted pine. The hills looked as if they had a stain, but she knew it was just the colors of the stone in the shadows. The valley was encircled by those hills, which provided a natural barricade from the other kingdoms. By nightfall they would reach the road that was carved into the mountain, leaving Stonehollow and joining with Fowlrox. They would probably reach Fowlrox before midnight.

She rubbed her legs and stood. The Kishion examined the contents of the saddle bags. There were some rations there—dried beef, fruit, nuts, figs, and cheese. An old heel of bread was removed as well. He tossed these to her, though kept some of the figs for himself.

"Do you even need to eat?" she asked him, tearing a hunk from the bread.

He shook his head no. "I enjoy the taste of food. But I will not starve to death or die of thirst."

She sat down by the edge of the stream, taking a nibble from the cheese. It was sharp but full of flavor. "You truly cannot die then?"

He nodded. "I do not know the magic the Arch-Rike uses to

give me this invulnerability. I have vague memories. I know about the Vaettir, the Preachán, the Cruithne. I am Aeduan, as you can tell on your own. I believe I have even visited all of the kingdoms. But I do not recall my past."

Phae sighed deeply. "I am sorry I was rude to you."

He gave her a curious look, pausing in his examination of the saddle bags. "You are a strange girl. I do not deserve your apology."

"That may be true, but I offer it still. I do not hate you, Kishion." She sighed again. "I wish you had a name, though. I do not like calling you that. It doesn't . . . feel right. When you have finished your task, I do want you to go find your true name. When you have, come and tell it to me. This is assuming my life is useful to the Arch-Rike in some small way."

A haunted smile passed over his mouth. "I doubt I will remember your request for very long. Now that you've killed a man, can you see why losing the memory is better? The guilt is crushing you."

Phae shook her head angrily. "No, I never want to forget what I did. I never want to do that again. I want to remember how it felt." She wiped her face, sighing again. "Is there anything else in the bags then?"

He poked inside the next one. "Ducats, mostly. Ah, here we are. A map." He withdrew a leather-bound parchment scroll. He uncapped the ends and slowly opened it, his expression keen.

"I see," he murmured.

"What is it?" Phae asked, getting to her feet quickly. She glanced at the scroll and saw a representation of the kingdoms. There was Stonehollow, featured prominently. She saw the city as well as the road to Fowlrox. There were other trails marked though, roads that were unfamiliar to her.

"They are looking for a new road into Stonehollow," the Kishion surmised. He pointed at the lines and the mountains. "See, they are drawing the different passes and marking each one they have tried with an 'X'. This is the gate where they were hiding. These are probably scouts, looking for a safe haven, another way of transporting stone and timber away from Stonehollow. Away from the only road in or out of the kingdom."

Phae looked at him curiously. "Why would they do that?"

"Because the strength of Stonehollow comes from its defenses. You cannot attack this kingdom because the only way in is through one of the mountain passes where they have carved a road through several enormous boulders. An army cannot cross those mountains except through that road. It is easily defended. It also means they can control all the stone and timber they sell, because they can tax what goes out through the road. If the Romani find another way to leave the valley, it will give them a way of manipulating the trading here. The Arch-Rike will wish to hear of this."

"I heard from my . . . friend that the Romani may not control the trade routes in the future. Is that true?"

The Kishion nodded. "Yes. There is a treaty with Wayland. This is useful information to have." He secured the saddle bags again and then climbed up on the saddle. Phae stared up at his face, feeling the mounting dread. Perhaps the Arch-Rike was not a person to fear. She had the sense that her life was about to change. If she embraced the change, perhaps her fate would not be as horrible as she thought.

He reached for her again and she clasped his arm and mounted behind him again. When she had first seen him, the scars on his face had frightened her but now she hardly noticed them. His eyes had seemed dead. They no longer did. There was something inside his eyes now, a longing for his past. But she also remembered quite vividly how quickly his mood could change and how dangerous he truly was. It made her shudder.

With a tap from his boots, the horse plunged into the shallow stream and emerged on the other side in moments. They managed an even pace to preserve the animal's strength. In the distance behind them, the haze from the brushfire could still be seen. She wondered what Master Winemiller was doing. Had he gone into Stonehollow to seek information? Was he traveling to the cabin at that moment? What of the Vaettir prince? Where was he? So many questions flitted through her mind.

"What do you know about my blood?" Phae asked him after they had been traveling awhile.

"You are Dryad-born," he said. "You also have the fireblood. I do not think there has ever been someone like you before."

"But do you know what a Dryad is? Do you know what makes that important? I do not understand what my father was hoping to accomplish."

"It does not matter," the Kishion replied. "His plan failed."

"Yes, but what was it? Do you know what he wanted to do with me? Why he sent someone to find me?"

He was silent for a while, and she did not know why. She did know that saying nothing would probably be best. Patience, she told herself. Let him decide he can trust you.

"He was going to take you into the Scourgelands."

Even Phae had heard of that place. Her skin prickled with gooseflesh. "But—nothing survives there. There is no kingdom even near it because no one can tame that forest. It is older than the world. In Stonehollow we teach that our valley was chosen as a way to protect us from the evil of that place."

The Kishion said nothing. She sensed a reticence falling over him.

"Have you . . . been there?" she asked softly. "Do you remember something?"

He shrugged. "I earned these claw marks somehow. I do not remember when I got them. I believe I have had them for a long time. It may have . . . something to do with that place. Your father had claw marks too."

123

Phae swallowed and pressed her cheek against the Kishion's shoulder. The hills began to rise and swell and soon they saw massive stone formations crowning the hills amidst the bristlecone pine and bur oak. The ridges were rugged country, impossible for a horse to cross. The sun began to set, turning the sky a fiery hue as it mingled amidst a bank of storm clouds. The wind swept through the lowland prairie, bringing the temperature down. In the distance came the rumble of thunder. The beauty of the land swelled inside Phae's heart. She still did not want to leave Stonehollow, but she could not think of a way to avoid that fate. Perhaps a storm would force them to shelter amidst the trees or inside a cave?

The horse was weary from the long ride that day and carrying two riders. But it was a stubborn beast and it continued to plod ahead, determined to carry them to the brink of the country. Phae nestled against the Kishion's back, drowsy with the swaying motion. She could feel the tension in his muscles, hear the heart beating inside him. He was a living creature. But he could not die.

"I hope you will remember me—when this is over," she said, stifling a yawn. "If I saw you again, I would be . . . sad if you did not remember me."

He was silent and the wind rustled the long valley grass. She swallowed, her eyes closing. His voice was barely more than a whisper.

"The strange thing is that I feel I already know you. Somehow. I cannot explain it."

Phae straightened. "We have never met, Kishion."

"Then why are you so familiar to me?" he wondered aloud. He sighed. "I feel as if I should know you. As if I should recognize you. The locket. The music. Your hair. Something speaks to me from the past." He sighed deeply. "There is the road."

Phae saw it too and her heart turned into stone. It was closer than she had believed. They had followed the valley to the northeast, cutting across the abandoned farmlands to reach the mountains and finally the road. They left the long grass to the finely packed dirt road leading up into the mountains. The constant trampling of oxen hooves and wagon wheels had made it impossible for anything to grow on the road. Markers carved from stone appeared on the road ahead, designating the distance to Fowlrox. They would reach it long before midnight.

As the horse climbed into the hills toward the mountains, the shadows thickened as the sun went down. Looming boulders flanked the road, making it impossible to leave the trail by horseback. This was the easiest path to leave the valley. It had the gentlest slope for the oxen to pull the massive granite rocks quarried from the valley and transported beyond. Each clop of the hooves made Phae mourn her past. She had a sickening feeling that she would never return.

Ahead, Phae saw the first tunnel. It was a square hole ponderously carved amidst an enormous boulder the size of a large cottage. The tunnel hole was wide and tall enough for a single wagon to ride through. It was also very deep, but she could see the dim light coming from the far end. The tunnel had been carved from living rock centuries before. She knew there were two more like it farther ahead. She had never passed its boundaries before.

Trees gathered thick around the edges of the tunnel boulder. Smaller fragments of broken rock were littered nearby. Phae was starting to drowse again when the Kishion stiffened in the saddle, jerking the reins so hard, it startled her. Shapes emerged from the darkness of the tunnel. Two men approached them. One was tall and broad-shouldered and walked with a slight limp. The other was shorter and walked to keep pace with the taller man. As they emerged from the tunnel facing them, Phae gasped. One was dressed like a Rike of Seithrall, though he was Vaettir.

It was Prince Aran.

The other man was taller, wearing a stained tunic and cloak and held a strange metal shape in his hand. Not a sword, but a device of some kind. He had reddish hair, cinder-colored, just like hers. His beard and temples were streaked with gray. His eyes were intense and stared at the Kishion deliberately. Phae sensed something about him, something familiar. Her heart started to hammer in her chest. He looked familiar, like a reflection in a dream.

The Kishion stared. "I killed you," he said in a low voice, as if he could not believe his senses.

There was the hint of a smile amidst the bearded man's face. "And I wanted you to think that, Kishion," came the reply. "I've come for my daughter."

"I once observed the Arch-Rike of Kenatos calm a quarrel between two very strong-willed merchants in the city. He invited both to a feast he had prepared for some prominent individuals. He told me this with a sly voice: 'If you wish to play peacemaker, seat adversaries next to each other where they must begin by being civil.' True it is, we only hate those whom we do not know."

—Possidius Adeodat, Archivist of Kenatos

XIII

F lee, *Druidecht. They are coming.*

Annon awoke with a start, hearing the voices in his mind. Nizeera was already pacing the edge of their makeshift camp, her tail lashing back and forth restlessly. Several spirits flitted about her ears, which swatted at them as if they were flies. Annon rolled to his knees and crawled over to Khiara and shook her awake. She roused instantly, her expression tightening with concern.

"Danger?" she whispered.

"Yes. We camped too near Boeotia," Annon answered. He listened to the trilling whispers from Mirrowen. "Wake Erasmus. I'll rouse Lukias."

She nodded and grabbed her blanket, folding it swiftly and plunging it into her pack. Annon scuttled over to Lukias, who slept soundly, his breath coming in and out like short curt breezes. He shook the man's shoulders firmly.

Lukias's eyes widened with terror, staring up at Annon for a moment. "What is it?"

"The Boeotians are near," Annon whispered. "We must go." *Nizeera, can you hear them yet?*

Not yet. But I can smell them. They have smoking torches. The same kind as before.

Annon whistled softly, feeling the prickle of gooseflesh run up his arms and make him shiver. He had nearly died protecting Neodesha's tree from the attack of Boeotians and the Black Druidecht. The thought of ever facing such people again made him sick with fear for the spirit would be unable to help him amidst the deadly smoke. He also remembered that the Black Druidecht had lost his arm and managed to escape.

"Come," Annon beckoned, pulling his cloak around his neck and starting to the east under a sky full of diamond stars. Erasmus hastily pulled on his boots and managed to catch up quickly.

Lukias fell in beside Annon. "I do not need to remind you that we are all dressed as Rikes of Seithrall, which would mean instant death if the barbarians catch us. We should have made for Brookshier as I told you."

Annon shook his head and scowled with impatience. "Brookshier is the last outpost north of Kenatos. It's under the Arch-Rike's control. We wouldn't be any safer there."

"You don't trust me," Lukias said with an accusing voice, his look darkening.

"It isn't a matter of trust, Lukias," Annon answered. "I'm a Druidecht. My power is here. We were warned in time to flee. If I didn't trust you, you'd spend each night tied to a tree."

Erasmus muttered softly under his breath, "A suggestion that I have mentioned more than once along this journey."

Nizeera padded up next to him. *They are closing quickly. Something leads them toward us. Dark spirits.*

Annon frowned, feeling his stomach churn with dread. He quickened his pace and noticed the others struggling to keep up. He was used to roaming the wilds, but never with spear-carrying nomads hunting him. Even the night sky could not hide the row of mountains in the northern horizon, the peaks gleaming with crags and ice. They had left Silvandom, skirting around the lake on the northern edge of the woods, and ventured into the grasslands separating the kingdoms from Boeotia. Lukias told them their destination was in the mountains north of the island city. It was unfamiliar country to Annon, who had never ventured farther north than Kenatos in his life. He had heard that Druidecht were welcome in Boeotia, but their disguises as Rikes of Seithrall would negate any friendliness his talisman would provide.

Annon and Lukias had struck an interesting comradeship along the way. The Rike was constantly amazed at Annon's ability to commune with nature and the evidences of the spirits of Mirrowen that were manifest around them. Lukias had watched Annon summon spirits to guide them, providing insights into the land, the location of wild berries or fresh game or roots. He was fascinated with Druidecht lore and continued to ask questions, though Annon did not do much to satisfy his curiosity. Much of the Druidecht training was verbal, passed on from mentor to student to be memorized and repeated—such as the names of spirits, their powers, and what persuaded them to aid or injure mortals. It was never allowed to be written down and Annon did not trust the Rike with the secret knowledge of how to commune with Mirrowen. It was enough that he could demonstrate the power to achieve Lukias's admiration.

Annon hoped that another day's walk would put them in reach of the mountain passes. That would bring them closer to Basilides, where Tyrus had implored him to go. Annon had no idea how he was going to infiltrate the lair of the oracle, especially knowing that the Arch-Rike's minions would be expecting him. He hoped that having Lukias on their side would help. He prepared himself, though, for betrayal.

Nizeera growled softly. *They are running now. I hear their approach.*

Annon's throat constricted. He licked his lips. "They are gaining on us," he said softly to the others. "They know we're here and they'll likely try to kill us."

"How do you know this?" Lukias demanded. He cast around vigorously. "I hear nothing."

"What should we do, Annon?" Khiara asked. "Do we stand and fight them? I will not kill but I can harm them."

"Foolish to face them in the open like this," Erasmus said. "They are trained hunters and survivors. How many are there?"

Annon sent out a mental thought to one of the spirits, who zigzagged away like a moth trailing green motes of dust. He shook his head. "We slept too long. It was not safe resting so near their territory."

"How many?" Erasmus pressed anxiously, probably wanting to comment on the odds of their surviving the night. There was a flash of light in the distance behind them. Annon felt a sick queasiness. The moth-spirit would not be returning.

"I don't know. To the trees over there," Annon said, pointing. "They are a scraggly bunch but at least it will provide some cover. Khiara, you float to the upper branches and wait there, ready to come down. I will try to startle them away."

"How?" Lukias asked. "The fireblood?"

Annon nodded. "Erasmus. You stay hidden and look for opportunities to strike. Nizeera and I will face them as we have before." He glanced at Lukias. "You seem proficient with a blade. Are you?"

"I know all of a man's vulnerable spots," he replied confidently. "I will stand with you. I have warred against Boeotians before. They are fearsome but they can be killed."

"Hurry then," Annon said, breaking into a run toward the copse of ash trees. His heart shuddered inside his chest, swelling with emotion. He remembered perfectly the battle where he had faced them before. Every part of it was burned into his mind, every word that had been spoken. Would any of those memories benefit him now? Reeder had died facing the Boeotians at the Dryad tree in Silvandom. Annon did not want any of his companions to meet their fate here.

They reached the ash trees quickly and entered the copse silently, moving through the skeletal limbs. Annon searched for a defensive position, quickly surveying the ground. His search was interrupted by the sound of running men, panting in the darkness behind them.

Nizeera growled again and Annon stroked her head, summoning his courage. He motioned for Khiara to float up into the trees, which she promptly did after taking in a deep breath. Lukias unsheathed his dagger and stood at Annon's left, arms folded, his face impassive but not fearful. Erasmus vanished behind them into the thicket. *Pyricanthas. Sericanthas. Thas.* Annon's hands began to glow.

The Boeotians slowed and entered the grove at a prowl, spears held low. There were no battle cries or warning. Their shapes flitted through the gaps of the trees, advancing on them in a wave. Annon tried to count the number of shapes and quickly abandoned it. There were at least twenty. He remembered how aggressive and cruel they were. Perhaps fire would frighten them. If not, he knew they'd be unleashing spears quickly. There was no reasoning with such men.

He recalled words that the other Boeotians had spoken. His memory was perfect now and he could summon the images by only thinking about them. Perhaps challenging them in their own tongue would surprise them.

"Atu! Atu vast!" Annon roared. Then he ran at them, bringing up his hands and unleashing his magic. The Boeotians were fighters. Annon did not think for a moment he could reason with them or talk his way out of a fight. The best thing to do was do something unexpected. Attack them first, make them feel that *they* had been drawn into a trap. Paedrin had called it the Uddhava.

Flames blasted through the woods, sending blooms of light to expose those he was attacking. He recognized the tattooed skin, the muscled arms and spears. His sudden attack caught them completely by surprise. Lukias shouted in fury and ran after him and Nizeera let out a feline scream that made even Annon quail.

Several Boeotians were caught in the initial blast of flame and went down, skin burning. Annon summoned a gob of fire in his hand and hurled it at another group. It streaked through the woods, blinding them with its brilliance and exploded into a tree, showering sparks as it struck. Boeotians dived away from him, unable to bring their spears up to throw. Nizeera vaulted into the nearest cluster of men, claws raking and teeth snapping viciously. Annon continued to charge, sending another sheet of flames into the next group. Fire began to lick the dried scrub at the base of the trees. Emotions swirled inside of Annon, feeding him with power and anger. Euphoria replaced the fear. At the fringe of the euphoria was madness.

Khiara dropped from the trees, landing amidst a group of Boeotians who were coming at Annon from the side. The copse was too dense for her to use her long tapered staff effectively. Annon glanced and saw her drop it and start using her fists and feet to cripple and break her opponents in the Bhikhu way. Lukias rushed up to the nearest Boeotian, dodging a thrust from his spear and threw his knife with deadly aim.

Several of the Boeotians started running for their lives. Annon saw more regrouping to press the attack again. They held smoking sticks in their hands, creating a haze of smoke around them. They were cursing and raging in their language, shaking their spears. If he could douse the flames somehow, he could summon spirit creatures to aid them. Annon focused on the burning brands and felt part of him connect with the smoking embers. He sensed the flickering tongues and fire, experiencing a kinship with it. They would pay homage to him. Muttering the Vaettir words in his mind, Annon tamed the fire in the brands. The smoke stopped.

Now! Annon beckoned to the spirits that were holding back, afraid of the smoke. Nizeera turned her bloody muzzle up, sensing the change in the air. She screamed again, launching herself at another cluster of men, savaging them with her claws. Annon's elation grew.

The Boeotians crumpled when the spirits began darting amidst them, stinging with magic and exploding in their midst with painful shocks and blinding light. The Boeotians roared with pain and fled the copse, sprinting away from the scene with haste.

Lingering in the air nearby, he sensed the presence of fell spirits.

We see you, Druidecht.

We know you, Druidecht.

Tasvir Virk will come for you. You are hunted still.

The thoughts fluttered against his mind and then they were gone.

The thoughts caused a chill to seep into Annon's bones, despite the flames dancing on his hands. He looked down and saw that he was standing amidst crackling flames that did not harm him. The woods were ablaze around him. He stared at the yellow licking tongues, hungering for the power contained inside them. He wanted the whole world to burn. He wondered, deep down, if he had the power to make it happen. Thoughts flooded his mind, seductive and yearning. Unleash the flames to their full potential. Let their true nature manifest itself at last.

The beckoning was seductive. It made his insides throb with excitement. What would it be like to experience that? What power would be unleashed?

Annon steeled himself, aware of the danger he was to himself and his companions. He remembered the Black Druidecht he had faced at Neodesha's tree. The man was already mad. Annon clenched his fists and walked away from the fire, back toward where Erasmus was skulking, examining the tattoos of a Boeotian corpse. Nizeera chased a few of the Boeotians even farther, but even she returned and sauntered up to his side as he emerged from the blaze. He released the control of the fireblood, letting the emotions fade and pass. Sweat trickled down his face. He had come close that time— dangerously close. He could remember the burning hut where his mother had died, lost in the furnace of flames. Tears threatened to choke him. He stood still, trembling. It took long moments to master his emotions.

Lukias approached and gripped Annon's shoulder, his face expressive with admiration. His eyes glittered and a wolfish smile appeared. "You are powerful, Druidecht. I can see why they hunt those with the fireblood. Truly, you frighten me."

Annon swallowed, glancing at the Rike with unease. The mixture of awe and fear in his voice was significant. Lukias was a man not easily impressed.

"I do not think they will hunt us now," he said huskily.

Lukias nodded in agreement. "I see why the Arch-Rike fears you as well. You see, he has the fireblood too. He fears you will usurp his place."

Annon stared at him coldly. "I do not seek his throne. But I do seek his downfall."

"The world is a book, and those who do not travel read only a page."

—*Possidius Adeodat, Archivist of Kenatos*

XIV

The sprawling mountain range north of Kenatos was jagged, brooding, and capped with dazzling white snow at the upper peaks. Below lay cracked foothills littered with boulders, as if some colossus with a hammer had repeatedly struck the mountains. There were no trees in the upper peaks, only slabs of blue-gray rock that provided a barrier to the twisted lands beyond—the place known as the Scourgelands. Passes led in and out of the maze-like range, but there were no trails or roads.

Annon and Lukias walked side by side, heads bent low against strong winds blowing down from the mountains. Erasmus and Khiara followed behind, and Annon heard the Preachán struggling to maintain his footing on the loose gravel. The vegetation was sparse, the prairie grass stiff and crackled as they trampled it. Nizeera padded a distance ahead, hunting for signs of spirit life.

"You said that you knew the Arch-Rike had the fireblood," Annon said, brushing dust from his eyes. "How did you learn this?"

Lukias craned his neck, staring up at the mountains with a grim look. "Many of the great men of this world have it. Some suggest it is merely an ample surplus of ambition. If you look through the histories, as I have, you will see its evidence. Band-Imas is one of the greatest Arch-Rikes who has ever lived. But to answer your question, I was warned of it when I was younger. It was said that the Arch-Rike is a calm man, but possesses a fiery temper. When angry, his hands begin to glow. That is one of the marks of the fireblood, is it not?"

"It is. But have you seen it yourself in him?"

Lukias nodded. "Yes, but only rarely. The last time was when Tyrus Paracelsus escaped the city, destroying the tower in his wake. I was in the room when the news was brought. His face went black, his eyes glittered, and then I saw his hands. The hunt began immediately."

Annon was curious to know more about their enemy. "How did the Arch-Rike come to power?"

"He was one of the many orphans raised in the city with a great mind for philosophy. Rather than joining the ranks of the Paracelsus, he devoted himself to the Rikes and rose quickly. He was wise for one so young and earned respect for his natural abilities as a leader. Men twice his age deferred to him for his unique wisdom. When there were problems, he solved them. I myself knew him as a younger man. He was the greatest among us. When the last Arch-Rike died, he was chosen despite his youth."

Annon rubbed his chin. "How did the previous one die?"

Lukias glanced at him, brow furrowing. "He was old, Annon. His heart gave out. You cannot understand the pressures that come with the position. When Band-Imas was younger, his hair was like yours. Now it is white."

"What I do not understand is why he stands in the way. Surely he has seen the destruction caused by the Plague. He has lived through it twice in his life, at least. Maybe three times. Is it merely ambition? He seeks to preserve his power?"

Lukias shook his head. "He and Tyrus were once very close. I think, at one time, he even considered Tyrus as a potential successor."

"Really?"

"Oh, yes. Something happened between them. Something regarding Tyrus's older sister. I do not know what it was. Both men are very private."

Annon mulled over Lukias's statements, adding them to the information he already knew from Tyrus. Something nagged at his mind.

"You said that the Arch-Rike was known for his wisdom, especially as a younger man. Do you know how he achieved it? Was he known to travel much?" Annon wondered if the Arch-Rike had been kissed by a Dryad.

"He did travel a great deal. He was an emissary for his predecessor and a shrewd negotiator and influencer. The only kingdom he would not visit was Stonehollow, for obvious reasons. They persecute those with the fireblood."

"Do you know why that is?"

"They have a pagan belief that those with the fireblood are immune to the Plague. It is nonsense, of course."

"Some myths have elements of truth," Annon observed.

"It is said that the Druidecht run naked through the woods performing secret rites." He looked at Annon quizzically, his mouth twitching with a smirk.

"That is not true," Annon replied. "Your point is taken."

"I have answered your questions about my master. Answer some for me."

"If I can. About Tyrus or the Druidecht?"

"You would doubt my motives if I asked about Tyrus. Yes, I see the look—you would. So tell me of your order. Why will the Druidecht not allow their lore to be documented? Clearly you run the risk of losing all power should the Plague strike Canton Vaud. It is not logical. I have never understood the reason."

Annon was pensive. It always made him uncomfortable when Lukias asked about the Druidecht or probed more about their plans following Basilides. While the ring on his finger helped him believe Lukias was not intending to betray them, he felt it prudent to withhold secrets, just as Tyrus had always done. He was beginning to believe that Lukias was sincere. But he did not wish to trust him recklessly.

"It is difficult to explain," Annon replied. "Some knowledge is precious. If used wrongly, it can cause great harm. A Druidecht is trained piece by piece, bit by bit. We prove ourselves worthy of new knowledge by faithfully using what we have been given. Only when we have mastered the obligations of the knowledge already given are we allowed to learn more. Writing it down would be a temptation for some to gulp the knowledge instead of only sipping it. Every Druidecht learns at their own pace, not according to age or race. This talisman that I wear"—Annon fingered it respectfully—"is proof that I have mastered the knowledge and have earned the trust to learn more. Were I too ambitious to learn or failed to demonstrate the knowledge properly, I would lose the confidence of the spirits and would lose the talisman eventually. Even if a Preachán stole it from me, it would do them little good in the woods. It would become very clear to a spirit that he had not earned it."

Lukias nodded sagely.

The gravel suddenly shifted under Annon's boots and he nearly fell.

Lukias grabbed his arm to steady him. "These foothills are treacherous," the Rike said, squinting at Annon.

"How far to Basilides?" Annon asked.

"Tomorrow we will reach the pass that leads to it." He glanced from Annon to his friends. "When you see it, you will understand why this quest of yours will fail. Just as it takes a Druidecht to understand the lore of the wild, it takes a Rike of Seithrall to navigate the shrine. You will not penetrate the interior without my help. It would be dangerous for you to attempt it."

Annon stood still and stared at him. "I do not ask you to betray your brethren. Only to lead us there."

Lukias shook his head. "I will not betray the order. I'm only warning you that it is dangerous. We spoke a moment ago about trust. I have tried to earn yours these last few days. Your spirit cat will attest that I have not tried to escape. I have made no contact with the order and I do not intend to betray you. Your rings verify my words."

Erasmus reached them, his expression wary. "Words are slippery things, Rike."

"They are indeed, Preachán. I was taught by the order that the Druidecht magic was a myth, a superstition. If that is not true, it puts in question the other things I've been taught. I am your willing prisoner right now. I hope to earn your trust to be included in your mission. Perhaps our two sides need not war any longer."

Annon smiled sardonically. "We'll see." He looked at the others. "The day is getting late, but we should go farther and then make camp. Onward."

Their heavy boots began shuffling deeper into the fringe of mountains.

☙

They sat around a small campfire in a cave made from fallen boulders. The enormous stones shielded the light and hid them from anyone passing by the foothills below. Scrub and rock littered the land, a boneyard of granite and fissures. They had seen many lizards along the way, some quite large. Serpents slithered away from them, unused to disruption by mankind in the inhospitable terrain. The shelter was large enough to provide cover for them. The ground was powdery dust.

Annon stared into the fire, reaching out through his talisman for spirits in the area. It was not the type of creatures he was used to in Wayland, but they responded to him immediately, coming in the form of moths and dragonflies as his companions ate their rations in silence, faces haggard from the arduous walk.

Greetings, Druidecht. May we be of service to you?

It was an oddly formal greeting, but it pleased Annon that they were not harsh or distrustful.

The Aeduan sitting next to me is a Rike from Kenatos. I would appreciate it if he fell asleep quickly.

He felt the throb of anger in their emotions. *Shall we poison his food, master? The Rikes are enemies. They poison these mountains.*

No—just sleep.

A colorful moth appeared from the shadows behind Lukias, hovering above his head. Fine trailers of dust came from its wings, sprinkling down on the Rike's head. Lukias was eating a hard biscuit, chewing it determinedly and Annon watched as his eyes grew heavy. He rubbed them, shaking his head in distraction. His eyes began to droop and the crust of biscuit dropped from his hand. Without a word, he stretched out on the ground and fell into a deep slumber.

Erasmus and Khiara stared at Lukias in confusion.

Annon smiled at them and nodded. "He will sleep all night," he said. "I wanted to speak freely with you."

Erasmus rubbed his mouth. "I recall a very similar feeling when we reached Canton Vaud and your friend, Reeder. Did I fall asleep that quickly as well?"

Nizeera padded into the firelight, returning from her hunt with a hare in her jaws. She nestled down deeper into the cave and started to pick at her meal.

Annon nodded. "Give me your prediction, Erasmus. Will Lukias betray us?"

"A one in ten chance that he will not," came the definitive reply. "I'm glad you asked, because I was beginning to worry about your judgment, young man. You speak too freely."

Annon scratched at an itch on his wrist. "It's a difficult balance when he has a ring himself. I believe he is not lying deliberately. But his devotion to and knowledge of the Arch-Rike may continue to be useful to us. You say he'll betray us. When?"

Erasmus took out a handful of nuts from his pack and started munching on them. "Not at the entrance of Basilides. He would wait until we were inside. Lost, perhaps. When we no longer have the upper hand in his confinement. He is adept at soothing fears. I do not trust him at all. Nor should you."

Annon nodded and gazed into the fire in the ring of stones. He stared at the variety of colors, at the whip-like tongues of flame leaping out from the brush they had gathered to feed it. "What of you, Khiara. What is your assessment?"

She shrugged, saying nothing.

"Please, Khiara. I would hear you as well."

"It is difficult to understand his motives in helping us," she replied softly, looking down at her lap. "I have spent time studying the ways of the Rikes of Seithrall. The prince and I—" She fell suddenly silent, not speaking for a moment. "There are many troubling aspects to their religion. They are skilled in argument and logic. They are students of the mind. The man we have been walking with has tried too hard to calm our concerns about him. That troubles me. He does not act like a man disillusioned by his training."

Annon sighed, concurring with both of their observations. "How long will he . . . live?" Annon asked her, glancing at her face. "How much time was he given when he was revived?"

She did not look up. "A fortnight. His heart will stop again before that time is through."

Erasmus shivered. "Reminds me of a Romani proverb. It's bad manners to talk about ropes in the house of a man whose father was hanged. You are sure he will die? He seems hale."

Khiara nodded. "His borrowed time came at a cost."

Shifting to get more comfortable, Annon glanced over at Nizeera. *What are your thoughts?* He asked her.

She snagged a thread of flesh in her teeth and yanked hard. *I wondered when you would ask me.*

I value your instincts. What do you say?

She ignored him for several moments, digging into the flesh while holding it still with her claws. *Why else did you wish to bring him?*

You know that already. To understand the thinking of my enemy.

Her head came up, her luminous eyes fixing his. Blood dribbled from her chin. *And what have you learned about your enemy so far?*

Annon thought the words that summoned fire and then began bathing his hands over the flames in the fire ring. Erasmus and Khiara watched him, transfixed.

"Nizeera asks what I've learned about the enemy so far. I want to make sure you understand my thinking as well. To see if I have any holes in my logic." He scooped up a thread of flame, using his mind to twist it into a sphere, which floated above his hand like a bubble. "The Arch-Rike is a tyrant, but a clever one. If he enslaved the people with the threat of bonds or prison, they would revolt against him. If he taxed them excessively, they would scorn him and rebel. He enslaves the kingdoms through ideas. People will always serve a cause higher than themselves." He chuckled softly. "It is the same principle Tyrus uses. We seek to end the Plague. The Arch-Rike seeks to preserve knowledge. Both are noble causes. Both are ideals. If the Plague ends, then there will be nothing to rally the minds of the people. The Arch-Rike would lose his power."

Annon swallowed, staring at the swirling flames. "The Arch-Rike has taken up an ideal set hundreds of years ago and has made it his own. He is a cunning man. He is wise. But just as a bubble can be pricked by a touch, so can an idea be punctured and vanish." He let the bubble of fire unravel and disappear. "I have the feeling that the dangers we face ahead will challenge our minds more than anything else." He fixed Erasmus with his gaze and then Khiara. "What we learn there may challenge our beliefs or assumptions. What we face there may make us doubt ourselves and our cause. This may prove as difficult a challenge mentally as facing the Scourgelands will test us physically. We are entering the lair of a man who has most of the known world under his thrall. To be honest, I'm terrified."

Annon removed his hands from the fire and brushed them together. The flames were as warm as bathwater. "I rely on you all to help me see through the illusions the Arch-Rike may use to protect his secrets. We must rely on each other. We will probably need to move quickly and think quickly. There is a reason Tyrus chose *us* to face Basilides. I feel lucky to have you all with me."

He looked over at Nizeera, who continued to stare at him. *Well said, Druidecht. You are truly our leader.*

"Having been a student of history for most of my life, I will venture a prediction. At some future period, not very distant as measured by centuries, the civilized races will almost certainly replace the savage races throughout the world."

—Possidius Adeodat, Archivist of Kenatos

XV

The day remained overcast, the gray of the sky blending in with the crushed rock filling the mountains. By midday, Annon and the others reached a river spilling from the mountains and flowing south to join the lake waters of Kenatos. The river was full of boulders and churning foam, making passage by boat impossible as well as reckless. The river was wide and full of flat rocks, worn smooth by the constant rush of water. Crossing it would be treacherous.

Lukias halted the group and pointed to shrubs farther up the river. "This is the road." A narrow trail followed the river north, and it was overgrown with shrubs and boulders. They would have missed it completely.

"Does it cross the river eventually?" Annon asked him.

Lukias shook his head. "No, but it is guarded by several threats. We must be cautious."

"What threats, Lukias?" Annon asked.

"I cannot divulge what the protections are nor the information you need to bypass them. As we draw nearer, they will test your resolve to enter Basilides. If you succeed, it will be by your own merits."

As they started up the steep incline toward the patchwork of shrubs blocking sight of the road, Annon began to feel a nervous warning in the pit of his stomach. He glanced around for the appearance of spirits, but saw none in the area. The place was devoid of life.

They crossed the hedge barrier and started up the shattered shale road, their boots crunching softly as they plodded along. As soon as they crossed the first bend, a feeling of intense dread struck Annon.

In the center of the small makeshift path was a waist-high stone boulder with a bronze disc mounted inside it, facing them. The bronze work was sculpted into the image of a face with a grim-set mouth and stern look. The eyes were vacant of pupils and knifed through Annon with shards of fear. Nizeera growled in warning, pausing at his side.

The feelings were terrible and real. Lukias continued to walk forward, but the rest had halted, staring in dread at the bronze work. He paused and turned back to them. "It is only fear," he said with a gentle voice. "Walk on . . . if you can."

It reminded Annon of the Fear Liath and his muscles constricted, holding him in place. He rallied his courage and put a foot forward. Then another. Khiara followed him but Erasmus was rooted in place, staring vacantly. His lips moved but his words were inaudible.

Annon could sense the waves of fear pounding against his own mind and realized that the Preachán was lost in the struggle. "Khiara, take his hand. Erasmus, close your eyes."

Khiara took his hand and pulled him after her. His legs shuffled slowly but soon he was walking, staring down at the broken rocks at his feet. Annon approached the strange marker, staring into the void-like eyes, steeling himself against them. "Is this a trap?" he asked Lukias, feeling the ring on his finger and focusing on the answer.

"It is here to keep away trespassers. That is all. Come."

They walked past the bronze work and the feeling immediately left them.

Erasmus twisted his neck and stared back at the rear side of the boulder. "You were right, Annon. It affects the mind most of all. I could only think of a thousand things that might be hiding up ahead. I couldn't move my legs."

Khiara patted his hand and released it, moving ahead down the way. The trail followed along the edge of the churning river. It began to grow colder as they ascended into the mountains, crunching on loose gravel as they walked. In some places, the path grew narrow as the side of the cliff was eaten away, spilling down into the river below. The defiles were dangerous but not too difficult to cross. Nizeera stayed close to Lukias, her tail lashing back and forth as if ready to pounce.

Farther up the road, another bronze work sculpture met them. This one did not radiate a feeling of fear. It looked similar to the one farther behind. As they approached it, the mouth of the sculptured face began to move. It spoke.

"This road is forbidden," it said in a wintry voice that was neither male nor female. "What is the seventh seal of the Ruby Goddess?"

Khiara stepped forward. "The Grave," she answered.

Lukias turned and looked at her in surprise and respect. "You know our lore surprisingly well, Vaettir. If you had not answered it properly, then the sculpture would have discharged energy into you that would have stopped your heart beating."

She said nothing in response. The bronze work fell silent. The group progressed up the road. Long before they reached the end of it, the sun started to set, draping shadows through the pass as they wound their way up the shattered rock, maneuvering past boulders and trying to follow the path of the river. Lukias insisted they proceed. Clouds began roiling in the sky, bringing with it a faint drizzle that turned heavier and began pattering down on the rocks, promising a squall before dawn.

Annon hugged himself for warmth, focusing on the hard march and the pace Lukias set.

"Will we rest at all tonight?" Erasmus asked impatiently.

"We are almost to the summit of this pass," the Rike answered. "You will see the advantage we gain by darkness soon. Farther."

Khiara said nothing but matched him stride for stride. Annon felt the presence of inquisitive spirits in the air, curiously reaching out to him with their minds. He tried to encourage conversation, but none of them responded. They flitted away in the darkness, timid as bats. He wondered if the black robes they wore had daunted the spirits. The light rain turned into flaky snow. He shivered.

It was nearing midnight when they reached the top of the pass, which opened into a vast intermountain valley. There was a lake ahead, the waters shimmering in the darkness, black as a void and full of crushed rock around the edges. A shrine made of white marble rose from the side of the road near the placid waters of the lake, forming the headwaters that became the river they had followed. The shrine was a series of four arches, each capped with a turret. The road there was surrounded by boulders blocking the way. A fetid smell lingered in the air, rising up from the foul waters below. This was unexpected for the waters along the river had not contained such a scent.

The path began to descend toward the shrine before winding around one side of the lake. As they approached, the smell grew stronger. The place reeked of decay. Erasmus stumbled on the wet stones and went down. He grumbled a curse and rose, patting his backside. The way down was treacherous and slow. They all had to be careful.

The outline of the shrine grew brighter as the moon appeared through a gap in the clouds at last. The snow turned into a slushy rain. The lake looked black.

"Is this Basilides?" Annon asked in a whisper.

"No," Lukias responded. "That is on the other side of the lake. This is a place we can rest until dawn. There are no servants here. It is a hostel only."

As they neared the floor of the valley and the structure, Annon heard a sibilant hissing, two threads bouncing off the rocks at odd angles. The voices he heard amidst the shushing noise were in his mind. It was impossible to determine the source.

Yes, I smell them too. Delightful to have visitors tonight.

Quite delightful. Vaettir blood as well. Delicious.

One is a Preachán, though. Tainted. You may eat that one.

A pity. We will do riddles for the Vaettir girl though?

Riddles will do.

"Hold a moment," Annon warned the others, listening to the discussion with growing horror. He did not want to alert the creatures that he knew their thoughts, but he feared they were blundering into a trap. They were some sort of spirit creatures. He dared not speak to Nizeera in his mind, lest they overhear him.

The sibilant hissing grew louder, making the others halt.

"Where is it coming from?" Erasmus asked. "Sounds like air passing through a vent. Is this crater volcanic?"

The voices spoke audibly this time. "Welcome to Basilides," said one.

"What questions do you have for the oracle?"

"I love questions."

"Quiet now, I am talking to them. You have journeyed a great distance. What are your questions?"

It was a trap. Annon knew it in his blood. Lukias stepped forward. "I am Lukias of Kenatos. We seek—"

His words were interrupted when an enormous reptilian head swooped down from a nearby boulder and swallowed him whole.

Annon stared in shock and horror. One moment Lukias had been standing there, just a few paces ahead. He could see the creatures now, their enormous lizard-like bodies a mix of white with black splotches. They blended in perfectly amidst the rock and snow. There were two of them, both perched on boulders on each side of the path heading to the shrine, as large as wagons with enormous bulging tails. They had held perfectly still, their eyes lidded shut. The one who ate Lukias flicked out a long fat tongue across the ridge of his mouth.

"What are your questions?" the other one hissed, more insistent this time.

Pyricanthas. Sericanthas. Thas. Annon's hands began to glow blue, bringing a rush of warmth into the frigid mountaintop.

The voices switched to his mind.

He's so polite!

Yes, he's a Druidecht. They're very polite before we eat them.

Bhikhu are polite too. I thought this one was supposed to be a boy.

I don't like Bhikhu. They taste like grass.

The cat is yours though. You can have her.

That is very kind of you.

"Nizeera!" Annon warned, but she had heard the voices as well and launched herself away.

The second lizard-creature lunged for her. Annon stepped forward, sending out a blast of fire into the massive head. The flames enveloped it in a wash of color and scorching heat. The creature snapped its jaws at Nizeera, but the cat had bounded out of its reach, hissing in fury. The flames swirled from Annon's hands but did nothing to the creature.

You did not think we would be set as guardians against your coming and not be protected?

Foolish of you to think that, Druidecht. Very foolish.

Annon saw the other one loom over him, coming down at blinding speed.

Khiara rushed to his side in an instant, holding her long staff between her fists in front of her, up at an angle so that the mouth could not close around her because the staff was too long and struck the inside corner of its jaws. The power of its strike knocked her down, but the mouth could not close around her. It recoiled and hissed.

Annon reached down and helped Khiara stand. "Fly!" he told her.

She inhaled deeply and shot into the air, rising above the boulders. Annon ran toward the shrine and saw a flicker of motion as the head followed him quickly. He dived to the side instinctively, just an instant before the head swiped down at him. He struck the sharp stones painfully and struggled to his feet. Fear made him quick. He had seen lizards stalk prey before and recognized the bobbing of the heads, the scuttling motion as they scrabbled from the top of the rock. Their necks were powerful and quick, their tails offering balance to keep from overshooting their victim.

He abandoned using the fireblood and sent out a call to the spirits of the mountains, pleading for help.

He runs! How delicious! Save the Preachán for later. He is hiding behind the rocks.

I want the Vaettir still. She would be very tasty.

I love how they wriggle. The one I ate is still struggling. We will gorge ourselves.

The panic inside Annon mounted as he glanced for a place to hide. The lizard-spirits were quick and crafty, coming down from the boulders and slinking swiftly to each side, trying to box him between them. Their plump tails dragged along the stones, speckled with black.

A rock sailed from behind the boulder and struck one on the side of the head. Erasmus grabbed another and prepared to hurl it too.

Khiara came down on one, jamming the end of her staff into its neck.

How pesky these mortals are.

Indeed. How tiresome.

The one she struck whipped its head around, snapping at her and Khiara barely managed to inhale fast enough to move above its reach. She began twirling the staff, getting ready for another lunge.

Nizeera launched at the one advancing on Annon, raking its side with her claws and teeth. It was like watching a cat attack a horse. It hissed, but the tail swished and swatted Nizeera away in annoyance.

Are you ready to die, Druidecht?

Are you ready to surrender?

Which do you prefer? The Arch-Rike will treat with you.

You could surrender.

Come closer and we will discuss it.

Come closer and—

One of the lizards writhed with pain and flopped on its back, twitching violently in spasms, its mind-shriek nearly knocking Annon down.

A slit opened up from its underside and Lukias crawled out, dripping with ooze and steaming in the cold air.

The other lizard-thing hissed with fury, rushing Annon viciously. As it lunged, Khiara's staff came down on top of its bulging eye, smashing it. Again, another mind-shriek of pain that nearly bowled Annon over with its intensity.

Erasmus appeared at its tail and grabbed a strange metal object bound around it and tugged it off. It was a metal band, as thick as an iron collar but fastened to its tail.

"Annon, now!" Erasmus yelled.

He realized that the band around its tail was its protection against the elements. Annon raised his hands, spoke the words again in his mind, and unleashed a plume of fire into the lizard's contorting bulk. This time the flames ripped into it, charring the scales and overwhelming it with pain. The creature thrashed recklessly, shrieking at the torture it was experiencing. It scuttled away from the plumes of flame, hissing in fury at him. It charged Annon, mouth gaping.

Scrambling backward, Annon unleashed the fireblood inside its widening maw. The flames wreathed around it, coursing and hissing, causing the beast to explode in a shower of ash. The flames consumed it entirely.

Annon retreated still, trembling, clutching the talisman around his neck. He knew he had almost died. He knew the Arch-Rike was expecting them and had prepared the creatures with protection against fire. He had nearly failed the others and doomed them to be ingested by giant lizards.

Lukias staggered toward him, his face pink with acid burns. He trembled as well, his eyes full of emotion and disgust at the ordeal he had survived.

"Khiara," Annon said hoarsely. "Can you heal his injuries?"

She floated down gracefully, tossing aside her elegant staff. When her feet reached the ground, she rushed to Lukias who bent double and began to vomit. She gripped him by his shoulders, murmured soft words in the Vaettir tongue that Annon did not comprehend. But the effects of her prayer-like utterance were immediate. The acid burns on his cheeks, arms, and hands began to heal, fresh skin replacing the blisters. He continued to tremble as her power surged through him, calming him until he was resting in her embrace. Annon recalled the pleasure of being healed by a Shaliah and was grateful she had chosen to join them.

"Thank you," Lukias said, bowing his head respectfully to Khiara. "The sensation of being healed so quickly is quite unnerving. I do not understand the power you possess, but I am in your debt."

"It was freely given," Khiara replied, rising and fetching her staff.

"What were those creatures?" Annon asked, staring at the gaping corpse of the one Lukias had slit his way out of. Erasmus knelt by it, studying it with obvious fascination. Nizeera prowled nearby, stalking back and forth and sensing the air for danger.

"I don't know," Lukias muttered. "I was not expecting them to be here. The protections I know of are inside the temple. They are equally dangerous, I assure you. This presages difficulties ahead. You recognize that, don't you, Annon?"

The young Druidecht stared at the flat lake, dreading to go any nearer to Basilides.

"I do," Annon answered softly, searching for a spark of courage in his heart to keep going.

"I heard this phrase once by a Vaettir, who are by nature very superstitious and believe in the existence of gods and spirit beings. It is wise nonetheless: Beauty is indeed a good gift of the gods; but that the good may not think it a great good, the gods dispense it even to the wicked. The same can be said for wisdom."

—*Possidius Adeodat, Archivist of Kenatos*

XVI

The encounter with Sanbiorn Paracelsus happened when Tyrus was twelve years old and lived in an orphanage in Kenatos. Even though Tyrus was young, he was uncommonly clever and quick to comprehend the world of adults. Though he lived in the orphanage, he was unlike the other orphans, since he still had family in the city. His older sister had brought her two brothers from Stonehollow when Tyrus was just a little baby, and so he had no memory of his birthplace. She loomed large in his life, a sister-mother who worked hard as an Archivist and was eventually chosen by the Arch-Rike himself to begin training as a Paracelsus. His sister was the most important person in the world to him, and he studied with iron will to master the lessons in the orphanage school so that he might be selected someday to become a Paracelsus. He was fascinated by the powers they manipulated. Occasionally, members of the order would come to observe the progress of the young. They were not easily impressed. Sanbiorn Paracelsus was one of those.

That autumn day, Sanbiorn arrived unannounced and began interrogating the students. He challenged them with material higher than their abilities and scoffed when they could not answer his questions. Sometimes he would withdraw a trinket from his voluminous robes and ask them to explain the swirling mist contained inside a gemstone. Some he would begin speaking to in Cruithne or Preachán to see what languages they had mastered. One could never anticipate the kind of questions he would ask. His intent and purpose was to make the students feel ignorant and unworthy. Tyrus hated him for it.

On that visit, Sanbiorn had begun quizzing other students but with lackluster enthusiasm. He was bored of them, he declared. No one had advanced very far since his previous visit. He chided the schoolmasters for producing such an inept crop of students. He roamed the room, skipping several completely with only a look of distaste to signal his rejection. Tyrus clenched his fists, feeling his fingers tingle with heat.

Suddenly, Sanbiorn Paracelsus was standing in front of Tyrus, gazing down his long nose at the boy. "*What hour does the south bell toll?*" he asked in the Vaettir tongue.

Vaettir was Tyrus's biggest strength. They did not teach it at the school. He had learned it from his sister. "*Dusk in the winter. Dawn in the summer,*" Tyrus answered.

The response caught Sanbiorn off guard. He switched his language to Cruithne. "*What is the best stone used to harness emotions?*"

"*Diamond, for it will not shatter,*" the boy replied in Preachán.

Again, a startled look. He proceeded in Aeduan. "What device do Lydian sailors use to navigate on the seas?"

"A lodestone compass, sir."

"Describe the principles of the lodestone magnet, boy."

Tyrus did, launching into an extensive treatise on the subject. Cartography and navigation had always fascinated him.

The Paracelsus's eyes were gleaming. Not with pleasure, but rage. Sanbiorn started on another series of questions, all of which Tyrus answered without hesitating. His mouth went dry with the effort, but he kept the older man's gaze, challenging him to test the depths of his knowledge. He would show him that he was not an ignorant little orphan to be intimidated.

Sanbiorn was growing flustered. Every question, regardless of the difficulty, was being handled by a mere child. There was a sickening pasty color filling his cheeks. His eyes bulged with animosity.

"Clever, are we?" Sanbiorn snarled, glowering. "Well then, how do you summon a Shain spirit? How do you trap it?"

Tyrus knew the answer. He nearly let it trip off his tongue. His sister had explained the concept of trapping spirits a year before and had used that exact example to educate her brother. Yet something about Sanbiorn's expression made him pause. He saw that proving his mastery of the craft at a young age only caused the other to resent him. In showing off his knowledge, he was creating enmity.

Sanbiorn mopped his sweaty brow. "Well? Shain spirits. Answer me, boy!"

The room was so quiet, Tyrus could almost hear the sweat trickling down his own back. He realized with dread that he had been a fool to reveal how much he knew to another man, especially a Paracelsus. Would it not be wiser to be deferential to men with power? What good would goading them bring ultimately? A momentary thrill of self-satisfaction? Was that worth a lifetime of the man's contempt? Why not appease the man's pride instead? Make him feel important.

Tyrus realized, in that moment, the danger caused by succumbing to pride. He realized he was enjoying the humiliation of a man who held so many advantages. What a costly mistake that could be.

Sanbiorn's expression began turning from desperation to triumph. He perceived the young man being flustered. He misunderstood it, but his emotions were too enraged to consider the facts. "You do not know? Really, I would think a little braggart like you would know something so simple."

"I'm sorry," Tyrus said bleakly. "There is so little . . . about that topic . . . here in the orphanage. I cannot say that I know even a portion of what you do." He felt his neck itching from the writhing emotions inside himself. *Let the man win. Let him triumph. Do not let him understand what you truly know.*

"Of course you don't!" he practically crowed. "Then I suppose you know little of Beetleflicks. Or Sylphs. Or any of the myriad wonders that exist in the wilds beyond Kenatos. Beings that would steal your courage in vapors of mist." His voice lowered theatrically. "You do not know these things, boy?" A smile began to curl on Sanbiorn's mouth.

Tyrus knew of them all. He stared helplessly at the Paracelsus, shrugging apologetically, feeling the scarlet rise to his cheeks. "I would give anything," Tyrus whispered hoarsely, "To know what you know."

Sanbiorn looked down at him smugly. His expression was completely altered from what it had been moments before. He glanced around the room disdainfully. "Someday, some of you may have the opportunity to study in the Paracelsus Towers. It is a great privilege. Only the best are chosen." He glanced down at Tyrus who looked at him with wide eyes. "I do not know if any of you will qualify. Probably not. In the meantime, keep studying. Work hard. The Arch-Rike is a worthy master to serve. There are secrets of power that cannot be shared in a classroom and must be foraged from the ancient books left down to us. Obey your schoolmasters. They will tell us which of you may be worthy someday."

Tyrus licked his bottom lip, nodding with every word. Sanbiorn left the classroom with the same huff of self-importance that he had brought with him.

The next month, Tyrus found himself apprenticed to the man.

One of the secrets to holding power over others was never revealing how much you really knew. That insight and habit, which Tyrus attributed to the classroom scuffle with Sanbiorn, had served him consistently over the following years. He gleaned what knowledge he could of others, but rarely shared what he knew himself. He found that the Paracelsus in the Towers loved to boast of their discoveries or the projects they worked on with or without the Arch-Rike's express permission.

Tyrus, on the other hand, mostly communicated the problems he was having and solicited ideas on how to solve them. He had already solved them himself, of course, but he liked to validate his thinking and see if he had missed an interpretation that he had not considered. He developed a reputation for a curious mind and one who tackled large, thorny problems. His peers sought him out for advice. He would often listen to their thinking first, offer to ponder the problem for a few days, and then return with an answer that helped. Even if he knew the answer immediately, he would adopt a pondering look and promise to think about it. Often the inquirer would solve it on their own before he got back to them.

His own work he kept expressly secret, only sharing his ideas with the Arch-Rike who encouraged the ambition of the scale of his projects. The Arch-Rike was one man he respected and admired, for he too was a keen observer of the nature of those with power. Tyrus shared much of his work with the Arch-Rike and made sure that he benefitted from Tyrus's inventions. But Tyrus always made two of everything he constructed. For example, the Tay al-Ard device. The Arch-Rike was the only other person who had the fully functioning kind.

One of the inventions he did not tell the Arch-Rike about was a soul-trapping stone. Since the craft of the Paracelsus involved trapping spirits into performing acts for a specified duration, he wondered if it would be possible to trap his own essence in a stone. His own spirit, for lack of a better word. He discovered the proper charm, a stone that was suitable for such an exercise, and crafted the small sculpted rock with the ancient Vaettir runes of power etched into it. He kept it always in his pocket, easily within reach.

When the Kishion had prepared to kill him, Tyrus had gripped the charm in his hand, squeezing it with all his strength. The force of his fingers had activated the magic. It was not instantaneous. It was not designed to be. But when the dagger had plunged excruciatingly into his back, he released his spirit into the stone, causing his body to collapse in the dirt. Just like a dead man. Any attempt to feel his pulse would indicate he had died.

From inside the stone, he was aware enough of his surroundings to feel the Kishion leave. He waited for good measure, just to be sure. Then deliberately, knowing the pain would return instantly, he used the charm to bring his spirit back into his body again. The agony nearly made him black out. He could feel his blood starting to flow again, sending dagger-pricks all over his body. The wound was deep in his muscles. His pumping heart would soon leave him dead. There were no lesser spirits of Mirrowen in the Fear Liath's lair. As his eyes fluttered open and he felt himself dying again, consciousness fraying around the edges, he summoned the Tay al-Ard from the bottom of the churning waterfall into his hand and invoked its power to bring him deep into the woods of Silvandom. A memory of the place was all he needed. It was a peaceful part of the woods, thick with friendly spirits.

Please, he beckoned with his thoughts. *Please save me. I am a friend of Mirrowen. I release your trapped brethren.*

The spirits of Mirrowen attended him immediately, healing the deadly wound.

Tyrus lay in the feathery growth, breathing deeply again, experiencing the fading of the agony in his back. The gash closed. The blood ceased to drain. He lay still, panting from the effort.

He wanted the Arch-Rike to believe he was dead. It would provide him time to set in motion the rest of his plan to conquer the Scourgelands and the Arch-Rike himself.

&

Phae heard the words from the man's own mouth. "I've come for my daughter."

It was her father. Tyrus of Kenatos. Tyrus Paracelsus. She stared at him in shock, her heart burning with a sudden unfamiliar feeling—hope. Her father had survived the Kishion's attack. He was limping slightly, she could see that, but he had survived. It meant that the Kishion was not unstoppable.

The Kishion slipped off the saddle, fast as a hawk. He pulled Phae down, catching her before she sprawled on her face. His arm was made of iron and fastened around her neck and she saw his dagger appear in his other hand. He did not stop her from breathing, but he was clearly claiming ownership of her.

Tyrus held up his hand. "If I had wanted to steal her from you, I would have waited in the tunnel and touched her as you passed by. Hear me out, Kishion."

She heard the Kishion's breath coming in short puffs. "I have orders to bring her to Kenatos."

"This is the only road to Kenatos," Tyrus said. "With one word, I can collapse this tunnel and delay your journey back. I am here to make you an offer. I wish you to join us."

The Kishion snorted. "I am loyal to the Arch-Rike. You waste your breath."

Tyrus shook his head slowly. Phae's heart trembled, wondering what he was going to do or say. Fighting him was impossible. She gripped the Kishion's arm, but did not try to pull it away. Her knees began to quake. The dagger was near her. She saw it poised, ready to plunge into her. *Please don't kill me*, she thought.

"I can help you," Tyrus said, his hand open calmingly, as if he were trying to soothe a skittish horse. "Let me tell you what I know about you. It may be more than you know. Here is my offer. I know how your memories can be restored. I can provide you the chance to learn who you really are and why the music from that little charm affected you so much."

The Kishion hoisted Phae up higher, keeping his arm around her neck. She felt the dagger tip press against her side and she began shaking all over, her breath coming in gasps.

"How did you survive?" the Kishion demanded. "My dagger went inside you. You are not protected by magic like I am."

"You are not protected by magic at all," Tyrus replied. "I know all of the types of spirits that can or have been harnessed, including the blade Iddawc. I also know that the blade Iddawc can kill you. It was designed to. The Arch-Rike claimed that it would be used by you to kill others. But it was invented to protect him against you. He fears you, Kishion. With good reason."

Phae felt the Kishion's body start to tremble. Her own was affecting his. She pulled slightly on his arm. "Please," she whispered. "I won't run."

His gloved fist was clenched and shook. He slowly eased his grip on her, but he did not lower the dagger. "I hold you to your promise," he warned.

Phae nodded, staring from her father to her captor. She turned and looked up at the Kishion's face, saw the whirlwind of emotions playing out there. He was desperately curious. She knew the knowledge being offered tormented him.

"What would you ask of me?" Tyrus asked, taking a cautious step closer. "I will not take her by force. I will not defy your mission. But think before you bring her back. Do you really want to go back to your cell in the Arch-Rike's dungeons again?"

"What?" the Kishion snapped.

"That is where he keeps you. His puppet. His killer who cannot be killed. He is afraid of you learning the truth about yourself. He fears you turning on him. He steals your memories to control you."

The Kishion's frown was terrifying. His jaw was clenched, the muscles in the corners bulging. "Tell me about the music. What is it?"

"It came from the Scourgelands," Tyrus said. "One could say it is even the hymn of the Scourgelands. Ancient spirits sing it still, which is why they are captured. The tune is melancholy. The song is part of you somehow. You are from the Scourgelands, Kishion. I know it. You bear the marks, the same as I do. Come with us back to your homeland. We will uncover the secrets of your past. There, your memory can be restored. I know how it can be done."

"But not here?" the Kishion asked, his voice full of distrust.

"No, the knowledge you seek can only be restored there. I need your help. I charge you to protect my daughter. She is the key to opening the door. There is no one else I could trust her safety to better than you. If you decide my motives are deceptions, you are free to fulfill your mission at any time. I do not force you, Kishion. Join us willingly."

The Kishion's voice was raw with emotion. "The ring I wear will explode."

Tyrus shook his head. "It will if you venture back into the Arch-Rike's domains. But even if it did, it will not harm you. You are not protected by magic, Kishion. You are what you are. You cannot be harmed except by the blade Iddawc. You are not trusted by the Arch-Rike. He does not want you to remember."

"Prove it," the Kishion said menacingly.

"I do not need to convince you," Tyrus said, shaking his head. "Your heart already tells you that I speak the truth. These are my motives. I seek to end the Plague. That is my goal and my destiny. I have assembled a mastermind, if you will, to help accomplish this. Just as the Arch-Rike has assembled one to prevent it, to conceal the knowledge that was lost. Tell me why the Arch-Rike seeks to thwart me? Give me his reasons? You cannot, for he has told you nothing. You are a slave to be sent to kill whoever crosses him. Then he strips away your memory under the false guise that he is saving your conscience. He knows how to stop it and conceals that knowledge to preserve his own power. Why else would he have summoned you to kill me? Listen to reason! You owe him loyalty because he tells you that you do? He cannot force you to obey him. Come with us and learn the truth. Protect my daughter from the dangers that threaten in the Scourgelands. Let us reveal the secrets that have long been guarded."

Phae was terrified at her father's words. She had no desire to enter the Scourgelands. But she knew that it had something to do with her being Dryad-born, that her ability to steal memories played a role in the absence of the Kishion's. She did not know why her father had abandoned her for all of these years. But seeing him in person, seeing the look of emotion on his face, she felt relief swelling up inside her as well as fear that he was gambling with her life.

She stared up at the Kishion's face next. "Please," she begged. "At least we can listen to him?"

The Kishion stared at Tyrus defiantly, his expression stiff and furious. "I cannot trust your words alone," he said. "Stand aside. Let us pass. Prove you won't interfere with my mission."

"Please!" Phae implored.

A voice came from above. It was like a whisper but it pierced her soul, the echo of it thrumming in her mind. It was as if the sky had spoken it. *Kishion, kill her now.*

Phae saw that they all heard the voice. She did not know where it came from, but it made her soul despair and her knees buckle. She faced the Kishion fully, gazing into his eyes with anguish. She would not run from him though he still held the dagger aimed at her ribs.

One breath. Two breaths.

She reached up and touched his face, feeling the grooves of the claw marks. Her touch brought his eyes down, meeting hers. She had contact with his eyes. She could snatch the memory away if she blinked. She could steal it all away.

She did not.

He stared at her in surprise, his expression a mix of anger and awe.

"Please," she whispered hoarsely. "Please protect me."

The dagger fell from his hand, sinking blade-first into the road. He gave Phae a quick nod just before shoving her away from him as hard as he could, sending her backward into the air as if a battering ram had struck her. He turned on his heel, sank into a crouch, as if praying, and exploded into a deafening blast of light. Had she been standing next to him, it would have killed her.

"One of the ancient Cruithne kings carved this into a monument
in his great city: He that is kind is free, though he is a slave.
He that is evil is a slave, though he be a king."

—Possidius Adeodat, Archivist of Kenatos

XVII

The explosion rang in Phae's ears, the blast buffeting them all and knocking each sprawling. Heat and a tingling pressure lingered in the air, sending streamers of smoke from her clothes. A strong hand grabbed her forearm and helped her back to her feet. It was the Vaettir prince, his expression stern and forceful. He said something to her, but the ringing in her ears prevented her from understanding him.

She shook her head and shoved past him, staring in shock at the Kishion's kneeling form. He was hunched over, head bowed, at the edge of a small crater. The blast ran out in a circle around him, charring the earth as if a stroke of lightning had landed there, though there were no clouds in the sky. Rock fragments were strewn about and pine cones and shattered branches rained from the nearby trees. The Kishion slowly stood and turned to face them.

The look in his eyes was haunted. She stared at him, realizing he had shielded her from the explosion with his own body, uncertain whether his immunity would save him from death. Her ears pierced with noise, but she approached him, staring down at his hands.

The gloves were smoking, charred with soot. He shook them off, revealing the ring on his finger. The sigils carved into it were marred and twisted. Slowly, the Kishion wrenched it from his finger and stared at it in his palm for long moments. Then he tossed it into the crater.

The Prince and Tyrus approached them.

"We must fly," her father said, his voice husky with emotion. "Come, both of you. Hold my arm."

Phae heard his words as if they were spoken under water. She saw him extend a cylindrical object, made of brass or gold with gems studded into the two ends. It was carved with peculiar symbols. The Prince rested his hand on the outstretched arm. Phae was hesitant, looking at the Kishion to see what he would do.

His voice was hushed. "Where do we go?"

"A safehouse. It will not take long before they start arriving. Grab my arm."

The Kishion did and Phae joined her hand to the mix. There was a queer feeling of power, a spinning sensation that made her lose her balance and she stumbled. The sky was suddenly darker, much darker than it was a moment before. They were in the woods somewhere, but the trees were different—cedar instead of bristlecone. The flavor of the air was strange, the night full with the sound of flies and other insects. Smoke from a wood fire met her nose and she struggled back to her feet, seeing that they were just outside a sturdy cabin in the woods.

"The root cellar," Tyrus said to the Vaettir, pointing to it.

The Kishion examined the area quickly, searching the yard and taking in the details. It was a woodsman's home, with several cords of wood stacked neatly with a round, gouged splitting block nearby. There was a shed nearby as well, but her father's finger pointed to the trapdoors of a cellar at the base of the cabin. Prince

Aran marched to it and heaved open the doors. The hinges were well oiled and opened soundlessly.

The main door of the cabin opened, spilling out lamplight. A wizened old man emerged, thickset and brawny. He hefted an axe in his left hand and a lantern in his right. Most of his hair was gone, with only a dusting of gray slivers across his dome.

"Tyrus?" the old man croaked.

"Hello, Evritt," Tyrus replied, stepping into the light.

The older man looked at the rest of them and then motioned for the cellar and then sat down on the rocking chair on the stoop. He cradled the axe in his lap. The chair began to creak as he slowly began to rock.

The Prince hefted the doors open and ventured down the ladder first. Tyrus strode to the porch, gripped the old man's hand firmly and with obvious affection, and then returned with the lantern and took Phae by the arm and brought her to the ladder descending into the cellar. He shone the light down, exposing the rungs and the Prince's waiting face.

The ringing in Phae's ears was subsiding. She climbed over the lip of the cellar door and hurried down the ladder, surefooted. The strong smell of musty roots filled the space, reminding her of mushrooms and worms. Fabric sacks were stacked neatly along the far wall. It was a small, cozy space, smaller than Winemiller's cabin in the mountains. She rubbed her hands together, feeling small and defenseless. She had three protectors it seemed, but she still felt vulnerable.

Tyrus came down with the lantern, revealing the supplies hanging from pegs on the frame. The floor was dirt but packed hard. Each scuff of her boot awakened a little plume. The Kishion came down last, reaching out and swinging the cellar door down behind him as he descended.

Phae walked hesitantly into the cellar, absorbing the heavy aroma in the air, feeling it sink into her bones. She saw another ladder at the far side and a trapdoor leading up to the inside of the cabin. Smart, she thought. More than one way to escape.

She looked at her father. "You are alive."

Tyrus seated himself in the center of the floor and set the lantern down in the middle. The Prince edged toward the ladder they had descended and remained standing for a moment, searching the room with his gaze. Then he settled on the floor as well.

"I am," he answered. "Sit. There is much we must say to each other."

The Kishion stared at Tyrus, his face impassive. "Where are we?" he asked in a whisper-like voice.

"Alkire," Tyrus replied. "But just for the night. It drains the rod when I bring others with me. It needs time to regain its power. We will be more difficult to track beneath the ground though. That should give us some time to rest. And to talk."

Phae rubbed her arms, still staring at the other ladder. She glanced back at the man she knew to be her father. Her heart was jumbled with conflicting emotions. That he was even alive was a shock and a thrill. But she was also wary and concerned about his motives. He had abandoned her as a baby and now had come to make her part of some deeper purpose. If that purpose was related to the Scourgelands, she wanted nothing to do with it. What was the proper way to greet such a stranger?

"Sit, child," Tyrus bid, motioning to the space on the other side of the lantern. "I'm sure you have many questions."

Phae stared down at him, studying the haggard look on his face. Yet he seemed genuinely pleased to see her. His eyes were fierce yet gentle, as if he tamed great emotions churning inside of him. He did not want to frighten her. She nodded and obeyed.

"What is your name?" he asked her gently.

"Phae," she replied.

The name seemed to startle him. "Really?"

She nodded. "That surprises you? Was I to be named something else?"

Tyrus half-sighed, half-chuckled in amusement. "Winemiller named you? How interesting. Yet there are no coincidences. I will have to ask him about it sometime."

Phae stared at him hard. "Why does it surprise you what he named me?"

He smiled at her in a broken-hearted sort of way, as if breathing caused him pain. "It was the name I gave your mother." He sighed, staring down at the lantern. In a moment, he had mastered his emotions again. His eyes were like flint. "What would you know of me?"

Phae folded her arms. "I am your daughter?"

He nodded.

"Why did you abandon me?"

Tyrus gazed up at the Kishion. "I am demonstrating my good intentions by speaking freely in front of you. With this knowledge, you will have power to stop me and my plans. I give it to you freely, because I believe you were meant to join in our quest. You took the blast meant to kill my daughter. For that, I thank you. You've earned my trust. I hope before this night is done that I have earned yours."

"I left the ring back in Stonehollow," the Kishion answered. "I think the magic was destroyed, but to be sure, I left it behind. That way the Arch-Rike will not hear you through my ears. I believe the connection between us is severed. The ring is what allowed it. Trust for trust. But I will hear what you have to say before making up my mind."

Phae glanced at the Kishion, saw the claw marks on his face vivid in the lamplight. She shuddered, knowing he was still very capable of killing her.

Tyrus turned his attention back to her. "I will answer you as honestly as I can. You may not like to hear what I have to say. It may trouble you. It will frighten you." He sighed deeply again, brow furrowing with consternation. "There is even a great possibility that my plans will result in your death. But know this, child. I will lay down my own life before I allow that to happen to you. So will Prince Aran. And so will that gentleman behind you. If we three cannot protect you from the dangers you face, then I do not know what else I can do."

He plucked the hair at his lips absently and then leaned forward, gazing at her. "Phae, I am determined to stop the Plague that wrecks our lands. I believe that the Arch-Rike is behind it. Either that or he knows its origins and conceals what must be done to vanquish it. Eighteen years ago, I rallied a group to my cause and we entered the Scourgelands to seek the Plague's origin. The Arch-Rike knew of our journey and the path we would take. We were set upon immediately and all were killed, save myself and a Druidecht girl named Merinda. She taught me, during our escape, that the guardians of the Scourgelands are Dryads. They are vulnerable creatures and cannot defend themselves physically, but they have a powerful magic that affects even the man standing behind you. A Dryad can steal memories. By stealing, I mean they can take a person's memory and embed it into the tree they are bonded with. The person forgets, but the Dryad remembers. Have you experienced this power?"

As he spoke, Phae felt a thrill and a tingle through her body. It resonated with her and she felt a flush rise to her cheeks. "Yes," she answered, looking down. "I have. It started to frighten me and so I do not use it very often. Only for little things."

Tyrus beamed at her. "How does it work? What have you noticed?"

She kept her arms tucked and began rocking slightly, back and forth. The light from the lantern painted eerie shadows across the walls. "I must meet someone's gaze. It cannot work in darkness. But if we look at each other, and if I blink, I can take memories from them. They do not stay with me. They . . . float away, you might say."

"Indeed," Tyrus acknowledged. "You have not bonded with a tree yet. Only then will you be able to experience the full use of that power. You are of the age, Phae, when a girl makes the decision to fulfill the obligation her blood requires. This is Druidecht lore, child, and I am not privy to all of it, but I know enough. Your mother . . . taught it to me. A Dryad bonds with a single tree. If the tree dies or is destroyed, the bond is broken and she is trapped and unable to enter this world."

Phae stared at him in confusion. "This world? What do you mean?"

Tyrus joined his fingers together and leaned his forearms on his knees. "There is an unseen world that we share. It is called Mirrowen. When one is calm and quiet, you can hear the whispers from Mirrowen. These are spirits, unseen to mortal eyes. Sometimes they appear to us in the form of animals, insects, or other woodland creatures. Only the Druidecht can hear them. The talismans they wear—that is the way they commune with the spirits. You are partly a spirit creature yourself, Phae. You are Dryad-born. You were also born with the fireblood, which you inherited from me. My goal, child, is to bring you into the Scourgelands so that you may bind with a tree there and re-learn the secrets of the Plague that have been lost for thousands of years." He leaned even closer. "I do not have the power to stop the Plague. But you do."

Phae shivered uncontrollably. Her heart raced with fear and panic. "But if I bond with a tree in the Scourgelands, will I be trapped there for the rest of my life? You said the bond is with a specific tree. That land is dangerous and evil." She felt the panic begin to surge inside her. She wanted to run for the ladder and flee out the trapdoor.

Tyrus nodded, his expression stiffening. She could sense he was very good at controlling his emotions, of hardening himself for unpleasant realities. "I cannot withhold the truth from you, child. Yes, you could be trapped there. But it is my understanding that the Dryads dwell primarily in Mirrowen. It is a place of peace and great beauty. They only come to the mortal world when someone approaches their tree. They are the guardians of the portals to Mirrowen. Phae, you must understand this. The process of bonding to a tree grants the Dryad immortality."

He looked at her imploringly. "I know what I am asking of you isn't fair. I imagine it is not your wish to be separated from Stonehollow and those you consider family. If there was another possible way to end the Plague, I would gladly take it. But all the evidence points to this. Something happened to the Dryads of the Scourgelands centuries ago. They are feared by their sisters. They are as ancient as the world. They have the knowledge that we need. They may be unwilling to give it to you without an oath to replace them. You can set one of them free by agreeing to take her place. A Dryad is not expected to remain bonded to a tree for all eternity. Only until their charge is fulfilled and they have given birth to a child to replace her."

Phae's mind whirled with confusion. She pressed her hands against the side of her head. She found herself gasping for breath. "How do I know," she asked in a quavering voice, "that you are even telling me the truth?"

Tyrus leaned forward. "What would convince you?"

Phae shook her head, trying to sort out her scrambled thoughts. "This is almost too much to believe," she said. "Yet, I know from my experience that some of it *is* true. I do have the ability to steal memories. I do have the fireblood. I feel that same power in you, strangely. When I was fleeing from . . . the Kishion, I came upon a Dryad tree in the woods. It felt . . . safe to me. A Druidecht was there."

Tyrus's eyes bulged with surprise. "Amazing."

She went on, her heart revolting at the memory. "He said that he was married to a Dryad. She was so young, but he was old and so . . . gray." Her face screwed up in distaste.

"Did she have a bracelet around her ankle?" Tyrus asked pointedly.

Phae thought a moment. "She did."

"He was her husband then. Your mother wears one. It is fashioned in the shape of a serpent. It is coiled around the ankle. She is his wife."

Phae looked at him in disgust. "She is sixteen?"

He shook his head. "The Druidecht is a lad compared to her. Dryads are often hundreds of years old, Phae. She is immortal and wiser than any youth. You must understand that time is very different in Mirrowen than it is here. What happened in the Scourgelands must have happened thousands of years ago. There are no records of it surviving. Believe me, I have inquired of the head Archivist of Kenatos, and he has read more than any other man. Not even rumors or legends. Nothing. It is deliberately so. To the Dryads of the Scourgelands, it may feel like it happened a fortnight ago. There is no sense of time. A husband is a fleeting thing to them."

Her stomach was sick with worry. "This is all too . . . new. How can I make an obligation such as that? I don't want to be trapped in a tree. I don't want to fall in love with a man and watch him shrivel like . . . like . . . like raisins while I stay young. The very thought is horrible."

Tyrus nodded sympathetically, but his resolve was iron. "Of course you feel this way. It is only natural that you do. You were raised in a vineyard in Stonehollow. You know what it is to see a family and to work with your hands, to stamp grapes into wine. You only know your world, the one you were raised to know. Imagine, if you will, that you were born to a Dryad and were raised as a child traveling back and forth between here and Mirrowen. What if you grew up expecting to live for hundreds of years? If you expected to love and lose and love again over time." His look was sad but compelling. "If you had been raised that way and I told you to leave the tree and go to Stonehollow, you would resist me and say it is unnatural." His voice dropped lower. "I know this is difficult for you. I know this isn't fair. I am asking you, child, to help save this forsaken world. It cannot save itself."

The words caused a spasm of emotion to surge through her. Her father had given up his life in pursuit of this dream, this goal, this *compulsion* to end the Plague. He had sacrificed everything to achieve it. He was not asking her to do something he was unwilling to do himself. He was asking her to do something he could not do himself.

Her breath came in quavering. "I don't know," she whispered, burying her face in her hands. "How can you ask this?" It meant she would never have a homestead of her own. She would never have a normal family. She would be parted from Stonehollow forever. A sick feeling of dread washed over her. Tears filled her eyes.

Tyrus shifted in the dirt and sat next to her. His arm came around her and pulled her close. His voice was thick with emotion. "If you knew how much it pains me to ask it of you . . ."

She drew up her knees, clutching them with her arms, and stared at the lamplight, tears trickling down her cheeks. "This is cruel," she whispered bitterly.

"It is," Tyrus agreed firmly. "But I must ask it of you still."

Phae sought for a way to escape. She resisted the words. Part of her refused to submit. A deep stubborn core inside her swelled. "The problem, though," she said, gaining a crumb of courage, "is that you sent me to live in Stonehollow. I need evidence that what you said is true. I cannot make my decision with just your word. I don't truly know you. I don't know if I should trust you."

Tyrus nodded sagely. "That is fair. I asked you earlier. What would convince you?"

Phae looked at him with her tear-streaked eyes. "I want to see my mother. Where is her tree?"

Tyrus stared at her, aghast at the demand.

"Where is she, Father?" she insisted.

His expression hardened following the sudden blow of pain and anguish. Emotions played across his face, ranging from anger to deep sadness. His jaw clenched. His eyes flashed. But he mastered himself, how she did not know. "The Paracelsus Towers. Kenatos."

Phae stared at him coldly. "Take me there. Now."

"No eulogy is due to him who simply does his duty and nothing more."

—*Possidius Adeodat, Archivist of Kenatos*

XVIII

Tyrus stared at Phae for several moments, unable to speak. The shifting emotions finally settled to a look of determination. His eyes were flecked with spurs of gold. The gray streaks in his beard and temples seemed to spread with the weight of his concerns.

He shook his head no. "Impossible."

Phae came to her feet, her emotions raw with fury. Her fingertips tingled with prickles of heat. "You would drag me to my death in the Scourgelands, but you will not let me see my mother? As if Kenatos were not the place to fear instead of the Scourgelands? You have some twisted magic that allows you to go from place to place. Surely it can bring us there?"

She caught the Vaettir prince's look of outrage at her insolence, but she ignored him. Tyrus allowed her to loom over him. He did not meet her anger with his own. "For your own safety, I cannot allow it."

"My safety?" Phae said, her voice shrill. She was cornered on all sides. These men in her life had all accosted her, threatened to or did abduct her against her will. She was furious. It roared to life inside her like a demon. "Is it safe to enter the Scourgelands? Everyone else you brought there died. What will make this time any different?"

Tyrus bowed his head, staring down at the lamp. "Sit down, Phae."

She covered her face with her hands, wanting to pound her fists into his chest. She wanted to kick the lantern and scream at all of them. She choked on her emotions. "Tell me why," she said with a savage voice. "If I must go into the wilderness with you, if I must bond with a tree as you say, then tell me why I cannot see my mother." Her breathing increased. She started to pace inside the thickly-shadowed cell.

The Kishion put a hand on her shoulder, stopping her. She looked up at his face, saw the hard look there—but it was not focused on her this time.

He gazed down at Tyrus. "The Arch-Rike knows of the Dryad in the tree," he said. "It is already weak from living in the city. He gave the order to have it cut down."

"No!" Phae gasped, clutching the Kishion's tunic.

He nodded. "I did not understand the reason, other than revenge, but the Arch-Rike cannot allow a portal to exist inside the city that he does not control. He is very careful who is allowed to use the gateways or where they can be entered from. It may take a few days for the order to be carried out, but I fear it is done by now."

Phae turned from the Kishion to her father, her heart despairing. "You cannot abandon her!"

Tyrus looked up, his face lined with a deep scowl. His eyes were haunted. "We knew the risks," he whispered. He shook his head. "I cannot shield her from the Arch-Rike's wrath as I wish to." His shoulders slumped. "You do not understand, child, what it cost her—what it cost us *both* to give you up. I would prefer another dagger thrust than to experience this pain. We knew a sacrifice would be necessary. Her instincts require her to provide a replacement for herself. She gave that up to try to save generations yet unborn. That has been my chief desire as well. I do not do this for glory or for fame. My only ambition is to correct the injury that was done in the past. No one forces me to do this. Believe me, it would have been far easier to quit long ago." He gazed into her eyes fiercely. "The tree is not destroyed yet. I know it is not, because I still share a connection with her. She is in peril. I can feel that. She is surrounded by enemies. But if we go to her now, and if we are detected, you know the Arch-Rike will destroy her in a hurricane of magic. He will use her against me. That is his nature. I will honor the sacrifice she made, though it pains me to my soul."

Phae stared at him, overcome with grief. "So he will kill her tree for certain if we go?"

Tyrus nodded. "I believe so."

Phae crumpled and sat down on the floor, all her energy gushing out of her. "How can I know this is even true then? Your excuses are believable, if not convenient."

Her father laughed bitterly. "The truth isn't often that way, I'm afraid. However, I propose an alternative."

She licked her lips, her heart too heavy to speak. She shrugged.

"There are others aiding in this quest. One is a young Druidecht, not much older than you. He is the son of Merinda Druidecht who I mentioned before. He protected a Dryad tree in the woods of Silvandom and earned her trust. She could teach you about your heritage." He reached out and drew a circle on the dirt floor with his finger. "Would that help convince you?"

Phae folded her arms over her knees. "I'll think about it. I am so tired, Father. So very tired."

"Get some sleep," Tyrus said. "We will have little rest in the days ahead."

Phae stretched out on the hard-packed floor, using her cloak as a pillow. Waves of weariness crashed down on her. Her entire life was hanging askew. Voices murmured in the stillness. She heard the prince speaking softly. Tyrus muttered a response. Her mind grew thick like churning butter. She tried to listen, but felt herself drifting farther away.

Then she heard the Kishion speaking to Tyrus. His voice was low, as it always was, but she felt the words cut through the veils of sleep falling over her.

"I will not let you force her to do this. She must choose it."

Daylight came through the uneven slats in the cellar door and Tyrus beckoned her to follow him up the ladder. Phae climbed the ladder outside, feeling her muscles ache with fatigue. The air was sharp and cold and she shivered, hugging herself for warmth as little puffs of mist came from her mouth. The old man, Evritt, greeted them from the porch with a small cauldron of porridge to stave off the chill. It was amber with honey swirls and tasted delicious. Fruits and nuts accompanied the meal along with water from a rain barrel on the far side of the cabin.

The prince practiced some strange morning ritual, standing stock-still, knees bent and legs flexed, his arms crisscrossing in a pattern of maneuvers that looked menacing. He rarely moved his legs, other than to shift the stance occasionally, as if his feet were slowly sinking into the earth. The motions were intriguing to watch and she studied him as she ate the porridge.

Tyrus conferred with Evritt on the porch, discussing someone named Hettie, a girl who had worked for him for some time. Not understanding the conversation, Phae abandoned the empty bowl and started to wander around the secluded grounds, exploring the various benches, curing sheds, and fire pits that had developed over time. Even a small stream trickled nearby and she went to find it, seeing a strange black-masked animal washing something in it with its paws when she arrived.

She stared at it and it stared at her, chittering in a friendly sound before slinking away up the stream bank.

Phae turned and saw the Kishion nearby, leaning against a cedar. "You are quiet," she said.

He folded his arms and gazed back at her. "What will you do?"

She crouched by the stream and ran her fingers through the chilly water. After rising, she approached him. "What do you think I should do?"

"What does my opinion matter?"

She glanced down. She was still frightened of him, but no longer feared he would stab her ruthlessly. "It matters to me. Strangely." She looked up at him, cocking her head. "I heard something you said last night. That you wouldn't let them force me to do this." She swallowed. "Thank you."

He shrugged as if it were of no importance. "Would you shove a man in front of a runaway cart to stop it from crushing five people? Or would you jump in front of the cart yourself? Either way, a person dies and five are saved. In one case it is murder and in the other the sacrifice is willing. There is a difference."

"Or you let the cart kill the five," Phae said. "I suppose I see your point."

The Kishion stared hard at her. "It is a sacrifice, to be sure. The obligation you face must be a great burden."

"Sympathy, Kishion?" she said, her mouth twisting into a smile. "From you?"

He looked at her calmly. "You have a choice in this, Phae. If you say the word, I will take you back to Stonehollow. You can hide in those mountains for a long time. It is outside the Arch-Rike's reach for now."

She frowned, her face pinching. "Now you are tempting me with freedom. That is not fair."

"You have a choice. Which is more than I have right now."

She picked a fleck of wood from his sleeve. "How would I live with myself, though? I am young and so have never experienced the ravages of the Plague before. I know my blood can save a few families from perishing. But if I could stop thousands of families from being destroyed? Could I be so . . . selfish? How would I feel watching so many die and wondering if I could have prevented it?"

"You've made up your mind then." It was spoken as a fact.

She gazed down at her boots and nodded. Her throat was too tight to speak.

He put his hand on her shoulder. "Then I will go with you. I have a feeling it is not the first time I've been there."

"Maybe you will remember again. When we get there."

He shook his head. "No. Not unless we find the tree where my memories are buried. Maybe I do not want them back."

She looked up at him, still feeling that visceral fear knowing he was capable of destroying her so quickly. "If you help me end the Plague, Kishion. It would go a long way in your redemption."

He nodded in silence, then cocked his head. "Danger."

Explosions screamed from the sky and then struck the cabin.

The ground rumbled with the impact. The Kishion grabbed her tunic and pulled her behind him and the tree. More whistling sounds came, followed by eruptions of flame and a spoiled egg smell. The woods began to catch fire and trees shattered in the showering hail of blazing pitch. Phae glanced around the tree and saw her father running toward them, the prince and the woodsman at his heels. A rock of burning pitch landed in front of them, exploding and splattering the burning black substance everywhere. Part of it struck the tree they sheltered behind and Phae felt it shudder and catch fire.

A howl of pain sounded and Phae could not tell which of the men it came from. The Kishion took her elbow and yanked her away from the tree as another whistling sound came from above and struck it directly, causing another plume of greenish fire and sending shards of wood and broken tree limbs every direction. The Kishion dragged her up as she stumbled and plunged into the stream.

The sky was raining fire.

Phae's boots sloshed in the water, her heart galloping in fear at the awesome force unleashed against them. It was as if ten thousand burning arrows had been launched at once and descended in a cloud. Tyrus was pulling the old man, whose arm was on fire with the burning pitch. Prince Aransetis grabbed Evritt's other arm and helped haul him toward them in the stream. The old man's face was knitted with pain and agony and he cried out. Tyrus removed the cylinder from his robes and held it out for them all to reach.

Another whistle sounded from above, coming straight at them. Phae took the Kishion's arm and closed her eyes as the world lurched and began to spin.

Trasen gazed at the monstrous city, listening to the sound of the oars lapping the waters and urging the boatman with his thoughts to put more vigor into his strokes. He was beyond worried. He was beyond desperate. He had searched the outer tunnel leading beyond Stonehollow for clues, for any trace of Phae's passing. What he found alarmed him beyond all reason—a blackened scorch mark on the ground, carving a huge tear in the earth's skin. He had discovered a twisted iron ring abandoned in the crater, which was now in his pocket. He had heard stories from Holt about the spells of the Paracelsus. He had never witnessed the magic himself.

In the dirt nearby he had found Phae's tracks. They were unmistakable. He knew the type of boot she wore, the size of her foot. His mind nearly went mad with grief and suspense as he tried to decipher the clues. Some sort of blast or explosion had happened. There were multiple prints as well, the size of men. There were also the prints of a horse coming along the road, mixing up the clues in a way that completely befuddled him. He wished Holt had been there and would have trusted his master's judgment.

Trasen began to nod off in the boat and jerked himself awake again. He had not slept properly in days. Poor Willow had gone as far as she could go and he had left her with a stableman at the settlement on the lakefront.

Phae had simply disappeared.

The tracks all clustered together, four people in total, and then there were none. It was as if some enormous invisible hand had snatched them away. Without a trail to follow, without anything but hope and the fires of love shoving him on, he had decided to press forward to their likely destination—Kenatos. Trasen would confront the Arch-Rike if necessary to save her. He would do anything to save her.

As he stared at the impassive city, swirling with gulls and pennants, the sense of dread and foreboding increased. He fished the iron ring out from his pocket and stared at it, turning it over in his palm, prodding it with his finger. It was a twisted, blackened thing—not a decorative ring. It had strange black sigils carved on it.

"What's that, lad?" the boatman asked, nodding to him.

"I paid your fare," Trasen replied hoarsely. "Leave me be." He felt the scowl etched in his own mouth. The thought of smiling was a distant memory.

"Don't be like that. What is it? A ring?"

Trasen stuffed it back into his pocket and folded his arms, feeling the aches all throughout his body. He had never pushed himself so hard or gone so long without proper sleep. His mind was a blurry fog of worry and pain. Would he ever see Phae again? He regretted that he had not confided in her his plans, why he wanted so much to join the Wayland army and save his ducats. He wanted to seek a homestead with her, to be with her always. He shuddered with suppressed emotions. He thought there was a chance she might feel more than just friendship. Not wanting to risk losing what they already shared, he had been reluctant to reveal his heart to her.

"Here we are," the boatman said petulantly. "Be on your way, lad. Keep your secrets then."

After the boat bumped into the pier, Trasen lurched to his feet and started to wobble toward the dock ladder.

"Don't forget your belongings!" the man said, exasperated. "You'll be leaving your brains behind next, I'm thinking."

Trasen apologized and grabbed his pack, slinging it around his shoulder. The docks were enormous, teeming with ships and freight. He tramped down the dock and found few in the lines ahead of him entering the city. Before long, he was standing before a brown-haired Rike who gazed at him with curiosity.

"Where are you from, traveler?" the man asked him politely. "You look bone weary."

"I am," Trasen replied, craning his neck to gaze up at the enormity of the city. "I'm from Stonehollow."

The Rike clucked his tongue. "Looking for work, then? The Paracelsus Towers are under repair. They need quite a few laborers."

"No," Trasen said, shaking his head miserably. "I'm looking for . . . a friend."

The Rike nodded calmly. "Well enough." He paused, his expression narrowing just slightly. "You won't last a moment among the Preachán in your condition. They'll rob you blind. Do you want to sit over there a moment and catch your breath?"

"No, I'll be all right," Trasen said, trying to wave him off. "May I pass?"

The Rike persisted in his interrogation, his face scrunching. "Do you have any . . . magic . . . with you boy?"

Trasen caught the subtle gesture from the Rike as he seemed to nod to someone elsewhere and gesture for him to come closer. He remembered the twisted ornament in his pocket and glanced at the beetle-black ring on the Rike's hand. He swallowed, knowing one did not lie to the Rikes of Seithrall.

"It is said that the Vaettir came in great ships across the sea. When the Plague struck their empire many thousands of years ago, they sailed across the turbulent waters in fleets and landed on the coast of what is now called Lydi. The ships returned for another convoy of survivors. They returned again a third time, bringing tens of thousands with them to safety. Alas, when the ships returned the fourth time, the empire was full of rotting corpses and abandoned cities. It is said that the deaths of so many, millions even, upset them such that the Vaettir swore an oath never to kill. They treat life as sacred, in memory of the forgotten generations that fell. They erected a temple in the mountains of Lydi—a place where they could pass along the traditions of their people. They named it Shatalin."

—Possidius Adeodat, Archivist of Kenatos

XIX

Hettie lunged at Paedrin with the dagger, aiming for his abdomen. The fading sunlight glimmered on the sharp edge of the blade. As Paedrin pivoted on his heel to let it pass by, he recognized that it was just a feint. Her arm never reached full extension and suddenly the dagger blade was jutting up to his neck. He accelerated his pivot, swinging away from her and then jumped high, bringing his leg around in a high circle, directly at her temple.

She ducked, of course, as he expected her to. His foot met nothing but empty air where her dark hair had been a moment before. With a quick sip of breath, he remained in the air, poised like a leaf caught on a draft, gazing down at her mockingly, as she was abandoning the leg sweep she had just commenced.

Snuffing out his breath, he dropped on her leg like a rock, pinning her to the ground. There was the dagger again, aiming for his back. He blocked her forearm with his, slid down to her wrist and closed his fingers around her hand. His eyes gleamed with triumph.

Her eyes glittered with fury. With a momentous pull, she jerked her arm backward and hoisted him, trying to offset his balance.

She lifted at his body with her pinned leg and Paedrin felt himself overcome by the act. He would have sailed over her shoulder if her leverage had been better. Instead, she managed to pull him right on top of her. The scratchy meadow grass crackled around them, leaving little burs in her hair. He sprawled on top of her, face hovering above hers. He still controlled her wrist with the dagger.

"That did not work out the way you intended," he observed dryly.

She squirmed beneath his weight, trying to get free. "Don't say you're not enjoying this, Bhikhu. I see it in your eyes. Get off!"

"Drop the dagger before I make you."

"What are you afraid of more? That I'll kiss you or stab you?"

"I'm not sure which would be more painful to endure," he shot back. "To be honest, the thought of the former hasn't once entered my mind."

She squirmed harder, trying to wrest him away with her leg. Then she tried to smash him in the nose with her head.

He jerked back in time, but kept her pinned. "Now you are trying to kiss me! Shameless, Hettie."

"I could really hurt you right now, if I chose," she said back through gnashing teeth.

He pressed his thumb at a spot near her wrist.

"Owww!" she groaned, wincing with pain.

"I'll wait you out. How long have your fingers been tingling?"

"How long has your brain been tingling?" she said, bucking harshly on the grass. Her fingers shot up to his face, hooked like talons.

"Tsk, tsk," he clucked, forcing his elbow around to intercept the strike and used his weight to push her arm back down. Now both of her arms were above her head. She tried to lash out again, but it was pointless. He could see her chest heaving with lack of air. Her fingers opened and the dagger thumped to the grass.

Submission.

Paedrin inhaled, smelling her sweat and the wonderful scent of the dried prairie grass cushioning them.

He lifted off her slowly, hovering in the air, and gazed down at her, hair sticking to her face, her black tunic slivered with grass. His heart ached with suppressed emotions. He would not give in to them though. Their friendship had expanded since leaving Kenatos with a whirlwind of seek and chase.

"You tend to slip back into insults when you realize I've won," he mentioned.

She stared at him, eyes narrowing with thought. "It's the anger of the moment. Sometimes you just aggravate me."

He nodded, satisfied. "Back to the mistake," he said, brushing his hands. "Your leg was trapped over here."

She stared at his face with a look impossible to decipher. Women were too complex to understand. He dared not even try. She snatched the dagger in the grass and rolled up to the crouching position. He set himself on her leg again, caught her arm as it plunged toward his back and gripped her wrist.

"What were you trying to do?" he asked her.

"Use your grip on me to pull you off balance," she answered. It was important that they were always communicating the thoughts behind the actions. "I wanted to throw you."

"I was on your leg," he stated, motioning down with his chin. During this part, they always moved very slowly, reenacting the previous combat. "Where is your leverage?"

She thought a moment. "Ah!" she said. "I was trying to pull you toward me. You flopped on top of me. I should have used the Unbreakable Arm and pulled you this way." Her arm went rigid as she twisted, pulling him backward. Paedrin felt the shift in his posture and the momentum carried him over onto his back, pulling her on top of him, knife blade still caught by his wrist, but now she was on top.

Her hair tickled his face.

"Correct," he praised. "That would have worked better."

She gazed down at him, her eyes narrowing slowly, her expression shifting into another of her mercurial moods.

"I'm getting closer now," she said softly. "Closer to cutting you. I don't think we should practice with the dagger."

"You weren't that close."

"Part of me still holds back though," she said, shaking her head. The tips of her hair were vastly annoying on his cheek. "I don't want to cut you."

"If I get cut, I deserve to be cut," he answered. "You are getting better though. I will admit that. Your hand forms need some work still. Practice your stretches for a while. There is still daylight left."

She nodded, tickling his face one more time with a smirk, then pushed up to her feet. She sheathed the dagger in her belt then extended one leg in front and curled the other leg behind. Leaning forward, she stretched, clutching her bare foot with her hands and pulled herself as low as she could. Paedrin's flexibility had been instilled since childhood. Hers improved vastly day by day. She never complained about the pain of the stretching. She threw herself into it, as if the knotting feeling in her stomach was a joy instead of agony. Pain is a teacher. She seemed to relish being a student.

Paedrin stood and brushed the grass from his Bhikhu robes and scanned the land ahead. They were well outside the range of the pack dogs of Kenatos, in the grassy hillocks south of Silvandom and north of Stonehollow. Another day of traveling would bring them inside the forests of Lydi. But even from the great distance where they were, they could see the flat blue line of the ocean. He had always imagined what that would be like. The vastness of it was beyond his previous imagination. The horizon stretched as far as he could see, nothing but a flat, gray-blue line. They were still several leagues away from it, high in the hills. A broad forest stretched out in front of them. But the port city of Lydi was clearly visible in the horizon to the south. There were easily thousands of ships anchored there, clotting the port like beetles.

The vastness of the ocean had caught him unprepared. It was not the smelly waters of the lake surrounding Kenatos, but the real, foaming oceans that his forefathers had sailed generations before. The anticipation of it was delicious. They had chosen to stop and train on the hilltop, providing a view of the land west as well as the path east where they had come from.

Hettie finished the stretch and then switched legs, leaning down the length of her leg, her back arched. Paedrin knelt in the grass behind her and placed both hands against her lower back and pushed.

"Harder," she said, stifling a groan. He put more of his weight into it and felt her breath quicken with pain. He leaned against her, seeing her jaw muscles clench with the suffering of the stretch and held it for several moments before easing up.

"Again," she panted, shaking her head. "Push again."

"You truly defy everything, including pain," he said, then obliged her. He pushed even harder, feeling her firm muscles. He waited longer, knowing it was excruciating to her. Yet she did not complain. He eased up the grip. She gasped with relief.

"I'll give you credit for your endurance," he said as she got to her feet. "I've seen younger men weep during the stretches. Now for some forms to practice. Sugar Plum Fist. Then Snapping Legs. No stopping between. Go."

Hettie nodded obediently and plunged into the routines with animation, despite her weariness. He noticed how being barefoot didn't bother her so much now. The calluses were forming swiftly. Her boots were nestled by the travel packs. She finished the first form quickly and then launched into the longer one. When she had first learned them, she had made many mistakes with technique. But instead of being angry when he corrected her, she had immersed into the nuances with a keen desire to learn. She was a gifted student and craved to memorize not only the movements but the names of the movements: Heron Gliding on the Water, Serpent Seeks the Pearls, Black Dragon Swings His Tail, Leopard Fist. It was the Bhikhu way not just to showcase movements and applications, but to describe the forces of nature that had inspired them. The tradition had been passed down for over a thousand years. Hettie was a natural.

When she finished Snapping Legs, sweat dripped from her nose. She stood at attention though, not moving until he released her with a salute. Paedrin walked over to their packs and sat down cross-legged. She joined him, wiping the sweat away with her hands.

"You didn't criticize me this time," she murmured, picking the fragments of grass from her clothes.

"Your form is improving," he said. "Give it another ten years and you'll be ready to face a five-year-old."

She chuckled, flicking away a speck. "Tell me, do you think it is odd that the Arch-Rike has not hunted us? Once we made it past the lake, there were no pursuers. Not even in the air."

Paedrin shook his head solemnly. The pain of losing Shivu had dampened his joy. While he often thought of witty retorts, he did not use them nearly as often. Traveling alone would have been unendurable. He was grateful to have Hettie to talk to and had enjoyed her companionship.

"He already knows our destination, Hettie. His forces will be waiting in front of us, not behind."

Hettie looked at him, startled.

"Always remember the Uddhava. Anticipate your foe. He has already sent others ahead of us to Lydi."

"How do we succeed?"

He did not want to poison her thinking with his own ideas. What they needed were fresh ones and so putting it as a challenge would incite her creativity. "You are a clever girl. Think it through as we go. We still have some time before we get there."

"It's a beautiful sunset," she said, folding her arms around her knees.

"I've never seen so many ships," Paedrin said. "Not even in the harbors of Kenatos."

Hettie nodded. "I've never been to Lydi before, but the Romani travel there. I heard the city is made of ships. There are no buildings, only reclaimed vessels brought to shore. It used to be a thriving city, ages ago. Now it is a graveyard of wooden hulls."

"If they are all made of wood, you would think they'd have decayed by now."

Hettie shrugged. "Lots of timber in the forest down below. They are the master shipbuilders, the Lydians. I do not know about their loyalties to Kenatos."

"Do you know anything of their customs?"

Hettie shrugged again. "No, not really. I've never met a Lydian before."

Paedrin stared at the sun, vanishing like a disc beneath the gray folds of the sea. It was a beautiful sight. Somewhere, past the Lydian city, somewhere buried and nearly forgotten was the Shatalin temple. His skin prickled with gooseflesh and his heart saddened again. His determination, however, only strengthened.

She noticed the subtle frown on his face. He saw it register in her eyes. "Let's go a little farther," Hettie suggested quietly. "I don't like being exposed on the hill like this. Let's go down to the woods before it gets too dark." She stood and offered him her hand.

Paedrin stared at it, feeling the swell of difficult emotions that always threatened tears. She was recognizing his moods now. When he wanted to banter. When he wished for silence. He gripped her hand and let her pull him to his feet. She then tugged on her boots and swung the pack around her shoulder. As they started down the hill, side by side, he felt her hand graze his. Part of him wanted to reach out and hold it, to cling to her grip like a rope to save himself from drowning in grief. He rebelled against that part of himself, the part that felt reassured by her presence. He needed to clear his mind.

Yet Paedrin struggled against the thoughts and emotions that kept flitting like inside him like a hive of enraged bees.

The following afternoon, Paedrin and Hettie studied the port city for a long while. From a secretive vantage point within the woods, they learned what they could from the safety of the forest. It was the strangest looking place Paedrin had seen. He had been impressed by the mountain towers of the Cruithne in Alkire. Silvandom, of course, had a special place in his heart with its majestic trees and stone-fashioned homes. Kenatos was a thriving civilization sprawled atop an island lake from end to end. Havenrook, on the other hand, was a painful memory and a place he never dared venture again—knowing that if he did, he would school the entire city in a lesson of pain. Yet he knew, by his Bhikhu training, that even scourging the city would not assuage his guilt.

Lydi was a city made entirely of sailing ships and a patchwork maze of docks and harbors. There were no warehouses or inns or taverns, yet the ships became all of these. Rather than constructing new buildings, the surplus of unused vessels had become the means for providing shelter and storage. The streets were the docks. Some ships had their hulls breached, and scaffolding and steps erected to provide entrances. Most hung with signs, featuring whether it was an inn, or a smithy, or a stable.

The population of Lydi, it seemed, had dwindled over the years. Derelict ships were everywhere, with no signs of life at all. During the time they spent observing, only four or five ships approached, all from the north, and docked in the harbor. There were people milling about in the town, but it seemed most kept indoors. Some of the ships were enormous galleons that had crossed the wide seas. Others were more humble vessels, only one mast instead of three or five. There were seagulls, of course, flitting above the town. Gulls were plentiful in Kenatos as well. Paedrin rubbed his chin, staring at the city.

"What have you noticed?" he asked Hettie.

"The woods have been cleared on purpose," she said thoughtfully. "They don't want to be approached unawares. I imagine they have lookouts all around the perimeter. I cannot make much sense of the arrangement of the ships. There are large ones and small ones jumbled together. That one over there is listing dangerously. I doubt anyone lives there. My advice would be to approach after dusk where it would be difficult to spot us coming."

Paedrin folded his arms. "Then what?"

Hettie glanced at him. "I would look to find a Vaettir first. A Bhikhu would be my first choice if we could find one."

"Because . . . ?"

"Because they would be the most honest in their intentions. If we are hunted by the Arch-Rike, they would try to arrest us quickly. No games. We'd know where we stood. They would also be the ones most likely to know of the Shatalin temple."

"True," he pointed out. "I noticed those things as well. What surprises me most is what I do not see. Very few people compared to the structures. The lack of trading. The place seems . . . sullen."

"That's a good word for it. The city has a strange feeling, doesn't it? It isn't lively, like Havenrook. It feels . . . depressed." She hesitated at the word and he knew why.

Paedrin stared at the city. "I agree. It does not feel like a flourishing town. It is decaying. So therefore, I propose we do the opposite of what you say. We enter the city now, in daylight. We enter a tavern or place to eat. Try to be gone before dusk. It may be a place, like Kenatos, that gets more lively, and by lively I mean drunk, after nightfall. I don't want to wait out here any longer. Let's go. If we don't learn about Shatalin quickly, we leave and make our way south along the coast."

She grabbed his arm. "I don't think that would be wise."

He shook his head. "I don't trust the Arch-Rike. This place has his taint on it somehow. Let's see what we can learn and then leave."

"We are walking into a trap, Paedrin."

He smiled impishly at her, part of his old humor returning. "Remember Drosta's Lair? I already know it's a trap. Let's set it off and see what happens."

"The wisest as well as the most dangerous men are

those who observe without speaking."

—*Possidius Adeodat, Archivist of Kenatos*

X X

The docks spread through Lydi like a maze. The creak of wood from the massive ships in the waters combined with the strain of mooring ropes and the squawk of birds. The air had the smell of dead fish, which Paedrin found revolting in the extreme. Many of the planks along the walkway were missing, creating treacherous footing. A few wandered the inner streets. No one had challenged them or even asked their names. A few glanced at them surreptitiously but no one engaged. If it was a trap, there was no bait to tempt them.

The races were a mix of Vaettir and Aeduan, a blending of the two races into something new. There were no Bhikhu, other than himself, and no signs of authority at all. There were carts packed with goods for sale on the docks, all small and very specific, most sold by small, gray-haired women. Debris and droppings littered the way.

Paedrin quickly picked a tavern and approached, but it was closed. Most of the ships were closed, the gangplanks missing.

A voice sounded from behind. "He's waiting for you at the Wharf Rat. Water's edge."

Paedrin turned and saw a young fellow, probably twelve, lurking past them both, pointing to the end of the boardwalk. He had flint-like eyes and a sallow face. An urchin, by his looks.

"Who?" Hettie asked.

The boy backed away, shaking his head. "I did what I was paid to do." He turned on his heels and ran.

Paedrin was about to go after him, but Hettie caught his arm. "Someone is watching us from that boat. He saw me look and ducked back. These people are frightened of us."

"No patrols. No Preachán trying to sell. Do we leave now or listen to the boy?"

"Who do you think is waiting for us?"

"I have no idea. Obviously someone who was paid to look out for us." Paedrin rubbed his mouth in frustration. It was the bait to the trap. But it intrigued him. "He said the water's edge, that way."

Hettie glanced that way. "Could it be a message from Annon?"

"Doubtful. This place is not very sensitive to nature. Let us go a little farther down this trail, Hettie. Be ready to fight."

"I am."

They continued down the pier until they reached the end. There were six boats moored there, each broadside and large. They had true sails and the tattered scraps of canvas. The farthest had a gangplank lowered. The sign was a cheap rendition of a blue-furred rodent. Some crew members were visible above, milling around on deck. The other boats were empty.

Paedrin was about to march up the gangplank, but stopped. "You stay here."

She shook her head, catching his wrist. "We go in together, Paedrin. If there is trouble, I'll jump overboard and you float away. We will meet in the woods where we studied the city. I think they will try to trap us trying to get out, not in. That's how traps work, after all."

"Agreed," he answered, pleased with her thinking. He walked up the notched gangplank and boarded the vessel. The deck was worn but serviceable. The crew looked real enough, wearing short breeches and belted tunics. They were the same Vaettir-Aeduan mix he had noticed earlier. They all appraised Hettie with undisguised admiration. One of the crew members pointed to a ladder going down into the hold without saying a word.

"After you," Paedrin said, smiling broadly. He saw the trapdoor lid and knew it would be too easy for them to bolt it after they had gone down.

The sailor shook his head. "He's waiting down below for you. It'll be a quick visit, I think."

Paedrin approached the ladder, staring down into the shadows of the hold. There were four members of the crew on deck. He glanced at the nearest ship and saw no one at first, but then he glanced up at the crow's nest and saw two figures hunching low and watching them.

"Who is he?" Paedrin asked.

"Men like him do not leave their names. But he said a Bhikhu and Romani girl would be coming and to let them board."

This felt just like a trap ready to spring. Part of him wanted to jump straight down and surprise whoever was inside. He could do that, but it would leave Hettie with four men on deck to deal with. Not that she couldn't handle herself, but it would make things more complicated.

"Describe the man who is down there," Paedrin said to the crewman. Before letting him reply, Paedrin grabbed his arm, bent his wrist, and flung him down into the hold opening. He whipped around, kicking the second crewman in the gut hard enough to steal his wind and hopefully break a few of his ribs. He glanced and saw Hettie subduing the third in an arm lock he had taught her, leaving only the fourth.

Paedrin waited a moment and then flung himself down into the hold where the surprised crewman was trying to recover from the fall.

Shadows were everywhere. The interior of the hold was not very tall and the crewman was holding his wrist gingerly and kneeling, seeming surprised to find himself on the floor and also in pain.

The sound of heavy boots thudded. The sound and the weight were familiar to Paedrin and a pit of dread opened up in his stomach. A man emerged from the shadows of the hold. A Cruithne—specifically, *the* Cruithne from the Paracelsus Towers.

"Nicely done," the Cruithne said, his expression bland. "You might want to call the Romani girl down now before they start shooting at us. It will not take them long to discover I've betrayed the Arch-Rike when the mooring lines are cut and we depart for Shatalin. I'm here to help you."

He gave Paedrin an expressionless look. He was fleshy about the face and lips, his bulk sturdy and formidable. He had dark crinkled hair that was graying at the sides, and the usual soot-black skin of his race.

Paedrin stared at him, saw the armor buckled to his body, the weapons secured but not drawn.

"You are wondering if you can defeat me quickly," the Cruithne continued. "Let me answer that for you. I was trained by Aboujaoude when I was a boy. And I'm a Cruithne, which would be the physical equivalent of kicking a boulder." He shrugged, opening his hands to show he brandished no weapon. "Your choice, Paedrin. Trust me or fight me."

The man had anticipated his thoughts. He was using the Uddhava. But what struck Paedrin was his demeanor. Calm and soft-spoken. If anything his words were a little slurred and hard to hear because they were spoken so softly. He presented himself as a threat on the surface but had said he was also in rebellion himself against the Arch-Rike. The Cruithne was the guardian of the Paracelsus Towers.

"Who are you?" Paedrin asked.

"Baylen of Kenatos. We met before."

"I thought you came to the temple to arrest us," Paedrin said.

"A fair statement. I wanted to try to talk to you before the Arch-Rike cornered you again. I'd rather not tell my story twice, and besides, she would probably do a better job telling whether or not I'm lying. The girl should come down here."

"Hettie," Paedrin called up the ladder. "You should see this."

She emerged down the ladder quickly, then paused on one of the rungs, staring in shock.

"Let me start with a few things you should know about me. First—I'm not like any Cruithne you've known. I don't like long speeches either, but you need information before you can trust me. I've been watching Tyrus for a long time. I had a feeling he was up to something. I figured it had something to do with the Scourgelands. He's very quiet about his plans. I mentioned I knew Aboujaoude. Well, he took on a street kid and taught him something useful. How to fight and survive in the streets. More importantly, how to watch other people. I learned later it was the Uddhava. I've been watching ever since. When the Tower exploded, I picked up a few of Tyrus's trinkets and thought they might come in handy or that he might come looking for them."

He turned and looked at Hettie. "I watched your trips to the Towers, Hettie. I noticed you each time." He stared at her, his expression dull. But his eyes were curious and the ghost of a wry smile passed quickly. "I didn't tell the Arch-Rike about your first two visits. When the two of you appeared inside without passing through the gate, I paid a Preachán to tell me where you went. I'm guessing that Tyrus is going back into the Scourgelands again. If so, I want to join and figure that you both are the easiest chance I have of finding him." He hunched his big shoulders, his eyes darting to Paedrin. "You haven't tried to attack me yet. I'll take that as a good sign. I'm fairly confident I could take you both though."

Paedrin breathed out deeply, shaking his head. "You set a perfect trap to catch a Vaettir and a Bhikhu. We're below deck, where my abilities are hampered. Confined spaces are an advantage to you. Yet you also know you have the advantage and gave it up by revealing yourself. Either you are crazy or trustworthy. Maybe both."

The Cruithne smiled briefly, pleased. "You should know that the only way to get to the Shatalin monastery is by ship."

The sailor on the floor rose cautiously on his elbows, eyeing Paedrin with anger. The Cruithne spoke down to the crewman. "Ready to sail?"

"Aye," the crewman said. "Assuming anyone is left on deck who can stand upright." He gestured to the ladder and Hettie came the rest of the way down.

"Cut the mooring ropes," Baylen said. "Draw the gangplank. Prepare for arrows and fire. You both look ready for a fight. Hope you are not disappointed it won't be with me. Once we go atop, are you ready to get attacked by the Arch-Rike's men?" he asked them with a smirk, a glimmer in his eye. "Because they will send everything at us at once."

☬

When the Cruithne mounted the steps to the main deck, Paedrin thought the ladder was going to break under his weight but it didn't. The orders were given and the ropes were cut and the boarding plank withdrawn. There were shouts of warning and curses from beyond. The ship began to move from the mooring and out into the sea. Paedrin inhaled and emerged from the hold below.

Baylen's words were prophetic.

Arcs of green fire lanced at the ship, coming from the nearby vessels. Paedrin saw the enemy now, the other Paracelsus on deck, sending wave after wave of magical fire at the sails. The flaming globes struck the sails with a hiss and crackle, but otherwise plummeted to the deck and were doused by the wounded crewmen. The sails did not look scorched.

The Cruithne glanced at Paedrin again, a half-smile on his mouth. "It helps to know their kind and their craft."

From a pouch at his waist, he withdrew a glass orb. He then clomped to the quarterdeck and held up the orb. He uttered a word. A fierce wind surged in the air, sending the sails billowing. The ship began to pick up speed. Winds surged and rushed, released from the orb in powerful gusts.

Men were running down the planks of the harbor, some screaming and shouting obscenities at them. The boat rocked and pitched as the furious winds intensified, shoving the vessels into the harbor. The Cruithne reached into his pouch and withdrew a smaller orange orb. He spoke the Vaettir word for fire—*thas*—and the orb burst into flame. With a powerful arm, he threw it at the docks behind and the orb shattered against it, sending a deafening explosion across the pier. He followed it with two more, Paedrin staring in amazement as the flaming orbs arched into the sky and landed in front of the rushing soldiers where they burst into explosions, devastating the docks.

Hettie joined them up on the deck, her hair whipping about her face. "What magic is this?" she yelled.

The Cruithne took a defensive stance, a Bhikhu one, and held aloft the orb, his legs sturdy against the gale. He gripped the wheel and turned, sending the ship knifing into the deep waters. A shaft of lightning came from the skies, striking the mainmast. An iron spike was at the top and the lightning made colors dance in the air, but the ship did not burn.

"Almost beyond their range!" the Cruithne shouted. "I thought they would unleash a *bejaile* on us by now, but they probably haven't thought of that yet."

Paedrin still could not believe what he was seeing. Why had the Cruithne joined their side? Was his connection to Aboujaoude more than a boast of his fighting abilities but also an indication that he could be trusted? Had Tyrus trusted him?

There was a flash of light on deck and a contingent of soldiers appeared wearing the tabard of Kenatos.

"Tay al-Ard," the Cruithne muttered. "Should have guessed that."

Paedrin vaulted over the rail, flipping in the air, and came down in the midst of the soldiers. He struck as a whirlwind, crippling knees and striking faces—using his entire body to press the attack. They were armored, which helped protect them from his blows, but he knew the vulnerabilities and struck quick and hard, moving this way and that to avoid swords and spears.

One of the soldiers threw an orb at him and he dodged it, but the glass shattered and burst into flames, racing across the deck. Paedrin grabbed the man before he could loose another one and chopped his neck soundly, dropping him. Every sense in his body opened like flower petals, absorbing the scene around him.

There was a boom of thunder on the deck as the Cruithne also dropped from the quarterdeck. He had a sword in each hand and moved like an avalanche, crushing through the mass of soldiers, using his elbows and the flat of the blades. Paedrin saw how quickly he moved, which was fascinating considering his girth, but he literally trampled the soldiers in front of him and sent others sprawling. The clash of swords against armor rang out on deck. The few sailors on board joined the fight.

Paedrin was struck from behind, feeling a blade slice into his shoulder. There was no pain at first, but he ducked, feeling the wet blade whistle over his head. Spinning around, he downed the man with a kick to his kneecap then swirled away from a blow aimed straight for his head. Blood oozed into his shirt, mingling with the sweat. He thrilled at the act of battle, ducking low and then inhaling to rise above his enemies, causing two to crash into each other as they attempted to tackle him. He moved liked a wisp, darting back and forth.

From the corner of his eye, he saw Hettie strike a man in the groin with her dagger hilt and then his ear with her fist. She kicked out, moving in a form he had taught her days before, slipping between soldiers like a silk shadow. Paedrin seized another man's wrist, arched it up and plunged his fist into the man's armpit, watching the man's grimace of pain. As he torqued the wrist and the blade clattered to the deck, he realized the fight was already over.

"Off with your hauberks," the Cruithne ordered, kicking one back down who still had some fight in him. "You'll soon be joining the fishes. You heard me. Off!" He sheathed his swords and grabbed one soldier by the collar and tossed him overboard. The others scrambled to remove the hauberks as one by one they were tossed over the side. There were twenty in all, and all were still alive, though some were unconscious. It was the Bhikhu way.

Paedrin stared at the giant of a man, feeling a dull ache in his shoulder blade. He was impressed with the Cruithne's quickness as well as his size. It was a rare combination in someone so big.

"Let me see that gash." He turned Paedrin to the side, frowning subtly at the wound. "Lucky blow. He only glanced you. A few stitches and you will be fine." He marched over to the ladder leading up and climbed it quickly. Paedrin floated up to it effortlessly.

Hettie climbed up the ladder next. The Cruithne took the helm and barked a few orders to douse the fire on the deck and then started rubbing the wood of the wheel absently. She marched up to him, her expression wary. "You got us safely away, but that is just the sort of trick we might expect from the Arch-Rike. He has used us before. Let me see your fingers."

Baylen held up one hand at a time, wagging his fingers at her. "No Kishion rings. But you are wise to be cautious. The Arch-Rike is the most cunning man I know. I also knew that I would never catch you two in time before reaching Shatalin. I did tell the Arch-Rike that you two had come to the Towers again, looking for something. I said I tracked you down to the Bhikhu temple and learned that you were heading for Lydi. I asked if I could help hunt you down. All true. He thought it would be useful having me on his side. He thought I wanted a reward. He should have looked into my motives more because I have always been loyal to Tyrus. I set up the trap in a way that suited our needs. That way, we can get to the Shatalin temple and back before word reaches there. As I said, it can only be approached by sea and we're the first boat headed there. Not even the Paracelsus know where Shatalin is, so no one can go there by Tay al-Ard. Is my presumption correct that Tyrus is leading another group into the Scourgelands and not a revolt?"

Paedrin and Hettie looked at each other.

"Thank you," he said, smiling. "You say more with your eyes than most people do with their lips. Now what I don't understand is why you are going to the Shatalin temple. I would think that is the last place you would want to go."

Paedrin looked at him quizzically.

"It is not far from here," Baylen said. "What I don't understand is why Tyrus would send you to the place where all the Kishion receive their training."

"*It was said by an ancient philosopher, Augour the Wise, that the purpose of all wars is peace. I wish I could believe that is true. History is rife with conflict. The wars and tumults of men are interrupted occasionally by the devastations of the Plague. Thus perhaps the purpose of all Plagues is peace.*"

—*Possidius Adeodat, Archivist of Kenatos*

XXI

Inside the confines of the captain's cabin, Hettie completed sewing the cut on Paedrin's shoulder. He felt the tug of the needle, but he did not flinch from it. The soldiers had done their best, but it was not enough. The three of them had scattered twenty men like leaves.

She clucked her tongue. "I'm surprised he cut you."

"One was bound to get lucky," he replied. "Are there any Romani quips about that?"

"Hmmm," she murmured. "Ah yes. A blind chicken finds a grain once in a while."

Paedrin chuckled with enjoyment. "So true. The Romani are very wise in their way."

Hettie bit the end of the thread after finishing the tie. "Done."

"Thank you."

Her hand grazed along his shoulder as she stepped in front of him. Her touch sent tingles throughout his body. She sat down on the small cot across from him. In the lamplight, he could see more of the red color coming out in her hair. He had noticed it before and asked. With a small shrug, she said she had stopped dyeing it after leaving the Romani. The dye would fade in time and her true coloring would emerge. He liked the hint of it in the lamplight.

"What is it?" she said, looking at him with concern.

"Nothing." She had caught him staring again. He cursed himself silently.

She leaned forward, resting her elbows on her knees. "Do you think we should trust this Cruithne?"

Paedrin leaned forward. Their noses almost touched. "As opposed to jumping overboard and swimming the rest of the way to Shatalin?"

"There is something about him that concerns me."

"I can think of about five concerns myself. He looks like a brutish Cruithne but he's as smart as a Vaettir. He knows about Tyrus and his plans. He outmaneuvered the two of us. He . . ."

She put her hand on his arm, silencing him. "How does he know about Kishion being trained at Shatalin?"

The door creaked open and Baylen pressed through sideways. Hettie withdrew her hand from his arm. Paedrin tugged on his tunic jacket and wound the belt around his waist. There was a pinch of pain in his shoulder, but it had stopped bleeding earlier.

"We will be at the monastery before nightfall," Baylen said. "What do you seek there?"

Hettie frowned.

Paedrin cocked his head. "You mentioned above deck that the Kishion train at Shatalin."

"And you want to know how I know that." He sighed with impatience.

Hettie folded her arms.

"Remember who my employers were. I was hired by the Paracelsus to protect them, not to count people entering the gates. If any are suspicious, I do not let them pass. Tyrus's nephew came recently. So did you," He nodded at Hettie. "And so did a Kishion.

He is known as the Quiet Kishion, a very dangerous man. I knew that someday I may be called on to protect my masters from him. With that possibility, I began to study what I could of him, including where he was trained. All Kishion come from Kenatos originally, but they leave the city for special training. Not many know this. Few even bother asking, but I made it a point to ask and then listen. If you want to know something, you eventually find a way to discover it. I learned from a man who knows the Archivists that the Kishion are trained along the coast. They said there was an old Bhikhu temple there called Shatalin. It is built on a cliff along the sea, south of Lydi. The only way to get there is by ship and climbing up very steep steps carved into the rock. The coast is known for recurring fog, so the monastery is shrouded most of the time."

Baylen rubbed his meaty hands together. "It gets worse. The one who trains them is blind. Those who are trained are blindfolded, forced to learn combat without sight. They say that looking at the blind master's eyes will turn you into stone. So again, I ask you: Why are you going there?"

Paedrin swallowed. "Rumors or truth?" he asked the Cruithne. "I wouldn't know."

Paedrin glanced at Hettie and saw the fresh concern in her eyes. Her expression was veiled, but he could see the worry. She stroked her hand through her hair, gazing at him, lips pursed.

Standing, Paedrin faced the Cruithne. "The Arch-Rike already knows what I am after. He knows because I once wore a Kishion ring and he heard Tyrus give me instructions."

Baylen's eyebrows lifted, but his expression was bland. "Those rings don't come off without killing the wearer."

"I speak the truth. I seek a blade—a sword. It is called the Sword of Winds. It is a weapon of power that will be used in the Scourgelands. Master Shivu also charged me to restore the Shatalin temple. The master there is known as Cruw Reon. I will defeat him."

There was a long silence as Baylen studied him, his expression continued to be bland, no hint of surprise. "Have you ever faced a Kishion before?"

"Twice. I failed both times."

"You lived. That is better than most. What makes you think you can defeat the blind master?"

Paedrin folded his arms. "Because I am not blind and I will have the sword when I face him. I trust you, Baylen. I may be a foolish Vaettir. Or maybe you have proven yourself as thoroughly as you can. You are welcome to join us. A question for you now: Have you ever faced a Kishion?"

Baylen shook his head. "No, but I did pull one out of a pile of rubble in the courtyard of the Paracelsus Towers. I imagine they are difficult to kill."

"I would imagine. Being a Bhikhu, killing one isn't my goal. Thank you for your aid."

The Cruithne shrugged and then squeezed out the door again, shutting it noisily behind him.

Hettie sighed. "Why do I feel like Tyrus is sending the goose with a message to the fox's den?"

He looked at her askance. "A goose, am I?"

"You honk like one, letting the whole world know the direction you are flying."

Paedrin smiled broadly. "I may honk like a goose, but notice I did not reveal your part."

☙

What the Cruithne said was true. The cliffs and the sea were shrouded in fog. Paedrin and Hettie stood above deck, smelling the salty air, feeling the moist kiss of the mist on their faces. The sound of waves crashing against stones haunted the air, but they could not see the breakers. The waters were green-gray, full of froth, and pungent, so different than the smell of the lake waters of Kenatos. The wind brought sounds from many directions, the slosh of water against the hull, the spray of the waves against rocks, the cries from gulls overhead. Paedrin leaned against the railing, staring into the fog, his stomach knotting with nervous energy. Baylen's words had unsettled him, but he was determined not to let them ruin his courage. Master Shivu would not have trusted this to him without believing in him.

Hettie leaned next to him. "I still don't trust him."

"You can have your opinions. Leave me to mine."

Baylen climbed down from the helm deck. "This is as close as we dare go. The crew says the rocks are very near. We will need to take a little boat to go farther. I will row you to the shore. Do your business and I will bring you back to the ship."

Paedrin nodded and they followed him to the edge where some sailors were using pulleys to fix the boat with ropes. Hettie and Baylen entered the small vessel and it swayed dangerously when Baylen boarded. It took three sailors to lower them down, their arms straining against the bulk. Paedrin waited on the edge and then breathed out, lowering himself down to the boat with a single breath of air to slow his fall. The Cruithne took the oars and rowed against the wild churn of the waves. Spray splashed against the side and the mist swallowed them.

The jolting of the boat was alarming as it responded to the surge from the ocean. Paedrin gripped the edge and prepared himself to float the rest of the way to shore if it swamped. He did not like being on the waters. Hettie hugged herself for warmth, peering into the gloom. Suddenly Baylen thrust out an oar and struck it against a jagged rock that appeared out of the water in front of them. The boat lurched violently, but he managed to avoid crashing into it. He took the oar in both hands and stroked vigorously. The mist began to part, revealing enormous cliffs and misshapen crags. The rock was thick with brown vegetation and moss, and puckered with clinging shells.

"There!" Baylen shouted, pointing to a cleft in the rock. Waves bounded against the cliffs, spraying them with white churn. The boat rocked violently as the crosscurrents hit it and Paedrin gripped both sides of the boat to steady himself. Hettie did the same. The boat pitched again as a wave caught it from behind and sent it shooting forward. Then the bottom scraped against rocks and it slowed to a halt.

Baylen cursed, rose, and jumped over the edge. The boat began to float again, and he gripped it with both hands and pulled them closer to the sheer cliffs ahead. "Do you see the stone steps?" He pointed straight ahead at the wall-like surface. Sure enough, the craggy rocks had been carved, forming a near-vertical stair upward, which disappeared into the mist.

"I see it," Hettie said.

"This is as close as I can get you until high tide," he said. "You'll have to wade in farther and climb up. I'll pull this boat up on a rock nearby and wait for you to come down again. If you don't come back in a day, I will come looking for you. Agreed?"

"Agreed," Paedrin replied, jumping out of the boat. He helped Hettie clamber out and felt the pull of the tide water against his legs. The power in the surf was incredible. Hand in hand, Paedrin and Hettie crossed the sharp surface of the reef, knee-deep in seawater, and closed the distance to the face of the jagged cliffs. He glanced back, spying Baylen climbing up on a pyramid-shaped boulder, the boat dragging behind him. The water was bitingly cold.

Hettie slipped on the slick stones and he tugged her back up as the water soaked her front. She uttered a Romani oath and pulled with him to reach the edge. The water receded with each wave, revealing enormous pockmarks in the reef. Colorful objects and plants grew inside the water-filled tide pools, amazing creatures he had never seen before. Some looked like flowers, except with quill-like ends instead of petals. Strange rocky creatures with five points clung to the rocks as if hugging them. Little crabs darted amidst the pools. The plethora of life was intriguing.

"What a forsaken place," Hettie muttered, staring up at the cliffs and not down at the teeming life in the tide pools. She brushed hair back from her face. Her expression was pained and wincing as she stared up the steep incline of the cliff. The water was down to their ankles now.

"What a mysterious place," Paedrin said. "The environment is harsh and punishing, but look at the forms of life around us. I had no idea things could survive in such a place."

She glanced down at the tide pools, looked at him with an arched eyebrow and then shook her head as if he were hopeless.

They reached the wall of the cliff, all jutting angles and sheets of dark rock. An inlet lay before them, where the sea had carved away huge portions of stone. Trickling waterfalls plunged into the sandy edge. There was a large flat rock near the base of the stairs—during high tide it would have provided an easier way to approach. The mist hung above them, about twenty paces, veiling the upper heights.

"Let me see if I can locate the temple first," he said. "You start climbing."

She nodded and Paedrin took a big gulp of air, rising despite the heaviness of his sodden clothes. He used the edge of the wall to pull himself faster up, gliding effortlessly up the face. The Vaettir would have no trouble ascending to such a place. The steps were undoubtedly there for others to use.

Paedrin entered the thick mist of the fog, which blinded him as he ascended. The rock face was steep, ascending at a gradual slope the higher it went, providing ample footholds and crevices to use. An idea began to blossom in his mind. He emerged above the sheet of fog higher up, which gradually tapered off, revealing the hulking outlines of an enormous temple structure. The Bhikhu temple in Kenatos was just a sprig compared to this. He was awed by the ancient stones, the curving rooftops and multiple levels of towers and parapets. It had been built over a great number of years, perhaps even centuries. The entire top of the rocky cliff was covered in structures, made of the same stone as the cliff itself, as if it had been painstakingly carved from the rock into the formation of towers and crenellations. Enormous statuary adorned it—bull heads and tigers and serpents and some creatures he could not identify. There was a giant wooden door at the top of the stairs, bound with rusty iron that gleamed red in the light.

The temple faced him majestically, more ancient than the Arch-Rike's palace. Yet as he stared at it, it did resemble the structure of the palace in Kenatos slightly. The design was reminiscent of it. There were no sentries posted on the walls, no sounds emanating from within. He did notice a shelf of flat rock without any structures on it near the cliff's edge partway around the temple. The blossoming idea went further. If he could draw attention by his approach and let Hettie climb the walls from behind, it would increase the chances of their success.

Paedrin let out his breath and sank through the mist quickly. His stomach thrilled with the sensation and he emerged beneath the cloud, finding Hettie climbing the steps barefoot, her boots tied to her pack.

He dropped down to her level and flattened himself against the cliff, grabbing handholds and footholds to steady himself. "I have an idea," he said.

"What is it?" she grumbled, wincing at the effort of the climb.

"Over that way, the cliff curves and emerges to a flat shelf at the base of the temple walls. It would be a good place to conceal yourself until dark. I will approach the main doors and seek admittance. My thinking is to draw attention to myself at the front of the temple tonight, drawing their gaze away from where they are concealing the sword. You climb the walls after dark and begin your search. I will distract them as long as I can."

"Draw attention to yourself? You mean insult them."

"It comes naturally to me."

"How do you plan on distracting them then? Parading the front tower in your smallclothes?"

Paedrin smiled. "I plan to challenge Cruw Reon directly for authority. Before I face him, he has the right to choose a champion to face me first. It is a Bhikhu custom. If I win, I earn the right to combat for authority. If I lose, it won't really matter anyway. You get the sword. When you do, whistle loudly if we should flee. I will come to you. If not, bring it to me and I will defeat him."

Hettie nodded. "So which way do I climb?"

He inhaled and started to rise again, crawling like a spider up the sheer face of the cliff. "The handholds are better over this way. Come on."

She followed, leaving the safety of the stone steps carved into the cliff. Paedrin searched ahead, looking for the best handholds and sturdiest places. It was an arduous climb and he could see the pinched look on Hettie's face as she struggled up the slope. The rocks cut at her fingers and feet, but she did not hiss or complain. They reached the veil of fog and the way became murky.

Paedrin drifted down to be closer to her in case she needed help. She bit her lip in concentration, judging each outcropping and angle to find the best position to ascend. He was proud of her willingness to try. The ascent was agonizingly slow.

"I'm getting . . . so tired," she said after a particularly difficult reach. "How much farther is it?"

Paedrin did not want to leave her side to determine it. "Not much farther. You are almost there."

They were not almost there though. Her pace slowed considerably. There was hardly any place to rest or catch her breath. She sagged against the cliff face, pressing her cheek against the rock. Time crawled forward. Paedrin stayed even closer to her, keeping a hand nearby just in case.

There was a bulge in the rock that had not been visible through the mist when they left the path. Hettie's brow furrowed in concern. "My arms . . ." she panted.

"Almost there," Paedrin said. He grimaced, knowing it was a lie. Hettie hung her head, breathing deeply, and then started up again.

Her foot slipped on the mist-slick stone.

Paedrin saw her fall. He reached and caught her flailing arms as she started to plunge down. His breath would not support them both and he felt them dragged down like an iron anchor at sea. Rocks scraped against them as they scrabbled down the cliff face.

"Grab something! Grab something!" he ordered, feeling the edge of the cliff give way to open air. Panic flooded his chest. He would go down with her. He would give his breath to slow the fall if he could. There was blood on her fingers, her cheek. Her fingers found a lip of rock, halting the fall. Her legs dangled in the air. Paedrin inhaled sharply, grabbed her by the belt, and pulled. Her arms, though tired, prevailed, and she managed to make it high enough to find purchase with her feet.

There, she rested, hugging the cliff face with her entire body, burying her wounded cheek against the rock. Her shoulders began to heave and tremble. She was coughing. No, she was crying. His heart twisted with anguish at the sound, for it caused him pain. Hettie tried to control her breathing, to stifle her sobs, and failed. Her hair shook with the quiet sounds. Below, waves continued to crash against the base of the rock.

He touched the small of her back, hovering in the air behind her. "I won't let you fall," he promised. "A little farther."

She nodded and reached up for the next handhold. The trek was impossibly difficult. It amazed him how high the cliff was without seeing anything above. The daylight faded. Hettie pulled herself up farther, one step at a time, one grasp at a time. Her limbs shook with the strain. He could feel the muscles in her back through the tunic.

The sun set.

Still, Hettie persevered. The moon rose, sending its silvery light to the glistening black rock. They were both feeling their way forward now, their sight diminished to the point of being useless. He stayed right behind her, guiding her and coaxing her.

Finally she reached the top, just at the base of the temple, in a little alcove just wide enough to fit them both, side by side. The rock sloped downward, just enough to make him feel they would slide off the edge of the cliff if they breathed wrong.

"You did it," Paedrin said to her triumphantly.

Hettie leaned against the hard stone of the temple wall, gasping for breath. She nodded with a leaden, slack expression. "I thought . . . I thought . . . the fall." She shook her head wanly. "Death. I thought I was going to die."

He patted her leg comfortingly.

Suddenly she grabbed him in a fierce hug, burying her face against his shoulder. Her whole body trembled and quaked. He put his arm around her, pulling her close, and stroked her hair.

"I wouldn't let you fall," he whispered. "I was there."

She shook her head against his shirt. Her face tilted up, lost in the shadows of the temple and the midnight sky. He could feel her breath hot against his cheek. "I ran out of strength," she whispered. "It was too much for me. Not even my stubbornness was enough." She gripped the front of his tunic. "I could have died tonight. I'm so used to being on my own. To relying only on myself. It wasn't enough. I wasn't strong enough."

He didn't know what to say. "It was you, Hettie. You did it. You conquered the mountain."

"No, Paedrin. It was you. You carried me up the cliff. You saved me from falling. I could have died. You've saved me so many times. In the cave where we found the dagger. You saved me then too." She shook her head and he could feel the hair tickle his cheek. Her shoulders trembled. "I'm so frightened, Paedrin. What if this task is too much for us? For you as well? What if the Scourgelands cannot be defeated? My father died there and he was Aboujaoude. He was better than even you. Now here we are, alone. I'm frightened. I don't think I've ever been this scared."

Paedrin put his hand on her cheek. It was wet with tears. "I will see you through this, Hettie. We will make it through this."

"But how?" She sounded so doubtful it pained him. "My best wasn't enough tonight. I failed. If you hadn't been there to catch me—"

"I was."

Her head thumped against his chest again. She clung to him, nestling against him as if he were the only thing in the world left to cling to—the only piece of comfort she had left in her fractured life. And he realized, with deepening awareness, that she was the only source of comfort left in his.

"Let us train our minds to desire what the situation demands."

—*Possidius Adeodat, Archivist of Kenatos*

XXII

The entrance to Basilides was carved into the face of the mountainside, a series of murals, intricate columns, and inset arches that gave the entire formation the appearance of an enormous hollowed skull. Scaffolding was erected on the left side where workers constantly hammered and chiseled the stone, expanding the openings and continuing the designs. It was three levels tall, with an open bronze-shod door where the mouth should be, and twin empty windows for eye sockets. Runes were carved throughout the design, arcane and impressive. It rose in the distance, at the rounded end of the valley. The waters of the lake had been dammed, providing space for the scaffolding and workers, but it was clear that when the monument was finished, the barriers would be breached and the entrance only approachable by boat and oars.

Annon crouched behind a massive fallen boulder and spied the creation, listening to the echoes of the hammer strokes off the jagged walls of the cliff. Amidst the haze of stone dust, he counted several dozen workers and a scattering of black-robed Rikes.

The trap they had overcome at the mountain pass behind them still lingered in his mind. His heart lurched with fear at how perilously close to dying they had come. He had assumed his fireblood would sustain him. The realization that he was wrong sent throbs of doubt and caution throughout his stomach.

Annon turned to Lukias. "How long has this been under construction?"

"A few years, no more. There are natural caves inside these mountains, creating a maze to confuse those who do not know the way. What you see there is just the outside works. The inner sanctum is guarded."

"By what precisely?" Erasmus asked, rubbing his chin.

Lukias glanced at him in annoyance. "Many things, Preachán. My advice would be to approach and seek audience with the Arch-Rike's emissary here."

Annon wrinkled his eyebrows. "And do what? Ask him for permission to use the oracle?"

Lukias gripped his shoulder firmly. "I told you before. This place is treacherous. You will not be able to navigate to the inner sanctum without my help or you risk wandering aimlessly and meeting your deaths in a dozen ways. A negotiation might be engaged."

Nizeera growled petulantly.

"I don't think so," Annon replied. "What can you tell me of the nature of the oracle?"

"Nothing," Lukias replied. "Just as you do not share your Druidecht lore with me. You must discover it on your own. Ours is at least written down in *The Book of Breathings*. Have you read it, Khiara? I would be surprised if you had not."

"Yes," she answered simply. "My cousin the prince has a copy of *The Book of Breathings*. It is very symbolic—we lack the true keys to decipher it."

Annon suspected as much. With only one entrance to the oracle, it likely would force a confrontation with the Arch-Rike's minions. Annon secretly hoped they might find a way to steal inside, gain the information they needed, and then return. Nearly fifty men guarding the entrance would prove a challenge, unless he resolved upon a strategy.

Turning to face the group, Annon rested his back on the boulder. "A thought to consider: I believe there are some spirits in the area here that may be able to help us. They seem to have hard feelings against the Rikes and would do them harm if asked. I know down in Wayland, woodcutters who violate the places the spirits deem special are often tricked or hindered by these spirits. I have no intention of harming the workers, but we need to get them away from the scaffolds and away from the main door. Fire would accomplish this. If the scaffolds are burning, it creates smoke to obstruct the view and would lead them to the waters to put it out. We use the confusion of the fire to enter." He shrugged. "I am open to other thoughts."

Khiara looked pensive and gripped her long staff, leaning against it and staring out across the lake waters. Erasmus took another peek around the boulder and studied the front.

"I know you have an opinion, Erasmus," Annon said.

The Preachán murmured to himself and then said, "Always smoke and fire with you. It will take a lot of smoke to hide us completely, but with our disguises, it will be easier than otherwise. Some of the workers will form a bucket chain to put out the fire. Some of the Rikes will go inside to warn the others. If we are close enough to follow their steps, they could lead us to the inner sanctum."

"That means I would need to be close by when the fire starts. Your prediction of the odds of success?" Annon added in a playful tone.

"Well over half," Erasmus answered curtly. He rubbed his throat and nodded with certainty. "Well over half, I should say. It's a good plan. How will you get close?"

"One person approaching will be more inconspicuous. I will see if the spirits will help me. Once the fire starts, wait for the smoke to billow and then approach quickly. The confusion will aid you. Nizeera will come with me and help track them inside the caves."

Khiara looked skeptical. "Shouldn't we wait until nightfall?"

Erasmus spat on the ground. "Too risky to wait. We don't know when the next arrivals will be. We also don't know how long it will take for the Arch-Rike to recognize that his pets are dead. The plan is solid, Annon. Surprisingly so."

The Druidecht smiled wryly. "Thank you, I think." He looked at the big cat. *Stay near me.*

I will not be seen by the mortals.

Annon emerged from the boulder and started along the edge of the trail, approaching it but keeping himself covered by the boulders interspersed along the way. As he walked, his nervousness increased, realizing he might well be seen long before he drew near. His breathing was quick and stressed. If he was challenged, he would need to think quickly. His thoughts reached out to the spirits in the mountains, probing gently to gain their awareness, hoping to beg their aid.

The response was immediate. *We sense you, Druidecht. How may we serve you?*

I thank you. Is there a means to shield me from their sight as I approach? You know by my thoughts that I am here to do mischief to these men who hammer at stone.

We understand your intentions, Druidecht. Walk amongst us and you will not be seen.

Annon felt their presence expand in the form of moths and gnats that began to swirl around him in thick clouds. He felt the vibrations from their fluttering wings and the natural urge to swat them away, but he remained surefooted and calm and continued walking forward. A shroud of magic enveloped him, providing a sense of ease and protection. Their power amazed him, and he felt a swell of gratitude.

I thank you.

The fluttering of moths billowed around him and he no longer guarded his approach. He did not know how it appeared to others, but he trusted in their power and approached the workmen and the scaffolding. The ding and clang of stone and chisel rocked the air, clashing harshly against his ears. Grunts from the workers, gray with dust, became more pronounced as he approached. Annon advanced to the far edge of the scaffolding, keeping his distance to the doors. He realized that, with the magic of the spirits, he could enter it by himself.

Are there enough of you to disguise my friends? he asked.

No, Druidecht. We are not sufficient in number.

He thought it best to proceed as planned. Reaching the edge, he glanced up at the figures standing on the scaffolding, working on the rungs and boards to provide the height needed to work. Some men were resting by the lake. The Rikes were clustered together, discussing something amongst themselves.

Annon reached out and gripped the lowest plank of the scaffolding. *Pyricanthas. Sericanthas. Thas.* His fingers began to tingle and glow blue. Seizing the plank, he focused the heat against the wood, watching it blacken. Smoke began coiling along the edge. He fed the flame slowly, not wanting to startle them with a sudden blaze. A few tongues of yellow fire began to lick at the wood. He stepped back, focusing on the wood, feeding it with his mind, letting it writhe and twist and begin its hypnotic dance. He stepped farther back, edging away from it. The fire began to crackle, but the sound was lost in the hammering strokes.

The length of the board burst into flame, its dry, desiccated wood ready to burn.

"Hold on there, look! Fire!" The cry of alarm came from the cluster of Rikes as one of them had finally noticed. "Fire!" he screamed even louder.

The hammering ceased all at once.

Annon, backing away, focused his attention on the flames and fed the blaze with his power. He willed it to burn hotly, to surge higher and higher.

"Get off!" someone shouted. A loud ruckus commenced, the scaffolding buckling as workers began to scramble across to the adjacent section, knowing that descending was perilous. Some jumped to the ground and rolled away in the dust and dirt. Smoke from the fire began to fill the air, bringing wheezing coughs and stinging eyes.

"Water! Fetch the buckets! Quickly!"

Annon saw the flames begin to lick into the upper planks, the fire coiling along the iron rungs and spreading. Men and bodies were everywhere, some jumping, others shoving to get away. Muttered oaths and curses met his ears. A few ran to the edge of the lake and began filling buckets. The first few arriving hurled the water at the flames, causing more billowing smoke to fill the area.

"More water! The whole thing will come down if we don't. Hurry, you fools! Run to the lake. Go!"

Walking quickly, Annon approached the main doors. He saw a black-robed Rike wrest open the enormous carved door and dart inside. The heavy door remained ajar. He thanked the spirits again and bid them leave. With the smoke and commotion, no one would think to notice him. He gained the edge of the door, listening to the footfalls of the boots as they disappeared into the dark swath of cave ahead. In the time he waited at the door, he studied the locking mechanism of the gates, the chains and pulleys that closed and secured the door. Nizeera padded up soundlessly next to him.

Nizeera, follow him.

She loped into the cave, vanishing into the shadows beyond. Annon stood by the door, impatiently waiting for his companions to come. Would Lukias betray them now, seeing them on the verge of success? He ground his teeth, staring at the smoke, wondering when they would arrive. Men toting sloshing buckets approached as they hobbled back to the scaffolding, trying to put out the fires. Annon ran his palm along the thick bronze band on the edge of the door. The wood was thick and heavy, the hinges enormous in size. Once fastened shut, it would not be easy to open, except from the inside. He hoped that gave them an advantage.

"Hold there. Who are you?" someone shouted in the fog of smoke. "Where did you—?"

The sound was cut off instantly. There was a bark of commotion, the sound of a fist striking flesh. From the plumes of smoke they came—Khiara, Erasmus, and Lukias. They sprinted to Annon and the doors and he waved them inside. Shouts of alarm sounded from the smoke, revealing the confusion of the Rikes.

"What is happening? Are you hurt? Who was that?"

"I swear it was Lukias."

"Are you sure?"

"I swear it! I've seen him before!"

Annon and the others shoved the doors closed. The cave was plunged into blackness. Annon summoned an orb of fire into his hand, providing an aura of blue-violet light. He pointed the light at the chains and pulleys. "Erasmus, can you determine the proper use of the levers?"

The Preachán was already moving, examining the intricate tangle of gears and chains. His eyes darted this way and that. Then he nodded and hefted on a pulley rope. The chains rattled and three crossbars, each a different height, came down and nested together, sealing the door shut from the inside. The workers and Rikes were stranded outside.

Excitement churned in Annon's stomach. He looked to the others quickly, his eyes dancing with energy. "We must be quick and find the inner sanctum. A Rike made it ahead of us and he is probably warning the others. I sent Nizeera ahead—"

"The cat will die then," Lukias said, his face flushed with emotion. "There are guardians here that can protect against spirit creatures. Magic defends these halls."

"Of what sort?" Annon pressed, holding the fiery globe closer to Lukias. "Either you help us or hinder us, Lukias. Which is it?"

The Rike's face twisted with conflicting spasms of emotion. "This is *our* lair, Druidecht. Your power will not prevail here."

"Which is it, Lukias? Will you aid us or thwart us?"

Khiara took a step closer, her face impassive.

"I truly did not believe you would make it this far," Lukias said through clenched teeth. He wiped sweat from his forehead. "While I was wrong about that, I'm convinced you will not make it past these defenses without my help. Let me go to the inner sanctum and plead your case. Let me see if they will treat with you. You are not helpless, that much is clear. Let me go on ahead of you."

Annon shook his head. "We've trusted you this far, Lukias. But it appears our truce is at an end. If you will not reveal the dangers ahead, then you are of no use to us."

Lukias's eyes narrowed challengingly. "Will you murder me, Druidecht?"

Erasmus's voice was thick with anger. "What do you call the attack at the prince's manor in Silvandom? Surely it was not an offer to negotiate."

The Rike looked at the Preachán disdainfully. "We were ordered to take you, if possible, kill you if not. Clearly our ends were not achieved. The Arch-Rike won't underestimate you again. Look at it from my side, Annon!" he said, grasping the younger man's shoulder. "They recognized me out there. I was seen with you. Either I am here under duress or willingly. My excuses vanish if I aid you. The ring tells you I speak the truth. I have been trying to save my own life. I gave you what you sought. I still believe you will fail. Will you kill me as well as yourselves?"

Annon stared into Lukias's fearful eyes. "I don't blame you. That is why I am giving you a choice. You have been wrong about our chances so far. You may be wrong about the future as well. If we succeed and the Arch-Rike falls, you have lost nothing you would not lose anyway."

"Persuasive," Lukias replied, "but not convincing. I die either way. I respect you, Annon. I do not lie. You have great power and a cunning mind. There is wisdom in you despite your youth. I know what dangers lie ahead. I know what you face. Believe me, I do not think you can succeed. The dangers ahead will kill you."

"We have no alternative but to succeed," Annon said. He glanced at Khiara and nodded.

With a swift blow, she struck the side of Lukias's neck with the flat of her hand. Erasmus caught Lukias as he fell. The Preachán withdrew a coil of rope from his pack and began securing Lukias's wrists behind his back and his ankles together.

"Help me," Erasmus said to Annon and the two hauled him to the side of the door. Erasmus withdrew a band of cloth next and then fixed it as a gag in Lukias's mouth.

"We should kill him," Erasmus said with a sniff. "It would improve the odds of our survival considerably. But I know the Vaettir are squeamish about such things even though he will die anyway, after the Arch-Rike questions him."

"No," Khiara said, her expression tightening with anger. "He will die when the *keramat* fails."

"We will not kill him," Annon replied sternly to Erasmus. "He had a chance to choose." He turned to the doorframe and discovered some unlit torches hanging in brackets along the wall. Using the flaming sphere in his hand, he lit several before handing them to the others and taking one himself. "Let's find Nizeera."

Erasmus sighed, rubbing his wrist as he held up the torch and let the light chase off ahead. "Remember the dark of Drosta's Lair, Annon?"

"I have a sense this will be more difficult than what we faced there, Erasmus," he replied, staring down the dark shaft of the tunnel. The uneven edges angled downward into the smothering blackness. The air felt stale and thin and had a moldy smell. The burning pitch from the torches did not improve on it.

"I agree with your prediction. Who is coming? Is that Nizeera?"

A glowing set of eyes appeared in the vastness ahead of them, reflected by the torches. Nizeera padded forward into the light. Her muzzle gleamed with blood.

"I have spent some little time delving into the studies of the Rikes of Seithrall. They are experts at the anatomy of all life forms, both human and animal. When you visit their temples, you see the remains of the skeletal lineaments, bleached white and fastened together with metal wires. They study these in great detail. They have large glass vials full of oil and internal organs. They are the masters of embalmment. When a pauper dies, rather than burying them in a public cemetery, the corpses are studied and meticulously recorded regarding the cause of death and the condition of the various organs and tissues. They harvest this knowledge that they may learn to prevent and treat illnesses and document their knowledge in The Book of Breathings. They truly are the overseers of death. It is even whispered amongst some in the population, the more superstitious ones, that the very touch of a Rike of Seithrall can induce death. This is, of course, a foolish belief."

—Possidius Adeodat, Archivist of Kenatos

XXIII

Annon stared at the cat's grisly maw. A sickening fear washed through him, turning his bones into water. *Nizeera?*

He is dead, Nizeera thought to him. The hackles on her back were ruffled and spiky. *These tunnels smell of the dead, Druidecht. There is great evil guarding this place.*

Annon knelt as she approached. *What did you see? Why did you kill him?*

She shook her head slowly. *Somehow he knew I was behind him. He invoked some magic that blinded me and then sent a crossbow bolt at me. When he missed, I charged and he fled toward an archway in the dark. Great magic lay beyond it. I knew if he crossed, I might not be able to follow. I caught his heel as he was nearly through and dragged him out.*

Her tail lashed and swayed.

He did not cry out. The portal beyond reeks of magic. Follow me.

Sighing with dread, Annon motioned the others to follow him. He was grateful the bolt hadn't struck her. His fear deepened. The darkness was barely dispelled by the light from their three torches.

It illuminated only a short way ahead as if the tunnel could swallow light. Annon felt his breath quicken as well as his pulse. Sweat began to trickle down his back as they walked, the weight of the mountain pressing heavily as they descended deeper. Tributaries branched off regularly along the way, like branches sprouting from a vine. Above each one, a stone piece of slate was fixed from iron pegs with symbols traced in chalk. He could not read the language.

"Do you recognize it?" Annon asked Khiara. "What does it say?"

"The script is ancient," Khiara replied. "It is not Vaettir. I cannot read it." Her mouth tightened into a worried frown. "I am sorry."

Annon glanced as Erasmus, but the Preachán shook his head with mute surprise. The dread in the Druidecht's stomach increased. They followed Nizeera deeper into the bowels of the tunnel. The torchlight hissed and spit, the pitch burning a brilliant orange.

Ahead, crumpled in a puddle of blood, lay the fallen Rike. His glassy eyes stared at them, his mouth frozen in a rictus of pain. Annon shuddered. Beyond the corpse stood a broad arch, carved into the stone in perfect symmetry. It was adorned with runes and strange symbols. The path beyond it was darker than ebony. Not even their torches penetrated it.

As they approached and carefully stepped around the body, Annon felt a presence in the blackness ahead. It felt like eyes were boring into him, unseen and hostile. He clenched his jaw, summoning his courage.

"Can either of you read the runes?" Annon asked. "The script is different than what we saw in the hall."

Khiara looked up at the archway, studying the letters. She was silent for several moments, rubbing her lip thoughtfully. Her jet black hair glinted in the torchlight. "It says, and I translate this roughly: *Beware the Ruby Goddess. The humble only may pass.*"

Annon stroked his chin thoughtfully. "What is the Ruby Goddess? Do you know?"

Khiara nodded, her expression brightening with relief at being useful. "It is an ancient belief. She is the Aeduan Goddess of Vengeance. She was greatly feared. The ancient texts say she punishes mortals. It is odd to find reference to her here, when the Rikes do not believe in the old myths."

"Remember the markers on the path leading here? This appears to be a temple built in her honor," Annon observed. His stomach twisted with fear. "Strange indeed, coming from the Arch-Rike. Is that all? Only the warning?"

"It is," she replied. She looked at the darkness nervously and stroked the edge of her arm with one hand. "This place feels cold."

"It is evil," Erasmus said. "The light does not penetrate the arch. Magic is at work. Can't you cancel it, Annon?"

Annon shook his head. "Our torches may not be of much use to us when we cross."

Nizeera prowled around the entryway nervously. *There is magic at work beyond. Spirit magic that is aware of us. It is waiting to strike at us.*

Pursing his lips, Annon stared at the cat. "How will it strike us?"

I do not know, Nizeera purred in warning. She started to hiss.

"What is it?" Erasmus asked.

"She senses something in the dark."

"I sense it too," Khiara said.

Annon swallowed. "We did not come all this way to turn back. We face it, whatever it is. We need to stay near each other. Erasmus, do you have more rope?"

"I used it on Lukias. I told you we should have killed him."

Annon exhaled sharply. "The torches will not be of use to us in there. We should hold on to each other's hands." He noticed the brackets inset into the stone arches, enough for six. He slid his torch into one of the brackets and motioned for the others to do the same. Then he reached out for Khiara's hand, offering his. She stared at his hand a moment and then shifted her staff.

"Hold Erasmus next and I will follow last. I want to hold my weapon in case we are attacked. This place is dreadful."

Erasmus took Annon's hand and Khiara took Erasmus's. Nizeera hissed and growled, pacing fitfully. Mustering his remaining courage, Annon stepped beneath the arch.

The magic responded instantly, and he realized that there was something they had failed to do, like a password uttered or a stone pressed. As soon as the blackness enveloped him, he felt the presence of an evil being stir awake ahead of them. The spasm of fear rocked him, for he recognized the presence from the waterfall beyond Drosta's Lair. It was the Fear Liath. There was no sunlight now to protect them. The creature moved in darkness and the place had been prepared to encounter anyone, day or night. He felt the presence in the chamber beyond, felt the fear coil inside his heart and melt his courage. As Khiara and Erasmus stepped inside, they also froze in panic.

Annon's heart raced, thudding painfully. Sweat trickled down his cheeks and neck. He trembled, unable to move. The fear blinded him to everything. He heard Nizeera hiss in the darkness next to him.

Be still! he thought to her.

A whisper of air brushed against his face. Something hulking loomed. His mouth was dry with terror. His legs could not move. What had he done? They had trusted him and now he had led them to their death. The Fear Liath had slain all of Kiranrao's men. Somehow the Romani leader had survived. Annon's knees strained with pain as they shook. They were going to die. They were going to be brutally murdered, their blood soaking the stones of the cave.

No! he screamed at himself. He tried to muster the words that summoned fire and could not remember them. His memory was blank. But how could that be? He had the Dryad's kiss. He should be able to remember everything. Confusion warped his sense of space.

"Annon?" Khiara whispered, her voice choked with fear.

"Forward," he said huskily. He pulled on Erasmus's arm but he did not move. He pulled harder. "Come."

A breath of wind came from his left. The darkness was consuming him. He wanted to tear his hand free and run. His breath came in ragged gasps.

"Forward!" Annon said again, pulling. Erasmus balked. Annon's arms shook. He could see nothing. White motes began to flicker in his blank vision. His eyes were starved for colors. He felt Erasmus sinking behind him, heard him gibber with fear.

He pulled tenaciously on Erasmus's hand, bringing him back to his feet. When he had faced the waterfall of the Fear Liath before, movement had helped break the grip of the creature's magic. Perhaps it was sleeping? Annon pulled again and forced Erasmus to follow. He took another step. Then another. The blackness engulfed him on all sides, numbing his mind. Which way should they walk? Which way lay the beast?

Sweat stung Annon's eyes. He tugged on his limp cargo again, drawing Erasmus and Khiara on. Suddenly, in the darkness ahead, two specks began to glow, as if a demon had suddenly awakened. The specks enlarged, revealing two molten eyes. The presence of shadow and night intensified, hurling at Annon with dread. The eyes bored into his. He froze in his tracks, watching the eyes, waiting for a snarl to follow. They had awakened the Fear Liath. He held his breath.

Nothing happened. He stared at the creature, waiting for a snort of breath to precede the claws.

Light.

It took several long moments to realize that he could see. The Fear Liath's glowing eyes could be seen. Did it mean that the darkness could be dispelled?

"There it is!" Erasmus whispered in a choking voice. "Ahead! See it?"

Annon shook his hand loose of Erasmus's. *Pyricanthas. Sericanthas. Thas.*

His hands glowed blue, breaking the iron grip of the darkness. The light began to expand as he summoned the licking flames to his palms. The darkness cringed and darted away, revealing a massive stone boulder ahead. Carved into the front of the boulder was the face of some creature, huge blackened face and narrow-slit eyes that burned with heat and malevolence.

The truth caused a gasp of relief. There was no Fear Liath, only its image. A coal-black smudge carved into a boulder. Somehow it channeled the creature's power. Yet it was a deception after all. Annon strode forward, examining the rough basalt surface. It was taller than a man, oddly lumped and misshapen. Only the creature's face had been blasted into the rock—and its eyes. The terror was passing. Annon turned and saw his friends, staring at him in dismay and shock. He motioned for them to advance. Slowly, hesitantly, they did. Courage began to replace fear. Nizeera was prowling low, chin barely brushing the surface of the ground as she came, ears flat, fur bristling.

Annon touched the basalt and it responded to the fireblood. A glowing aura shimmered where his hand touched. The light from the eyes winked out.

Glancing around the room, Annon saw another archway on the far end of the cave. Finding it in the dark would have been tedious.

"Come," Annon bid them, walking confidently toward the next trap the Arch-Rike had created for them.

☙

The tunnels twisted endlessly, branching off like a maze that befuddled even Erasmus. Fortunately, Nizeera was with them. As they approached a cavern that branched different ways and they were unsure which path to take, Nizeera came forward and tested the air, breathing in the scent. Always one path had a more human smell than the others and her senses brought them that way easily. Each room and chamber brought an increase in confidence from the perils they had faced. But time was running short and they knew they needed to hurry. Lukias would revive and start wriggling free from his bonds. Once he succeeded, he would open the doors and the Rikes would enter. They certainly had the means to bypass the traps, and so each delay caused the worry to gnaw deeper inside Annon.

He was not sure how deep they were beneath the mountain, but the trail led them eventually to another bronze-shod door. It had a rounded top fixed beneath another archway. The columns on each side were flat with rectangular reliefs carved into them, around six panels high. Chiseled into the stone above the door was the single word: *Calcatrix.*

Annon stared at the word, for it was not familiar. "Is it Vaettir?" he asked Khiara.

She nodded. "It means 'trackers.' Someone who hunts."

He was grateful she was there. "Thank you. Let us see what danger awaits us then."

Erasmus studied the panels by the archway, running his fingers along the edge. "There are no hinges. The door swings inward."

"Any locks?" Annon asked.

"None that I can see. We push it, by the look of it."

Annon took a deep breath, mopping his sweaty face on his sleeve. "Nizeera, any sound of pursuit?"

The cat went back down the tunnel, ears pointed and still. *Nothing.*

Annon approached the door to shove it open, but Erasmus caught him. "Better not to be standing in the way when it opens. We should open it from the edge where the hinges likely are. Could be rigged with darts or bolts. You never know."

"Good thinking," Annon said. They separated, Annon and Nizeera on one side, Khiara and Erasmus on the other.

Together, they pushed on the edge of the door. It swung open with little effort, the hinges oiled and soundless. As the door opened, the room beyond was suddenly lit by smokeless glass stands, the same as the kind used in Kenatos to light the streets at night. The stands were taller than a man, and the cavern beyond broad and wide. There were enough poles to illuminate the entire chamber, revealing its vastness as well as stalactites and stalagmites, protruding from the ceiling and floor, interspersed through the room. There were statues throughout as well, stone carvings of men and women in various poses and positions. In the vastness of the high ceiling, they could hear the flapping and fluttering of wings. Annon supposed they were bats. Pockmarks and crevices showed various entrances and exits in the room. It would take some time to search them all.

Not bats, Nizeera thought. *I sense beings here. Spirit beings.*

It is the lights, Annon thought in return. *There are spirits trapped in them. It is the same in Kenatos.*

They entered the high chamber, walking amidst the interesting columns of light as well as the jutting crags of rock. With the interspersed obstructions, it made it difficult to see the walls. Annon was wary and walked cautiously as a result, studying the floor, the light columns, glancing up at the pockmarked ceiling. The sound of fluttering wings whispered through the room.

Nizeera prowled again, tail lashing in vexation. Erasmus glanced from side to side, trying to take in the scene. Khiara walked last.

Suddenly the flapping of wings sounded from behind, swooping down on them. Khiara gave a cry of warning and spun around, swinging her long staff from one side and struck something heavily plumed and solid, sending it careening into one of the stone sculptures nearby. The creature hissed in pain and aggravation, a mass of scales and wings and—

"Don't look at it!" Erasmus roared.

Annon glanced at the Preachán, his eyes wide with terror. Erasmus stared away, looking at the ground. "The statues! They aren't carvings. They are people, turned to stone. These creatures have magic that will turn us to stone! Out! We must get out!"

The flapping of wings sounded like an avalanche from above. From his side vision, Annon saw dozens of the plumed avian creatures dropping down from the pockmarked ceilings, rushing down at them in a frenzy. He shut his eyes, his heart quailing in panic, and the creatures attacked him savagely. He held up his arms to ward off the attack and felt talons ripping at his skin, beaks snapping into his flesh, shredding his robes. One landed on his back, gashing the back of his head with its hooked beak. Cries of pain from the others erupted all around.

Annon's emotions went wild with desperation. He summoned the fireblood, spraying the flames everywhere above him, and the bird-creatures squawked in pain and rage. Some flopped to the ground, their bodies burned and smoking. Annon tried to get clear and ran into a statue, striking sparks in his eyes. He reached back and grabbed the plumage of the bird creature on his back and hurled it away.

Erasmus and Khiara cried out in pain as they fought back the savage things clawing and pecking at them. *Look at us!* the creatures seemed to be saying. *Look!*

It took all of Annon's mental will not to open his eyes. He heard the sound of wings and dropped low. Nizeera screamed in fury, swatting at the ones assailing her. Annon felt the rake of the talons again, this time on his back. He flipped around, wind-milling his arms to dislodge them. Blood oozed from the razor wounds in his skin. Pain lanced throughout his body. The cuts stung tremendously and he realized with dread that the room was full of their victims, all in poses of warding and defense.

Fury engulfed him and he sent another sheet of fire blazing into the ranks of the creatures, reducing them to ash in a sweep of his arms. What were these creatures? He struggled to search his memory for any Druidecht lore that would help. *Calcatrix.* A Vaettir word. Was there another word, in another language then? His memory, sharp as a knife's blade, remembered. His Druidecht studies referred to these creatures with a warning—*for out of the serpent's root shall come forth a Cockatrice, and his fruit shall be a fiery flying serpent.*

That is what they faced.

Calcatrix was the Vaettir word for Cockatrice, a creature that did not exist in Wayland, but was warned of in Druidecht lore.

More wings fluttered. Ribbons of pain sliced into Annon's elbow. He grabbed the creature with his other hand and sent the fireblood coursing into it, making it explode. He was bleeding from many places now, the blood and sweat mingling.

Before they had faced darkness. Now the room was light. He made the connection instantly. Without light, the Cockatrice had no ability to turn them into stone.

"Khiara!" Annon shouted, swatting away at others who ravaged at him. "The orbs! Crush the glass! Darkness will save us!"

Annon let out another plume of fire and spread it out in a wide net, trying to keep the next ones back. His heart churned with the magic, the temptation to loose it completely and turn the entire chamber into ash. The pain sickened his thoughts, adding to the compulsion to kill. He squeezed his eyes shut, near delirious from the itching pain in his arms and back.

The sound of shattering glass echoed. The chamber dimmed slightly. Annon crawled away from the base of the statue and scrabbled to another, trying to change positions. More of the Cockatrice fell on him, pecking and stabbing him with beak and talon. He kicked and shoved them away, willing his eyes to remain closed. Another burst of glass sounded. Then another.

He could imagine Khiara in the air, using the sense of light from her eyelids to draw near and then pulverizing the orbs with the butt of her staff. Another went out. The room was darkening and the Cockatrice increased the ferocity of the attack. One of the creatures went straight for Annon's face, clawing his cheek. He huddled low, burying his face in his arms, and brought in his body. They swarmed around him, pecking and tearing at him.

Another orb shattered amidst the fury. Darkness descended around them, closing in like a veil. Khiara had broken most of the columns around them. As the light failed, the Cockatrice grew confused and began flapping around the chamber wildly, as if chasing something. Or someone!

"Khiara!" Annon croaked, fearing for her. The sound of breaking glass happened farther and farther away. He knelt, dragging himself forward, listening to the sounds of wings and malevolent cawing.

The explosion of glass from the final orb plunged the room back into darkness. Annon writhed in pain on the floor then, twitching with agony. The whoosh of the wings disappeared as the Cockatrice return to their roosting place.

Erasmus moaned somewhere nearby. Khiara's voice came from the gloom. "Where are you?"

"Here," Annon said, trying to sit. He heard the soft tread of her boots as she approached and knelt by him. He was feverish with suffering, skin burning with itching and cuts.

"Hold still," she breathed, resting her hand on his back. A flood of relief surged through him, emerging from her hands to tame the wild pain and soothe the tormenting itches. The venom of the Cockatrice purged from his body, and he lay gasping with relief and comfort. It was amazing. He had never felt such torture in his life. It felt like his back had been a field harrowed by a farmer and now it was soaked with healing waters and soothed. He sat up, breathing deeply.

"Thank you, Khiara," he said, meaning every word. "I heard Erasmus over there."

"Yes," came the reply through clenched teeth. She found him and applied her hands again, using the *keramat* to heal him. "I would have paid ten thousand ducats for that," Erasmus said with a blissful sigh. "Sadly, I do not have a hundred anymore. But I do thank you, Khiara. Death by stone would have been easier, I should think."

They all stood, listening to the rustling sounds on the floor around them of the dying Cockatrice, those who could not fly. An idea sprouted in Annon's mind.

Nizeera shared it instantly. *Wise, Druidecht. Turn the enemy's weapon against him.*

"Before we depart," Annon said. "I think we should bring the Rikes a gift when we visit."

"*There is news in the city. All shipments of goods from Havenrook have been halted to Kenatos. The Arch-Rike has negotiated a new treaty with the king of Wayland to transport grain, fruits, and timber. In retaliation, we have learned that the Romani are attacking the shipments and destroying the caravans bound for our docks, seizing the goods and stockpiling them in Havenrook. Confrontations like these are inevitable, but it is curious that the Preachán act as if they alone have the right to control trade. I pity them, for the king of Wayland has a massive army and the Preachán are vulnerable. The woods that surround Havenrook will not protect them long. The Arch-Rike's pragmatism is truly inspiring. I hope these skirmishes do not provoke a war between our kingdoms.*"

—*Possidius Adeodat, Archivist of Kenatos*

XXIV

The end of the tunnel trail concluded at a set of massive stone doors hung on iron brackets. A series of tiles covered the ground in front of it, revealing patterns of dusty footprints showing frequent traffic. Torches were suspended in sconces on the wall, their flames blazing away the dark. Annon stared at the doors, his stomach churning with nervousness. Were the torches always lit or was it a sign that their arrival was expected?

Khiara brushed away her dark hair, cocking her head as she examined the stone doors. Nizeera approached the edge of the tiles and dropped her muzzle close, sniffing the air.

Erasmus scratched the back of his neck, mulling over the scene. "The doors open toward us," he whispered. "Do you see the crossbar over there?"

Annon stared and noticed it. "Strange. Why do you think the lock is on this side?"

Khiara stepped forward. "To trap inside whatever is in there. I don't like the feel of this place. There is ancient magic at work here."

She rested on her long staff, staring ahead and squinting with a look of revulsion and worry.

"Test the tiles," Annon suggested. "They may be trapped."

Khiara approached and nudged the first tile with the butt of her staff. She tested several, pushing hard against them. She shook her head.

"Do you have the Cockatrice?" Annon asked Erasmus, who patted his travel pack and watched as the creature inside thrashed. He kept a sturdy grip. "Good. Khiara, you pull the door ajar. Erasmus, let loose the straps and fling in the pack. I'm suspecting there are Rikes inside. Maybe it can do some damage to them first. Ready?"

Khiara advanced to the doors with a surefooted grace. She reached the first and grasped the thick iron handle. She nodded to Erasmus, who approached next and unslung his pack. He readied the straps and stood by the edge.

Annon advanced as well, thinking the words to tame fire in his mind. His stomach squirmed with dread. It seemed as if they had been buried beneath the mountain for days. *Nizeera, can you hear anything?*

The doors are too thick. Nothing comes from behind.

Stay near me.

She brushed against his leg. Annon took a deep breath, steadying himself. Then he gave a curt nod to Khiara.

The Vaettir woman yanked against the door. It groaned with weight, swinging slowly on its thick hinges. It opened into a room beyond lit with greenish light. The smell of strong incense wafted toward them, fouling the air with its musty smell. Erasmus flung the pack into the room, where it landed with a thud. The Cockatrice fluttered free and let out a vicious shriek of rage, its wings flapping aggressively.

Annon stared at the floor, controlling his vision.

Cries of alarm came from inside the room.

"What is that thing?"

"Don't look at it!"

"Roth! Over there! Roth!"

A brazier toppled over, sending a plume of flame that immediately extinguished. Cries of fear and terror sounded as the men inside were caught unaware.

"Shut the door!" Annon called. "Grab the crossbar!"

Erasmus fetched it while Khiara and Annon shoved hard at the door. The Preachán slid the iron bar in place as the first attempt to flee struck the stone door on the other side. The iron crossbar rattled in place. They all stepped back, preparing for attack. The hinges groaned and the door shifted, but it did not open. Annon's nerves were as taut as bowstrings. He ground his teeth, fingers tingling with buds of flame. He stared at the door. It shuddered again, the muffled sound of screams inside. Erasmus stared coldly at the doors, his expression grim. Khiara sighed.

The shuddering of the door ceased.

Annon made them wait. Nothing happened. No sound came from the stone doors. The torches sputtered, startling them. Erasmus grunted in surprise, rubbing his arm nervously. Nizeera was tense as well, hackles bristling. What lay beyond?

The effort of drawing on the fireblood was wearying him. Annon nodded to Erasmus finally and motioned for him to remove the crossbar.

"Pull," he whispered, preparing himself to go in first as a leader should. Nizeera was crouched at his heels, shoulder muscles bunching.

Erasmus and Khiara pulled on the door handles, causing them to groan. Sweat streaked down Annon's back. He marched forward, ready to enter the room and face whatever horrors lay beyond. If the Cockatrice had survived, he was ready to reduce it to ash. As the crack in the door parted, he saw the statue of a man, face turned back to the room, his arms frozen in the motion of pushing on the door. Two other statues were there as well, both turning to look back into the room. All three were made of stone.

Annon glanced down at the floor and stepped between the statues and entered the circular chamber. There was another man, on the floor, also made of stone, his arms and legs bunched in a cowering position.

Blue fire erupted from Annon's left, sending a blast of flame that tore into him and engulfed him, but did not harm him. Annon strode forward, exiting the sheet of flames, and faced his attacker, a man half-hidden behind a pillar. The flames came from a ring on his hand.

"Now!" the man shouted from behind the pillar.

Nizeera hissed and Annon flattened himself on the ground, dropping to the tiles so hard his bones rattled. Streaks of lightning lanced at him from pillars around the room, exploding into stone and sending jagged fragments into the air. Explosions rattled his ears and he rolled to one side, another bolt searing the ground where he had been a moment before. He was surrounded on all sides.

Nizeera! The order came from there! He's the leader!

Annon scrabbled toward a nearby statue of a Rike, using it to block the blasts of white lightning streaming through the room at him. Khiara sailed into the room from above, her white staff gleaming.

There were many more than the Druidecht had expected. Bits of stone spattered off his cloak as the lightning continued to strike against the statue. He glanced at the room, trying to understand it. Pillars stood around the circumference but there were openings between them at various intervals. Stone altars or biers stood in a circle as well, probably twelve in all, each with the effigy of a sleeping corpse engraved onto the surface. Were they sarcophagi? All of the altars faced the center where a large bronze circle had been inset into the floor in the middle of the room. At the far side was another set of large stone doors with scrawling letters engraved above it: BASILIDES.

A blast of energy struck Annon in the shoulder, searing with pain and flinging him like a doll. His shoulder burned as if it has been stabbed with a hot poker and he let out an involuntary cry of pain.

Exposed now, Annon knew he had to find shelter again quickly. Trying to force down a moan of pain, he crawled toward one of the biers and then found his feet and ran. The tiles behind him cracked with the impact of energy. Khiara could not be seen. Neither could Erasmus. Nizeera shrieked with savage fury as she rushed the hidden man and he sensed her mind suddenly go black with terror. She had charged at the Rike with the ring, the one who had shouted for the others to attack. A wall of frenzied fear had struck her, reducing her mind to a gibbering mass. She fled from the pillar, cowed, unable even to think to Annon, unable to communicate anything.

Annon made it to the nearest bier and dropped behind it, feeling a blast of lightning zoom over his head, smashing into the stone wall across from him. He pressed his back against the firm stone, breathing in gasps, trying to think. What could they do against so much magic? How could they defend—?

The memory struck him. In the prince's manor, when the Arch-Rike's forces had attacked, Tyrus had uttered a single Vaettir word that had disabled all the devices and even killed many who held them.

The kiss from Neodesha brought the word to his mind instantly.

"*Calvariae!*" Annon shouted.

Nothing happened. The blasts continued to slam against the stone behind him.

"Hold your attack!" came a voice from behind the pillar, the one that had driven away Nizeera.

The hail of lightning stopped.

"You uttered the sacred Vaettir word," the voice said, ghosting from behind the pillar. "Surely you did not believe we would let that trick happen twice? Think, Druidecht! We know so much about you. We know so much about Tyrus. Fool us once, yes. But not a second time."

Annon craned his neck, trying to catch a glimpse of the hidden man. He felt totally alone, defeated. They had charged into the enemy's lair. Surely the Arch-Rike would have prepared for the arrival. Surely he would have taken precautions.

"Why do you seek Basilides?" the voice said. It was moving now, showing the man had changed positions.

Annon shifted, preparing to duck around the corner of the bier. His mind worked frantically to find an escape. "Knowledge," he replied.

"Hardly," the other man said. "This is a trove of treasures, Annon of Wayland. This is where the kings of old are buried. Which treasure did Tyrus send you to steal? He sent the Bhikhu and the Romani girl to claim the Sword of Winds. A precious relic, yes, but an equally foolish venture. The Kishion train where it is kept and your friends will not survive the ordeal of blindness. I guarantee it. Which of the many artifacts here did Tyrus send you to claim?"

Annon was baffled by the man's words, but he wanted to learn what he could. "If you know so much about us, you tell me." He turned his head and examined the lid of the sarcophagus. It was half a hand thick and made of solid stone. Would he be able to budge it? Would it slide off or was the stone fitted and needed to be lifted to open? If this truly was the lair of dead kings, perhaps they were buried with items that would be helpful to him, especially if he could free the trapped spirits inside.

"We know you brought Lukias," came the voice, much closer now. He seemed to be approaching steadily from the center of the room. "He is loyal to us."

Annon bit his lip. The next bier was not far away. With a running start, would he be able to shove it off? Open it enough? If the lid was lying flat, he might. He took several deep breaths.

"I know the Arch-Rike prizes loyalty," Annon said, drawing up his knees, getting ready to run again. "Does he also punish those who fail him?"

"Most severely, Annon. Quite so. You are surrounded. I have no qualms killing you. But you are worth a great deal if I can bring you to Kenatos alive. You passed the outer defenses. You showed great courage coming to this place. Tell me what Tyrus sent you to find here? What relic do you seek?"

Annon dropped low, planting his fingers on the ground soundlessly. He arched his back, ready to run. "You know I spoke truth, if those black rings truly do not lie. I came for knowledge."

"Ah, I see. Then you seek Poisonwell. The source of the Plague. It is in the Scourgelands, boy. Only one thing here will help you conquer that place and I wear it around my neck. That land is a maze of madness and disease. We alone hold its powers at bay. It seeks the death of all knowledge. You would unleash it on us again."

"I would destroy it," Annon replied. Poisonwell? The name made him shudder. He did not understand why.

"You cannot destroy the Plague," the man said with a laugh. "Some curses cannot be undone. Will you surrender or do you intend to commit suicide?"

Annon lunged for the nearby bier. Crackles of energy exploded into the place where he had been crouching moments before. He abandoned the plan to shove the lid, knowing instinctively that it would be too heavy. As he slammed into the stone, he saw the damage done to the other bier, the one he had come from. The convergence of energy had cracked open the lid at the corner where he had been crouching. A faint mist crept from the dark void.

He hoped beyond hope.

"*Calvariae!*" he said again, taking a risk he prayed would work.

There was a blinding flash of light and then groans of pain. Annon crawled on his hands and knees, blinded by the flash. The presence of a spirit touched his mind.

You have freed me, Druidecht, boomed the voice inside his head. *In return, I will disarm your enemies.*

Annon blinked furiously, trying to see. The sarcophagus lid flung at the Rike who was approaching him, crushing him beneath it. A pillar of light emerged from the gaping maw of the sarcophagus. From all corners of the chamber, brilliant shards of lightning struck at it, but it only made it glow brighter. The being of light began to zigzag through the chamber, faster than a wisp of sunlight, causing grunts and shrieks of terror. It moved so quickly, going from column to column. The knot of light finished its bounding tour and then came back to Annon, revealing itself as a small, gnarled man with a long, hooked nose, gripping a small cudgel. The being nodded to him with wizened eyes then vanished.

Amazed at the reprieve, Annon slowly got to his feet, his knees wobbling. Smoke drifted in the air, clinging to the floor from a spilled brazier. A muffled groan came almost unheard nearby. Annon saw the man pinned beneath the sarcophagus lid, a trickle of blood coming from his mouth. The Druidecht approached him warily.

The man's eyes were feverish with pain, his lips pulled back in a snarl of agony. His head turned slightly, his gray eyes piercing Annon. "You . . . will . . . still . . . die . . ."

"Khiara?" Annon called. She emerged from behind a stone pillar, her robes singed. Erasmus poked his head in from the massive stone doors.

Annon crouched by the crumpled Rike. "Where is Poisonwell?" Annon asked him.

"You . . . will . . . still . . . die . . . "

"Help me lift this off him," Annon said and the two hurried to him. Together, knees bent, they struggled to raise the lid. Muscles bunched and limbs strained. The lid came off and they dumped it nearby.

The wheezing Rike stiffened with anguish, his neck twitching. Then he fell still.

"Khiara?" Annon asked.

She knelt by him, placing her hand on his broken chest. He was already dead, his eyes fixed blankly at the domed ceiling. A strange jeweled ornament was fashioned around his neck, offset with two deep blue gems. It almost looked like a necklace except it did not connect in a full circle. She looked up at Annon and then nodded toward the other interior doors. "We do not have much time. We know the Arch-Rike can send people quickly through the aether. We should enter Basilides now."

Annon nodded and motioned for them to follow. The doors they had entered began to groan shut. In a panic, the three charged back to the doors, but they closed solidly behind them. The crossbar landed in place.

Erasmus cursed colorfully and scanned the room. Smoke from incense hung in the air, giving it a charred, unhealthy smell.

"Nizeera?" Annon called, searching the room for her. She emerged from behind a set of pillars, all hunched with hackles.

I am ashamed.

He looked at her, saw the whipped countenance. *What happened?*

He wears a torc. It is anathema to me. I could not approach him nor attack him. It causes terror in animals. The Cockatrice could not have harmed him. No wild creature could.

Do not be ashamed, Nizeera.

She growled. *I failed to protect you.*

Annon stared at her and shook his head. His heart was still settling after the near encounter with death. He stared at the individual biers, counting twelve in all. One was marked with the name of Wayland. Another with runes written in Vaettir. Each was from a different kingdom, each representing a fallen ruler from the past.

"Erasmus," he said, looking at the Preachán hopefully. "Study the room. See what you can learn. Khiara, come with me."

"How will we get out of here?" she asked him.

"First, we seek the oracle. Over there." As they approached the doors, Annon noticed something unusual. It was Erasmus's observation all over again. The crossbar was on their side of the door. It made him pause.

"What is it?" Khiara asked.

He stared at the door, at the great carved letters above it: BASI-LIDES. The crossbar held the stone doors shut. It was there to keep something out. His mind jumbled the pieces together. Two sets of doors, both facing the same direction.

It made him think of a castle fortification, multiple barriers to provide a defense. A defense from what? What were the doors meant to hold back? Were they there to protect the Rikes? From what? From Basilides itself?

He stared at the doors, at the carved text. The massive stone doors. Strong enough to hold off battering rams. Sturdy enough to wall them inside to die. It came as a flash of insight. Annon took an involuntary step backward.

"What?" Khiara whispered, gripping the staff defensively.

"I know where that door leads," Annon said numbly. "We've been traveling into the mountains, north of Kenatos. These tunnels go underneath the mountains. What is on the other side of the mountains, Khiara? What do these mountains protect us from?"

She stared at him, the dawning horror spreading across her smooth face. "The Scourgelands."

He nodded. "This is a doorway into the Scourgelands."

"It must be so," Erasmus said, muttering to himself. "Annon, Khiara! Look at this! Look! It is the only explanation that makes sense. By the fates, I cannot believe it!"

Annon turned to the Preachán. "What did you find?"

"Look at these!" he said, waving his arms at the various biers. "Alkire. Havenrook. Silvandom. Lydi. Boeotia. Kenatos. Wayland." He gasped with some vision inside his head. "These are not crypts for the dead. Look—the one that broke over there. No bones inside. Just folded clothes and weapons and jewelry. Coins from the past. These are not crypts, Annon. These are not the remains of the dead." Erasmus started to pace, his hands gesticulating broadly. "These are masks."

"What are you saying?" Annon demanded impatiently. "Erasmus, help us understand your thoughts! You are going too fast!"

The Preachán trembled with emotions, his face seeming to shrink with the massive weight of the thought he was experiencing. His lips contorted. "The race immune to the Plague. Yes, that must be it. The missing race. The nameless race. The persecuted blood. He's part of it, Annon. The Arch-Rike is not who we think he is. He masquerades as one, but look—look!" He rushed over to one of the biers. "This one—Kenatos. The name on the crypt is Band-Imas. It is the name of the current Arch-Rike, not a dead one. Look at that one—Wayland. It bears the king's name and he is *alive*." Erasmus struck his forehead with his hand. "The Arch-Rike . . . this is his illusion."

Annon could not comprehend what Erasmus was raving about. "I don't understand, Erasmus. What do you mean? The Arch-Rike isn't a man?"

Beware! Nizeera growled. *They come from the walls!*

Khiara cried out in warning. "On the floor, Erasmus! Behind you!"

The Preachán barely heard her, but he lazily turned and saw it too. An enormous black cobra, thick and sinewy, gliding through the haze toward the Preachán. There were more, slithering through the smoke. Annon cried out in warning as well, watching in horror as they converged at them from all sides.

Erasmus saw the serpent's hood flare as it rose toward him. His eyes widened with utter terror and he twisted to flee.

Annon cried out in warning.

The serpent struck Erasmus from behind, sinking its fangs into his leg. The Preachán let out a howl of pain and fell to the ground, writhing and twisting in agony as the venom coursed through him. The twitching lasted for only seconds. Then he was still. Then he was dead.

The hissing serpents surged at Annon and Khiara.

"War is indeed upon us. Reports arrived of an attack in the woods of Alkire by the Preachán and Romani from Havenrook. A great fire engulfed the woods and burned for days. You can see the smoke from Kenatos. It is absurd that the Romani attacked the Cruithne if their quarrel is against Wayland. They will be trapped between two opposing kingdoms now. Fortunately the King of Wayland has mustered a large force and is preparing to march on Havenrook."

—Possidius Adeodat, Archivist of Kenatos

XXV

The burning pitch on Evritt's arm caused him to wail in unceasing pain. Phae winced as she watched him thrash, his face a mottled twist of veins and suffering. Tyrus knelt by him, grabbed his shoulder, and waved his hands over the tongues of flame. When the fire died, Phae saw the blackened skin and had to turn away or risk vomiting. Dizziness from the magic that had transported them away mingled with her revulsion at seeing Evritt's injury.

"Be still, be still," Tyrus soothed.

"Where are we?" Prince Aran asked, crouching near.

"Silvandom, near the border. Let me try to summon a spirit."

The Kishion put his hand on Phae's shoulder, steadying her as she started to wobble.

Evritt moaned. Tyrus offered soothing words. "They won't heed me. Aran, we must get him to a healer quickly. The Arch-Rike will trace us here and let loose others to hunt us."

"We should divide then," the Prince said. "If we stay together, it will drain the Tay al-Ard. We stayed at the cabin too long, allowing the Arch-Rike time to put forces in place to bombard us."

"We should keep moving." Tyrus agreed and stood. He came to Phae and Kishion. "The Arch-Rike has tools to sense magic when it is used. It will take him time to locate this place. Take Phae and hide her in the woods. Canton Vaud is in Silvandom right now. They may shelter you."

The Kishion snorted with ill humor. "The Arch-Rike has a spy in Canton Vaud. We knew you were hiding there. He was unwilling to risk an open confrontation with the Thirteen at that point."

Tyrus's expression hardened. "Do you know who the spy is?"

The Kishion shook his head.

"Fair warning then. We must avoid Canton Vaud while concealing our presence in Silvandom. The Prince told me that Annon and the others will assemble at a Dryad tree in the woods, somewhere to the north and west. This forest will provide ample places to hide. Here, Phae—" he reached into his pouch and pulled out the necklace with the blue stone she had left behind at the Winemillers—"Take this. With it, we will be able to find you again, wherever you are."

"How did you . . . find it?" she asked, staring.

"Prince Aransetis took it when he went after you and gave it back to me. He has the stones that will find it."

Phae took the necklace, examining it with relish. She had grown up wearing it and was grateful to have it again, especially if it would always help them find her. "Thank you."

Prince Aran helped Evritt to his feet and then supported him. The old man's face was blanched white from clenching his jaw. He smelled of cinders and brimstone.

Tyrus sighed deeply. He reached out and cupped Phae's cheek. "I hate to be parted from you. But you are safer with him than you are with me."

She nodded awkwardly, not sure what she should do. "I have decided, Father." She let out her breath. "I will help you, if I can."

The ghost of a smile drifted across his mouth and was gone. He swallowed suddenly, his eyes intense and almost fearful. Unable to speak, he patted her shoulder. Phae was an affectionate person, so she embraced him, pressing her cheek against his broad chest. She felt his beard against her hair. He squeezed her once and then departed, assisting Evritt.

The Kishion looked at her, gazing at her curiously, and then nodded in approval. They both started into the woods, heading northwest.

&

Phae and the Kishion walked in silence, crossing the forest in broad strides to put as much distance as they could from the place where they had entered Silvandom. The forest was a maze of moss-covered evergreens, with slanting descents and rugged climbs, full of fern sprays and fragrant juniper shrubs. Insects buzzed and clicked throughout the lush woods, interrupted occasionally by a woodpecker or a jackdaw. Fallen trees lay rotting across their path at regular intervals. There were no paths or roads, just the unlimited expanse of ancient trees and furrowed hills.

Around midday, they stopped to rest at a small pool fed by a trickling waterfall. The water was clear and clean and Phae cupped it in her hands, drinking deeply. The Kishion produced some roots and sour berries for her to eat. The flavor of the berries made her scrunch up her face. He smiled faintly at the look.

After gulping down another long drink, Phae wiped her mouth on the back of her hand. "I've decided something. You need another name."

His eyebrows lifted, but he said nothing. When she looked at him, she could not help but see both facets of his nature. He was a ruthless killer. He could also be gentle and compassionate. Both aspects seemed to always be at war with each other. It filled her with a sense of dread, as if watching storm clouds pent up with lightning.

Phae sat by the edge of the pool, gazing across the sunlight twinkling on the water's surface. If his dual nature were still conflicted, she wanted to do something to shift the balance. "I can't keep calling you Kishion," she said softly, barely meeting his eyes. "I know that is *what* you are. But it is not *who* you are. It would be a temporary name though. Until we find your real one."

He stepped closer, his boots just at the edge of the water. "And did you have one in mind for me?"

"I have your permission then?"

"Names are not important to me. The truth is."

She rubbed her arms, nodding slowly, grateful he had not responded angrily. "What my father said about you—being in the Arch-Rike's dungeons. That he is secretly afraid of you. I would be very angry, if I were you. I would want to know the truth as well."

"Tyrus is either very foolish or very wise. Perhaps a little mad. Who else would have let his enemy protect his only child? By trusting me so implicitly, he compels me to be honorable." Slowly, he sat down next to her, facing the cool waters. Taking a pebble from the edge, he flung it carelessly into the pool, rippling the waters.

"Trust is powerful," Phae said. She looked at him seriously, feeling emboldened. "I trust you. The Arch-Rike ordered you to kill me, but you did not. Why not?"

His expression darkened. "Did you want to die?"

"Tell me."

He did not meet her gaze. "I couldn't."

She waited, letting the silence do the goading.

He glanced at her, then back at the waters. His expression was deeper than a lake, his eyes lost in some inner void. "I could not do it," he whispered. "I know I have been trained to take life and think nothing of it. I look at you and see a thousand ways I could kill you. You are truly defenseless. But there is something about you . . . something familiar. As if I knew your voice from sometime before. Your smell. The look in your eyes . . ." He frowned, but not with anger. It was more frustration . . . an elusive memory nagging him. "When the Arch-Rike sensed my unwillingness, I knew that he was going to use the ring to destroy you. That he would kill you in front of your father in such a brutal, merciless way, reveals his desperation and utter ruthlessness. I cannot serve a man like that. If Tyrus spoke the truth about things, then I will face the Arch-Rike. Since that Romani thief has the blade Iddawc now, there is nothing to protect the Arch-Rike from me."

The menace in his voice sent chills racing down Phae's arms. "I pity him."

"You, of all people, have no need to pity him. What name have you decided for me?" He looked her in the eyes and it caused a warm flush to run through her.

"It will not be for long," she answered, looking down at her lap. "I just feel that you are no longer a Kishion. It is silly, probably, but I want to be able to call you something else." She sighed. "I think—Shion."

"Shion," he murmured, letting the word roll over his tongue. "Very well."

Phae sat cross-legged then and leaned forward, peering across the pool. There was an enormous blue butterfly perched on the moss on the other side. It was dazzling in color, as vivid as the sky. A feeling of dread and nervousness struck the pit of her stomach. The butterfly lifted up and started to dance in the air. "Father mentioned that there is a Dryad tree here in Silvandom, but only the Druidecht know where her tree is." Phae rose.

He nodded in agreement and stood. The feelings of dread intensified.

"When you were chasing me through Stonehollow, I was

warned of the danger. There were these moths and butterflies that kept flitting around me. I see one right there, across the pond. I just noticed it and felt the same warning I did then." She glanced back the way they had come. "I think the Arch-Rike's minions are getting close."

"I see it," he said. "The blue one. It's beautiful."

"In Stonehollow, the moths led me to the safety of the Dryad tree. Maybe they will this time as well. Come."

The feelings of dread began to lessen as she followed the butterfly into the woods. They increased their pace, leaving behind the small pool and its trickling fountain, and plunged deeper into the terrain. When she ran from him before, the feelings were much more intense and ominous. The blue butterfly winged ahead of them constantly and it was easy seeing it amidst the dark browns of the tree trunks and loam. Ferns whipped at their legs as they crossed, keeping pace with the flitting spirit creature.

"Do you know about Mirrowen?" Phae asked.

"The Rikes teach that it is a superstition of the Druidecht, but some know the truth. The spirit creatures in Kenatos are all enslaved. The woods of Silvandom are said to be the last bastion of safety." Another blue butterfly flitted from the side, joining its brother ahead. "There is another one, joining the first."

There was no path that they followed, but the butterflies seemed to know it instinctively. The ground suddenly ended, opening to a steep decline into a broad gulch. The butterflies flitted across the open air to the other side and then landed on a tree stump, their wings opening and closing.

Shion frowned, gazing down at the steep incline and then motioned for her to stay. He started down the side of the gulch, body low and hands plunging into the muck on the side to steady himself. Tendrils of tree roots poked through the side, offering handholds. It was very deep and steep and she watched him proceed with surefooted grace. About halfway down, he motioned for her to follow.

Phae stepped down the side of the gulch too. Her boots sank into the muck as she scrabbled down, trying to keep from slipping. She was not nearly as graceful as he had been, which irked her, but she bit her lip and continued the descent. Partway down, she slipped and slid down, but he shifted his body and caught her legs, stalling the slide. She clawed through the muck with her fingers to regain control as he continued the rest of the way to the trickle of gully water at the bottom. She joined him shortly after, rinsing her muddy hands in the rank waters.

Three butterflies flitted down from above and started down the gully trail ahead of them. Their boots made sucking sounds in the muck. At some points ahead, the gulch was so narrow they had to go sideways to clear it. The dazzling butterflies were soon joined by others, both in front and behind. The muck dragged at Phae's ankles, making it difficult to walk. Exposed roots brushed against her face and hair, causing flecks of dirt to shower over her. Rivulets of water streamed down from the top of the ridge above. The air smelled rich and spoiled, like the loam pits behind the Winemiller shed.

The ravine widened to an immense opening. It was a pit sunken into the midst of the ridge, exposing a bracken-covered pond. In the midst of the pond was an enormous tree. Instead of rustling leaves, the branches held thousands of blue butterflies, clinging to each branch and twig. It was the most beautiful sight Phae had seen in her life and she gasped. The butterflies that had thickened ahead joined the writhing mass of the tree. More came from behind, dancing in the air past them, rushing toward the tree and its enormous canopy of blue leaves.

Phae paused to catch her breath, gripping Shion's arm. "Look at this! I've never seen anything like it. So beautiful."

He said nothing, his expression impossible to read. He stared at the tree, shaking his head. His lips pursed. "I think I have been here before."

Some butterflies left the tree, flitting before them, coaxing them forward. Phae stepped into the murk of the pond, her boot sinking into the mud, the water just below her knees. The air smelled sickly sweet.

He grabbed her wrist and jerked her back. "Wait."

Phae struggled against his grip. "Let go of my arm. These are spirits. They want to protect us. We should go to them."

"Look around," he said, motioning with his other hand. "The pond is dead. Everything is decaying here. You can smell it."

"The tree is alive," Phae said. "Look at the leaves."

"Those aren't leaves," he answered harshly. "Come out of the water."

Phae felt the compulsion to join the tree grow stronger. "No, we will be safe there. They were warning us. The water is not deep. We can cross."

She tried to pull away from his grip, but it tightened painfully. Anger burned inside her. She tried to pry his fingers away from her wrist. "You're hurting me! Let go!"

"Trust me, Phae. This doesn't feel right. There is no life here. We were lured here."

She looked at him, seeing the vivid scars on his face. His eyes were blue—a dead man's eyes. Fear exploded from the marrow of her bones. She had to get away from him. She had to run, to escape. Desperately she tried to rip her arm free, bucking and twisting. She wrenched with enough force that his boots slipped in the muck on the bank and they both tumbled into the brackish waters.

The smell and taste of the waters was loathsome and thick with slime. Phae gagged and thrashed in the water, her hands plunging into the mud at the bottom, but she felt something hard and round, a large rock. She seized it and shoved herself up out of the foul waters, impulsively bringing it down on the Kishion's head with her free hand.

He deflected the blow, then hoisted her by the waist and flung her back to the mouth of the ravine. She struck the ground hard. Her hair was plastered to her face. The taste in her mouth was putrid. Sputtering and choking, she scrambled to get to her feet, ready to plunge back into the pond.

She stared down at the rock in her hand. Only it was not a rock. It was a skull.

The Kishion, dripping wet, emerged from the pond, his face contorted with anger. He snatched the skull from her hand, whirled, and hurled it with all his might, sending it arcing across the pond where it struck the midst of the tree with a loud cracking sound.

Instantly the air was a cloud of blue butterflies, revealing a skeletal tree in the midst of the pond. The limbs were cragged and silvery, gaunt as bones. Her mind snapped awake instantly, realizing in shock that they had been led into the lair of some horror.

He grabbed her tunic at the shoulder and hauled her back into the ravine. The swarm of insects caught up with them in moments, a blizzard of blue wings and tickling legs. They both raised the cowls of their cloaks and fought down the path, tromping through the slick, fetid waters as they tried to go back the way they had come. She felt the insects all over her body, wriggling inside her clothes. Phae shrieked and convulsed at the feeling, unable to walk, contorting against the writhing creatures that tickled and pricked against her skin.

The Kishion's firm hand pulled her after him, half-dragging her through the muck. The farther they went, the less frantic the feelings became. Phae's breath was ragged and choked with tears. The wave of butterflies crested and then faded, leaving only a few dancing tauntingly in the air nearby. She stared at them, twitching with raw emotions, and nearly summoned the fireblood to destroy them.

Her boot struck a tangled root and she went down. Sprawling in the wet ravine, wet and miserable, she stared up at Shion. His face was no longer an eerie exaggeration that she had seen by the pond. In fact, she barely noticed his scars at all. Instead of dead eyes, they were full of emotion. He knelt next to her in the mud and debris, gripping her shoulder.

She flinched, afraid he was going to strike her. She tried to control her breathing and failed.

"Are you all right?"

Concern was not what she had expected. She shuddered. "It was . . . awful. I still feel them wriggling . . ."

He nodded in agreement then he froze. He put his finger to his lips, his eyes looking up the wall of the ravine.

Voices drifted along the air, coming from above. "I know . . . I heard it too. It was a scream. A girl's scream. This way. Can you see anything, Finder?"

"The tracks are over here," came a reply, farther back along the ravine. "The two sets only. One belongs to her."

Phae's eyes widened with shock, unable to believe the voice she had just heard. It was a voice she would have recognized anywhere. It was a voice from her past and it brought a surging flood of different emotions.

It was Trasen.

"*Even wild beasts feel kindness, nor is there any animal so savage that good treatment will not tame it and win love from it. It is a true principle. And it is even more true when dealing with men. Men can be persuaded to many things through small acts of kindness.*"

—Possidius Adeodat, Archivist of Kenatos

XXVI

The Kishion's filthy hand clamped over Phae's mouth and he pushed her against the ravine wall, pressing himself against her. His mouth brushed against her ear, his voice the smallest of whispers.

"I recognize his voice. The boy from Stonehollow. Do not cry out. The Arch-Rike is using him to find us. Possibly to kill you. Do you understand me? Nod if you do."

A sickening wave of fear and desperation tore through her and nearly made her crumple. What was Trasen doing in Silvandom? She was desperate to see him. The urge to jerk free and scream to her friend was nearly overwhelming. Instead, she nodded and he removed his hand.

"Don't hurt him, Shion," she pleaded. "Promise me."

"I will not," he said curtly. "He is no threat to me. He is hunting you. This is how the Arch-Rike does his work. He goes where the feelings are strongest. You are not safe with this boy."

"I *must* see him," Phae said, grabbing a fistful of his cloak. "He may be a hostage."

The Kishion smirked. "Then I will free him. Stay down here. Stay hidden."

Trembling seizures of cold began to shake her and she hugged herself, nodding glumly. He looked up the sharp edge of the ravine and sinuously began to scale the roots and dirt, his arm muscles thick as coiled wagon ropes. He pulled himself up the edge of the ravine, spattering crumbs of dirt and silt down. She crouched nearby, hidden in the shadows, cold and dripping from the plunge into the pond. Her wet hair clung to her face and she brushed it back, trembling uncontrollably.

The Kishion snaked his way up the ravine edge before disappearing past the lip of the ridge. He was silent, but the men above were making plenty of noise. The sound of boots trampling through brush. Voices murmured from above.

"I don't see anyone."

"Should we go down?"

"There are no boot marks on the other side." Trasen's voice. "The floor of the ravine is too dark to see. I'm going down."

"Don't be an idiot, boy. You won't last long against that one. The Quiet Kishion. He's a killer of children. Sick in the head."

Another voice. "The ravine goes both ways. Should we trail them both?"

"Where is Heap?"

"What?"

"Where's Heap? He was over there. I don't see him."

Phae could not stop trembling, listening to the sound of their voices. So close. They did not realize how close they were to their prey—or to becoming prey themselves. The mud smelled spoiled and tainted. The air was stifling.

"Heap?"

"How old are these tracks, boy? When did they pass?"

It was Trasen again. "Not long ago, by the look. The marks are fresh. If you shout any louder, Badger, they will hear us coming."

"What about the girl's scream? How far away do you think that was?"

"Sounds travel oddly in the woods," Trasen said. "It sounded like it came from over there. I think we should follow it this way."

"I saw someone! Over there! A shadow."

"Heap?"

The sound of running and thrashing from above. Weapons came loose from scabbards. Phae flinched, digging her nails into her hands, stifling her gasp on the back of her fist.

"There! I see . . ."

"Scatter! Get back to Gorman. Go!"

The sound of a fist striking flesh. A man grunted and collapsed into a mass of fronds. The men were fleeing into the woods, crying out in panic and dread. More noise came as some fell, struck down by a silent attacker in the woods. Phae heard someone scrabbling down the side of the ravine, heard boots splash in the trickle and mud.

"Phae?" Trasen called, charging up the ravine neck. She heard him splashing, heard the muck clinging to his boots as he struggled. A frenzy of emotions whirled inside her. She was desperate to see his face. But what if it was a trick? Conflicting doubts and feelings assailed her, making her heart hammer violently in her ribs. She had to know. She started toward him, shaking with cold, clawing at the mass of dirt along the ravine wall as she stumbled.

Then he was there. Trasen—his curly dark hair, angled face. The look of shock and relief in his eyes brought tears. He recognized her—his expression was one of pure delight and the first embers of hope amidst ashes.

"Phae!" he breathed in triumph, a wide grin splitting his face. He rushed and embraced her, grabbing her with strong arms and pulling her close. He had not bathed in days, it was true, but he still smelled like himself—like home. A muffled sob burst from her chest and she squeezed him hard.

"I need to get you out of here," he said, pulling back.

"No, Trasen," she said, shaking her head. "You are the one in danger. Why are you with these men? Who are they?"

"They are hunters. They trap bears. They have special ropes and nets. They're going to trap the man who abducted you. Now that I've found you—"

"No!" Phae cried, pressing her hand against his mouth. "I am here willingly, Trasen. But you have to go. Leave these men. Go back to the Winemillers. Tell them I am safe."

"Safe?" he said, aghast, his face crinkling with outrage. "Look at you! You were kidnapped by the Arch-Rike's most—"

Phae clamped her hand over his mouth. "Listen to me! He is my protector. My father is alive. I need to go into the Scourgelands, Trasen. I won't be . . . I won't be coming back. I chose this. No one is forcing me. I can end the Plagues."

He shook his head free. "Is that what your father told you, is it? Your father, Tyrus of Kenatos? He's a liar, Phae. Whatever he's told you, it's a lie. I've spoken to the Arch-Rike. I've been to the city. This . . . I'm trying to save you!"

A shadow loomed just before the Kishion landed in the muck behind them. Phae gasped with fright and Trasen whirled. He pulled a short axe from his belt and Phae saw the sparkling onyx stone set into the sigils along its blade. The stone shimmered with light, growing brighter as the magic was summoned.

"Trasen, no!" she begged.

The Kishion had landed full on his feet, a raven in his dark cowl and menacing eyes.

"Run, Phae," Trasen said warningly. "I won't be a victim this time."

The Kishion's face was grim. He did not unsheathe any weapons. He looked equally deadly without any.

There was no way she could make Trasen understand. No words would make sense to him, not after the Arch-Rike had woven his lies around Trasen's mind. What mattered most to her was that he was safe. She did not want Shion to kill him or even injure him. Trasen would not be safe if he continued to track and hunt her. He would follow her. He would follow her all the way into the Scourgelands. She would have done the same for him. Of all the sacrifices she would need to make, this would be the hardest. She knew what she had to do.

Phae grabbed Trasen by the cloak and pulled him around until he faced her. His expression was hard with determination, his jaw tensed and thick with stubble. She saw him swallow. His gaze shifted, surprised by her sudden action. She took his face between her palms and stared into his eyes. His eyes were bluish green and wild with energy and determination. She stared deliberately, connecting them. Then she blinked.

She took away his memories of her. All of them.

When the fierce maelstrom of sobbing had finally ended, Phae felt drained, desolate, and hollowed as a gourd. Her nose was puffy and tender and she dried her face with her hands, wiping away the vestiges of grief from the corners of her eyes. Her head throbbed. Sitting across from her in the dense scrub, silent as a stone, was the Kishion. He was a silent observer of her suffering, but though he had not spoken, his expression was full of compassion and sympathy. His mouth was a tight, drawn line, his lips curling with shared pain, as if her suffering somehow was his. The look in his eyes was haunted, full of anguish for her.

"I'm sorry," Phae whispered hoarsely. She wiped her chin and then pressed her temples with her fingers. "I needed to mourn him."

"You loved . . . Trasen, didn't you." His voice was soft, not judging.

She licked her lips, staring at him and then down at her boots. She nodded. "I didn't realize it. I didn't see the pattern until I gathered all those memories together in one. He loved me as well. I saw it then, but it was too late. They flitted away . . . like leaves. I could not hold onto them. They're gone now. Forever." Saying it out loud caused the crushing weight in her chest to press harder.

"You saved his life," he said. "He will be of no use to the Arch-Rike now."

Phae nodded, the misery a dull ache still. "I'll never forget the look on his face though. I was a stranger to him."

He reached out and touched her shoulder. "I understand a little of what he was feeling when he left. Confused, frustrated. He is in the woods of Silvandom and he doesn't realize why he is here or why he came. We told him to go back to Stonehollow and keep the orphans safe. His memories of them may return. At least we sent him out of danger and to the right place. It's more than anyone has ever done for me."

She bit her bottom lip, glancing into his eyes. "I pity you, Shion. If my father is right, your memories will return when this is over. I hope so, for your sake."

He gave her the hint of a smile. Then dropping his hand, he leaned back slightly. "It was painful to watch you grieve. I wish there was something I could do to take it from you. It wasn't just pity that I felt." He stared off into the woods at the thickening shadows of twilight. "Memories hidden. Locked away. Insurmountable grief. I understood your pain as if it were my own." He sighed deeply and fished in his pocket. There, in his hand, he cupped the locket.

Phae stared at the charm, blinking. She reached out and took it, fingering it delicately. From deep within the Kishion's chest, a sound emerged. He started humming the tune she had last heard emitted by the locket. The sound that came from him was rich and languid, as if he had been an accomplished performer on a stage. He stopped, catching himself.

"You can sing, Shion?" she asked, surprised, her eyebrows lifting.

He stared at the locket as if it were a hot coal that could sting him despite his imperviousness. "Perhaps I can," he said simply. "When I hear the music from that locket, it invokes feelings, as if I recognize the song. As if I've sung it before."

"It is a song of grieving," Phae said, pinching the locket between her fingers. "When we were in the abandoned homestead that night, when you opened the locket and the music came out, it made me think of suffering and grief. It is how I feel right now. I loved Trasen without realizing what it was. Because I love him, I set him free. Love is painful. I never knew that." She shook her head, scraping clumps of hair behind her ear.

"Pain is a teacher," he said quietly, picking at a twig and twirling it between his fingers. "A harsh teacher. I would spare you this lesson, if I could."

Phae sniffed and wiped her nose. "Thank you for not killing Trasen."

"The axe gave him confidence he did not truly earn. I promised you I would not. So I did not. Are you hungry?"

She nodded weakly and pulled open her sack. Fishing around inside, she withdrew a pear. It was a bit ripe and bruised, but she sank her teeth into it and relished the taste.

"Do you ever hunger?" she asked.

He shook his head no.

"But you still enjoy the flavors. Let me get one for you then."

"No, you need the strength more than I. You eat them." He gave her a nod and waved it away.

She took another bite and then handed the fruit to him. "A bite then? Please?"

He stared at it a moment and then took it, staring at the pale flesh of the pear and then took a respectable bite with his white teeth. He offered it back to her, and she accepted it, feeling a strange sense of intimacy sharing it. Her stomach rumbled with hunger, and she devoured the remaining portion.

Exhaustion stole over Phae's body. Her clothes were damp and mud-stained. The maze of trees surrounding them brought a canopy shielding them from the glitter of stars. Branches swayed in the light breeze, causing a shushing sound as soothing as a mother's caress. She blinked, realizing her eyes had been drooping.

"Sleep," he said. "I'll watch over you."

Phae was too weary to argue, especially remembering that he did not require sleep himself. She stretched out in the matting of pine needles and scrub, using her pack as a pillow and huddling inside the cocoon of her cloak. She stared at him, sitting across from her, hands clasped around his knees.

"Back in the mountains, when I ran away from you," she said, her words beginning to slur. "I finally collapsed. I was so exhausted. You sat near me and watched as I fell unconscious. Do you remember that night?"

"Of course I do."

"What were you thinking?" She yawned expansively.

"Your very vulnerability brought feelings of protectiveness in me. I can't explain it, other than your Dryad blood. But I felt almost a . . . a duty."

Her eyes had closed again and she tried to keep them open. "A duty to what?"

"A duty to look after you. To keep you safe. I feel it now." He smiled down at her. "Sleep. I will be watching."

"Will you sing to me?" she asked. "I love hearing men sing. After the harvest, on the nights we crush grapes into wine, there is always singing. I love the songs of Stonehollow."

As she shut her eyes, sinking into the cushion of her pack, she heard his voice. It started low, blending in with the deep vastness of the woods. There was power in his voice. She could almost call it magic. The sound wove a blanket around her. There were no words, only a plaintive melody that wrapped around her mind and soothed the pain and the despair. Phae tried to stay awake, savoring each strain. She was used to folk songs and cherished the sound of clapping and dancing around a blazing bonfire. In her mind, she went back to Stonehollow, remembering all the things she loved. The heat of a bonfire, the smell of baked bread, the sweet flavor of mulled wine given to all the children after they turned ten. Memories trailed through her mind, dug up like earth from a spade.

The Kishion's melody stitched all the memories together, creating a theme that bound them. Stacking wine barrels. Culling the grapes. Walking barefoot on the sandy dirt by the vines. The vibrant green of the grape leaves. Clapping and whistles of the dancers. The large vats full of fresh grapes. She was there with Trasen, gripping the edges to keep from stumbling, pants rolled up to their knees as they squished the grapes with their feet. His hand brushed against hers. She looked up and instead of seeing Trasen's face, she saw Shion's. The juice from the grapes, the pulp from the skins sticking between her toes. The sweet honeyed smell. She touched his fingers, gazing into his eyes, not certain who she was seeing in her mind's eye. The memories transported her far away.

The Kishion's voice lulled her asleep.

"We are surrounded by various histories and fragments from the ages. Some are true. Some are only the approximation of truth. Some truths are hard to accept. If you believe only what you like in the histories, and reject what you don't want to believe, it is not the truth you seek, but a confirmation of your own opinions. You will never find truth that way."

—Possidius Adeodat, Archivist of Kenatos

XXVII

Phae's legs burned as she tramped up the steep hill. Sweat trickled down the side of her face and her stomach twisted with hunger, her throat parched with thirst. Foraging for food in the woods had proven more difficult than she expected and the hunger had robbed her energy and made the climb more difficult. She did not complain, but she wished they had encountered something more substantial to eat. The trees blocked the view ahead and the progress of the sun, but the day was warm and mild and puffy clouds scudded across the sky.

Shion paused at the top of the ridge, waiting for her to catch up as he studied the downward slope. As she reached it, she noticed the forest change suddenly, the trees become white-barked birch with teeming leaves. The trunks were slender and peeling and Phae touched several as they started down. From the ridge they could see forest in every direction. They were in the middle of Silvandom with no view of cities or roads in any direction. The world felt incredibly vast to her and she sighed in wonder. Each step down jarred her knees and she felt dizziness swim in her mind. She stumbled, catching herself on Shion's arm. He slowed the pace and when they reached the bottom of the hill, he paused to let her rest.

"Thank you," she breathed, sitting on a fallen tree. The grove was bathed in beautiful sunlight, and full of the sounds of insects and birds. The trill of a songbird caught her ear and she listened, hearing the babbling of water. "A stream?" she said, cocking her head.

Shion nodded and motioned for her to follow him. A red robin swooped in front of her, and she admired its brilliant plumage. But-terflies flitted through the air. Not the blue kind they had encountered the day before, but with multi-hued wings of red, gold, and yellow. The drone of giant black bees caught her attention as they swooped lazily in the air around her, not threateningly but curiously. She saw little lizards pop up their heads and then dart away. Crossing the glen, they reached a small brook winding its way through the lowest part of the terrain. The waters looked inviting and calm. Phae knelt by it and scrubbed her hands together, washing away the dirt and mud. She cupped some in her palms and drank deeply while Shion filled his water flask.

Movement caught her eye. Looking downstream, she saw a large stone at the edge of the stream. A small mat of big green leaves covered it like a blanket and on the leaves were a pile of berries of various sorts. She stared at it in surprise.

Shion followed her gaze. "That wasn't there when we arrived," he said thoughtfully.

Phae approached the stone, smoothing her tangled hair back from her neck, and stared down at the treasure, her stomach aching to see them. She glanced around, seeing the creatures of the forest all around her. Some chittered softly. Slowly, she extended a hand to the berries. A large black bee buzzed nearby, almost warningly. She stopped.

"What do they want, Shion?" she asked, glancing back at him. "Is it a gift? I feel something is missing. I shouldn't just take it."

He stared at the rock and then at her. "You should offer a gift in return. The spirits are responding to your need."

Phae thought a moment. "I don't have anything to offer except myself."

"Maybe that will be enough."

Phae sighed, stared down at the food hungrily. Then she nodded and summoned all the feeling of gratitude she could muster. She was grateful for the gift, so grateful for food she did not have to collect or hunt. She smiled at the woods, trying to show her gratitude with her mouth.

"Thank you," she whispered. "I am so very hungry. May I eat these?"

The drone of a black bee hovered near her. It landed on her shoulder, its furry black body creeping along the fold of her cloak. Then it lazily went away and she felt a feeling of peace settle inside. Gingerly, she reached for a berry. Meeting no resistance, she took it and plopped it in her mouth. The juice and flavor were dazzlingly sweet.

"Shion, have one!" she said, offering a plump blackberry to him. "They are very good!" He took it, smiling at her, and ate it.

Phae devoured the gift left on the stone slowly, savoring each berry as a sacred gift. She cooed with delight. Motioning for Shion to sit by her, she encouraged him to linger. When she turned back to the stone, it was nearly overflowing with berries of various sorts. Each was a treat, a delight. She ate until she was full, feeling strength and energy begin to warm her. The water from the stream provided what she needed to quench her thirst.

"Can I borrow your flask please?" she asked him.

He offered it to her and she knelt by the stream and poured it out on her hair, scrubbing through the strands to free the dirt and mud away. She dipped the flask three times into the brook before feeling like her hair was finally clean. It hung wetly down her back, but it no longer smelled of the rot and stink from the pond she had plunged into. After filling the flask the final time, she stoppered it and handed it back.

"How did you know that pond was dangerous yesterday?" she asked him. "I was so sure it was leading us to safety, yet I was wrong. It twisted my mind somehow."

He crouched by the edge of the brook, circling his fingers in the water. He was quiet for a while. "It felt familiar. As if I had been there before. I had a premonition of warning."

"Do you think it was a Dryad tree? It looked dead once all the insects were gone."

He shook his head. "No, I don't think it was. Just as there are good spirits, there are also terrible ones. When I tried to kill Tyrus, he took me with his device to a waterfall deep in the Alkire. I felt the presence of a spirit creature there, a terrible presence. It radiated fear. Whatever creature was lurking in that bog was probably like that one. The butterflies were a trap. The waters were likely poisoned."

She shuddered at the memory of the butterfly swarm. The experience in the glen was much different. She felt safe, that the creatures of Mirrowen were guarding them.

"Look," Shion said, his eyes narrowing.

Phae turned her gaze. Across the brook behind them was an enormous white stag. Its breath came in little puffs of mist as it breathed. Huge pronged antlers crested its head like branches of a sharp thorny tree. The feeling of peace swelled inside of her, along with something else. A deep sense of longing rose up inside her. The feeling was hard to describe. It was a yearning—a desire to belong. The feeling was deep inside her, thick with essence and it permeated all through her. She stared into the stag's eyes, seeing intelligence there. Another puff of mist came from its beautiful nose. She longed to stroke the velvet skin. A thought brushed against her mind.

Follow, Dryad-born.

Phae rose obediently to her feet.

The stag led them through the tangle of woods, always choosing a path easy to follow. The berries had completely restored Phae's flagging strength and it was much easier keeping pace through the forest. The birch gave way to oak and cedar as they crossed over ridges and delved deeper into the reclusive woodlands. Signs of spirit life were evident everywhere around them, colorful birds trilling and the aroma of flowers that she could not see. Phae felt at peace and safe, as if the woods were a mantle shielding her from the probing gaze of the Arch-Rike's minions. A queer hunger to belong grew inside her as she marched. She could not speak for fear of weeping. Her emotions had been struck by some invisible chord of music and she felt oneness with the woods that she had never experienced before. Strangely, it was as if she were coming home.

The intensity of her feelings continued to mount as the sun started its fading arc in the sky. Gnats swirled in the air, dancing like dust motes. The stag's pace did not flag, but it suddenly stopped, dipping its head to the ground, drawing attention there. It had stopped before a patch of charred earth, as if sniffing it. Then it continued a little way farther, stopping again to smell a heap of ash on the forest floor. Phae and the Kishion approached, staring at the sudden shift of color and smell. Oaks with charred trunks appeared as they got closer and the air contained the scent of smoke. Farther still, a skeleton lay sprawled near a tree, fragments of clothing rotting in the woods, alongside a spear. It startled Phae and she grabbed Shion's arm.

He stared at the remains. "Boeotian," he whispered.

The stag led them into a grove of blackened trees. The forest floor crunched beneath their boots, but already new growth was beginning to poke up from the dense tangle of blackened scrub. After the burning circle of trees, Phae's heart leapt with emotion. A gnarled oak tree lay in the center of the scorched ground with hulking limbs and an enormous axe-bit wound into its bulky trunk.

"It's her," Phae breathed, feeling the familiar presence of her kindred. She tightened her grip on Shion's arm. "I can feel her presence." It reminded her of the Dryad tree in Stonehollow she had fled. There was no Druidecht here now to frighten her. Biting her lip, Phae let go of Shion's arm and hesitantly approached. Her boots disturbed the soot and ashes, bringing up an earthy smell that was not unpleasant. It was like smelling a candle wick after it had been snuffed out.

Phae stared at the ancient tree, mesmerized with its beauty as well as its savage scar. The wound was already beginning to heal, covered over with a layer of dark sap. Amidst the crooked branches were clumps of mistletoe. Phae closed the distance, hands wringing in front of her nervously. She had the sudden sensation—an impression, really—that the Dryad would not appear with Shion standing near.

She glanced back at him. "Will you wait for me?" she asked. "I need to speak with her alone."

He looked from her to the tree, his expression suddenly wary. She wondered what he was thinking.

"I'll be all right," she said simply. "She won't . . . hurt me."

The look of resistance in his eyes lingered and she said nothing, waiting for him to get used to the idea. She inhaled the smell of the woods, listening to every chirp and tick coming from the forest. The wind rustled the massive branches. Then Shion nodded to her and stepped away from the glen, vanishing into the shadows. She knew he was still there, nearby. But she could not see him.

Phae took a deep breath and turned to face the Dryad tree. She found herself peering into the green eyes of a girl no older than herself, a girl peeking from behind the tree.

"Hello," the girl said in Aeduan.

Phae bit her lip again. The connection between them was strong, as if they each shared a single heart. Phae blinked rapidly. "I am . . . one of you," Phae said in a small voice.

"I know," the girl said, stepping cautiously around the tree. She wore a pretty dress that matched the color of her eyes. Her hair was long and blond and as straight as wheat sheaves. She had an unearthly beauty that made Phae suddenly self-conscious. The girl looked over Phae's shoulder, her expression crinkling with worry. "He is near. Are you in danger? You will be safe with me. I can make him go away."

Phae held up her hands. "Please no," she begged. "His memories have already been stolen. Do you have a way . . . of restoring his memories? Could you help him to remember?"

The girl made a frown, her lips pouting. "Yes, there is a way, but the idea is loathsome to me." She stepped away from the tree, but never lost touch of it. She stared again over Phae's shoulder. "A Dryad's kiss would make him remember. But it is a gift we rarely give for it binds us to that person. We only do it if someone saves our tree from destruction and lingers to claim the boon." She looked at Phae and smiled prettily but with confusion. "Who are you? Where is your mother?"

Phae wanted to reach out and stroke the bark of the tree, but she dared not, unsure whether it would be offensive to the other girl to do so.

"It's all right," the girl said encouragingly. "You may touch my tree."

Phae looked startled. "Did you . . . did you know my thoughts?"

"No, I read your expression. The eyes say much. I made the choice to become a Dryad a long time ago. I know the nature of you mortals. Especially the unspoken ways you communicate with each other. That man you came with. You clutched him as if he were a . . . brother . . . or a protector. But he has a dark cast to him. A blight in his soul. I smell blood from his hands."

Phae nodded seriously. "It is true. But he is starting to change. His mind was stolen away and he was persuaded by his ignorance to do savage things."

The girl frowned and shook her head. "I pity him. He is your protector then?"

"Yes."

"Who is your mother? I cannot place you by your smell. You have been to many lands in a short time. They each cling to your skin. Each land has its own scent. You are from . . .?"

"Stonehollow," Phae answered. "But my mother was not. She is a Dryad from a tree in Kenatos. The Paracelsus Towers. My father is Tyrus Paracelsus."

The look on the girl's face gave away much. She stared at Phae with open astonishment, her eyes narrowing with suspicion as well. "I sensed the presence of kindred magic in the woods. I summoned the stag to lead you here, but I did not realize who it would be. You are . . . Tyrus's daughter?"

"I am." Phae bowed her head.

The girl stiffened. "Who is it that is with you? Speak his name?"

Phae looked startled. "He has no name."

"The Kishion," the girl hissed.

Phae held up her hands placatingly. "He no longer serves the Arch-Rike."

The girl had a panic-stricken look on her face. "And I helped lead him to my tree? Call for him. I must take his memories. He cannot remember this place. All would be at risk."

"No, please!" Phae implored. "He is no threat."

"His presence is a threat," the girl answered, looking fearful. "The ring he wears—"

"He no longer wears it," Phae replied. "He shed it days ago. There is too much to say and not much time, sister. Can you . . . can you see my memories? It would help you understand. Do not take them, but I give you permission to see them. I need your help. I don't know how . . . to be a Dryad, even though I am Dryad-born."

"Look into my eyes," the girl said. "I promise that I will not steal your memories if you promise not to steal mine."

"I promise," Phae said gratefully. The two girls clasped hands and stared into each other's eyes. Phae felt a strange sensation in the pit of her stomach, a churning feeling that made her dizzy and nauseous. The world seemed to tip and she felt herself wobble, but the girl's grasp on her hands steadied her.

It was finished.

Phae blinked, feeling as if she had dozed. She looked up and saw tears glistening in the other girl's eyes. The girl rested her slim hand on Phae's cheek.

"What strong memories," the girl whispered to Phae. "You are Dryad-born."

Phae shuddered. "Can you help me? I must learn how to be one of you. If I am to go to the Scourgelands, I need this knowledge."

The girl nodded slowly, dropping her hand. She suddenly squeezed Phae's hands with her own. "I could help you, but I shouldn't be the one to do so. I was taught of this life by my mother. She prepared me for what I could not know any other way. Mothers and daughters share a special bond. These trees are portals. We daughters are the guardians of these portals. They connect this world to Mirrowen. They also connect us to each other. Your mother is the Dryad in Kenatos. I will trade places with her. She will guard my tree and I will guard hers. Just for a moment. If you should be taught of our ways, it should be done by her."

Phae gasped with astonishment, her heart shuddering with emotion. "Can you? Can you do such a thing?"

"I can. And I will. Stay here." Suddenly the girl's eyes widened with surprise and a flash of sudden intense emotion. "Annon!" she gasped, as if seeing something Phae could not. Her fingers dug into Phae's. "No," she moaned, her face turning livid with emotion.

"What is it?" Phae asked, her own heart panged.

The girl shook her head, her expression engulfed in misery. "He is . . . there is danger. So much danger! I feel it." She started gasping, struggling for breath. "He . . . is . . . no! No!" The Dryad girl crumpled to her knees, hands covering her face.

"What?" Phae begged, dropping to her knees, clutching the girl tight. "What do you see?"

The girl moaned, shaking her head. Then her eyes blazed. "Serpents! The Preachán is dead. They are coming. Annon, don't move! Don't move!"

"*There is great agitation at the Temple of Seithrall in Kenatos. The war crisis between Havenrook and Wayland is threatening to spill over across all the lands, Boeotia included. There are reports of barbarian incursions into Silvandom, once again threatening our great city. If the southern kingdoms are not united, it will leave the city practically undefended against the treachery of the invaders. Always it is civil unrest and tumult. Gratefully, the Arch-Rike is wise in sending a delegation to mediate with the Preachán. There is even talk of asking the Druidecht of Canton Vaud to settle the dispute that we may unite against a common enemy. All is in an uproar.*"

—Possidius Adeodat, Archivist of Kenatos

XXVIII

When Paedrin was a child, he had watched the older Bhikhu fight amongst themselves. They did not hold back in punches or kicks, knowing that the temporary pain of an injury would lead to swifter reflexes after the healing was done. He admired their unwillingness to express pain and he strove to emulate it amongst his own peers. Paedrin had always been a quick learner and he noticed how Master Shivu gave him special attention, as if they shared some unspoken secret that acknowledged that Paedrin truly was the best student in the temple. The memory touched his heart with sadness, but it did not diminish his determination.

As the young Bhikhu crouched on the temple walls of the Shatalin temple at dawn, bathed in dewdrops from the swirling fog, he watched the activity in the courtyard below. Just before dawn, the interior doors had opened to the training yard and a group of twenty men emerged, of various races. A tall Vaettir master led them through a curt series of training exercises to warm up their bodies, speaking the commands in sharp, crisp language, but not participating himself. Paedrin was struck by the immense discipline of the men. There was no joking or jostling. They were riveted at attention and followed the drills with audible claps and grunts, in perfect unison and harmony. The tall lanky master walked amidst the twenty, head slightly bowed, and snapped orders, which were obeyed promptly. The tall master was a Vaettir with long flowing hair.

This went on for a good while and Paedrin continued to crouch, invisible amid the crenellations. He counted the men by races: five Vaettir, five Aeduan, five Cruithne, and five Preachán. The symmetry was not lost on him. The tall master snarled a quick command and the men lined up along the interior walls. He barked out two words and a Cruithne and Preachán emerged from the line, facing off against each other. The size difference was immense, for the Cruithne towered over the smaller Preachán. Paedrin leaned forward slightly, watching with fascination.

Another curt command—a signal to commence fighting. The Cruithne was bulky but he was quick. The Preachán was even quicker. Like a blur, the smaller man ducked and tumbled, diving out of reach, flitting around like a hummingbird to strike at the bigger man's calves, the back of his knees. The Cruithne swiveled around and tried to snatch the puny opponent, but could not touch him.

Paedrin rubbed his mouth, watching the fury of the exchange. The little man ducked away from a solid punch aimed at him and suddenly the Preachán had his wrist and the big man flipped down, crashing on his back. Like a bee coming in for a quick sting, the Preachán somersaulted over him and landed by his head, hammering down on the Cruithne's nose. A fountain of blood spattered from the blow. The Cruithne grabbed the Preachán's leg and wrenched, jerking the smaller man off his feet. There was a sickening crack as the leg broke. The Cruithne swung the body and hurled it across the yard where he slammed against the far wall before slumping to the ground.

The Cruithne, wiping the blood on his sleeve, rose ponderously to his feet.

The crumpled Preachán did not move.

A pit of disgust welled in Paedrin's stomach. No one went to the fallen Preachán to see if he were even alive. The Cruithne lumbered back to the line, taking his place again. Blood smeared his face.

Paedrin stared at the crumpled body. The tall master gave another order and an Aeduan and two Vaettir were summoned. It was clearly a mismatch but with a whistle the three launched into combat, the two Vaettir against the one fellow. Not a favorable contest, but the Aeduan attacked like a mountain cat, leaping with grace and kicking down one of the Vaettir as he tried to float away. The other was defeated only moments later, brought down by a vicious punch that knocked his air away, bringing him crashing down. He did not stop until both Vaettir were unconscious at his feet. He saluted to the lean master and went back to the line.

Glancing again at the fallen Preachán, Paedrin saw him start to twitch. He was trying to sit up, his head hanging low.

They were in the practice yard, fighting and maiming each other in various combinations of brutality. There was no discussion or instruction. Sometimes they were given weapons. Other times they fought with wrists tied behind their backs. Paedrin watched and studied them, feeling the mist roil around him. He did not shiver though. He willed his muscles to be calm. He waited.

Just before midday, or what Paedrin assumed was such without the presence of the sun, there were only several men left standing. Each had been called to fight multiple times. Their chests heaved, faces bathed in sweat and some with blood. The tall master, the Vaettir, whistled again and all went rigid. He barked a curt order, which sounded like a question. No one moved. The tall man paced in the midst of the square, hissing at them like a snake. He asked the question again, so low that Paedrin could not hear it. He paused, waiting. No one moved.

The tall master clapped his hands twice and the men started back toward the doors leading inside the temple. There were at least a dozen left behind, sprawled out in the training yard, either unconscious or unable to get up.

Paedrin did not think he would get a better chance than that. If the Kishion in training beat themselves up every morning before the midday meal, what better time would there be to challenge the tall master's authority than just after? They were tired and spent. They were used to fighting each other. They were not used to fighting someone like Paedrin.

The tall master started back toward the doors, pausing every few steps to walk around one of the crumpled bodies sprawled in front of him. Paedrin's legs were burning from holding the crouch so long, so he delicately stretched and let the ache in his muscles wane. He waited until the tall master was almost to the doors.

"Cruw Reon!" Paedrin shouted.

The tall master froze in place as Paedrin's voice echoed throughout the courtyard.

He did not turn. He stood erect, almost aloof. He was long and sinewy, his hair a curtain of black. The long hair sent a nagging memory in Paedrin's mind. He looked . . . familiar. Too tall, but familiar still.

"Who challenges me?" snapped a voice from the courtyard below. It was like a whip crack and echoed sharply.

"I do," Paedrin said, taking in a deep breath, and jumped up, floating above the courtyard like a gray raven. "I am Paedrin of Kenatos. I am Paedrin Bhikhu. I am the last Vaettir of the *true* temple. I come to claim what is mine. I name you a thief. I name you a traitor." He exhaled sharply, letting himself come down hard in the center of the courtyard. "And I can smell your bad breath from over here."

The tall master stood like a granite slab. "I have been expecting you, Paedrin Bhikhu," replied the voice. The man's voice was suddenly familiar. A growing sense of dread welled inside of Paedrin's stomach. From above, he had not recognized anything special about the sharp commands or the tone of voice. His mind began to shriek at him to flee. He stood still though, willing himself to face the worst. His goal was not to defeat the man. It was to provide Hettie sufficient time to steal the sword.

"Yes, I have expected you. But you are somewhat mistaken." He turned around, his hair swishing. "My name is not Cruw Reon. It is Kiranrao. But you are correct. I am a thief. And I am a traitor."

Paedrin would have recognized the voice anywhere. He stared into Kiranrao's dark eyes, the wicked smirk on his mouth. There, at his side, was a sword that flickered in and out of view. He exhaled sharply, feeling his insides coil and twist with shock and surprise. Kiranrao of Havenrook. A traitor. A Vaettir. The man who trained new Kishion for the Arch-Rike? He reeled from the surprise, from the shock of it.

"I see by the gaping fish mouth that you had not figured it out before coming," Kiranrao said with keen pleasure. "Oh, but how I have been waiting for you, little boy. Come to avenge the death of the Bhikhu temple. Poisoned by my orders." He took a menacing step forward. "You've come for this weapon, have you not?" He motioned to his side. Looking at the sword made it disappear. Paedrin blinked furiously. "Or are you here for the blade Iddawc? You wish to take my place, to become who I am? Is that your wish?"

Paedrin steeled himself, feeling the sweat streak down his ribs. How had he not recognized Kiranrao before? The mist had obscured some of the courtyard, but the walk and the gait had not revealed him. It was too formal, not the lounging, lazy way of the Romani lord.

"You are unworthy to be a Vaettir," Paedrin said in a low voice. "You are not even a Bhikhu. This shrine is no longer yours. Step down, or I will make you."

"And how will you make me?" Kiranrao replied in a silken voice. "We both know that you were beaten by lesser men than me."

"I don't think it is possible for there to be a lesser man than you." Every nerve in Paedrin's body tingled with anticipation. He knew that most fights were won or lost in moments. By judging correctly or incorrectly how your enemy would first act or react. He knew that Kiranrao was trying to unsettle him, to make him act rashly. It was certainly working, but Paedrin was not a fool.

"If you wish to claim the Sword of Winds," Kiranrao said, pulling the scabbard around. He tugged on the belt and the scabbard and blade unhasped. There was a glimmering green stone set in the pommel. "You must be able to draw it. It cannot be drawn by any man. You must defeat the one who holds it first. Is this what you want, Bhikhu? I could give you this sword, but it will not come loose from its sheath until you vanquish me. Is this what you crave? Is this the right you desire?"

"What I desire is that you eat your own dung and drink your own piss," Paedrin replied with venom. "After I have *made* you do that, I will take that sword from you and use it to free this world of the Plague. When that is done, I will see you locked in chains in a dungeon with no light and nothing but gruel. You will be helpless and alone as you truly are. Do I make myself clear, Band-Imas? I know you can hear me. This is my promise to you, Arch-Rike. I will put you down, the lowest of men. Death would be too merciful for you."

The cold eyes of Kiranrao went flat with hatred. Clutching the shaft of the scabbard, Kiranrao raised it so that the stone in the pommel met Paedrin's gaze. A sickly green light emerged from the stone. Then it flashed suddenly, sending searing pain into Paedrin's eyes. It felt as if his eyeballs were stabbed by hornets. He screamed in pain, shutting his eyes, but it was too late. The magic of the stone had already begun its work, causing agony inside his eyes. He almost crumpled to the ground, but instead, he jumped high, sucking in breath despite the torture searing his entire face and soared upward into the air. He had to get away. He had to flee.

A foot struck his stomach, right where he held his breath and he felt it gush out, dropping him like a rock to the courtyard floor. Despite the torturing magic, Paedrin lunged out, a whirlwind of fists and feet. He listened for the sound of movement, for any intake of breath. Then he dived to the side and rolled, dropping into a low crouch, arms brought into a defensive square, ready to block an attack. A fist struck him in the back. Pain ripped through his lower muscles, making his legs weak. In retaliation, he back-kicked and felt it strike the man, sending him sprawling. Like a tiger, Paedrin vaulted after, hammering down on the body until he realized it wasn't Kiranrao at all but one of the Kishion in training.

The deft scrape of a foot behind him.

Paedrin flipped up in the air, sucking in painfully, and felt a body pass below him. He knifed downward, his face afire, and dropped the man below. As he was straightening, a meaty hand grabbed his wrist. It was a Cruithne. He knew his arm would be dislocated in a moment. Paedrin used Unbendable Arm and stepped in sideways, swiveling the Cruithne over his back, and hurled him to the ground. With a wrenching feeling, the grip on his wrist vanished and he was free.

Paedrin could sense the heat from the bodies as they converged around him. He struck fast and hard, squeezing his eyes shut to try to block the torrid pain, but he could hardly think past the scream he refused to allow out of his mouth. Dropping low and then high, he struck and parried, blocking the blows that rained on him from all sides. His knee was taken out from behind and he staggered down. A kick to his face brought stars as well as more pain. Flopping on to his back, Paedrin rolled back over his shoulder, shoved against the ground into a handstand and sucked in another gulp of air to start rising again. If he could reach the walls . . .

Something struck the side of his skull, and all went black.

"The delegation to Havenrook failed. The ambassadors were ambushed and robbed. It baffles me that the Preachán would do this, despite the advantage of their own interests to meet with the delegation. Several Bhikhu bodyguards were murdered. I fear that we are past the possibility of diplomacy now."

—Possidius Adeodat, Archivist of Kenatos

XXIX

As the first silver shades of dawn emerged through the immense fog bank, Hettie decided to start climbing. Her arms and legs were still weary from the ordeal of ascending the jagged cliff to the outer edge of the Shatalin temple, but it was a good place to conceal herself. Before Paedrin left, he had floated up the outer wall and discovered the highest tower directly above with a broad stone balcony set into the side, overlooking the vast ocean. It was tall enough that it protruded from the continual mist and provided a single overlook to the domain. Paedrin had taken the rope from her bag and tied one end to the stone buttresses supporting the balcony and brought the rest down to where she crouched. Scaling the wall would have been slow and dangerous without it.

She chafed her hands, fingers raw and still oozing from the climb the day before. Not even her blanket and cloak had kept her very warm and both were dripping with moisture. After rising slowly, she shook them off, rolled them up, and folded them away. She gazed up the slender rope that disappeared into the mist above. Paedrin was gone, scouting the perimeter and preparing to provide the distraction she needed. A gnawing, sick feeling—worry—grew tortuously inside her stomach. She knew he was capable and brave. He was also reckless and too sure of himself. A tiny spasm of fear accompanied the worry. She was not anxious to begin climbing again.

Knowing that daylight would rob her of natural advantages, she prepared herself mentally. Hettie checked her weapons, making sure they were snug. The arrows were bunched together and tied off to prevent them from rattling inside the quiver. She re-laced her boots again, just to be sure they were tight; the soles were padded to prevent sound. From a pocket, she produced her shooting gloves and tugged them on.

The Bhikhu training had begun to occupy the foremost thoughts in her mind. Deliberately, she had to recall the lessons of the Romani. How to move with perfect stillness. How to control her breathing. The inner mechanisms that made locks function and how to release them without a key. The art of disguise and the myriad of subterfuges she was capable of. But it was different now. Before she had been serving the interests of Kiranrao in claiming the lost Paracelsus blade, the one known as Iddawc. She had been his puppet. That secret and the trust of her brother and Paedrin had cost her something. Now that she was free of the accursed earring, she felt a lightness in her chest she'd never experienced before. Yes, a Romani may try to threaten her again. Kiranrao might attempt to poison her—but she felt much more capable of avoiding the fate of other Romani women. Tyrus's quest to banish the Plague had resulted in the banishment of her captivity. He had offered her a chance to live in Silvandom, safely beyond the Arch-Rike and the Romani's reach. She gladly clung to that strand of hope.

With a supple spring, Hettie launched herself up the rope. She pulled with her arms and also pushed with her legs, twining herself up the vast length with easy grace. The quiet stretching of the rope mixed with little bursts of breath, which fogged out of her mouth and joined the vapors shrouding the land. But those sounds were tiny compared with the colossal crash of the waves against the rocks beneath her. The outer wall of the temple was covered with lichen, but it had been crafted of enormous stones and seemed determined to endure through the ages. Up she went, one pull at a time, gliding her way up to the tower.

The fog boiled around her, obscuring the encroaching sunlight. Her fingers burned with pain but she persevered, feeling the steady grip of the leather shooting gloves accepting the strands of rope snugly. Each pull was flawless. She ascended quickly. The light became more pronounced as the mist thinned. She emerged from its folds and found the dawn sky above her, bright and blue with traces of lavender. She reached the top of the wall but the tower continued up. Sounds reached her, reminding her of the training yard of the Bhikhu temple in Kenatos. Vivid memories of that place stung her mind—its life as well as its death. She heard grunts and the sound of fighting and bodies colliding. She wondered where Paedrin was, hidden in the mist somewhere near the main gates. As she continued up the rope, she listened for sounds from him. Her arm muscles throbbed with the effort, but she was strong and had only grown stronger with Paedrin's training.

Scaling the tower wall, hand over hand, she paused for a moment and stared at the buttresses above. There were no stairs or ledges leading to it. There were no windows in the tower itself. She wondered, with it being a Vaettir stronghold originally, if there were even any stairs within it. An enemy would be hard-pressed to attack a place that could not be breached without tall ladders. She heard a voice coming from the training yard, but it was too distant to recognize the words or the identity of the speaker. With a smirk, Hettie was suddenly grateful for Paedrin's bombastic side. She would have no trouble hearing him.

Hettie reached the lower edge of the buttress and grabbed the stone, admiring the quality of the knots Paedrin used to fasten it. She debated with herself on whether she should untie it, but decided that it would be best to leave it as a possible way to escape. She gripped the stone and pulled herself up to the buttress, which curved out, supporting the weight of the balcony. She paused for several moments, listening for any sound other than the crash and foam of the sea, the training yard, or anything else. The balcony faced away from the temple and so it would not give her a good view of the grounds below. Comfortable with her decision to wait, she then crept along the edge of the buttress and gripped the bottom edge of the balcony. Holding her weight with her hands, she peered up between the thin stone columns of the balcony rail. There were two stone urns, one on each side of a wooden door. The balcony was tiled with intricate stone chips of different colors. The balcony was small. The rail was wide enough to form a stone seat in a semicircle. There were no windows.

The roof was similar to what she had witnessed in Silvandom, steep and sloping. The crown of the roof had an iron cage. There was some sort of metal contrivance inside the cage and a large bracket of some kind. The wind whipped against her suddenly, causing her grip to strain. She pulled herself up on the balcony ledge and then waited, watching and listening. She was too high up to hear the training yard. The wind was all she could hear and it was as cold as winter.

Hettie stared at the door, examining the hinges and how it was made. She studied the mosaic of stone chips, admiring the pattern, but searching for cracks or grooves that would reveal the presence of a trap. The urns were slightly green with moss on one side. Her eyes went up to the strange cage at the top of the roof. It looked tall enough for a man to stand inside. The edge of the roof was low enough that she believed she could jump and reach it and pull herself up. But the stone shingles looked noisy and loose and she dared not risk it.

Now that she was at the top of the balcony, Hettie felt her mind come alive with all the years of Romani training. She assessed the shapes and structures, looking for anything out of place. She was carefully tuned to her feelings, seeking that telltale jolt of apprehension that would warn her of danger. As much as she hated the life, there was a certain degree of thrill in what she was doing. She caught herself smiling and then scowled. How long would her loyalties be divided? The mixture of feelings was difficult. She was grateful to have the skills she needed at this moment—skills that Paedrin lacked. Her plan was simple. Start with the highest tower, usually the place of power. Probe the edges to test its defenses. Then break past the defenses and search for the missing Sword of Winds. It was either on Cruw Reon's body or it was likely hidden in the tower. Determining which was crucially important.

Hettie crept along the edge of the stone seat, avoiding the puzzle-like stones below. It did not feel threatening, but she did not wish to risk it. The door was thick and solid, likely sealed by a crossbar on the other side. Not a problem for her. As she crouched near the wall, she studied the outer rim of the tower, looking for an alternative way inside. She was surprised by the lack of windows. Cautiously, Hettie stepped on the edge of the balcony floor, careful to avoid the colored design. She waited, listening. Then, slowly, she began to stretch over the ground, sliding out like a snake so that it spread her weight evenly as she moved. That was usually a way to circumvent many troubles that might be in the way, but her instincts felt that the balcony was not rigged. When she was fully stretched out, her head near the door, she cocked her ear at the seam at the bottom and listened, waiting patiently. She waited a long while, letting the sounds of the wind wash over her, letting her senses reach out to the world around her. The air from the bottom of the door was stale but she detected the odors of ale and wine. Curious. She also felt heat coming from the seams, just enough to caress her skin. Thinking back, she realized she had seen a flue jutting from the rooftop on the other side—a tiny one. A sparrow might squeeze in it, not her.

Convinced there was no one beyond, she lightly touched the handle, a stout iron ring flecked with rust. Grasping it by the collar, she waited, breathing in slowly, her heart starting to race. She pulled at the ring. The door opened a fraction. She waited, shutting her eyes so that she could hear better with her ears. Another little tug on the door. It opened farther. There was no crossbar securing it. With her other hand, Hettie loosed her dagger from its sheath and brought it out, holding it underhanded. She pulled the door until it parted open, just a fraction. She kept herself pressed against the door itself so that she would not be seen. Again, she waited for sounds to reveal the presence of someone.

Nothing.

Taking a deep breath, Hettie jerked the door ajar, keeping herself back out of sight. She wanted it to seem like the wind may have gusted it loose. If someone were asleep inside, they would come to investigate. Nothing happened. Hettie peered around the edge of the door, into the room.

A small fireplace contained a crackling fire and there were glowing orbs set in the wall inside, revealing the room with light. The dancing flames first caught her gaze, as they appeared to be the only movement in the room. She waited for several moments, watching the flames whip as the hot air joined the swirling winds outside. Hettie stepped around the edge of the door, peering inside curiously. It was a small tower, a single room. It was, however, very full.

Hettie's boot tapped against an empty wine bottle as she took her first wary step inside, knife balanced for throwing. There were bottles throughout the chamber, cluttering the floors and tabletops. A bed sprawled to her right, the blankets and sheets rumpled, but not occupied. There was a huge chest at the foot of the bed, nailed with leather and bound with iron straps. She shut the door behind her firmly, knowing it would open with a strong kick. The room was deliciously warm and had the yeasty smell of ale and the pungent smell of spoiled grapes. A second door was directly across on the far wall, of the same design as the one she had entered through. Two doors and no windows. A small coffer sat on the table, its lid open, spilling an assortment of gems and ducats of various mint—Havenrook, Cruithne, Wayland, but mostly Kenatos. There was a shaggy rug in the center of the room. She went to it quickly and lifted one of the corners, trying not to let the empty bottles rattle too much. She expected a trapdoor beneath, but there was none. A book lay on the table near the coffer. It was open to a page with ink scrawls marking names, races, ages, and recording injuries sustained. She flipped several pages, seeing the ledgers full. Many names were crossed out. The swipe of the ink looked ominous. A half-empty goblet sat by the tome, a small circle of ale froth showing its remaining contents. There was a small chair by the desk.

By the bed, on the far side, was a huge bracket full of swords. She raced to it immediately, counting at least seven. A solitary brace showed one was missing. She studied the remaining blades and scabbards, seeing various fashions of blades. All had gems mounted to the pommels and she could feel the sense of power radiating from them. Seven blades. One was missing. She swore under her breath. However, if the empty brace was where the Sword of Winds was normally kept, it would be an asset to know that now. She studied all seven, noting the make and length of each. She memorized the order and the details.

Across the wall on the other side of the tower, Hettie noticed a hanging cabinet. There was a lock on it. It was too small for a sword, but the lock caught her attention immediately. She approached it, studying the curve of the wood and noticed it was sturdy and solid. The lock, however, was no match for her skills. With a wire and a prod, she tripped it open and unfastened the cabinet latch. She expected to find bottles of wine or ale, but instead, a cold creeping fear clutched her stomach. There were vials of poison inside. Each had a label, scrawled with a delicate hand. She stared at one of them, tucked away in the back.

Monkshood.

Just seeing the words made her stomach clench with dread. The heat of the room became suddenly oppressive. Bile rose in her throat.

Next to it, almost cradling it, lay a small leather pouch. She stared at the pouch, her mind quickening. She snatched it from the cabinet and untied the drawstrings. It was a tiny pouch. There was a single, decaying leaf inside. The leaf was so old, it seemed to be collapsing into dust. Her memories stirred. As a child, Hettie had watched the effects of one of her sisters poisoned with monkshood. Just before the girl had died, they had given her a cup of tea to drink and the symptoms finally vanished. A strange tea. Hettie had always wondered what the tea was made from. She never knew, because the Romani men guarded the cure steadfastly.

Hettie took the small pouch and delicately slid it into her pocket. A surging thrill went through her body. And an idea sprouted inside her mind. It came with sharpness and clarity. The room reminded her of Havenrook. Discarded bottles of ale and wine. Rumpled careworn sheets. Ledgers and coins. Even the lights in the room, except for the fire, had the markings of enchantment. She stared at one of the glowing spheres, reminded of the lights of Kenatos.

A muffled noise caught her attention, striking her with dread and alertness. It was a shout from far away. Or a scream. Hettie raced to the other door, the one facing the courtyard. She tugged it open a crack, and heard the sounds rising up from below. The mist had cleared slightly and she saw bodies sprawled down in the training yard. A Vaettir was floating up, thrashing, attacked on all sides. It was Paedrin. Her heart lurched with dread. He was attacking as a drunken man, trying to fight foes as if he could not see them. As if he were blind.

There was no way down. No stairwell or ladder waited at the crest of the balcony. Only a Vaettir could enter or exit the balcony. Only a Vaettir. A Romani Vaettir with monkshood. Hettie's eyes widened with shock and a spasm of dread went through her. No—it's couldn't be.

Hugging the edge of the door, Hettie watched helplessly as Paedrin was brought down. She shuddered, seeing the savagery with which they treated him after he had collapsed. His limp body was dragged over to a giant stone pillar at the edge of the training yard, his wrists bound behind him and around the pillar with shackles. He was unconscious, head lolling against the cold stone as the others left him there, a vanquished foe. Hettie groaned inside, furious that she had been too slow. But what could she have done? There was no way down unless—she saw the mane of black hair as another Vaettir below took flight, heading up like a gust of breeze toward the tower where she crouched.

She would have recognized Kiranrao anywhere.

"*War is a grisly necessity betimes. The Waylander army has secured the borders of the ruined forests of Havenrook. The Cruithne march down from the mountains in force. Hammer meets anvil. The iron of the Preachán is about to be shaped into a new future. The Romani are scattering like leaves in the wind.*"

—Possidius Adeodat, Archivist of Kenatos

X X X

The door squealed as it was thrust open. Hettie watched the boots as they entered. She cowered under the huge bed, hidden in the shadows and near the rumpled blankets. She willed herself to be small and silent, shrinking deep within herself, doing her best to calm her thoughts, afraid that even the smallest spark of imagination would alert him to her presence. His shadow spread across the floor as he stepped in front of the fire, chafing himself vigorously. Then turning, he marched over to the table and reached for the ale cup, downing it in a single swallow. Her guess had been correct and a surge of relief went through her.

"Who's there?" he barked suddenly, his voice dark and menacing. She went cold, unable to move. Cold sweat trickled across her body.

He took a few steps into the room, muttering something under his breath. The cup suddenly flew into the wall, banging with a loud sound. It nearly made her cry out, but she did not. She saw the scuff marks on his boots. Normally they were quite polished. That was strange.

"Where is it?" he muttered darkly, swinging back to the desk.

She heard the cork pop free of another bottle and this one he held by the neck, taking a loud slurping draw from it. He slammed the bottle on the table, shoving the cask and scattering coins. Hettie tried to get a better look at him but decided it was not worth the risk of making noise. She heard him sigh deeply. He stood still a moment, breathing deeply. Then a glow began to illuminate the room, coming from his presence.

"I must speak with the Arch-Rike," Kiranrao said in a low voice. "I have a report."

He waited in silence, pausing occasionally to sip from the bottle. There was no answer, but he stood still. He cursed under his breath.

After an interminable wait that caused the hairs on the back of Hettie's neck to raise, a voice answered. "What is it?"

"You took your time," Kiranrao snarled.

"I was in a war council," came the terse reply. "What has happened?"

"I caught the Bhikhu."

"Paedrin?"

"Yes. Paedrin. He's as you described him. I've got him chained down in the training yard. I blinded him with the sword."

"What about the Cruithne?"

"He was found this morning, guarding a little skiff at the base. I doubt he will be able to climb this high. Leaving him be for now. He's a big brute, but mine can take him. Not a concern."

"Kill him. He's no use to me. What about the girl?"

"No sign of her."

"What?"

Hettie smirked. She was as still as a cat. Kiranrao swore softly again, his breath starting to quicken.

"No sign of her yet."

"She's the most dangerous of the three. Probably skulking nearby. Search for her. I'm sending over one of my Rikes to bring rings for Paedrin and Hettie. Then you can commence their Kishion training. Hopefully one of them will survive it."

A snort followed. "Who is your man? What is his name?"

"Aeldwyn," the Arch-Rike replied. "He will not stay long."

"When can I leave this cursed place?" Kiranrao's voice was almost begging. "You promised me—"

"I know very well what we agreed to. You are doing your part. Let me do mine."

"Ooogh," hissed Kiranrao, pain in his voice. "Aeldwyn will come soon? Very well. I will wait for him at the summoning chamber. Send more Stonehollow wine with him. The last batch of Waylander ale was spoiled, I think. Remember your promise."

Silence was the reply. The glow in the room faded.

"Blast my insides," he growled, wheezing suddenly. He muttered more under his breath, complaining that he had swallowed pins. Hettie stared at the shadow on the floor, watching him bowed over. He would realize it soon enough. But she had also heard enough to realize something herself. Comprehension dawned on her.

"Every moment it gets worse," he gasped. He sat back against the table, jarring the contents. He stiffened suddenly, bending double and wheezing loudly. "No," he gasped. "No . . . it can't be." Lurching forward, he staggered over to the other side of the room, over to the cabinet fixed onto the wall, near the bed, near the fallen blankets, near Hettie. He withdrew a key and unlocked it, pulling open the cupboard door violently. His fingers jittered as he fumbled through the vials of poison, searching.

"Gone," he whispered breathlessly. In shock and despair, he sat down on the bed, his weight pressing on the mattress, pressing on her.

Hettie plunged her dagger into the side of his knee and jerked the blade hard. He howled in pain and fell off the bed, his scream muffled by the blankets he collided with. Hettie struggled to free herself, clawing her way out as he thrashed in the blankets. Her heart pounded in her ribs, knowing she would not have long to bring her victim down.

As she swung herself free, she found him rising, holding up the scabbard, and saw the pommel begin to glow. She swept her cloak over the pommel and using a Bhikhu maneuver, she grabbed his wrist and then rammed her elbow against his extended forearm, dropping with her weight. It broke his arm and another scream ripped from his mouth. Hettie kicked him hard in the stomach, choking off his breath, and then jerked the scabbard away from him and tossed it to the far side of the room.

He was on one knee, his other bleeding profusely, his arm hanging loose at his side. His face was contorted in anguish. She slid another dagger free and kneed him in the chest, knocking him back against the cabinet, and then put the dagger to his throat.

"You are not Kiranrao," she said with disdain at the imposter. She knew what the real Kiranrao was capable of. "You are a drunk and a wretch, and you've been poisoned by monkshood, as you already know. I've stolen the cure and even if you managed to kill me, you will not find where I've hidden it. You will die, very soon, crumpled in pain and agony. If you wish to live, you will start answering my questions."

His eyes glittered with hatred, his mouth a snarl of enmity. "I'm bleeding to death."

"Hardly. The poison will probably kill you before that happens. You just won't be able to walk very well. Sit down on the bed." She grabbed him by the tunic front and shoved him on the bed. He gasped with pain as he collapsed.

She waved the dagger at him. "How can you wear Kiranrao's face? What magic gives the illusion?"

He licked his lips. "I wear a Druidecht talisman," he gasped. His face contorted and tears squeezed from his eyes. "The pain! Lass, it'll kill me soon!"

"Give me the talisman," she ordered, holding out her hand.

One of his arms was useless, but with the other, he reached up to his collar and she saw the cord she hadn't noticed before. He fished it from his shirt and she recognized the design from the one her brother wore.

"Take it off slowly." Her voice was full of menace. She hefted the dagger, ready to throw it.

His face contorted again and he began gasping.

"I swear, I will kill you right now and take it from you," she promised.

"Have you ever tasted monkshood?" he said savagely. "Oh by the gods, it hurts! The cramping. I swear it, lass, you will die. I will kill you. I will—"

"A postponement till morning is a postponement forever," she interrupted. "Give it over!"

He was reluctant. She could tell. But he could not see any other way and slid the talisman over his head. His entire body seemed to collapse upon itself, a grape shriveling into a raisin in moments. The illusion was gone. Sitting on the edge of the bed was a wiry Preachán. The only part of him that had not changed was the expression of absolute hate. She blinked in surprise at the complete metamorphosis. There was something familiar about him.

"It's you," she whispered, realizing the deep truth finally. He was from Havenrook. He was one of Kiranrao's closest men. He whipped the talisman around by the cord and it struck her on the side of the face. The metal bit hard, causing a rip of pain as her skin tore. The blow was so sudden and hard that she dropped her dagger. Suddenly he lunged at her, grabbing her shirtfront and pulling himself forward, his teeth widening to dig into her.

Hettie managed to bring her arm up in time and his teeth sank into her flesh, biting hard enough to shear through her skin. Their bodies tangled and they fought, each as desperate as a savage alley cat. Though her arm was bleeding she would not cry out with pain. She kneed him in the groin twice, dug her thumb into his eye, and finally managed to twist herself free from his terrible grasp. Grabbing the hair at the base of his scalp, she smashed his face into the floor. Blood exploded from his nose, the blow dazing him. Hettie found her fallen knife nearby, grabbed it, and brought it up to plunge into his back.

Only she did not.

The Preachán lay gasping on the floor, his body convulsing. His face was smeared with his own blood and hers. Her arm hurt from the bite marks. Gritting her teeth, she stared down at him.

"Kill me," he begged. "Do it! The Bhikhu should have killed me. He should have killed me in Havenrook. I killed them all. The whole temple. Please . . . you must kill me."

Hettie stared at him with loathing and understanding. This was the Preachán that Paedrin had fought defending Erasmus's house in Havenrook. A man whose arm was broken and blade claimed and then the spirit trapped inside was freed. The man who had come to Kenatos and poisoned the Bhikhu well with monkshood.

The man's eyes were full of desperation. "You are Romani," he said, his voice quavering with agony. "Kill me, or the Arch-Rike will."

Hettie noticed the Preachán's hand and saw the Kishion ring around his finger.

"Close your eyes then," Hettie ordered.

The man complied, his breath heaving with pain. Hettie grabbed his wrist, and pulled it away from his chest, exposing his heart.

"Answer my questions first and be quick. How does the talisman work?"

"You must know the person you intend to mimic. You must know them very well." He grunted with pain as the poison continued its terrible work. "A casual glimpse is not enough. You must know his voice, his mannerisms."

"Where did you get it?"

"The Arch-Rike. He wears one as well." He started to moan. "Quickly, lass!"

Hettie swallowed. "The Sword of Winds. Where is it?"

"On the floor where you threw it."

"Tell me about it."

"Little. I know little. Oh, the pain, lass. The pain!"

"Pity the Romani girls, not yourself. They live in fear of it. What of the sword?"

"Even in the sheath, it is powerful. With it, I can fly like a Vaettir. Even better . . . than a Vaettir. Faster. It is very fast. It cannot be drawn though. Only the champion can draw it. Anyone else who tries will be blinded. The stone in the hilt stings the eyes."

"Is the blindness permanent?" Hettie asked.

"No. The Bhikhu's vision will return. It's the Kishion test. To be the master here, one must wrestle the champion for the blade. No one can defeat the champion, though."

"Cruw Reon," Hettie said. "He's the champion. Where is he?"

"No one knows," the Preachán snarled. "No one dares to fight him. He's the Arch-Rike's champion. His bodyguard."

Hettie gasped. "The Quiet Kishion?"

"Yes. He's the master of the blade. He's the only one who can draw it without being blinded. I'm going to die anyway! Just end it now! Give me the blade. I'll do it myself. I don't want him in my mind. I don't want him spoiling me again. Please, girl! End it!"

Hettie grasped the Preachán's wrist, staring down at the iron ring on his finger. It was the same kind of ring that Paedrin had been forced to wear.

"Hold still," Hettie whispered.

The trembling Preachán sucked in his breath. He held as still as he could, though his body trembled.

With a quick stroke of the dagger, Hettie cut off his hand and tossed it beneath the bed.

The Preachán screamed in pain, his eyes open and livid. His face was a mask of shock and despair. Hettie grabbed a nearby blanket and stuffed it against his stump. With some cord from her backpack, she tied a tourniquet around the wound and sliced away the excess fabric. He began sobbing in pain and despair.

"Why won't you kill me?" he groveled. "I murdered them all at the Bhikhu temple. Even the young. The Arch-Rike swore he could remove the memory of it. He could take away the guilt."

Hettie found the discarded talisman and slipped it around her neck. Then she went to where the sword lay and strapped it to her belt. She stared down at the quivering Preachán, his face ashen. She tugged the small leather pouch from the side of her boot and withdrew a fleck of desiccated leaf and held it above his tongue.

"Just kill me," he whimpered. "I beg of you. If not with a knife or sword, let the poison do it, at least! I would rather die than live."

Hettie crouched lower, staring into his eyes. "If I were a Romani still, I would oblige you. But as you can see, I no longer wear the earring. I am free and so are you. I am a Bhikhu now. We do not seek revenge, even for the worst wrongs. Pain is a teacher. Let this pain teach you. What is your name, Preachán?"

His upper lip quivered. The hate seemed to leak from his eyes. "I am Janis-Stor. They call me Stor."

Hettie sheathed her dagger and placed the fleck of leaf on his tongue. "I spare your life, Janis-Stor. I will not kill you, though you are worthy of it. Go back to Havenrook and join your people. Fight the Arch-Rike's dominion. There is a rope dangling from the balcony facing the sea. Use it to claim your own freedom."

"You think I can climb like this?" he said bitterly, his face twisting with the futility. "Or swim?"

"You have a great strength of will," she replied. "You are relentless. Use it now for a better cause than greed." She touched the side of his face, trying to ignore the stinging pain in her own skin. "We seek to abolish the Plague. The Arch-Rike tries to thwart us. Through your failure here, you help us be successful. I pity you, Preachán. But I do not hate you."

His eyes closed and he started to sob.

Hettie stood and left him crumpled in the corner, weeping. Wearing the Druidecht talisman around her neck, she began to imagine herself looking like Kiranrao.

"I have heard that in moments of extreme terror and suspense, our minds can deliver to our aid a remedy for the situation if we have the courage not to flinch from it. Too often we are doomed to fail simply because we believe too quickly that we will."

—Possidius Adeodat, Archivist of Kenatos

XXXI

Erasmus was dead. It had happened so quickly that there was no time for Annon or Khiara to prevent it. Staring at the body of his fallen friend brought a swell of grief and a shattering earthquake of rage colliding inside Annon's chest. The serpents converged on him and he unleashed the fireblood in a torrent of flame, sweeping his arms around in a circle to scorch the ground in every direction. The serpents recoiled from the brightness, but he saw immediately that their scales were not harmed by it, just as the lizard-like guardians in the mountain pass had not been affected either. The rage turned to sudden icy terror. The Arch-Rike had prepared his defenses.

"Fly!" Annon shouted to Khiara.

"I won't leave you alone," she argued. "The flames are useless, let me try my staff." It was long and she swept it in against the serpents, striking at their flaring hoods and pin-prick fangs. The serpents struck at the staff, one latching onto it and slithering up the post. She brought it down hard, dislodging it.

"Behind us!" Annon warned desperately.

She pivoted the staff between her hands and swung it down in a sharp arc on the other side, crushing one of the serpents with the blow. Others hissed and struck at the staff again, coming closer to their boots. There were too many. They were too quick.

"Fly!" Annon said, grabbing Khiara's arm and shaking her.

Her eyes looked desperately into his.

"One of us needs to survive!" he pleaded. "One of us needs to warn the others."

He saw the determination in her eyes. With a quick motion, she struck another serpent with the butt of the staff, breaking its body. Then she inhaled and rose above Annon, but she gripped his hand with hers as she floated upward. He wondered if she would attempt to pull him up with her. It seemed impossible.

Don't move.

It was only the whisper of a thought. Khiara hovered in the air, her eyes closed, her mouth whispering words in a language he did not understand. He felt power surging from her into his skin, healing his injured shoulder, infusing him with life and vitality. Her whispers echoed through the circular chamber, sounding behind his eyelids, down to his very toes. The connection of her fingers against his was full of energy.

Don't move.

Annon saw the serpents gather at his feet, hoods flaring. He saw the little forked tongues and felt pure revulsion and fear threaten to unman him. He shut his eyes, unable to bear the suspense, wondering if the *keramat* that Khiara was performing would save him from the fangs and the poison. He waited to feel the needle-like fangs pierce his legs. He tamed the fireblood, knowing it was useless. There was no defense against such an attack.

A serpent slithered across the top of his boots. He wanted to shudder, but he willed himself still. Clenching his jaw, he dared not even breathe. He waited for the jolts of pain.

"Annon," Khiara whispered.

He would not speak. His jaw hurt from the pressure of his grinding teeth. Moments passed in silence. Another serpent slithered across his feet, one brushing against his ankle. He felt them continuously, snouts butting against his boots, prodding. He sank deep into himself, preserving the air in his lungs. His heart began to slow.

"They aren't striking," Khiara whispered. "They are searching for something. Searching for us. Annon, they cannot see us."

Annon opened his eyes. He almost wished he hadn't. There were probably a hundred or more. The floor of the room was a twisting, writhing mass.

Nizeera? Annon beckoned with his mind.

I am behind you, atop a tomb. They cannot strike me here. I am still.

Growl, Nizeera. Let them hear you. Tell me if they react to your noise.

He heard the low growl in her throat coming from behind him. The growl increased and then became a high-pitched shriek of anger. Annon stared at the twisting serpents, trying to see if any responded to it, but they did not. They were slithering randomly now, each serpent going its own way, prodding at the stones, tasting the air with their split tongues.

"They cannot hear us," Annon whispered. "For some reason, they cannot hear us." It was unnerving, feeling them glide around his body as if he were nothing but one of the stone columns in the room. "Nizeera, are you moving or still?"

"She is still as a stone," Khiara replied, still floating above Annon's head. Her body swayed slightly, up and down, as if she were floating in a pond. "Nizeera—move and see if they see you."

The serpents began to converge, darting around him and gliding purposefully to the object behind Annon. He did not turn his head to see, but he saw that the serpents were responding to something.

"They see her," Khiara said softly. "Nizeera, stop."

"What is happening?" Annon asked, feeling sweat trickle down his neck.

"She stopped pacing. The serpents are . . . their heads are coming back down. They are tall enough to strike her when roused. They are searching again. Movement, Annon. They respond to movement, not sound."

"Test it again," Annon said. "Nizeera—growl again but do not move."

She growled from behind, the sound a threatening and menacing one.

"No change," Khiara said. "They cannot hear us."

"Or see us only so long as we do not move," Annon reminded her. "It forestalls our death but does not eliminate the risk. I can't remain standing here forever. I see a bier on my left . . . how far is it away?"

"There are snakes between you and it, many of them," Khiara replied. "They are everywhere and they are quite tall when roused. I don't think it would protect you. There is the broken sarcophagus over there, though. That one might if you could make it inside. Where were they hiding before?"

In the walls, Nizeera thought with a low growl. *I could sense them but not understand what it was. They began to enter soon after the Rike perished.*

Annon thought a moment. "Nizeera says they were hiding in the walls. Obviously there are other chambers here. They must be fed somehow. Something keeps them at bay—" The thought bloomed in his mind, the distinct memory. "Of course! The Rike wearing the torc! He was the leader, I think. The torc repels creatures. It kept Nizeera from attacking him. It keeps all creatures at bay." A surge of hope and joy sprung into his senses, causing a thrilling wave. "Yes! I remember hearing Tyrus talk about the creatures of the Scourgelands. They are terrible to face, quite vicious. That torc repels them. This allows the Arch-Rike or whoever he sends to enter the Scourgelands unharmed. It also keeps the serpents from entering the room. Once he died, its power failed—"

"The serpents were no longer barred from coming in," Khiara finished. "He said we were going to die. He knew the snakes would come and bite us."

"The doors leading back the way we came are locked from the outside," Annon said. "They were barred. The only way forward is to enter the Scourgelands."

Annon's upper lip was salty with sweat. He glanced around the dimly-lit chamber. This entire place was a deception. It was also a gateway. He understood why the Arch-Rike had guarded it so carefully. There were secrets here that he could not figure out. The Rike had mentioned that he thought they were seeking Poisonwell. Annon did not know what that meant, but logic told him it probably had something to do with the Plague. Each sarcophagus was chiseled with the herald and name of one of the kingdoms surrounding Kenatos. Erasmus had figured out what they all meant. But he had died before he could explain himself.

"Annon?" Khiara asked.

"Sorry, I was thinking," he replied. "We need to get that torc somehow. It is important. It may be crucial. Nizeera, can you jump to another bier? Maybe you can distract them and have them follow you away from us. If you can clear the ground here a moment, I might be able to get the torc."

"The biers are not very close together," Khiara said. "If she missed, she would land in the middle of them. Let me do this. If I shove away from you, I can drift to the other side of the chamber."

"Be careful, Khiara."

Nizeera growled. *I can make the jump.*

Let her try, Annon thought in response. *Please, Nizeera. Trust me. I have failed you.*

He grit his teeth, feeling the blackness of her feelings. *You are helpless against these forces. It is not your fault. Courage, Nizeera. You will aid me in the Scourgelands. We must survive this first.*

The growl in reply was sullen, but did not argue.

Khiara pushed off from Annon's shoulder and floated away from him. Using her staff like a ferry pole, she maneuvered away from a nearby column and then came to land on a carved sarcophagus lid. She straightened, setting her balance. Then she swished the staff around in a broad circle, again and again. The serpents hissed and converged on her, slithering in haste to reach her. A broad smile passed on Annon's mouth. Many of the serpents went over his boots and around him to reach her. There were still too many nearby to risk moving.

"They followed me," Khiara said. "I will go farther."

"Be careful," Annon pleaded. His knees and ankles were restless.

With another gulp of air, he watched her lift off and soar across the chamber to another bier, even farther away. When she landed there, she began circling the staff again, in long broad sweeps. The serpents attacked again, slithering straight toward her with ferocity. The floor by Annon was nearly bereft of the creatures. He waited, watching them writhe toward her, as if hypnotized by her gleaming pale staff. She stopped suddenly, bewildering the serpents and then leapt again, moving to the next stone lid.

There were only three serpents nearby, all three of them investigating Erasmus's body. Annon stared at them, willing them to follow their brethren away. Khiara began sweeping her staff in circles again, drawing the snakes to the farthest portion of the chamber. He could make her out in the dim light, but only barely. The three serpents were not following the others. In his mind, he summoned the words to tame fire and then brought a small orb of blue flames into his hand. He stared at the pulsing colors and then noticed all three serpents had stopped and were staring at him. He released it, tossing it over them and watching as it rolled across the stone like a magical ball. The three serpents hovering around Erasmus rushed at it, hissing and striking at the flames, though each was unhurt by it.

As they streaked away, Annon watched for signs of others. Finding none, he moved, walking swiftly to the fallen body of the Rike who had been crushed by the sarcophagus lid. Dried blood had formed a rivulet on his cheek. Annon glanced up at Khiara and saw snakes had spied his movement and were coming at him, slithering across the stone swiftly.

He grasped the cold metal of the torc and then twisted it around so that the open ends were in the back of the man's neck, facing the floor, instead of being open at his collar. Being so near the corpse made bile rise in Annon's throat.

A prick of danger in his mind warned him too late. Nizeera growled and screamed and launched herself from the bier. He heard her land behind him, whipped his head around in time to see her snatch a serpent in her teeth and then hurl it away. He saw the bristling fur, the rage in her eyes as she faced the advancing serpents, planting her claws forward defensively.

Annon grasped the ornamental torc with both hands and yanked with all his strength. It was a tight fit around the Rike's neck and resisted. Planting his foot down on the dead man's back, he pulled a second time, wresting it free. It came loose suddenly and he flew backward, colliding with the sharp edge of the broken sarcophagus. Pain caused spots to dance in his eyes.

"Nizeera, go!" he shouted, scrambling to his feet.

The great cat hissed and struck at another serpent, catching it with her claws and flinging it aside.

"Nizeera!" he shouted again, springing up and inside the sarcophagus, clutching the torc to his body. She raced away and vaulted up onto another carved lid, her tail lashing triumphantly once before falling perfectly still. He felt the surge of pride come because she had risked herself for him as well a flood of relief. Their emotions were always mixed together.

"Do you have it?" Khiara called from afar.

"Yes," Annon said, smiling. He stared down at the twisting design, made of bronze it appeared. The symbols were more decorative than arcane, but the look was ancient and had many nicks and scratches. There were two blue gems, shaped as polished spheres, set into each end. Staring closely at them, he could see swirling mist inside each, and little fireflies of magic within. He wished he could hear the spirits trapped inside.

I will free you, he promised. *When our journey is through, I will free you. I will free all of you.*

He stared at the torc, wondering if he should put it on himself. He remembered how Paedrin had been overcome when putting on a ring the Arch-Rike had given him. He wondered if he would even be able to control its magic.

There was a grinding noise nearby. Annon's head jerked suddenly at the sound as one of the doors they had entered through was dragged open.

"Annon!" shouted a familiar voice, thick with fear and dread. It was Lukias.

He saw the Rike emerge into the chamber, his face wet with sweat, his expression tortured with worry. The serpents began to converge on him.

"Lukias!" Annon shouted. "The serpents! Shut the door!"

"You survived? By Seithrall you are blessed! Do you have the torc? It repels the snakes."

"Yes, but they are coming at you! Their venom is—"

"—Fatal, I know! Use the torc. The activation word is Iddawc. Put it on, now!"

Annon stared at the Rike, cringing by the door. He then stared at the torc in his hand. Would it harm him to wear it? Would it subvert him? He did not know. Erasmus had given his life for their quest. He was willing to do the same. The snakes slithered with a frenzy to reach Lukias. The door was ajar. Had Lukias truly come to save them? Or was he there as a spy to reclaim the Arch-Rike's treasures? He did not have time to reason things through. He needed to trust his own judgment and take a risk.

"Nizeera," Annon shouted, loud enough so that Khiara could hear him as well. "If the torc harms me or my mind, keen three times." Inside his mind, he thought to Nizeera, *Then help Khiara escape this place of death.*

Annon felt the great cat panic as he fastened the torc around his own neck.

"There are reports that the Arch-Rike has made an embassy outside the city. This is a rare occurrence and a sign of the gravity of the situation. His personal ship left the port before dawn and was seen to be sailing westward. He is a great pragmatist and I am certain he would not have left the city himself unless his own persuasive voice was necessary to interrupt the war's violence. I have not found a more moral being than the Arch-Rike of Kenatos. A moral being, by my definition, is one who is capable of reflecting on his past actions and their motives—of approving of some and disapproving of others. He is always learning."

—Possidius Adeodat, Archivist of Kenatos

XXXII

The torc was cold around Annon's neck. Breathing heavily and fighting off a wave of sudden nausea, he waited in the echoes of his own mind for some sign of power or acknowledgement of the beings trapped inside the device. Finding none, and feeling himself quite alone in his thoughts, he invoked the command word.

Iddawc.

The taste of the word in his mind invoked feelings and memories: the cold dark well of Drosta's Lair. The ravening hunger to kill that came from the blade he had taken. Cold sweat gathered across his brow. The word Iddawc contained fear, like a man cupping poisoned water in his hands and about to drink of it. Invoking the word in his mind made Annon shudder.

The blue gems in the torc began to glow dimly.

He felt the stirring of energy, the portent of power. The metal of the torc was uncomfortably hot. He felt the gathering power; the sudden surge brought tingling gooseflesh down his arms. The serpents recoiled. Nizeera's mind went black with fear and she crouched, head low, tail limp, ears flat. The serpents fled the circular chamber, disappearing into small crevices made from the designs on the lower edge of the wall near the floor that had been invisible before. In moments, not a single serpent remained.

"Well done," Lukias said triumphantly, breathing a sigh of relief and staring at Annon. "I knew you would tame it easily. What a gift you have, that strength of will. Not many could have done that, Annon."

Khiara floated down and came forward, her expression wary. She approached Annon and touched his cheek with the back of her hand, as if testing for a fever. "Tell me your name."

"Annon of Wayland," he said. "What is it, Khiara? My mind is my own."

"Can you prove that?" she asked, her expression darkening. She rounded on Lukias. "How did you get here?"

He held up a hand calmingly. "You feel aggressive. It is the magic from the torc. It affects us differently than the beasts. I feel it myself. My heart is racing. I have the urge to smash something. It is a physical reaction to the torc's power. When the serpents are beyond its radius of influence, the power will lessen."

She scowled and took a step toward the Rike. "Answer my question. How did you get here?"

"I freed myself from the bonds. It took a while, as you can imagine. Erasmus was thorough. I had a choice to make. Face the Arch-Rike and perish or help you escape. The Arch-Rike is here in Basilides. There are at least fifty soldiers immune to fire marching this way. If you wish to live, as I do, we must go. This instant."

A shiver of dread went through Annon. "The Arch-Rike is here?"

"I assure you that he is here in person. Basilides is a carefully guarded secret, Annon. When you overcame it, he summoned his personal legion to fight you. I will take my chances with Tyrus and the rest of you. We must go. Now!" He gestured at them with his open palms.

Annon swung his legs over the rim of the sarcophagus. "I do not wish to do this, but I think the only way to escape will be through those doors." He pointed to the ones across the room with the markings that said BASILIDES. "It leads into the Scourgelands."

"It does," Lukias answered gruffly, shaking his head and holding up his hands warningly. "It is death to cross that gate. There is another way out."

"Where?" Khiara asked.

"The same way the Arch-Rike arrived. There is magic here—a portal controlled by Tay al-Ard spirits. The soldiers are arriving through it as we speak. I noticed you survived the Calcatrix lair by extinguishing the light spheres. Clever move. Darkness is the way to cross that way unharmed. The chamber is vast. If we can get there quickly, we can hide and wait for the soldiers to pass. There will be a few left to guard the way back, of course, but between us I think it won't be a problem. We reach the Tay al-Ard and then go."

"Where?" Annon asked.

"Wherever you desire," Lukias replied with a grin. "It can only take you somewhere you have been before. You will choose the destination, Annon." He pursed his lips. "I see by your expressions you still doubt me. How else can I prove my loyalty? If I wanted you captured, I would have only done nothing. The torc was the only way to escape the serpents. I gave you the activation word." He tossed his hands. "What else can I do? The soldiers are coming. If we argue much longer, we are all dead."

Annon glanced at Khiara. Her expression was still fierce but it was slowly calmed as her thoughts conceded his points. She nodded curtly.

"Lead on," Annon said. He shoved the outer doors open all the way and released his mental control of the torc, allowing the stones to cool and subside. "The chamber will be swarming with snakes in a moment. We best hurry."

Lukias gave him a cunning smile and shook his head. "I hadn't even thought of that. Well done. Come."

With the release of the torc's magic, Nizeera padded off the stone lid and came after them as they exited. Feeling the urgency of the moment, they proceeded to run back to the Calcatrix chamber. Annon sent Nizeera ahead to scout and she willingly did, darting ahead of the others with her longer stride. It was still shut and she waited while they caught up.

They reached the doors and stopped to catch their breath. Annon wiped sweat from his brow and listened at the door. A pang of sadness stabbed him, realizing that Erasmus was no longer with them. A prediction would have been handy at the moment. He shoved aside the mounting grief and pulled at the doors, leading into darkness.

"Take my hands," Lukias said, offering his to both of them. "I know the safe path in the dark. The cat can smell us easy enough. We need to hide quickly."

As the door shut behind them, they were immersed in utter blackness. Their boots crunched on the broken shards from the glass spheres. Lukias took them to the right, keeping along the edge of the wall. Each step echoed on the cold stone. Above, they heard the flutter of wings and a sickly clucking sound from the creatures lurking above. Hisses came as well. Annon remembered the pain from their talons and started to tremble.

"Sshhh," Lukias warned, slowing. "Do you hear it?"

They come, Nizeera thought to Annon. *The ground trembles with it.*

"They are almost here," Annon whispered.

"Against the wall and crouch low. We dare not move with all the glass."

They all hunkered down in the darkness. Moments later, light split the wall across the chamber, knifing into their eyes. Annon shielded his face, his breath quickening. A mass of leather-hard boots clomped into the room. A few held strange torches, not made of pitch or flame, but with a strange crystal at the top. The light did not radiate, strangely, but seemed to gather like honey to a stick. They heard a voice warn to follow the lead lights and not wander off. The sound of marching men filled the chamber, causing wave after wave of vibration to tremble the floor. The scraping and grating of the broken shards ground beneath dozens of boots caused an uncomfortable shiver up Annon's spine. Mutters and oaths came from the mass of men. Links from hauberks jingled. The cooing from the Calcatrix above intensified, as if they were hungry for human flesh below, but could not see.

The marching reached the far doors and again light spilled into the chamber. Annon caught a glimpse of a black cassock and silver hair. The marching continued and then the doors closed and darkness reigned again.

"Good," Lukias whispered at last. "It will not take long for them to reach the other chamber. We must go."

Lukias pulled on their hands and they rose and quickly walked along the outer edge. "I will let go of your hands now," Lukias said. "I need to feel for the door. We can't risk missing it. Follow my footsteps." Once the grip was lost, Annon felt like a ship without a rudder. He grabbed Khiara's arm so that the two of them wouldn't stumble against each other in the dark. Nizeera prowled behind Lukias until he found the gap in the stone he was looking for.

"Over here," he offered.

They joined him just as the crack of light appeared again, blinding them. Annon saw Lukias's shadow on the floor and followed as he exited the chamber. The hallway beyond was deserted.

"How did you manage to survive it?" Lukias asked over his shoulder at them, his eyebrows raised curiously. "Most people would have looked at the creatures attacking them and been turned to stone first. Did someone warn you?"

Annon shook his head. "It was Druidecht lore, actually," he answered. They all walked at a fast-paced clip. "I remembered it in time."

Lukias snorted. "You have quite a memory. But then Druidecht are known for their good memories. You must memorize the lore, after all. This way—the tunnel branches off. It is a maze that few know the passages through."

They walked swiftly, feeling the tension and dread of knowing soldiers were behind them. Annon sighed, wishing he had done something else to delay the Arch-Rike. "We should have decoyed them," he said, frowning. "If we had opened the bars leading to the Scourgelands, it may have tricked them into thinking we had gone in there. With the doors barred, they will know we did not."

Lukias glanced back at him again. "You use the Uddhava as well? Impressive. But then, you traveled with a Bhikhu. I'm sure he taught you."

"He did." Annon glanced back the way they came. He asked Nizeera to keep them alerted of pursuit.

"It is not much farther," Lukias said.

Annon glanced back one more time and when they turned the corner, they saw three Rikes standing in a small cluster in front of a massive wooden door. It startled all of them.

"Ah!" Lukias said, raising his hand to hail them. "There you are! There was some trouble with the soldiers crossing the Calcatrix Lair. What a mess that was left. Do you have any more of the light sticks? All of the orbs have been broken."

"Who are you?" one of them asked, a grizzled fellow with a gray stripe in the front of his beard. "Are you from Kenatos? I didn't see you—"

Lukias struck the man in the stomach with his fist and then squeezed his inner arm with his fingers, making him yelp with pain. Khiara brought her staff around, dropping the second man before he could move. The third reached for a cylinder in his robes and found Nizeera's jaws clamped down on his wrist. Then Khiara struck him in the skull as well and he fell to the floor.

Lukias shoved the Rike he had captured into the door. "How many came from Kenatos?" he hissed angrily.

"You traitor!" the other Rike snarled, his eyes livid.

He struggled for a moment, but Lukias slammed him again. "Answer me, or you'll wish you had."

"There were fifty, fool. Do you think the Arch-Rike will let you live after this, Lukias? You are the world's greatest fool."

Lukias kneed him in the groin and the man collapsed in a whimpering mass on the floor. He brushed his hands and yanked open the door, waving them to join him.

Annon stared at the hateful eyes of the Rike on the floor as he passed him.

They are coming, Nizeera warned. *Running.*

"Quickly," Annon said, shutting the door behind them. He glanced around the room. It was not very large. A few stone benches were set against the walls. On the far side was a black onyx platform with silver runes carved into it. It was wide enough for five or so across, no more. In the center of the onyx floor hung a black iron lantern, fixed from a rung in the ceiling on an enormous heavy chain. There were no glass slats on the lantern, only immense stays. In the center of the lantern was a brass cylinder, not unlike the one Annon had seen Tyrus use. It was fastened into the lantern, suspended in the middle. Only by reaching through the slats could people grab it. Annon realized that it also prevented anyone from stealing it.

"It is a Tay al-Ard," Lukias said, approaching it swiftly. "Only five or six can surround it at a time. Join me on the stone." He stepped onto the onyx platform and crossed to the center. Khiara glanced at Annon and he nodded and followed himself. Nizeera stared at the door and a low growl sounded from her.

"Nizeera," Annon beckoned. He strode to the suspended lantern.

"You think about a place you have been," Lukias said. "As long as you have been there personally, it will take you there. You lead us, Annon. Where do we go?"

Annon looked at Khiara. "Silvandom?"

Lukias shook his head before Khiara did. "The Arch-Rike has been there, remember? You want to go to a place where he cannot immediately follow us. A place of safety. Quickly, Annon. Decide." He glanced at the door.

Annon reached through the bars and grasped the cylinder. It was scalding hot and he jerked his hand away, banging his fingers on the bars.

"Hot!" he said in amazement.

"No," Lukias said. "Cold. But your body reacts as if it were heat." He looked at the door again, his expression quickening to a look of panic. "A Tay al-Ard needs time to rest between uses. If the Arch-Rike brought fifty through here, it is well spent."

"How long must it rest?" Annon asked.

"We don't have time," Lukias said. "Abide the pain. We must leave!"

Annon stared at the cylinder. He had never been burned before. He was not familiar with the sensation. His palm tingled where he had touched it.

"Do this, Annon," Khiara said, her eyes full of trust. She put her arm on his. Lukias did the same.

The sound of boots echoing down the corridor grew louder. From behind the door, they heard the muffled cries of the Rike they had sprawled on the ground. "In there! Quickly! They are inside!"

Annon stared at the Tay al-Ard. He reached through the bars again, his arm heavy with the added weight of their hands. Nizeera pressed against his leg and he gripped the skin above her neck with his other hand.

Closing his eyes, he clenched the cylinder, experiencing the freezing burn of the Tay al-Ard explode up his arm and thought of a place of safety. A place he longed for more than anywhere else.

He thought of Neodesha's tree.

The door shuddered open on its hinges as the world lurched and began to spin.

"Hear the other side. What is usually lacking, when there is trouble, is the lack of listening. So quick we are to rush to judgment. We would do well to listen more. There would be far fewer disputes."

—Possidius Adeodat, Archivist of Kenatos

XXXIII

The look of alarm and misery on the Dryad's face wrung Phae's heart. She rushed to the other girl, clutching her arms. "What is it? What do you see?"

The other girl's eyes were wide with terror. "I cannot see it. It is what I feel. Memories flitting through the aether, summoned here because of the bond we share." She gripped Phae's forearms with surprising strength for one so slight. "He may die! Annon, be still. Be very still." The girl shrank against the trunk of the oak, huddling small, like an acorn. Phae lowered with her, still holding the girl as if she were one of Dame Winemiller's orphans.

"Who is it?" Phae asked, stroking her shoulder.

The girl shuddered as the memories assailed her. "A moment. There is danger. So much danger. If he dies, I will know it. Our bond will be severed." She put her face in her hands and wept softly.

Phae hugged her, nestling against the bark of the tree, feeling wave after wave of emotion passing from the Dryad. She was quiet herself, just being there to comfort the girl—her sister in some strange way. The wind rustled through the trees, bringing the smell of soot and forest. They hugged each other, sharing the lack of words, the surging feelings. In time, the Dryad's panic began to ebb.

"Thank you." The girl patted Phae's arm. "Normally I am the one who comforts. The threat is still there, but I do not sense the same fear. He has survived the danger for now."

Phae bit her lip. "It must be awful to feel such premonitions but be unable to help."

The girl shook her head. "I can help, in a small way. If he is calm in his heart, my thoughts can reach his mind. The talisman he wears aids in this. The Druidecht have always been our fiercest guardians. We need them, you see. They are the way we can be free of our duty."

Their voices were soft, nearly whispers. "He can free you by marrying him, is that how it is?" Phae asked solemnly, eyes downcast with embarrassment.

The girl smiled. "It is not as you probably fear. Annon saved my tree when the Boeotians came to hack it down. His friend perished, right over there. He could have fled. We share a special bond. I'm not sure it has grown yet into love." Dimples appeared within a timid smile.

"How old are you?"

The Dryad looked at her as if she had asked a strange question. "Age means nothing to me anymore. How many leaves are in a forest? Does it matter? Why bother counting them?"

Phae shook her head. "Is it . . . miserable at times, being Dryad-born? Are you very lonely here in the woods?"

The girl straightened, her look turning to amusement. "You misunderstand a great deal. I guard this portal. I control access to who may pass and who may not. I protect memories. But I do not live here. My home is Mirrowen. When someone approaches my tree, I sense their presence. To me, a year passes quickly, like a moment. A man may age and die in a single day. I am never lonely. There are my sisters, of course, to keep me company. And there are others who have earned the right to live in Mirrowen. And then there is the Seneschal." She lowered her voice reverently.

"What is that?" Phae asked, leaning forward.

"The Seneschal is a title—it is an ancient title. It means the oldest servant. He holds the Voided Keys. He is the one you must see if you are to accept your powers. He is the one who will perform your oath. He will bind you to your tree with a Key." The Dryad reached out and gently brushed a lock of Phae's hair away from her face.

"Does the Seneschal have a name?"

The girl nodded. "He will tell it to you. I cannot speak it." She sat straighter, looking worriedly into Phae's eyes. "So you are the one who was chosen? You would enter the vast Scourgelands and seek our fallen sisters? You must awaken them to the oaths they made. We do not speak of what happened. Only the Seneschal remembers it and he does not say. It is a great sadness, I think. The younger ones, like myself, have asked. The knowledge is lost to all of us."

Phae nodded slowly. She felt so comfortable with the Dryad. "What can you teach me? I know so little about us."

"I should fetch your mother. It is proper that she should teach you."

"I would like to see her," Phae said, her heart swelling with emotion. Tears pricked her eyes.

"Then I will seek her. I will be gone but a moment."

Phae blinked and the girl was gone. Startled, she stared at the spot where the Dryad had been. Slowly, Phae stood, trying to quell the sudden tremor that started in her knees. She longed to see her mother. A burning ache began to swell inside her heart. Phae grazed the bark with her fingers, staring down at the fallen leaves, waxy acorns, and stubble. Another breeze stirred the air, sounding like a sigh. Phae shivered.

The Dryad girl reappeared around the side of the oak, her face downcast.

A stab of pain struck Phae's heart. "She did not come?"

The girl shook her head slowly. "She cannot leave her tree, even for a moment. It is dying, Phae. The air and pollution of Kenatos is choking its life. Her presence is the only thing helping it survive. She must stay to preserve your father's memories. If she leaves, even for a moment, the tree will die and she will be banished from this world." With a look of sorrow, the girl approached and gave Phae a hug. "She bid me embrace you. And she charged me to instruct you in her stead." She kissed Phae on the top of her head. "She loves you, sister. More than I can express."

Tears spilled from Phae's eyes, and she caught them on the edge of her sleeve. "I wish I could go to her," she whispered mournfully. "I told my father to take me to Kenatos."

The Dryad shook her head vehemently. "There you must not go. The air is sick. I could smell it in her bark. Her tree is just a husk now. There are so few leaves and only a few sprigs of mistletoe left. She clings to its life, to preserve the connection with your father. To give him the wisdom he needs to fulfill the task."

Phae bit her lip, nodding. "It is my task now as well. Tell me what I need to know."

The two girls held hands and lowered back to the base of the oak. "It may sound strange to you, but I will do my best to describe our world. You should have been taught this as a child. If you had, it would have been easier to believe. You must trust me. Things may seem strange to you at first. Do not let your natural doubts crowd out the truth of what I say. All right?"

Sighing deeply, Phae nodded, clinging to the girl's warm hands.

"Let me teach you first of Mirrowen. It is the gateway to the lands beyond the reach of death. There is no death in Mirrowen. It does not exist there. How can I describe it? It is like a kingdom . . . no, that is not the right word. It is like a manor house only more beautiful than any king could construct. There are no bastions or walls or gates. There are gardens and bridges and waterfalls. There is no night. Every tree produces the most precious fruit. The flowers and plants are beautifully tended by the Seneschal. There are other servants, of course. But . . . that is not what they really are. Many are Dryad-born, like us. Some are spirit creatures who serve the Seneschal because they choose to do so."

"What is he like?" Phae asked.

The girl bit her lip, her expression pinching in thought. "He is very tall. He looks similar to a Vaettir, except his hair is not black but a dark brown. He is ageless, eternally young. He is wise. So very, very wise. When you speak with him, you learn something new every time. He is patient. Mostly though, he is meek. Do you know anyone who is meek?"

Phae's brow wrinkled. "I'm not sure I even know that word. It is not a common trait in Stonehollow, I think."

The girl laughed softly. "No, it is not common in this world at all. It is difficult to describe. He does not anger quickly. But when he does, when he is disappointed, you feel it in your bones. He is patient though. You gain patience tending gardens."

"So the Seneschal is a gardener then?" Phae asked, shrugging.

The Dryad smiled knowingly. "In a way. You see, the garden he tends is very precious. There is a tree. The fruit of that tree is what makes us immortal. He decides who can pluck a fruit from the tree."

Phae's eyes widened.

"Don't let your doubt cover your eyes," the girl said. "What I say is true. I have partaken of that fruit. It is . . . bitter. So very bitter. But it changes you. When you eat it, your body no longer ages. That allows you to dwell in Mirrowen and this world. In order to earn a piece of that fruit, you must perform an oath in front of the Seneschal and accept the responsibility of preserving the portal and the tree's memories. The responsibility passes from mother to daughter. A Dryad can never bear a son. When you have found a man you deem worthy, you can make him your husband. You fashion a bracelet around your ankle as a token of that vow. It ends with the man's death. When you have a child, you train her to make the oath and take your place. As I said before, time is not the same to me as it is to you. Kingdoms come and go. I was here before the Vaettir arrived. I am ready, I think, to pass on my knowledge to a daughter."

Phae's heart was swarming with conflicting feelings. What she heard sounded preposterous in some ways. But she did not speak her doubts openly and stared at the Dryad. She patted the girl's hand, thinking of a thousand questions.

"Why is the fruit bitter?"

"I don't know. It just is."

"I know I can steal memories. I have that power now. How do I embed them into a tree?"

The girl smiled. "When you make the oath, the Seneschal will kiss your forehead. When he does, your memory will be perfect only so long as the tree lives. Your responsibility to guard and care for it isn't permanent. When you pass on the duty to your daughter, you will not be able to take all those memories with you. The burden will pass to another."

Phae's brow wrinkled. "And I will have the power to restore someone else's memories? You said that you could do it with a Dryad's kiss, but it is—"

"It can be loathsome, yes. If a man has saved your tree from destruction, you owe him a boon. It is a debt that must be fulfilled. If he lingers for one day, you must appear to him. If he looks at you, then you can steal his memories and he will forget the debt and leave. If he does not look at you, then you must give him your true name. That is the name that the Seneschal gives you. With it, the man can force you to obey him. That is why we try to trick the man into looking at us and make him forget. A man with that power over us can prevent us from fulfilling our duty. It would prevent us from returning to Mirrowen." She shuddered. "That is why the Druidecht guard this lore so carefully, to prevent the young ones from taking advantage of us. Wisdom comes with age not with youth. If you give the man your name, you may give him a Dryad's kiss, which allows him to bond with you and gain access to your thoughts as well as your perfect memory. If he dies, the connection ends. If the tree is destroyed, it is also severed.

She squeezed Phae's arm sadly. "This is why Tyrus of Kenatos seeks you to enter the Scourgelands. There are Dryads there who are bound to this world and no longer visit Mirrowen. Their trees are ancient, as old as the world when it began. They are cut off from Mirrowen now and are poisoned with hate. They will not speak with us. If you can find the mother tree, the one who controls all the others in the forest, you can enter Mirrowen there and seek the fallen Dryad and remove her burden. That would give you the knowledge Tyrus seeks. No doubt she contains many secrets and many mysteries."

Phae felt a surge of alarm. "But what if she does not relinquish it? What if she refuses? Does she have that choice?"

The Dryad nodded. "She must willingly give it to you. She may well be mad by now." She cupped Phae's cheek. "There is great risk in this journey. The Scourgelands are guarded by evil spirits that act as sentinels to keep away the living. They will try to kill you, even though you are Dryad-born."

Sighing in despair, Phae wiped her face, her emotions churning. The possibility of success was even more remote than she believed. They would have to fight their way deep into the Scourgelands, surrounded on all sides by enemies seeking her death. How would they even find that mother tree? Would they have to search every tree in the forest? How long would that take?

"You are despairing," the girl said softly. "I feel it in you."

"This quest feels impossible," Phae murmured.

She shook her head. "No, sister. When Tyrus ventured into the Scourgelands last time, it was impossible. Despite his failure, he gained the key he needed. Through patience and cunning, he has arranged for you to succeed where he failed. It will be difficult. It will be the most difficult thing you ever do."

Phae bit her lip. "I wish I could have met my mother." She sighed again, feeling the tears sting her eyes.

"You will," the Dryad promised, tears glistening on her lashes. "When her charge is complete, when her tree finally succumbs to death, as all trees must eventually, she will be free to join you in Mirrowen. She has earned her place there."

Smiling, Phae reached out and hugged the other girl. It was a mote of hope. A tiny little speck. But it was something.

"Could I enter Mirrowen from your tree?" Phae asked, staring at the bark, wincing at the damage done to it by a vicious axe.

"No, not yet," the Dryad replied. "Only those oath-bound may enter Mirrowen through a Dryad tree. You are not oath-bound yet." She clasped Phae's hand between hers. "I sense in you that your power is fully ripe. You are sixteen, or will be soon. If you do not take the oath by that time, you will not be able to enter Mirrowen at all. You must choose this life or abandon it forever. It must be your choice, freely made."

Phae breathed through her nose, smelling the fragrances of the woods around her. It was not Stonehollow. She would miss the beauty of her homeland. But perhaps the wonders of Mirrowen would surpass it? She hoped so.

"I make the choice," Phae said. "If it can prevent the death of innocents, I will do so."

The other Dryad smiled proudly at her. Then her eyes widened suddenly and she sat up straight, blinking rapidly. "He's here," she whispered, her voice filling with delight. "I sensed him enter the woods. He is coming this way!"

"Who is?" Phae asked, rising with the other girl as she rushed to her feet.

"Annon, my Druidecht," she said, her eyes shining. "How did he get here so quickly? He was leagues away." The girl's fingers dug into Phae's arm, her expression darkening. "There are others with him. I sense powerful magic coming from him. I cannot be seen." She bit her lip, staring into the woods toward the sound of crunching foliage.

Shion appeared in the ring of trees and his presence made the Dryad vanish. He strode up to Phae purposefully, his hand on a dagger hilt. "Come, others approach," he whispered, pulling her by the arm away from the tree.

He had that dangerous look in his eyes again, the look that made her insides shrivel with fear. It was a look that said he would kill anyone who tried to hurt her. She wondered, deep down, if she would ever be free of him.

"There is a great Bhikhu proverb that I have always admired:
I found thee not without, Wisdom, because I erred in

seeking without what was already within."

—*Possidius Adeodat, Archivist of Kenatos*

XXXIV

As Paedrin slowly became conscious, he was immediately aware that he was blind and that the blindness hurt. The pain was so intense that he feared his eyes had been gouged out and sought to touch his face to verify it, only he could not. His wrists were bound in iron shackles, his arms bent backward around a stone column. His chin rested against his breast and he felt drops of sweat or blood coming from his chin. His ravaged eyes were excruciating and he began to cough.

For a moment, he could not remember what had happened or how he had come to be trapped in chains. Then the images came back into his mind, darting like spiders and sinking their fangs into his mind. Kiranrao was at the Kishion training yard. He possessed the Sword of Winds. Everything they believed about him had been a lie. Paedrin flexed his arm muscles, testing the strength of the chain and the amount of slack. He heard the metal scrape against the stone, allowing him to shift slightly.

Pain was a teacher.

Paedrin wondered what lesson he was going to learn this time. Had they truly blinded him? Or was it magic of some sort that caused the pain? His breath became ragged gasps, his shoulder convulsing with the suppressed agony. He would not cry out again. He would bear it like a Bhikhu.

He heard footsteps in the yard. Several sets, in fact, the sound of training.

"You are too slow," he heard the man say. "Lower! Feel the stretch in your calves. Push harder! Lower that stance. Lower! The Arch-Rike's emissary is coming. He must see you working harder."

The voice seared Paedrin's mind. Kiranrao.

It was Kiranrao who had freed him from the Arch-Rike's dungeon. The legend was that he was the only man who had ever stolen from the Arch-Rike and survived to flaunt the exploit. How had they missed his treachery all along? It was brutally clear now. When the battle had commenced with the Arch-Rike's forces in Silvandom, Kiranrao had vanished after Tyrus had given him the blade Iddawc. It was a weapon that Kiranrao craved above all others. But he had stolen it the second time for the Arch-Rike.

Paedrin hung his head, jaw clenched, suffering the pain.

"The Bhikhu," someone said. "He's rousing."

"It does not matter. Leave him be," Kiranrao said condescendingly. "A nod is as good as a wink to a blind donkey, eh? And as the Romani say, a secret is a weapon and a friend."

Paedrin almost replied with a biting retort, but he was afraid to open his mouth. He tested the chains again, feeling the hardness, the implacability of his situation. He was surrounded by enemies. The Arch-Rike's minion was coming for him, most likely to place a ring around his finger and bind him with a curse of service.

Never.

Paedrin's heart boiled with fury at the thought. He had been starved of light and food and trapped in the Arch-Rike's dungeon when they had last tricked him into wearing a Kishion ring. It would not happen again. He refused to submit to the fate. They could blind him. They could whip him. They could sear his skin with burning pokers, but he would never submit to that ink-black, oily feeling of the Arch-Rike invading his mind. He would die first.

That left him one option.

Escape.

Paedrin crossed his legs, letting his head hang low to hide his expression from the men training in the yard. His lips quivered with wrath. He would escape the chains. He would escape the courtyard. He would claim the blade from Kiranrao and use it to free the land of the Plague. Where to start, though?

He needed freedom.

There was a time he had sat by a fire at night in the woods with Hettie. She had described her bondage to the Romani. He had told her that she was already free. Freedom was a state of mind. Fear could shackle a person as much as any fetter. What was Paedrin afraid of? Being forced to submit to torture? Being forced to wear a ring? He could not allow that to dominate his thinking. Rather, he needed to spend his thoughts finding a way to escape.

Freedom was a state of mind. Pain is a teacher.

Paedrin drew deep inside himself, plunging into the void of his thoughts like a swimmer diving for pearls. What knowledge did he have that could rescue him? A column of stone pressed against his back. Could he shift it? Could he topple it in some way? The stone weighed as much as a mountain. He would never be able to budge it. The chains then. He needed to be free of them. He began twisting his wrists in circles, keeping the movements concealed. The cuffs were tight against his forearms. There was a little give, but not enough to squeeze his fingers through. He tried squeezing his fingers together, pulling against the bonds with his shoulders, trying to work up sweat to make it slippery.

The lack of sight sharpened his other senses. While he worked at the cuffs, he heard the slaps and groans as the men in the training yard acted on the instructions. How many were there? In his mind, he could count around a dozen. He could almost see them in his thoughts, where they were positioned in the courtyard. Every sound gave him new information. Who was heavy. Who was slight. He began to discern the variety of the races.

"Come on," Kiranrao urged. "Do it again, but much faster. Heron Gliding on the Water, like I showed you. Then Serpent Seeks the Pearls. Faster though. Much faster."

A memory tugged in Paedrin's mind.

"The Vaettir is trying to work himself loose," one of the men said. "I see his wrists."

"He's more to be pitied than laughed at. Ignore him."

The pain in his eyes made him squint, but he still could not open them to see if he had any vision at all. The metal from the cuffs was working with him now. He broadened the circles, trying to tug against the bonds while he worked. All he needed was one wrist free. Just one.

Deeper into himself he went, trying to understand the truth about his situation. What was he missing? What facts had he observed from the wall above the training yard before he had spoken out? He had not realized it was Kiranrao at once. Why not? What had blinded him?

Maybe he was looking at the truth upside down. It was a spark of insight. Down inside his pain, the flicker happened.

What if the Vaettir in the training yard wasn't Kiranrao at all?

Careful not to douse the tiny spark, he cupped it inside his mind and breathed on it. The Arch-Rike of Kenatos knew they sought the Shatalin temple. He had plenty of time to prepare for their arrival. What person could he send—what *imposter* could he send on ahead that would aid in his goal of thwarting Paedrin and Hettie? A man whom both of them knew and feared. A man known to have a tapered sword that gave him great power. The light of the truth began to flame more brightly. Did the Arch-Rike possess the power to send a decoy? Could a Vaettir Kishion be sent and mimic Kiranrao's mannerisms? Or could magic assist in the illusion? Yes, that had to be it. It was the Uddhava, of course. Always the Uddhava. Anticipate your enemy's goal. Provide a counter to it and force him to react to you.

The man in the training yard was not Kiranrao.

Who was he?

Someone who knew Kiranrao's mannerisms well enough. But not someone who could know everything they had said together in their journeys. Romani sayings were one thing. What about the past they had shared? He had to test it.

"Kiranrao," Paedrin said, raising his chin.

"Everyone is wise until he speaks," came a sardonic reply.

"How could you betray us?" he said. "You swore an oath to Tyrus that you would support our mission!"

"I made no such oath, sheep-brains. He who pays the piper calls the tune."

Paedrin stiffened. The words were said in Kiranrao's voice, but the way it was said reminded him of . . . Hettie.

He had to test it. "Every bird relishes his own voice."

"A blind chicken finds a grain once in a while."

The last one was all he needed. Hettie had told him that one on a hill outside of Lydi. Kiranrao had not even been there. Somehow Hettie had discovered the false Kiranrao. She was using whatever power that enabled the disguise to mask herself. She was standing in front of him with the sword they had come for.

"Do you have it?" he asked tautly.

"I do," came a quick reply. "If only you could fly, Bhikhu." He heard the boots approaching him.

"When I am free of here," he said, uncurling his legs and rising. The chains dragged against the stone. "When I am free, I swear you will suffer as I do."

"The blindness isn't permanent. But unfortunately for you, the Arch-Rike's emissary will be here shortly."

Paedrin felt the weight of the chains. He tried to inhale and see if he would rise. The weight of the chains prevented it. Very well. He set the edge of one foot against the base of the stone pillar. He dropped into a low horse stance, pulling his arm into position.

"What? You think you are strong enough to break a chain?" came Kiranrao's mocking voice.

Paedrin exhaled. A Vaettir floated when breathing in deeply. The opposite was also true. Paedrin breathed in quickly and then exhaled just as quickly, pulling against the chains with all of his might. He felt the iron dig into his wrists. His neck muscles strained. His legs quivered.

"You're a fool! You cannot break these chains!"

He felt the irony in the voice, the pleading with him to keep trying. Paedrin's head grew dizzy from the lack of air. He rested a moment, sucking in breath again in several generous gulps, then expelling it all out and tested the iron chains once again. He strained. The chains went taut. He groaned inside of himself, drawing on the pain in his eyes to fuel his strength. The iron would not give.

Paedrin paused again, choking on his breath. He puffed more air inside him and then expelled it for the third time, drawing every bit of power he could from his legs, his hips, his shoulders, pulling and forcing the chain. The muscles burned. His thoughts grew dizzy again from the lack of air.

An iron link of chain snapped.

The sound of it reported off the walls in every direction. One of his wrists felt heavier than the other, meaning the chain had broken unevenly. As he staggered away from the stone column, he felt it drag and scrape.

He was free.

Still deep inside himself, still hunkered down in the core of his strength, Paedrin felt as if another set of eyes had suddenly opened. The pain was gone, buried beneath thick layers of resolve. Even though the skin of his eyes was wrinkled shut, every sound came at him and spoke to this new sense . . . this seeing but not seeing. He heard the grunts of shock and surprise. He heard the training Kishion charge at him, the echoes assailing him from nearly all sides.

Paedrin met them head on.

He swung the loose chain over his head, around and around, building momentum. He lunged into the midst of them, swinging the chain in a deadly circle. He felt it hit the first man, striking him in the face with enough force to crush the cheekbone. Without losing the momentum of the attack, Paedrin sidestepped, swirling the chain around in another arc, taking another man on the chin. Paedrin ducked low, sweeping the chain like a dragon's tail, catching two off guard and sending them sprawling. He dived forward, rolling over his back, and was up again, sweeping the chain in two circular motions. Someone came from behind. With a shift in his stance, Paedrin sent the chain out into another man.

"Grab the spears! Get a staff!"

Paedrin sensed where the bodies were crumpled nearby him and he skillfully stepped around them, whipping the loose chain out again and catching a fleeing man on the ankle, dragging him back. He delivered a powerful blow to the man's ear and then shoved him down, starting to swirl the chain again, lashing it over and over against the stones until it sparked.

The main gate of the Shatalin temple exploded. Fragments of wood and cinders sailed through the air, bringing a billowing cloud of black smoke. The noise was nearly deafening.

"It's Baylen," Paedrin heard Hettie say.

Paedrin could feel the rumble of the stone tiles as the massive Cruithne entered. Shouts of outrage sounded. Paedrin heard something whistle in the air over his head, followed by the crunch of glass and another explosion. Paedrin's jacket fluttered from the impact and he felt the heat from the flames on his neck, but he could no longer feel any pain.

The sound of two swords clearing the scabbards appeared, followed by the clomping steps. "Best leave in a hurry," Baylen said. "Your eyes look a little pink, but I think you'll survive."

Hettie grabbed Paedrin's arm. "They're coming with spears."

"I'll take those three," Baylen said. "Head to the gate."

The massive boots thudded against the stone as he charged them. Paedrin heard the Cruithne strike a spear out of the air with his twin blades. Then another sound as he launched himself at the others, striking down the long poles and spearheads and snapping one of them in half with a cutting motion.

"Can you see?" Hettie asked in his ear.

"In a way, yes. You have the sword?"

"Yes. With it, I can fly like a Vaettir. Only faster. I went down to Baylen and told him to climb up and help get the gate open as a distraction. He was coming to break your chains, but I guess you did that on your own."

"Who needs a Cruithne to break a chain?" Paedrin scolded.

"Indeed. When did you realize it was me?"

He was so grateful she was by his side he nearly kissed her. "As soon as I smelled your breath. The illusion isn't perfect, after all. A clever trap."

They entered the plume of smoke and Paedrin felt his chest constrict. They coughed and choked their way through until they reached the edge of the landing.

Paedrin lifted his face to the sky. The thrill of victory throbbed inside him. He had faced down one of the Arch-Rike's threats. He had conquered the Kishion's lair. He turned back to the gate.

"What are you doing?" Hettie said.

"I'm not finished here," Paedrin replied. "Let me hold the sword."

"You cannot unsheathe it. Only Cruw Reon can and he is no longer here."

"But it still works. Let me hold it."

She handed it to him and he gripped the thin wooden sheath in his left hand. He felt the power surge inside it and lift him up to the top of the wall. After reaching the top, he stood on the crenellations, feeling the haze of smoke and hearing the battle down below. Paedrin lifted the blade into the air.

"I reclaim the Shatalin temple!" he shouted in a booming voice. "I will return with an army of Bhikhu. If any of you are here when I return, I swear by the stars that I will throw you off the walls at low tide. I am Paedrin Bhikhu and I claim this temple!"

"*Before they perform a marriage ceremony, the Rikes of Kenatos counsel with the couple to discern the motives for the union. If the motive is driven by ducats, they counsel against it. If it is driven by force, they will oppose it. If it is driven by fear or jealousy, they will refuse to perform the binding. To these they say: He that is jealous is not in love.*"

—*Possidius Adeodat, Archivist of Kenatos*

XXXV

The Cruithne's huge arms wrestled with the oars, making the skiff cut through the waters toward the awaiting ship. Hettie observed the seawater dripping from his nose, still reeling from the shock of seeing him leap from the top of the cliff into the water below. The splash he had made was no bigger than if a boulder had been flung from the mountainside, but he emerged from the depths quickly enough, stroking his way to where the boat had been secured and climbing aboard. Paedrin and Hettie had floated down through the veil of mist and gracefully landed nearby.

The thrill of Vaettir flight was still a new experience for her, but she loved it already. The sword gave her the power, even when strapped against her hip. The queer feeling in her stomach as she had descended from above was exhilarating.

"Why the grin?" Baylen asked her, and she noticed he had been studying her face.

"We made it out of there alive," she replied, sidling closer to Paedrin on the bench. "We bested the Arch-Rike again. I enjoyed that."

Baylen shrugged. "The plan was sound. I may have killed one of the Kishion. On accident."

Paedrin snorted. "At one time that would have bothered me."

"Are you still blind?"

Paedrin's mouth twitched. "For now. The pain is gone and I cannot see, but my senses are . . . sharper. I know exactly where you are, where Hettie is. Every slap of the waves against the hull. I'm blind but I can still see. It is a strange feeling."

"Are you wounded, Baylen?" Hettie asked him.

"A scratch."

"Let me see it."

"The Kishion was aiming for my back. He didn't realize I had a sheet of metal sewn into my tunic in that spot. He took the liberty of adjusting his aim. I'll be all right."

"Can I row for you?" Hettie asked, leaning forward.

A small smile met her. "I'll be well enough until we get on board. There are some healing runes I can sleep on that will help. Where do we go from here?"

Paedrin folded his arms, staring blindly into the open sea. "Silvandom."

Baylen nodded. "I thought as much."

They were hailed by the sailors as they approached the massive vessel. Ropes were thrown down and Baylen secured them to the oarlocks.

Hettie stood and then gripped Paedrin's arm. She inhaled deeply and so did he. They both floated up from the boat and quickly crossed to the main deck. The sailors met them with cups of steaming broth thick with vegetables and noodles. The other sailors hauled on the ropes and pulled the heavy load up the side. It would take a while to bring it back.

After giving direction to the helmsman about their destination, Hettie took Paedrin and the soup back to their shared quarters.

Being away from the ship had made her legs a little unsteady, but she quickly got used to the swaying motion. Paedrin sat down on the edge of the cot, burying his face in his hands.

"Eat, Paedrin," she said, handing him the cup.

Holding it with both hands, he took a sip of the broth. "It's good."

Hettie was ravenous herself and sat cross-legged on the cot opposite his and wolfed down the soup. The vegetables were crunchy and there was just enough salt to flavor it. The two slurped in silence and Hettie mopped her chin on her sleeve.

"I could get more," she suggested, staring across at him. He was brooding.

"One is fine."

"What are you thinking?"

He rubbed his wrists, which were still bound by the cuffs and chain. She could see blood on his skin. She waited for him to speak, wiping the edge of the bowl and then licking the salty broth from her finger.

"I meant what I said about the Shatalin temple," he said in a determined voice. It bordered on being a growl. "That place was meant for Bhikhu to train. How did it get overrun?"

"I doubt we'll ever know. The first thing we must do is fix that gate."

His mouth twitched and he cocked his head as if looking at her. His eyes were open but not focused. He stared just to the left of her. "We?"

She set the bowl down on the edge of the cot. There was that look on his face again. She saw him swallow.

"I haven't finished my training yet, *Master*," she said softly. She put just a little bit of emotion in her voice, an unspoken promise.

He stared dully at her and said nothing.

"What did you think I meant?" she asked, leaning forward, studying his face for any sign of a reaction.

"Well, you said 'we.' That implied that after we conquer the Scourgelands—"

"Which we will of course," she interrupted, shifting herself off the edge of the cot so that she was even closer to him. She saw a little flush creep into his cheeks. He was trying very hard to pretend not to be affected by her closeness. She had been watching him struggle with his feelings for days now. Good.

"You think so?" he asked curiously. "It destroyed the last group that went there."

"They were not us."

"But they also thought they could defeat it."

"We have knowledge they didn't have. But go on, Paedrin. I didn't mean to interrupt you."

He cleared his throat. The faint flush in his cheeks began to deepen. She was certain it was driving him mad not being able to see her expression. He was listening to her words and trying to discern more than the literal meaning.

"I was saying that I intend to return and toss out those imposters. Obviously I won't be returning to Kenatos and teaching there."

"Obviously."

"But when I said that *I* would be returning, I did not think that perhaps *you* might want to come as well. You have your freedom now, Hettie. You can go anywhere you want to go."

She smiled at the uncomfortable expression on his face, as if he were writhing with emotions inside and barely able to suppress them. It was difficult not to laugh.

"What?" he asked, his face perplexed.

"But I have not finished my training yet," she said. "You promised to train me."

He swallowed again. She was torturing him and she knew it. "Is that what you wanted then? You wanted more training?"

"Of course. You have knowledge that few possess outside of Kenatos and Silvandom. I wish to learn it."

"Oh," he answered, his voice sounding disappointed.

"I also need to thank you," she answered in a low voice, rising from the cot. "You saved my life when I fell from the cliff. You've saved it more than once. It is a debt that I must repay in the Romani way."

His head cocked. "What is the Romani way?"

"This," she answered, dipping her head and pressing her mouth against his. She grasped his neck, entwining her fingers to hold him in place, and pressed a long, savory kiss against his completely befuddled mouth. She tasted the salt from the soup. The fireblood stirred inside of her. Possibly it was something else. It took several moments before the shock passed and he started to respond, to kiss her back, to kiss her in earnest.

She pulled away.

"That is the Romani way," she said, pleased at the silly grin she found on his face.

It took a moment before he found his composure or his voice. That was gratifying too.

"How does a Romani say you're welcome?" he asked, his eyebrow lifting.

She sat on his lap, stroking the stubble on the dome of his head. "You wish me to teach you the Romani ways, do you?" she asked, grazing his ear with the tip of her nose. He shuddered.

"I wish I could see your face," he said softly. "You have me at a disadvantage."

"You've always been blind, Bhikhu. Only now you have realized it."

The camp smoke from a hundred fires hung in the night air like a shroud, threading through the gaps of the trees. Only a thin sliver of moon radiated from the sky, peering between the branches. There was a sentry in the shadows, spear held upright so that the edge of the tip would not glint in the moonlight. He was paying attention, ignoring the sounds wafting from the army as they washed over him. He stared into the night's darkness, vigilant. Kiranrao thrust the blade Iddawc into his ribs, watching the magic of the blade snuff his life out instantly. There was a plume of memories released and Kiranrao inhaled them, discarding most until he found the one he was after—the location of the pavilion where the King of Wayland slept. The rest of the memories he scattered to the breeze and then entered the camp.

Gripping his sword pommel with one hand, he was invisible to all but the most astute Finder. The magic of his blade allowed him to pass unseen, his very essence the semblance of a blur. In his other hand, he gripped the blade Iddawc. He almost always carried it unsheathed, listening to the faint whispers of promised death. It exposed the vulnerabilities of any man, the most efficient way of killing them.

That one, fidgeting with his stew. He's weak on his left.

That one, crossing the camp believes he's a sword master. He's a fool. Get in close and he'll panic and drop his weapon.

Over there—see the Finder? He's looking our way, but he hasn't seen us yet. You may have to kill him next.

Over and over the whispers came to his mind, spoken by the blade's hunger to kill. It worked best when he had a target in his mind. The blade seemed to sense everyone around, probing for weaknesses and assessing their vulnerabilities. It was a useful tool. No wonder the Arch-Rike had paid so handsomely for it. It revealed the weakness of others so perfectly, it allowed Kiranrao to kill his victims in a single thrust. It unmasked everyone.

That way, where the flames burn brightest. The king is there. Kill him.

Kiranrao moved through the camp like a wraith, fueled by pure desperation to murder. The Wayland army was closing fast around Havenrook. The price of meat and bread had tripled in the last two days. No caravans had arrived in a fortnight. The road to Alkire was infested with Cruithne bringing their goods down the mountain roads but bypassing Havenrook along the way. The city was shriveling. Kiranrao's vast wealth followed suit. The Romani attacking the armies along the border did insufficient damage to lift the blockade. Perhaps a dagger in the king's chest would suffice.

Kiranrao burned with anger and hatred. The empire he had created around the trading hub was unraveling. How had it happened so quickly? How had the Arch-Rike managed to outmaneuver him so? His breath was quick in his ears. A bold move—an assassination—would shift the tide. He was certain of it. Isn't that why Tyrus had yielded the blade to him at last? All his talk of a fool's errand into the Scourgelands was a feint. Tyrus wanted the Arch-Rike dead. He wanted the King of Wayland removed. He had held the blade tantalizingly as bait until Kiranrao had snatched at it.

He nearly collided into an approaching Paracelsus and shifted his path just in time, almost cursing. That was sloppy. It was unlike him to be sloppy. Kiranrao was no fool. He was still the wealthiest man in all the kingdoms. His fortunes may have begun a landslide, but he would rally them again. The Arch-Rike had coffers enough to plunder. So did the King of Wayland. He would regain every ducat he had lost through this farce of war. Kiranrao's lip curled into a sneer of anger. He shuddered with the emotions. The Romani were being systematically hunted down and slaughtered, yet they bore the blame for starting a war when they had never so much as lifted a dart to hurl. The hypocrisy was galling. Romani poison could not injure the army for the Arch-Rike knew the cure and every victim was quickly remedied. Well so be it then. The course of history would change on this night. The King of Wayland had a young wife and a little boy. They would grieve the loss of husband and father. And then he would spit in their eyes.

There it is. Go quickly. The guards at the front are Outriders. Easily dispatched. He will likely have a Kishion as a personal bodyguard. He will be no match for us.

Kiranrao went to the far side of the pavilion, where he anticipated the shadows were gathered like berry bushes. Instead, tall poles wreathed in blue flame were set into the ground on each of the four corners of the pavilion. They cast a brilliant hue around the entire pavilion and filled the air with a steady plume of white smoke.

He studied the pavilion shrewdly, looking at the seams, the tent stakes, the curving poles, and pennants fluttering from the top. Voices murmured within, discussing, undoubtedly, the progress of the siege of Havenrook. Kiranrao boiled with fury. This night would be spoken of in frightened whispers. No one would ever again risk the wrath of Kiranrao.

He was impatient to be finished.

Studying the hem of the pavilion, he saw the widest opening, the fringe tugged down by stakes. It was narrow enough that a man could slide under if a stake was pulled up. He glanced at them all and felt the blade nudge him toward the weakest one. He nodded and stalked forward, a wisp of night himself.

After dropping to one knee, he tugged at the tent stake and it came up effortlessly. He heard the fabric stretch softly, the pressure removed from the cords fastened to the stake. There was a pungent smell in the air, an unfamiliar one. Wrinkling his nose, he dropped low and laid himself down on the ground, parallel to the skirt of the pavilion. He saw furs covering the dirt floor, plump cushions, a few ironbound chests and an armor rack with the king's armor hanging from it. The helm with the white plume was especially well crafted.

A few soldiers were gathered around a hide-bound stool, sharing some plans with the man seated on it. The King of Wayland, his goatee flecked with streaks of gold and rust, his hair long about his shoulders. He was a handsome man, except for the receding hairline, and his nose was a bit too bulgy. But he had a charming smile and a reputation of ruthlessness that had finally been confirmed. Kiranrao would enjoy killing him. He stared at him, waiting for the pulse from Iddawc revealing the man's weakness.

None came.

Kiranrao stared at the man, the covenant King of Wayland. Something about him felt . . . wrong. The gloved fingers stroking his beard were the best money could buy. His chain hauberk was fringed with intricate gold trim along the collar and sleeves— another fortune. There was a necklace of some sort around his neck. A Druidecht talisman? Kiranrao could not tell. He nodded as the men continued to speak to him, treating each with respect and patience.

The king's eyes flickered to where Kiranrao was lying. He blinked slowly. A small, delighted smile twisted up one corner of his mouth.

Their eyes met.

The blade began to hiss in fear and fury in his grip. It caused an ache to rush up his entire arm. He nearly dropped it, feeling the hideous sensation inside his flesh, as if a thousand grubs were wriggling beneath his skin, trying to burrow into his bones. He almost dropped the blade. But he did not.

That one look told Kiranrao that it was a trap designed for him and that he had blundered his way into it. Rolling away from the pavilion, Kiranrao made it to his feet. Soldiers appeared from the dark.

"He's over there, boys. Look at the shadow on the ground. Aim at the shadow!"

The light from the torches. Of course. The magic fire burning in them revealed those hidden normally from sight. He had not noticed the shadow he was leaving on the ground behind him. He had to give the King of Wayland credit. He truly had thought it through.

As the crossbows began to fire, Kiranrao whipped one direction and then another and took in a big breath of air, rising above the torches. The light from the flames had no canvas on which to paint his shadow. He floated above the pavilion, watching as some of the bolts tore gashes into the fabric. He scudded like a cloud, breathing even deeper until he rose as high as the monstrous trees. With a kick in the air, he angled his way to the upper branches and grasped a hold of the trunks. The soldiers down below scurried like ants from a kicked hive. He stood on the slender branch, keeping his breath carefully measured so that it would easily support his weight. The throbbing feeling in his arm began to settle. How close he had come to losing the blade! He did not think for a moment he had come close to dying. He was far too clever to ever risk that.

Watching as the army of Wayland began to search the camp, he nearly shouted his laughter from the tree tops. Instead, he slunk away, vowing to return and drive the blade deep into the king's chest. The siege would continue to choke his people. Murderous rage continued to burn in his heart.

Shoving away from the tree, he rapidly descended into the camp and made his way through the confusion of the raid. Soldiers were talking about an intruder in the camp. A man had been seen. The thief Kiranrao. His name was said with contempt. It made him grind his teeth with fury. He would kill them all. One by one if he had to. One soldier at a time. But would that be fast enough to save his wealth from vanishing? The cask was caved in, the wine already spilling out. He wanted to save as much of it as he could. He was frantic at how quickly his wealth was vanishing.

Kiranrao killed another sentry on his way out, leaving the man crumpled in his bones. He did not even bother lingering to taste the man's memories. It was not a great distance to the Romani hideout.

They were lurking all around the camp, awaiting orders to launch a raid or strike at the enemy's supply lines. They were waiting for him to return with news of the King's death. They had waited in vain.

He released the pommel of the sword and shrugged off the magic that hid him from the sight of others. He would sleep in a bed tonight. In a bed on a wagon. He wanted to get drunk. He craved it with a great thirst. He would not give in to the craving. Not tonight. He would plot the king's death again. He would find a way to stop the assault. He would rally. He always did.

As he approached he found the Romani alert, as always. Beckett was a Preachán with a sharp nose. He was digging beneath his fingernail with a jeweled spike.

"He's here," Beckett said, nodding to the unhitched wagon at the far edge of camp.

Kiranrao looked at the little man, scrutinizing his face. "What?"

"I said he's here. Arrived a little while after you left. Offered a bet that you wouldn't succeed."

Kiranrao's scowl made some of them step back. "And how many of you craven dogs took that bet?"

Beckett flicked a rind of fingernail away. "No one bets against Tyrus of Kenatos."

☙

Kiranrao shut the door of the wagon, narrowing his eyes at the small candle flame illuminating the face of Tyrus. The Paracelsus was a large man and he seemed to dwarf the size of the wagon interior. There was a half-wince of pain in his expression.

He has pain in his back from a knife wound that did not heal fully. It was a death blow but he survived it. Below his shoulder blade. His neck is exposed. He has magic protecting him but if you move quickly, you can kill him before he brings it to bear. See his right hand?

"How did you find me?" Kiranrao asked softly, glancing at the strange brass cylinder half-hidden behind the big man. Was it a weapon or a defense?

"I know how to find those I seek," Tyrus replied evasively, as Kiranrao expected he would.

"I should kill you now. You are at a disadvantage."

A small smile. "A scholar's ink lasts longer than a martyr's blood."

"What is that supposed to mean?"

"It is what has always motivated me, Kiranrao. I care not for ducats or duchies. I want to leave a legacy in this world. I want to be known as the man who stopped the Plague. You will help me achieve this."

Kiranrao leaned back against the door, studying the Paracelsus quizzically. "Why would I care to do that? If you could not tell, I have my own problems to sort through."

"Because, as the Romani like to say, the enemy of my enemy is my friend." Tyrus leaned forward, his expression haggard yet intense. "Your enemy is not the King of Wayland, Kiranrao. He is only the Arch-Rike's puppet."

Kiranrao stepped closer, smelling the other man's scent for the hint of fear. He was so close. One thrust from Iddawc would end him. It would end all of his tricks and mischief. What toys and trinkets did he hide within those robes?

"And you can bring down the Arch-Rike?" Kiranrao asked with silk in his voice.

"When the Plague is conquered, the Arch-Rike's power will fail. With no more threat of death, do you think people will willingly submit to living in that pus-pool of a city? It is truly a prison, Kiranrao, as you well know. Only those confined there are confined voluntarily. Fear keeps them inside its walls, nothing more. Remove the fear and you remove the prison. When the Arch-Rike falls, his power falls. And so does his grip on the King of Wayland's leash."

Kiranrao rubbed his finger on the edge of the wooden wall. "You know as well as I do that the Arch-Rike will still hold power even if the Plague ends. Men like us do not yield power. It must be forced."

"How does it feel, Kiranrao?"

"You grow tiresome, Tyrus. Perhaps I will kill you now."

"Your weakness is your lack of imagination," Tyrus replied with a hint of arrogance in his expression. "You think that I am trapped here, come to barter with you for your aid but defenseless against you should you turn on me. I assure you I am not. My knowledge of the Paracelsus ways is invaluable to you. I know how to breach their defenses. More importantly, I know what the Arch-Rike secretly fears. I have a weapon against him."

Kiranrao arched his eyebrows. "Another weapon?"

"This weapon is a person. You know of the Quiet Kishion. You abandoned us to him back in Silvandom."

"What else did you expect me to do? Keep my word?"

Tyrus shook his head. "You did exactly what I did expect you to do. You took the blade far away. The Arch-Rike fears the Quiet Kishion. He fashioned that blade to defend himself against him. And I have turned that Kishion to my side. He aids in the quest."

"You lie!" Kiranrao said, disbelieving Tyrus though the ring on his finger did not warn of any falsehood.

Tyrus leaned forward. "This is how it ends, Kiranrao. I have the Quiet Kishion on my side. He will dispatch the Arch-Rike when this is through. I have left nothing to chance. The last time I led a group into the Scourgelands, I was defeated by my own ignorance. I've learned much since that failure. I have everything I need to succeed except one thing." His eyes narrowed. "You."

"What?" Kiranrao looked at him in annoyance.

"You heard me, Kiranrao. I truly believe that we cannot defeat the Scourgelands without you. Every piece is important. But yours is crucial. You will not do it for the cause. You will not do it to save the world. You will do it because you stand to gain more wealth than anyone else should the Arch-Rike fall."

There was a trick hidden inside the words. Kiranrao knew there was. He was determined to pry it loose.

"Back in Silvandom, you said that there was another to join the quest. You refused to tell me before who it was. Was it the Arch-Rike's minion then? Was it the Quiet Kishion?"

Tyrus smiled in chagrin. "I see it is very difficult to hide the truth from you. I cannot succeed without your help. You cannot succeed without mine. We are bound together, you and I. If one of us stumbles, both of us fall."

Kiranrao stared at the Paracelsus, feeling the sweet urge to kill him, to prove him wrong. Somehow their destinies had been entwined together. It was time to sever that tie.

"You are the only man I know of who has been inside the Scourgelands," Kiranrao whispered. "What can you possibly have that can defeat it?"

There was a glint in Tyrus's eye. From the folds of his robe, he raised the strange scepter he had been concealing. There were gems fastened inside it, scroll work and fluting that made the Vaettir's eyes bulge. It was truly a rare specimen.

"I have this. It is called a Tay al-Ard. With it, I can travel to any place I have ever been. You arrive there instantly. Imagine having a magic such as this. There are only two in existence. The other one is held by the Arch-Rike of Kenatos. When he falls, his will be yours."

There was a deep ache that started in Kiranrao's belly. He stared at it, transfixed.

"I am going back to Silvandom now. Come with me."

"Sometimes even the wisest of scholars and archivists are fools. They think much learning gives wisdom. They are doubtful of every person and argue over trifles. I have found the opposite to be the better approach. Stineo said it best: Seek not to understand that you may believe, but believe that you may understand."

—*Possidius Adeodat, Archivist of Kenatos*

XXXVI

Being in the Dryad grove brought memories to Annon both pleasant and painful. It was this place where his friend and mentor Reeder had been murdered. Though the body had been taken to Canton Vaud, Annon recognized the spot and it was where he had summoned them to through the magic of the Tay al-Ard. The forest of Silvandom was awash in colors and scents, the air alive with the presence of myriad spirits. Their thoughts brushed against his panicking mind, for his heart was still racing from their flight from Basilides. The narrow escape had cost them dear. Poor Erasmus was added to the dead in Tyrus's quest.

There are others here, Nizeera said, her tail lashing. *I sense them near the tree. It could be a trap.*

Annon raised his hand, stopping Khiara and Lukias.

"What is it?" the Vaettir girl whispered, drawing near him.

"We are not alone," Annon answered, rubbing the stubble on his chin. He prepared to tame the fireblood. "Be ready."

Who are they? Boeotians or Bhikhu? he thought to Nizeera.

I cannot smell them yet. I heard movement in the trees, over there, in the shadows.

Annon marched forward, preparing to defend the tree again. As they approached the inner ring of oaks, he saw the jagged gash in the trunk of the Dryad tree, the raw skin now blistered with sap. He observed motion through the screen of trees on his left and turned to face it. Someone was approaching, quickly, a man by his shape and size.

"There," Lukias warned, stepping forward, pointing.

The intruder emerged from the cover. It was the Quiet Kishion.

Annon's heart quailed at the sight of him. His bowels turned to water. There was no Tay al-Ard to rescue them this time. How was it possible that he had found the Dryad tree? Annon stared at him in shock and dread, Nizeera lowering on her haunches, preparing to spring and defend him.

Khiara reacted first. With a vault forward, she swung her staff around to try to clip the side of his head. He easily ducked the blow and moved like a pool of quicksilver. She twirled the staff over her head and brought it down a second time. He caught the pole, jerked it from her grip, and tossed it away. She did not back down, but launched herself at the Kishion, her eyes focused and determined. There was a flurry of arms, strike and block, grunts and the clack of limbs, and then suddenly she bowled over, clutching her stomach, and dropped to the forest floor, writhing.

The Kishion's eyes were blue and fierce as he surveyed the other two. Annon knew his flames were useless. He called for aid from the spirit realm, begging for power that might defeat the Arch-Rike's champion.

Nizeera growled and hissed, clawing the earth. *Back,* Annon warned her. *He will kill you.*

The Kishion stepped forward, then shifted like a serpent and struck at Lukias next. He stepped behind the Rike's heel, grabbing his arm, and jerked, levering the man so that he fell backward over the Kishion's leg and tumbled to the mat of leaves. Lukias shrieked with surprise as his arm was torqued and wrist bent. He did not resist, his face grimacing.

"He will kill us," Lukias moaned with dread.

He heard the whisper from Neodesha's tree in his mind. *He is not your enemy, Annon. Be still.*

Fly, Druidecht! Nizeera warned, letting out a keening growl of challenge.

Annon was racked with indecision. He recognized Neodesha's voice in his mind. It conflicted with the panic and fear from Nizeera. The Kishion dropped to one knee, keeping Lukias's arm at a terrible angle, one that caused immeasurable pain. Lukias gasped.

Trust me, the Dryad whispered.

Annon stared at the Kishion, the realization beginning to dawn on him. Why had he attacked the Rike? As a servant of the Arch-Rike himself, would he not have gone for Annon instead? He was deliberately subduing the other man, not trying to strangle him as he had with Hettie.

"Wait," Annon said, holding out his hand calmingly. His mind and heart were aflutter with conflicting reactions. What was the right course to take? "He is on our side. He is one of us."

The Quiet Kishion raised his gaze to Annon, his expression hard but not cruel. "This is Lukias, a Provost-Rike of Kenatos. I know this man. He is not your ally."

The spasm of fear that had constricted in Annon's chest began to unclench. "And are you?" he asked. "The last time we met, you vanished with my uncle and killed him."

The Kishion's eyes narrowed. "Tyrus is alive."

The revelation made Annon's hands drop to his side. "What did you say?"

"You heard me well enough, Druidecht. I will go into the

Scourgelands with you. But this man cannot be trusted."

"You?" Lukias said through clenched teeth. "You say that about *me*? A fine jest, Kishion. He wears a ring on his hand. The Arch-Rike controls him through it. Do not believe him."

The Kishion snorted, exchanging his grip on Lukias's wrist with his other hand. He held up his fingers and showed them to Annon. "The Arch-Rike tried to destroy me with that ring. It was left in Stonehollow. I am free of his influence now. This man helped lead the raid into Silvandom against you."

"I know," Annon said. "Please. Stop twisting his arm. Let him sit and I will explain. Khiara, are you feeling any better?" He noticed the Vaettir girl struggling to rise and helped her straighten. She stared at the Kishion with fear and confusion and then nodded slowly to Annon.

The Kishion watched her warily, his blue eyes alert for any motion. He kept them all within his sight, shifting around to the other side of Lukias, and then untwisted his arm. The Rike massaged his wrist, his face twisted into a frown of pain.

"I will warn you all right now," said the Kishion. "Do not try my patience. If you attack me in any way or try to flee, I will not be merciful. Now you, Druidecht. Explain how this wretch is among you."

Lukias shook his head, his face contorting with anger. "You question him about me? You are the Arch-Rike's killer. If you are not here to execute us, then I cannot imagine why you are here."

"Silence," the Kishion warned. "Not a word more, Lukias. I don't trust you. Speak, Druidecht. Quickly."

Annon stared at the man, amazed at the turn of events. "There are questions I would also ask you."

The Kishion shook his head no. "Answer mine."

Annon was still amazed at the revelations and he struggled to master his thoughts. What could he tell the Kishion? Would anything he said be safe to reveal? Was this some trick? If Tyrus was still alive, why had he not contacted them? Maybe he had but could not track where Annon and the others were going. Too much confusion.

"Speak!"

Annon sighed deeply. "Tyrus sent us to find Basilides. Do you know of it?"

The Kishion nodded.

"Lukias was *persuaded* to help us find it. He attempted to convince us along the journey that we would be better served surrendering to the Arch-Rike. He led us there, but refused to grant us any knowledge that would bypass the defenses. He bargained for his life, as any man would. We were attacked by Boeotians along the way, and he assisted us. He was even . . . ingested by one of the defenders along the outer pass and cut his way out with a long knife. Our truce has been tentative, I assure you. But Erasmus perished inside that horrible place and Khiara and I would have probably perished as well if he had not freed us and led us to the Tay al-Ard that provided the escape. The Arch-Rike himself was leading the hunt for us. We only just escaped."

The Kishion's eyes narrowed. He looked at Khiara warily. "What is your role in this, Vaettir?"

"I am a Shaliah. My skills are needed to heal."

He then gazed down at the prone man. "I will not bother asking you for your motives, Lukias. Surely you can lie well enough to deceive even a black ring."

"True enough," Lukias replied evenly. "How did you survive the detonation of the ring?"

The Kishion frowned. "My immunity protects me still."

Lukias shook his head slowly. "No. What truly protects you, Kishion, is the veil over your memories." He grunted with pain and slowly stood. "Have you recovered them yet? When the ring burst, did they flood back?"

The Kishion gestured that they had not.

Lukias nodded, as if he had expected that answer. "In every kingdom, there is a man chosen and sent to do the vilest of duties. We all know the King of Wayland is a cunning and ambitious man. He has many rivals. There are many who attempt to topple his power. To preserve it, he thrusts his knife into the vulnerable parts of his enemies. He threatens their kin. Especially their children. Do you even know, Kishion, how many children you have killed? I thought you always wore gloves because you could not bear to see the red on your hands."

Revulsion and horror swept through Annon. He tried to control his composure, but he could feel the twitching of his cheek muscles, and bile rose into this throat. The Kishion stared at Lukias solemnly. He did not deny it.

"So why would you have joined this quest?" Lukias challenged. "My motives are clear and rather obvious. I believe Tyrus will win. With you to aid him? Even the Preachán would have said the odds improved enormously. If the Arch-Rike falls, another power will step into his place. The King of Wayland is the one to watch. Or Tyrus of Kenatos. I lay my wager with the Paracelsus over the cunning king. I know that I will not earn Tyrus's trust until his quest is successful. Why are you here, Kishion? What does Tyrus trust you to do?"

There was a snapping of twigs and another shape visible through the trees. "He is my protector."

Phae stepped through the ring of trees, watching those who had come, and approached the Kishion from behind, standing beside him, but slightly behind him. She rested her hand on his arm, trying to reassure him with her presence. She saw the clenched jaw, the distrust so clearly etched in his expression. She wrestled with her fear of him, but she was determined. She pushed a strand of hair from her face and stared at them all dispassionately.

"My name is Phae," she said, looking at each of them. "I am Tyrus's daughter."

They were each very different. The Vaettir girl was naturally quiet, reserved. She was dressed as a Rike herself, which was odd. But then, the appearance of Prince Aransetis was the same as he had worn the tunic too. She had long black hair, a bruise on her cheek, and a scrape slashing the end of her chin. The middle one, the Druidecht, looked young. He was handsome, but his expression was haunted. The news he had experienced was causing a churn of emotion inside of him and he was wrestling with it still. He wore something around his neck, a piece of jewelry of some kind with glittering stones at the ends. There was a creature just behind him, some strange mountain cat with a beautiful pelt. The final man was a Rike, silver-haired, and his look made Phae distrust him completely. He was goading Shion, trying to unhinge him with secrets from the past. Was Shion a child-killer? Was that why his memories were veiled? She was the one who had encouraged him to seek his past. What if that past was truly too horrible to relive?

While she had waited in the seclusion of the grove, she had listened to the conversation and decided to reveal herself at last. She was alarmed at their presence, but she understood why and how they had come.

"I'm staring, I'm sorry," she said, offering a weak smile. "We were attacked by the Arch-Rike's forces and had to flee. Tyrus brought us to Silvandom, but we split up because one of us was wounded—"

"The Prince?" Khiara interrupted, her face drawn with worry.

Phae shook her head. "No, he is safe. There was a man we met in the mountains of Alkire who sheltered us. Evritt is his name. He was injured in the Arch-Rike's attack and they took him to the city for a healer. The two of us have been evading the Arch-Rike's minions. We found our way here. I think you all know . . . what I am."

Annon stared at her in awe. "You are Dryad-born."

Phae nodded. "I am. There is something I must do here though. I do not know how much time we have before Tyrus finds us again. Or the Arch-Rike for that matter. Annon, would you join me? The others must wait outside the rim of trees. Shion . . . will you keep the others away?"

He glanced at her in concern and hesitated, his fists clenching.

"I will be safe with Annon," she whispered, squeezing his arm. "The Dryad will keep me so."

He nodded finally and then gestured for Khiara and Lukias to retreat the way they had come. They obeyed, vanishing into the woods. Phae studied the young man, who was barely older than her. He stared at her in return.

☙

"You look like Tyrus," Annon told her, shaking his head. She wore a ribbed shirt and trousers with a thick leather belt. It was not the look or the fashion of Wayland, but he had seen those from Stonehollow wear such clothes before. It was a dusty place, thick with stones. Her hair was lighter than his, but still bore the telltale sign of their fireblood. She looked fit and hale, her hair clean and slightly damp. Her clothes were a bit tattered and frayed.

"Is that a compliment?" she asked, wrinkling her brow.

He approached her and took her hand with both of his. "You've seen your father, then?"

"I have."

He closed his eyes, relieved beyond words. "I thought he was dead."

"He was dead, Annon. Shion killed him with a dagger. Well, if there is one thing my father knows how to do better than being a

Paracelsus, it's to survive. Prince Aran found me in Stonehollow, but I snuck away not trusting him. I wish now that I had. I was found by Shion and he took me captive and was bringing me to the Arch-Rike when Tyrus and Aran discovered us. This has all come about very fast. But I know who I am. I know what my father intends for me." She swallowed, her look nervous. "I have accepted my fate. I believe you are the only one he told everything to. Which is why I wanted to speak to you alone, and not in front of the others."

Annon smiled at her. "If only Paedrin and Hettie were here as well, we would be ready to face the Scourgelands right now. I have learned of another way to enter. A way that will bring us close inside. Tyrus has a Tay al-Ard. I have the knowledge of the location. I think this bodes well for our success."

He glanced over at Neodesha's tree, longing to speak to the Dryad again.

Phae must have caught his look, for she tugged at his sleeve. "This is why I wished to speak to you alone. She wants to see you again, Annon. She knew as soon as you arrived. Go to her."

"One can never predict the true course of action in a war. It is by nature unpredictable. But knowledge is surfacing in the city that there was a thwarted assassination attempt against the Arch-Rike as he traveled to counsel with the King of Wayland. These are surely tumultuous times."

—Possidius Adeodat, Archivist of Kenatos

XXXVII

Annon winced at the gashes in the trunk of the mighty oak. The foliage that had been burned was already beginning to heal and revive. It constantly amazed him how fire caused a forest to be reborn. They were as natural companions as water and wind. His fingers grazed the jagged bark of the tree.

He heard Neodesha's voice before he saw her.

"I told you the injury to the tree does not harm me," she said lightly, a smile lilting the sound. She appeared around that side of the tree, wearing the same dress he had seen her in before. Her bare feet crunched on the leaves.

"I've not forgotten anything you've told me," he answered, his heart suddenly in pain with longing. "How far does our connection reach, Neodesha? I could swear I heard you in Basilides."

She gave him a pretty smile that tortured him. "It is not so much the distance as the state of your emotions. I felt your terror, Annon. When you are calm or quiet, I cannot hear or see you very well. I'm grateful you survived."

He smoothed the back of his hand across the bark of the tree, gazing up at a sprig of mistletoe and feeling the strong urge to kiss her. He tried to control himself.

"You have suffered much since we parted," she whispered. "The loss of a friend. The worry over whether you can trust the Rike in your company. You are conflicted about Tyrus's death—or that he survived but did not tell you."

"How easily you read me."

She shook her head. "It is not difficult. Dryads learn much about the mortal world through our calling. It is a tumultuous existence. There is no death in Mirrowen. I wish I could bring you there."

"Some Druidecht are allowed, eventually, to visit. Isn't that so?" She nodded.

"How does one earn that right?"

"I have never known anyone who has earned it. It was more common in the past, I think." She gazed shyly down at the forest floor.

"So you do not know?"

She shook her head and looked down at her feet. "I do not."

"What is it?"

Neodesha glanced up at him. "You've changed me, Annon."

He cocked his head, his heart starting to burn again. He felt a small tremor begin in his knees.

"The change you wrought on me is more obvious," he said. "I see the world differently now. Being able to remember everything is a blessing as well as a curse. When I think of Erasmus, my heart throbs with pain. It is an ache that will never dull. Yet when I think of you . . . I feel quite differently but equally powerful. How does one tame such emotions?"

"I wish I knew," she said, coming around the tree and standing before him. "But I am struggling myself. I was content to be a Dryad. There is much solace and peace in our existence. Dangers do not threaten our trees very often. I existed between both worlds. Time has always been ephemeral to us. Until now. The boon I gave you bound us together. I worry about you now. I seek your safety and welfare. I do not want you to go to the Scourgelands."

Annon's stomach roiled with confusing emotions. He saw her hand resting against the tree trunk and he yearned to hold it. He remembered laying against her lap, reliving the emotional memories of his past. Her very presence comforted him, soothing the guilt and anguish of his life. He had no desire to return to Wayland, not for all the slices of honeyed bread Dame Nestra could bake.

"But I must go there," he said softly.

"I know," she answered with a sigh. "I . . . care for you, Annon. I will worry."

She had said it and he felt a rush of relief, grateful to believe that he was not totally alone, that his feelings were not solely at risk. It had not been long, yet their connection was powerful. He nudged closer to her, staring at her hand.

"In the many years that I have guarded this tree," she said softly, trying to meet his eyes, "I have thought often on my duty and the peace of my existence. I have not felt the desire to relinquish either." She bit her lip. "Until now."

He felt his throat tighten. "You know I must go," he said in anguish.

"You misunderstand me. I do not seek to stop you. There are memories there, Annon. There are memories lost to the world. Reclaim them for us. It is your fate. The dangers of the Scourgelands are equally great. I will worry about you. And I will wait upon your safe return." Her hand lifted timidly and brushed aside of lock of his hair.

Her touch caused a jolt of heat throughout his body. "Neodesha, I . . ." he whispered.

She put her fingers on his mouth, covering his lips. "Say not my name," she said. "There are too many nearby. I would hate to be bound to anyone else . . . but you."

He gently took her wrist and then kissed her fingertips. She smiled shyly.

"I will return when it is done," he promised. "Nothing will prevent me. Not even death."

She hesitated a moment and then stepped into his arms, burying her face against his chest. She trembled as he wrapped his arms around her like a blanket, holding her close, feeling the warmth from her body seep into his. The terror of Basilides was tamped. Smelling her hair brought a measure of peace and shards of pain.

Her face lifted, her eyes full of conflicting emotions. "I will wait for you," she promised. One moment he was holding her. Then she was gone, vanished again into the tree.

Annon was suddenly cold, bereft of her comforting presence. Pain consumed his heart. He gazed around for her, bewildered at the suddenness of her departure. Turning, he saw Tyrus standing in the grove behind him, the Tay al-Ard in his hand.

The look in Tyrus's eyes was full of hostility.

"What do you think you are doing, lad?" Tyrus said hoarsely.

Annon stared in surprise. "How did you find us?" he demanded, his emotions caught in a wrenching vice. "You are alive?"

Tyrus walked closer, motioning for Phae to approach. He loomed larger than a giant, though with a slight limp in his step. "You are fooling with emotions you know little about," he said with clenched teeth.

"What?" Annon said, staring in confusion.

"The Dryad," Tyrus said with a hoarse whisper. "There is a reason why the Druidecht do not teach this lore to the young ones. You are too young for this, Annon."

"Too young for what?"

"To be trifling with such powerful feelings. You know where we are going. You know the task at hand. I need your mind sharp as a dagger's blade. I need your heart as hard as stone. You will not survive the terrors of the Scourgelands if you are feeling desolate about a pretty young girl. When this is over, if we survive, that is the time to court such feelings. They will only distract you from the purpose at hand."

A hot flush of shame came across Annon's cheeks at the scolding. He saw Phae wince for him, her eyes full of anger at her father's words. His body shook with suppressed feelings.

"I am not a stripling from Wayland," Annon said, grinding his teeth. "I am a Druidecht."

"Then act like one," Tyrus replied. "Master yourself. You must clear your head of misty-eyed thoughts. We have a duty at hand. I do not know how many of us will even survive it. It is for your good that I speak plainly."

Annon took a shuddering deep breath. In the past, he would have bristled at such a reproach. But he knew Tyrus had sacrificed so much himself. He could respect that, despite the sting of the accusation. "I will do as you say. How did you find us?"

"The same way Prince Aran found her to begin with. The necklace she wears brought me straight here. Were you successful? Did you find Basilides?"

Though Annon's heart was still chafing, he was determined to keep his composure. "We did, though Erasmus perished. There is a chamber in the center of Basilides, a doorway to the Scourgelands. This torc I wear will help keep beasts away from me when I activate it."

A pleased smile came over Tyrus's mouth. "That will be very helpful. It may save your life more than once against the enemies we face. What of the secret lair? What was it like? Was there an oracle?"

"Not as I was expecting," Annon replied. "There were tombs—sarcophagi—one for each kingdom. Erasmus noticed a pattern. He deduced something inherent about the format, but the room was infested with serpents and he was bitten and died before he could reveal what he knew. I can tell you what he said, though. I remember it perfectly."

Tyrus held up his hand. "Hold that knowledge." He glanced suspiciously at the woods around them. "You survived the ordeal. I'm proud of you. Nizeera and Khiara made it as well? Without Khiara, we cannot succeed. We need a Shaliah to heal us."

"They are both over there." He looked at Phae. "They are with the Kishion you converted to our cause. And a Rike of Kenatos named Lukias who has also joined us."

The look on Tyrus's face filled with dread. "Who?"

"He is a Provost-Rike . . ."

"I know who he is," Tyrus said. "What I cannot understand is how he is with you. He is here, now?"

"Over there. The Kishion does not trust him either."

"Yet you did?"

Annon choked back a retort before he accused his uncle of trusting the Arch-Rike's personal bodyguard. "He guided us to Basilides, Tyrus. He even betrayed the Arch-Rike to free us from the trap. The Arch-Rike himself came hunting us there with at least fifty soldiers. They were on our heels but it was Lukias's knowledge of the Tay al-Ard device in Basilides that helped us escape capture. I do not trust him fully, Tyrus. I have not trusted him with the knowledge you gave me. If you would send him away, do so. However, you should know that a Shaliah recovered him from death. His time with us will be limited. Perhaps you should speak to him first."

"I intend to," Tyrus replied. "Where is he?"

"This way."

Annon led them past the ring of trees and warned Nizeera that they were coming. He felt her impatience and could sense she was pacing the woods, uneasy by the storm of emotions Annon was feeling.

Khiara was leaning back against a tree, her shoulders slumped with fatigue. Lukias was also seated, but he rose when they approached, crackling through the foliage to arrive. The Kishion was already standing, keeping an eye on their prisoner.

"Lukias," Tyrus said curtly, his eyes narrowing.

The Rike brushed his arms boldly, meeting Tyrus's distrustful gaze with one of his own. "Tyrus." He folded his arms. "Are you going to slay me now or let the Kishion do it?"

"I must first ask you a question," Tyrus replied. "One that only Lukias would know. We met in my study about four years ago. You sought information from me. What about?"

Lukias rubbed his chin thoughtfully. "A good question. That was quite a while ago."

Tyrus said nothing, only staring at the man.

"If I recall the occasion . . . as I am sure that you do . . . we discussed the vulnerabilities of the Romani trading system in Havenrook. You were of the opinion, I believe, that to topple the Preachán it was best to invest heavily in trade with them. You said it would collapse all on its own."

There was a whisper of a breeze through the grove, the faint rustle of branches.

"You satisfy me," Tyrus replied. "Now that I know who I am speaking with, I ask you another question. Why should I trust you?"

Lukias smiled warily. "You should not, naturally. That is the only proper answer in a circumstance such as this. There is nothing I could say that would establish your confidence in me. However, I do have knowledge that would benefit you. Prove its worth by keeping me alive. Let me vindicate the trust over time. We are both of us too clever to deceive each other properly. Let me be blunt. When this is finished, I perceive that the Arch-Rike will fall. There will be a power struggle after that. You stand the best chance to succeed him. You will reward those who had faith in your vision, in your quest. I stand much more to gain by siding with you now."

"You also stand much to lose," Tyrus said after a scrutinizing look. "Those who ventured into the Scourgelands with me last time all perished."

"I have already perished once facing you, Tyrus Paracelsus. You struck down one of the Arch-Rike's most trained cohorts with a single word. You've claimed the loyalty of the Arch-Rike's most feared minion. I like your chances. If you send me away, I will skulk in the woods until word comes back of your success. Clearly returning to Kenatos is no longer an option I have."

Tyrus stroked his beard, observing the other man keenly. "What can you tell me that will injure the Arch-Rike most?"

He responded with a curious look. "How do you mean?"

"Give me information that will harm him. A vulnerability he has."

"You seek to kill him yourself then?"

Tyrus shook his head. "Toppling his power does not require his death."

Lukias smiled knowingly. "A horse resists the reins but submits because of the bridle. The Arch-Rike does not use a bridle or a bit. Instead, he shapes the path he wants the horse to travel on. Where does his path lead now, Tyrus? Do you see it?"

Annon felt a wrinkle of worry at Lukias's words. Somehow Erasmus had discerned the pattern of the Arch-Rike's strategy. But the Preachán's words had been a jumble of phrases, all disconnected.

The race immune to the Plague. Yes, that must be it. The missing race. The nameless race. The persecuted blood. He's part of it, Annon. The Arch-Rike is not who we think he is. He masquerades as one of these, but look—look! This one—Kenatos. The name on the crypt is Band-Imas. It is the name of the current Arch-Rike, not a dead one. Look at that one—Wayland. It bears the king's name and he is alive. The Arch-Rike we face is an illusion.

Tyrus interrupted Annon's thoughts. "I'm more interested in what you know and how you can help us."

Lukias nodded sagely. "Of course. You already know that it is the Arch-Rike's stated goal to preserve all knowledge. That tradition began long before his reign."

Tyrus nodded.

"What most do not realize is that he plots to overthrow *every* kingdom. Havenrook is only the first to fall. So will Wayland, Alkire, and Silvandom. Lydi is already his. Even the Boeotians will be forced to submit. Stonehollow will be the last. Stonehollow is his goal. Even now he has been plotting to overthrow it, finding another way to invade your home country. His home country. He began paying Romani to seek alternate paths inside to circumvent the tunnels."

Annon noticed Phae and the Kishion turn and look at each other.

"Thank you," Tyrus said simply. "You've answered my question."

Streamers of dust began to flit through the air, zigzagging with color and radiance. Annon felt the surge from the arrival of spirit beings from Mirrowen, a thick onslaught of them arriving with chiming noises and spectral streamers of magic. Their voices were rushed and urgent.

They come. They summon you.

Druidecht, they come. Be ready.

Annon tensed, feeling the suppressed giddiness of the voices. Khiara got to her feet, gripping her staff. The lights were dazzling as they infiltrated the glen.

They come, Druidecht. Be ready. The Thirteen seek you.

Canton Vaud calls.

Come. You must come.

Annon sensed the presence of others in the woods, watching the forms begin to emerge from the trees. There were Bhikhu mixed with Druidecht, approaching.

Lukias's head jerked and his face went ashen. "Who are these emissaries?"

Tyrus turned to Annon, gazing at him. *Can I trust you?* he seemed to be asking.

They come, Druidecht. They are here.

Canton Vaud summons you.

Come.

Annon stared at Tyrus and nodded firmly.

"Despite what I may think of their beliefs, the Druidecht hierarchy known as Canton Vaud are the most trusted and respected of individuals throughout the kingdom. They are the only ones known to be welcomed as honored guests even beyond the borders of our lands. Even the Boeotians pay them respect."

—Possidius Adeodat, Archivist of Kenatos

XXXVIII

Phae was not always certain how she felt about her father. His moods were mercurial and his behavior seemed to alter depending on who they were with. When they had spoken in the cellar below the woodsman's lodging, he was thoughtful and even tender. She had seen him scold Annon and flinched for the pain he was causing the young Druidecht. She had watched him interrogate the Rike known as Lukias with brutal efficiency and could fully understand his cold distrust. He shifted his communication depending on the circumstance, almost like a performer would in front of an ever-changing audience.

She knew he was powerful, but also that he had powerful enemies. She was beginning to realize that his power may not lie so much in his knowledge of magic as it did with his knowledge of influencing people. There was a hazy feeling of suppressed danger in the air whenever he was near. It made her want to be closer to Shion, just in case another terrible danger tried to destroy her father. Shion was the only presence amongst the group where she felt a small measure of safety. Maybe it was when he took the blast of the Kishion himself to shield her. Someone who would do that, not knowing if it would destroy them, deserved her trust. She saw his eyes constantly alert, his body tense as a bowstring. He was trained as a killer, yet she trusted him with her life. She still feared him though.

As the new arrivals appeared, consisting of two Druidecht and several Vaettir protectors, Phae noticed Shion step next to her. It was as if an invisible chain appeared between them, binding them together. She watched Annon stare at the newcomers, his face mixed with different emotions.

Annon looked back at Tyrus. "Palmanter," he whispered. "He's one of the Thirteen."

"I know him," Tyrus responded distrustfully. "Let me speak first."

Tyrus stood at the head of the group. Phae watched his hand slip into a pocket. She stared at the arrivals and blinked quickly. She had never seen so many Vaettir before and wondered if the rumors were true, that they could fly. Their Bhikhu robes were plain and gray and many walked with polished staves. Of the two Druidecht, one was a man and the other a woman. The man had a thick mane of gray hair. He was tall, as tall as her father, and built strongly. His eyes were keen and appraising, glancing quickly across each of their faces. The woman looked more frail, with a pinched nose and auburn hair cut short. She looked like a form of a bird, but her expression was serious and probing.

"Greetings again, Tyrus," the gray-haired Druidecht said. His expression was decidedly nervous. "It has been many weeks since you sought refuge in Canton Vaud."

Tyrus replied with a measured voice. "Which you refused to grant, if I recall."

"Do you have enmity now against Canton Vaud?" the woman asked pointedly.

Tyrus gazed at her. "I do not, Stoern. How did you find me?"

Palmanter held up his hand to prevent her answering. "Annon—it is good to see you as well. You wear the cassock of the Rikes now. Has your allegiance shifted? I see your talisman still?"

Annon folded his arms. "I am a Druidecht. These clothes do not change that."

"Why are you here?" Tyrus pressed, stepped forward.

His step caused Palmanter to flinch. Great beads of sweat appeared on his brow. He was clearly nervous.

"Why do you fear me?" Tyrus asked. "I am no threat to you."

"Truly?" Palmanter asked, his voice thick with distrust.

"You did not grant me sanctuary, but I do not resent it. The Thirteen have a truce with Kenatos, but we are not enemies. I respect Canton Vaud."

"Your actions in Silvandom would say otherwise," the woman, Stoern, said archly.

"What actions do you speak of?" Tyrus pressed.

Palmanter held up one of his meaty hands. "We wish you to come to Canton Vaud, Tyrus. To answer . . . some questions."

Phae felt Shion's arm brush against hers. His eyes were pointed like daggers at the two arrivals, his jaw set in a scowl. He seemed ready to attack them. Something was not right. This was not an introduction of allies.

"This conversation does not inspire trust," Tyrus said. "What actions do you mean? Speak plainly."

Phae noticed that the Bhikhu were slowly detaching from the two Druidecht, slowly positioning themselves on each flank, their weapons ready. Her throat went dry. She could feel the tension bubbling up.

"It would be better if we spoke at Canton Vaud," Palmanter said evasively. "Will you come with us?"

Tyrus chuckled darkly, his visage grim. "I am harried on all sides it seems."

Annon stepped forward, Nizeera at his heels. "The spirits say what you refuse to. Speak it openly, Palmanter. We are not your enemies as you fear."

Palmanter looked at Annon coldly. "You owe your obedience to Canton Vaud, Annon. If this comes to blows, you will not intervene. Your participation in this requires an inquest."

"You may command me," Annon said. "That is your right. But we must speak openly. Your words and actions make this feel as if we're walking into a trap if we come with you."

"It is for our own safety that we do this," Stoern said. "After what happened to the Arch-Rike's emissaries. Your attire only confirms suspicion."

Annon stared with composure. "I know how this must appear. But we should not dissemble, not with each other. I am a loyal Druidecht. I will speak openly if you will not. What I have come to learn is that the Arch-Rike has been imprisoning spirits from Mirrowen to harness their powers. It is the craft of the Paracelsus." He put his hand on Tyrus's shoulder. "They are conflicted because of the Arch-Rike's explanation of the confrontation in Prince Aran's manor. It contradicts ours rather decisively."

Stoern's expression contorted with anger. "You were told to be silent!" she snapped at Annon. Her face was mottled with fury. "Will you come peacefully, Tyrus? Or must we compel you? There is much you must answer for."

Phae swallowed, shrinking from the hostility in Stoern's voice. She did not want to go anywhere with that woman.

"Your meaning is clear, Madame," Tyrus said. "You have been given reports that concern the Thirteen. Naturally you wish us to submit to your questions to ascertain the truth of the matter. But you are predisposed to find me guilty. What would you do if you were in my place?"

"If I were innocent," Stoern said, "I would come to Canton Vaud and seek to clear my name. If I were guilty, I would slay the ones who knew the truth."

"Your thinking is limited," Tyrus replied. "But I see your intentions now. Let me speak plainly, since you will not. We were attacked by the Arch-Rike's minions in Prince Aransetis's manor in Silvandom. We fought for our lives and we prevailed."

"So you say," Palmanter said. "Allow us the opportunity to challenge your version of the events."

"Or confirm it?" Tyrus asked mockingly.

"We have witnesses," Stoern said.

"As do I. Believe me, nothing I say will satisfy you. You have witnesses right here. Annon was there. Khiara Shaliah was there. Prince Aransetis was there. So were these two—Lukias is a Provost-Rike and helped lead the assault against us."

"And that man over there," Stoern said, pointing to Kishion. "His presence here is highly suspect. We all know who he is. Will you turn him loose on us, Tyrus?"

A cold smile came to her father's mouth. "You were brave to face me, fearing me as you do. We will come with you peacefully. I have nothing to hide. I will plead my cause before the Thirteen. But first, you must answer my question. How did you find me?"

Palmanter looked relieved. "We did not know you were here, Tyrus. There are Bhikhu monitoring this portion of the woods to protect the Dryad tree. We were alerted when the Quiet Kishion arrived."

"And you brought something you could capture him with," Tyrus said shrewdly, nodding. "Some magic from Mirrowen, no doubt. I advise you not to attempt it. He is impervious to spirit magic. If you do not harm us, you will not be harmed. Not even the Bhikhu you brought will be enough. Trust me on that."

Stoern glowered. "Now that our motives are laid bare, will you come with us?"

"We will," Tyrus answered. "I have no quarrel with Canton Vaud."

Phae felt dread in her heart. She remembered Shion's warning that the Arch-Rike had a spy in Canton Vaud.

It was good being back in his old Druidecht clothes again. Annon had gratefully discarded the black cassock and returned to his pack for his old attire. He kept the torc around his neck. Canton Vaud no longer held the allure it once had. He had visited it before and had found his friend Reeder camped there in a small pavilion. He knew Palmanter was one of the Thirteen and he wanted to trust him, but the reception they had received had troubled him greatly and Stoern's rebuke had rattled him. He was used to the respect afforded his position as a Druidecht. The thought of losing his talisman and being cast off from the order filled him with dread. He believed the order was fair. If he could persuade them of the dangers they faced, that the Arch-Rike was a mutual enemy, he hoped to get them on their side and win their trust.

After crossing the woods of Silvandom back to Canton Vaud, they were brought to an expansive pavilion to rest, eat, and change before being summoned to the presence of the Thirteen. The long walk had not afforded the privilege of private conversation, so he had not spoken to Tyrus at all along the way.

After changing his clothes, he approached the man cautiously, noticing Khiara had already changed as well and sat in a meditation position, head bowed. Tyrus picked from a platter of food, tasting an assortment of nuts and cheeses. Phae was resting on a small pallet, speaking in low tones to the Kishion. Lukias brooded and paced, his eyes traveling across the pavilion, taking in every detail.

"What is it?" Tyrus asked, motioning Annon over. "You have questions."

"I was a little surprised you chose to come willingly," Annon said. He nestled down on a cushion and took some fruit from the tray. "Do you think we are safe here?"

A wry smile flickered across his mouth. "Of course we are not safe here." His voice dropped very low. "The Arch-Rike has a spy in Canton Vaud."

"What?" Annon asked, leaning forward. His stomach clenched. "Who?"

"I am trying to figure it out. Probably one of the Thirteen. I have been trying to reason it out myself."

"Do you think it is Stoern?" Annon whispered.

Tyrus shook his head. "No, she is too easily ruffled. Someone more subtle. What do you know of Palmanter?"

Annon's anxiety went into a full raging panic. "Reeder was friends with him. He is the one who told me some of the Dryad lore. He revealed the boon and counseled me to stay by the tree."

Tyrus stroked his beard. "You look unsettled."

"Shouldn't I be?" Annon said with a gasp. "We are in the middle of Canton Vaud, surrounded by the most powerful Druidecht in the lands. There are spirits here, powers we cannot understand."

Tyrus met his gaze, listening intently.

Annon edged closer to him. "Which is why I was surprised you would bring us here." He grabbed a handful of nuts and began eating them. They were heavily salted and tasted delicious. Nizeera was coiled near the door, head on her paws, watching them closely.

Tyrus leaned forward. "You must trust me, Annon. Trust that I know something about the spirits of Mirrowen. Trust that I know every possible way of taming them. The situation has changed since we were last here. The Arch-Rike attempted to murder us in Silvandom. There were corpses left behind. He has also lost one of his most valuable allies. He has invented a story to lay the blame on me. You saw how they treated me. I am not afraid of the truth.

Whether or not they choose to help us, we will continue. The pieces are starting to come together."

Annon hated cryptic comments like that. "What do you mean?"

"All in good time, my boy." Tyrus smiled knowingly.

Phae was drowsy and the blankets were very soft and comfortable. She blinked slowly. She shook her head and sat up. "I fell asleep, didn't I?"

Shion nodded, sitting on the floor next to the pallet. "You should rest. The others are, except for Tyrus."

Brushing hair around her ear, Phae looked across the dimly-lit pavilion. Annon was curled up next to Nizeera, his expression showing possible nightmares. Khiara was still in her trance, head down, black hair veiling her face. Lukias was spread out on another pallet, breathing softly.

"There is a smell here that reminds me of Stonehollow." She looked around and then noticed the cask of wine and the pewter cups. "Ah."

He glanced where she was looking and then looked down at his hands. She could see him wrestling with himself.

"What is it?" she whispered, touching his sleeve.

"I'm conflicted," he murmured softly. "Something Lukias said gnaws at me."

She remembered the comment perfectly. She tightened her grip on his arm. "Promise me, Shion. When this is through, you will confront your memories. You will face your past."

"Do I dare?" His voice was just the ghost of a whisper.

She lowered her face closer to his. "You must. I feel your anguish. Not knowing is certainly worse than any deeds you have done. You did not do those things on your own. If other men paid for the deeds, they are the ones who bear an equal share of the blame." She frowned, angry at the men who had dominated his life. "There is some hope. If the truth is so unbearable . . . I can take it away." She looked him in the eyes pointedly.

He shook his head. "I would not want you to carry my burdens. You least of all."

"I'm not sure how it works. I learned much visiting the Dryad tree. But if I can help you, I will."

He met her gaze. "Something tugs at me when I look at you. A memory buried away." He sighed deeply.

She patted his arm. "I trust you, Shion. You will not let anyone hurt me."

He nodded gravely, his expression suddenly concealed by a shadow as Tyrus stood. Her father approached and settled down on a cushion next to the pallet.

"Did you learn what you need to know at the tree?" Tyrus asked her.

"I believe so," she replied. She paused. "I do not think I am meant to share it."

He held up his hand, smiling inwardly, and made a motion to forestall her. "I would not ask it of you. If you need to return and visit the tree, you can later."

"Why don't you sleep, Father?" she asked him. "Shion can guard us."

He nodded sagely, glancing from his daughter to her protector. "They will call for us soon. There is something about midnight that strengthens a Druidecht's power. They seek every advantage in this confrontation." He brushed something from his pants. He looked at Shion shrewdly. "We may have to fight our way out of Canton Vaud. I would ask you to spare their lives. I hate to bind you, and you will need to use your own judgment. But I would prefer not confirming their worst opinions about me."

Shion shrugged noncommittally then motioned for the pillow. "Sleep," he bid her.

Phae shook her head. "I'm not tired."

A dark scowl came across Tyrus's face. "You will be," he said softly. "We must be well rested when we enter the Scourgelands. We will get little or no sleep once we do." She saw his expression harden and felt the sparks of memory exploding in his mind.

"What will we face?" Shion asked.

"I will tell you all later," he replied. "I would not brook fears until we are ready to face them. It is a dark place. It is a terrible place. Fire seemed to work the best. I hope it will still." He reached out and took Phae's hand. "You will need to fight as well, Phae. Not even your friend here will be able to protect you from all dangers. You must use the fireblood to protect yourself."

Phae felt a shiver of fear go down to her boots. "I'm frightened of it," she whispered.

"If you weren't, I would worry even more. Use it. Do not overuse it. That way leads to madness."

The look in his eyes showed her that he knew what he was talking about. He was haunted by his memories. Slowly, he turned and stared at Annon's sleeping form. Nizeera's head popped up, her whiskers twitching, her ears alert.

"They've come for us," Tyrus said, his voice black with dread.

"*The Vaettir have a saying that is ripe with wisdom: The gods judged it better to bring good out of evil than to suffer no evil to exist. They will not willingly take a life for fear of destroying that potential inside us. We all have tendencies toward evil, some more than others. Each of us must constantly root away those evil tendencies lest they prevail into our character. We each carry within us the bud of true goodness as well as evil. Which we nourish determines our destiny.*"

—*Possidius Adeodat, Archivist of Kenatos*

XXXIX

As they were escorted into the grand pavilion of the Thirteen, Annon swallowed hard, not certain what to expect but fearing the outcome. It was just past midnight, according to the stars peeking from amidst the tree branches, but there was still a general buzz about the camp. He noticed streamers of magic lingering in the air, and the flames of several of the torches fastened to iron poles sticking around the perimeter of the pavilion burned a strange blue color and chased away shadows. There were several Bhikhu guarding the main entryway.

Annon ducked slightly as he entered and found the pavilion full of bodies. The Thirteen were a mix of the races and his eyes jumbled at the sight of all of them and his pulse quickened with worry. Each wore an ornate talisman over their clothing, which were varied depending on the country they hailed from. As soon as Annon straightened, he felt several sets of eyes on him, staring at him shrewdly, judging him. They were all much older, several well silvered, but none of them were very old, as he had been expecting. They all had accoutrements of some kind—chokers around the neck, some with bracers or rings. Some even had torcs, similar to the one he wore, but without the glowing gems fastened to the ends. It was an intimidating group and Annon felt himself shrivel being in their presence and under their intense scrutiny.

The others assembled into the pavilion with him, Tyrus taking the lead and striding to the front of the council, his bearing confident. He had stood before them previously seeking asylum that had not been granted.

Palmanter spoke first. "Welcome to Canton Vaud. You are safe here. Be at ease." He sat on a comfortably padded chair, his arms folded, one hand tapping his cheek. "Introductions, before we begin." He motioned to Tyrus.

Tyrus nodded in acceptance. "You are quite aware of who I am. Let me introduce the rest. This is Annon of Wayland, son of Merinda Druidecht." He paused deliberately, his hand cupped toward Annon.

"She died during your last foray," one of the Thirteen muttered darkly.

Tyrus was as hard as flint. He did not respond to the comment. "Khiara Shaliah of the royal house of Silvandom. Friend of Canton Vaud." There were nods in respect to her. Annon saw her bearing as aloof. She gripped her long, tapered staff, almost leaning on it. Her knuckles still bore the scars of their troubles in the mountains. Tyrus motioned next to the Rike. "Lukias of Kenatos. Provost-Rike." There were murmurs at that, some looking at each other askance. He then gestured at the Kishion. "This man is known to many of you, in rumors if not by name. He is one of the Arch-Rike's Kishion. He aids in our quest."

"*Your* quest," one of the Thirteen muttered, a man.

Tyrus then motioned to Phae. "This is my daughter, Phae of Stonehollow. She is Dryad-Born."

Annon saw the ripple of shock go through their faces. The

looks varied from shock, resentment, fury, and disgust—the blend
conjured made Annon doubt whether Tyrus should have mentioned
the last part. The girl herself seemed to shrink at the sudden hostility in their gazes.

"Impossible . . ."

"A cruel trick?"

"This cannot be condoned . . ."

"Patience," Palmanter interrupted, motioning for the others.
"The time for questions will come in due course. Be silent, Stoern.
Kepniss, hush. I will introduce us, as there are many faces here that
are strangers to you all." Palmanter rose, a tall man himself, of the
same height as Tyrus. He looked older, but only because his hair
was silver. He paced slowly in front of the others, his head bowed
low in thought. He started at the far end of the semicircle of chairs.

"Stoern of Stonehollow," he said, gesturing toward the bird-like
woman who had met them in the woods. She was very distrustful,
her expression one of open contempt and wariness. She had auburn
hair and Annon wondered if she possessed the fireblood. As each
name was spoken, he felt the gift of the Dryad kiss working and he
was able to memorize instantly each of their names as well as the
kingdoms from which they hailed.

The man sitting next to her was tall and bluff, his face square.
He had black hair that was fringed with gray along the temples.
His skin was dark and he had the look of a man who could wield a
hammer and chisel. A small smirk curled the corner of his mouth.
He whispered something to Stoern. His robes were rumpled and
dusty. "Zannich of Stonehollow," Palmanter said.

The next was another woman, a Vaettir who wore the talisman.
She was not a Bhikhu or a Shaliah. Her hair was cut short in a bob
and she had an intense look. Not one of judgment but of great
curiosity. She was leaning forward in her chair, her eyes taking them
in. "This is Jinna of Kenatos. The only Vaettir among the Thirteen.

She was an Archivist in the past." Annon noticed Tyrus's sudden interest in the woman.

The next man was part-Vaettir, though larger around the shoulders and fairer haired than Annon expected. "Skogen of Lydi." The man was shrewd looking, nodding to them respectfully. His eyes were probing the Kishion's. There was a sleek spirit animal next to his chair, a spotted cat with a long, thick tail. Its eyes were also probing them. Annon felt Nizeera brush against his leg, as if reminding him she was there.

Palmanter stood next in front of three Cruithne. They were all dark skinned but one was an exceptionally big-boned woman. "Rajas of Alkire," Palmanter said, motioning to her. She looked at them imperiously, as if she were a queen, her eyes glinting with condescension. She dipped her chin to them, but looked as if she would prefer summoning a tornado to destroy them all.

Next to her was an older man, the oldest of them all, with thick streaks of gray in his beard. He rubbed his bottom lip, staring at all of them as if they were diseased. "Bryont, also of Alkire. And next to him, Obie of Alkire. She is the newest member of the Thirteen. These three are our experts on the Paracelsus order." Obie had darker skin than the other two Cruithne and did not share their girth. She was looking at Phae with sympathy, her expression troubled.

Annon looked at the next three, for all were Preachán and smaller than the rest. The first was a woman, with chestnut brown hair. She was slight but wore a variety of necklaces and jewelry. The cut of her tunic was very fashionable. She was probably fifty. "Kepniss of Havenrook. Next to her are Koth and Moolien. They both speak the Romani tongue fluently and are experts in the trade disputes going on between Alkire, Havenrook, and Wayland. They have heavy accents and are sometimes difficult to understand."

"You malign us," Moolien said. He was bald and bearded and gestured with annoyance at Palmanter. "I will have you know we have memorized each line of the agreement scrolls and can cite them by annotation as well as by age of the parchment." He was a small man, very feisty and energetic. "Where is the Preachán you had with you previously, Tyrus? Where is Erasmus?"

"Dead," Tyrus said flatly, his eyes piercing the smaller man whose eyes filled with shock.

The other Preachán looked injured. He was Koth and his hair was well silvered. "He was a brilliant man."

"We are in agreement on that at least," Tyrus replied gravely. He nodded to the three Preachán solemnly.

"Deaths have already begun even *before* your departure," Stoern pointed out snidely. "How unfortunate."

Palmanter waved her silent and then introduced the final two. The first was a woman with gold hair flecked with slivers of steel. She was a handsome woman, elegantly dressed in form-fitting robes with elegant needlework patterns. "Mitrisin of Wayland. The king's cousin." She nodded respectfully to them and reached out and patted Koth on the arm, as if comforting him.

"And Psowen, also of Wayland." He was a turtle of a man, his hair receding and he had bulging eyes that gave him almost a frog-like look. His hair was well silvered too and he looked as if he'd enjoyed too many pastries over his life. But despite his looks, he stared at them with keenness and scrutiny.

Annon recounted their names once more in his mind, fixing their features and looks. He did not know the process of being chosen as one of the Thirteen. Each one of them wore a talisman that had a different look than his did. Theirs seemed more ancient, as if it had been passed down for many generations.

Palmanter took his seat, his big arms folding imperiously. "Who would ask the first question?"

"How did Erasmus die?" Moolien asked, his jaw quivering with emotion. He leaned forward in his chair.

Tyrus held up his hand and took a step forward. "You have summoned me here to answer questions. Rather than submit to them, I propose an alternative. Let me explain what I am doing here, what these friends are doing here with me, and what our intentions are. Then I have a few questions of my own to ask the Thirteen. Are we agreed?"

Zannich snorted. "We summoned *you*, Tyrus. Not the other way around."

"I came here willingly, as a friend of Canton Vaud. I understand there are some suspicions regarding my recent activities. It is probably best if I address them directly."

"You may try," Zannich muttered darkly.

Tyrus seemed to focus on him first. "We are countrymen, Zannich. I understand your skepticism. Let me speak freely then, if you are agreeable?"

Palmanter looked at the frog-eyed man, Psowen, who nodded, his face impassive.

"Thank you. I do not wish to claim all of your time. My motives remain as they have always been. I seek to banish the Plagues. I know how this may be done. These, along with a few others, have agreed to journey with me into the Scourgelands. Our intent is to depart immediately and face the horrors there once again." It was clear some of them were going to interrupt by the way they shifted in their chairs, but Tyrus waved them silent. "Please, I must beg your indulgence further. Hear me out. I will be brief." He clasped his hands behind his back. "As we gathered in Prince Aransetis's manor house in Silvandom, we were viciously attacked by the soldiers and Paracelsus and by the Arch-Rike of Kenatos himself. We were outnumbered, caught by surprise. We defended ourselves and many of the Arch-Rike's servants were killed in the battle. I admit this freely. There was no offer to treat with us. To put it plainly, they tried to destroy my quest before it could even begin." He gestured broadly. "These are the witnesses, including two of the Arch-Rike's servants who have since changed sides. This is my evidence. I have been hunted and attacked nearly every day since I fled the prison city of Kenatos. The Arch-Rike seeks my life. He wishes to stop me."

Mutters and words began to mix.

"Are you saying," Kepniss said with a thick accent, "That the Arch-Rike of Kenatos attempted to murder you? You know this is what he accuses *you* of."

"Of course he does," Tyrus replied, folding his arms. "One of us is a liar. There can be no other conclusion. Against every treaty, against common sense, and even against wisdom, he led a group of armed men into the jurisdiction of Silvandom with the express intent of murdering me and those who follow me. When they failed, with corpses as proof of that failure, he needed to concoct a story granting his arrival some semblance of legitimacy."

Stoern shook her head. "You have the same burden of proof as he does. You cannot prove your story any more than he can. We have a long history of relations with Kenatos. The Vaettir are his sworn allies. If he wanted you turned over to him, he would only have needed to ask."

"Curious then, isn't it, Stoern?" Tyrus replied, locking his hands behind his back again and giving her a shrewd look. "With such good relations with Silvandom, you would think he would have been welcomed into their kingdom as an honored guest. Why the secrecy and treachery? He was anticipating killing us all and ridding our bodies as evidence. That begs a very important question." He paused, letting his words sink in. "Why would he seek to thwart my quest at all? If his intentions are as good as he claims, why not leave me alone?"

"Because," answered Koth grumpily with a look on his face as if he'd bitten into something very sour, "your intentions are no more honorable than his own. The Arch-Rike holds great influence and power, but he is dependent on the goodwill of the kingdoms to maintain it. You have always been jealous of that influence. I remember when you last ventured into those dreaded woods. Everyone died." He snorted. "Except for you."

Annon saw the cheek muscle on Tyrus's face twitch.

"I have since learned," Tyrus said in a low, steady voice, "that my last quest was compromised before we even left. We walked into a trap and were butchered. The Arch-Rike himself was behind our failure. I have the tools needed now to be successful. And I will use them. Believe me or not, it does not matter. We are going anyway."

"But it does matter," Mitrisin said imploringly. "Tyrus, you know I admire and respect you. You have a reputation to be envied. But you are ambitious. This ambition clouds your vision. If there was a way to penetrate the Scourgelands, *we* would have discovered it long ago. The woods are our domain, Tyrus. Not yours."

"You are blinded by what you do not see," Tyrus answered.

"You are the one who is blind here," Moolien said savagely.

"Please, let us not provoke one another," Kepniss said calmly. "Tyrus, you know I respect you as well. You are without peer. But it is said, and whispered by many, that you have the fireblood. That you are of the forgotten race. Do you deny it?"

Tyrus bristled at the question. He looked at Zannich and Stoern, both of whom eyed him with great hostility. Annon remembered hearing that those from Stonehollow persecuted people with the fireblood.

"No, I do not deny it," Tyrus replied. "I am not bound to answer your questions. I chose to do so openly."

There was an audible murmur.

Kepniss shook her head. "It is also said that those who possess the fireblood often go mad. There are words they use that tame this power. But if those words are not used, well, that is how the madness begins. It is incurable."

"Who taught you this lore?" Tyrus asked her. "It is not Druidecht."

"I did," Jinna said, her Vaettir eyes probing. "It is written in the Archives."

"It is true," Tyrus replied. "The lore, that is. My own sister succumbed to madness." His eyes blazed with unbridled fury. "It pains me, even now." His voice dropped low. "And I am the last person in the seven kingdoms who would allow it to happen to myself. I know the dangers of fire. So does the Arch-Rike. He has the fireblood too. I have seen him summon it."

There was another burbling of gasps in the pavilion.

"What proof does he have?" Zannich muttered.

Tyrus spread out his hands. "Let me be quite clear. I do not seek your permission to enter the Scourgelands. I do not seek your support for my quest. I am not a Druidecht nor am I bound by your customs. You say the woods are your domain. Very well. Prove it. Do any of you have the courage to join me?"

"You have already persuaded a Druidecht to join you," Obie declared. "He is just a boy. Your daughter is little more than a child herself. Can you safeguard their lives as you failed to do before?"

Tyrus stared at her and then shook his head.

"Why should we let you go then?" Zannich demanded, leaning forward, nearly coming out of his chair.

The look in Tyrus's eyes was cold and it froze the Druidecht. "What makes you think you possess the power to stop me?"

Annon saw some of the Thirteen glance at each other. There were a few curt nods. They were planning something. He could see the stiffness in their shoulders. He could see the looks of distrust. They had no intention of letting any of them go free.

"I have a question," Bryont said sagely, leaning back in his chair. "It's a simple one, really." He stroked his grizzled beard. "You said your daughter was Dryad-born. I presume that has some relevance to this or you would not have brought her or sired her. That knowledge is not in any book in Kenatos. How did *you* learn that lore?"

Tyrus smiled grimly. "A good question, Master Bryont. You always go straight to the crux of the matter. I like that about you. I have been honest with all of you so far. I first learned the lore from Merinda Druidecht. Now I have a question for you. For all of you. How long have you willingly harbored one of the Arch-Rike's spies in your inner circle?"

Palmanter leaned forward. "What did you . . . ?"

"You heard me well enough, old friend. One of you is in the paid service of the Arch-Rike of Kenatos. Shall I have Lukias name the person for you? Or will you confess it willingly? I know who you are."

Psowen's face twitched with rage. "Bhikhu!" he ordered sharply. "Attend us!"

The flap of the tent fluttered as the Vaettir began to enter the pavilion.

"Please, don't do anything rash, old friend," Palmanter said warningly, making a gesture to the Bhikhu entering. "We are turning you over to the Bhikhu. They will investigate your claims before any are delivered to Kenatos. You are a dangerous man, Tyrus. You are dangerous to these friends, as you call them. For the good of everyone, we must question you further."

"*It is one of the bad habits of kings and those with power to attribute the virtue of truthful speaking to those from whom there is no further risk of hearing it.*"

—*Possidius Adeodat, Archivist of Kenatos*

X L

Paedrin entered the pavilion first, gripping the chain ring in his hand. He was used to its heft and ready to begin whipping it about the room. He quickly observed the situation, saw Tyrus standing in front of the others and immediately assumed a defensive posture, tightening the chain between his fists loudly so that the links clashed when they went taut. Hettie entered next, the charm she wore around her neck disguising her as Vaettir-born, the Bhikhu robes perfectly disguising her and gripping the hilt of the Sword of Winds. Kiranrao and Prince Aransetis came next, taking up position, four Vaettir in all. Baylen was stacking the bodies of the unconscious bodyguards out of sight.

It was good to see the others again. Annon looked greensick, a lad taken before his masters for punishment. If scolded, he might vomit. He saw the Quiet Kishion with dread and respect, amazed that Tyrus had tamed him. He hoped it was not a trap, for he did not relish the thought of fighting the Kishion a third time. He was willing to though. His vision was whole, his body healed, and he had enjoyed an especially savory dish of rice and peppers for supper earlier.

Judging by the looks on the Thirteen's faces, none of them had realized their bodyguards had been dispatched yet. All Vaettir looked the same to foreigners.

One of them, a pudgy man with a sallow face, pointed to Tyrus. "You will submit to us. We are well aware of your capabilities, Tyrus. We know you can vanish through use of a magic device. We may not be able to stop you, but you will not take many of these with you on the mad quest you insist on. Annon—you owe us obedience and allegiance, stand aside. The rest are offered clemency if you desist immediately. You are in the middle of Canton Vaud. Do not be foolish to presume that you will all escape."

Tyrus's reply was classic. "You are the one who is presuming much, Psowen. Allow me to introduce the remainder of my group." Paedrin could not keep the smirk from his mouth. It was a brilliant use of the Uddhava.

"This is Paedrin of Kenatos, last Bhikhu of the temple. The others were poisoned to death and the Arch-Rike did nothing to help or cure it, though he did not lack the antidote or the knowledge of it. Hettie, who appears to you as a Vaettir girl right now, is also the child of Merinda Druidecht. Kiranrao of Havenrook you will recognize and perhaps even sense the presence of the blade Iddawc in his hand. There is Prince Aransetis, of course . . . I am sure you overlooked him since he is not dressed as a Rike currently. And lastly, here he comes, is Baylen of Kenatos, guardian of the Paracelsus Towers."

Tyrus took a meaningful step forward. "It may not have escaped your notice that there are twelve of us. Had Erasmus been here, it would have been an *even* thirteen. Threaten us again and you will find that your talismans will not save you from me. I have not come this far to be thwarted by Canton Vaud."

Palmanter held up his hands. "Easy, my friend. Do not be hasty."

"Am I your friend?" Tyrus asked coldly. "I have told you the truth. The ring worn by the Arch-Rike's spy confirms it. We can ask one by one if we must to prove this. But let us hasten the game. Name her, Lukias."

Paedrin glanced at the Rike who stared at Tyrus with a mixture of awe and respect on his face. "Well done, Tyrus," the Rike said with a half-chuckle. There was a clap of shocked silence.

"The spy?" one of the Druidecht muttered nervously.

"Who do you mean?" a Preachán asked pointedly to Tyrus.

Tyrus turned to the Rike nearby and gestured for him to disclose it.

"It is Rajas," the man said simply. "The ring is on her right hand and is disguised in a gold filigree design of a scarab. She is your spy. The Arch-Rike told me himself."

All eyes turned suddenly to a corpulent Cruithne with an imperious and completely bewildered look. The shock was so sudden and evident on her face that for a moment she could only splutter.

Tyrus tapped his mouth. "I do see a ring on her hand. It bears a startling resemblance to a scarab."

The shocked expressions, the utter bewilderment thrilled Paedrin. Their entire shared minds were fumbling over themselves, reacting to the news.

"How . . . dare . . . you!" Rajas uttered lividly. Her cheeks went chalky white and she fixed a finger at Lukias.

"Do you deny it, Madame?" Tyrus said simply. Then his voice pitched low and throbbed with warning. "Do you *dare* deny it?" He glowered at Palmanter. "You invited me here to answer questions. Instead, you intended all along to turn me over to the Arch-Rike."

"No, Tyrus," Palmanter said gravely. "The Vaettir are wise and honorable. Cunning, too, it would seem. They are investigating what happened at the manor house. Surely, if what you have told us is true, there is ample evidence of your innocence." He looked over at Rajas with disgust. "You have also done us a great service, Tyrus. We will deal with her immediately."

"Hold a moment," one of the other Druidecht said, standing up. "We aren't letting him leave . . ."

It was Zannich. Annon saw the wariness in his face and instantly distrusted him. There were possibly more in league with the Cruithne woman. His heart was overjoyed at Tyrus's duplicity, grateful for once that he was a man who guarded his secrets so well. He recognized Paedrin and Prince Aran. He would never forget a man like Kiranrao. And the girl Tyrus had claimed to be Hettie did not look familiar at all, but he trusted that it was magic disguising her. The Cruithne who had entered with his other friends was not a stranger to him either. He looked at the man and instantly recalled having seen him before, at the Paracelsus Towers.

"Hold a moment, Zannich. We must consider what he has told us," Mitrisin said gravely. "Rajas might not be the only one of us who has betrayed the Druidecht. Are there more traitors among us, Tyrus?"

Tyrus gave her a probing look. "We must go. Our journey will be difficult. We will leave you. Gather around me," he said urgently. "All of you."

"You cannot leave!" Zannich said fiercely. "You've leveled accusations against the Arch-Rike of Kenatos. You must stand behind those accusations. We will summon him to Canton Vaud. If he refuses to come, then it proves the validity of your words. If you leave now, it puts everything you said before in doubt."

"You and Stoern already doubt every word I have uttered," Tyrus said. "My intention is *not* to topple the Arch-Rike. It is what

I declared it to be in the beginning. I will stop this Plague from ravaging the lands. We cannot delay."

"You must delay," Kepniss said. "There is a war raging between Wayland and Havenrook. The whole world is in turmoil. Only delay a fortnight, that is all that we ask."

"We will not," Tyrus said flatly. The others began to gather around him. Annon saw the Tay al-Ard in his hand, clutched just out of sight of the Thirteen. Annon stood by him, staring down the Druidecht, those to whom he owed his allegiance.

"Annon of Wayland," Psowen said thickly. "You will not go! You are not strong enough to face the dangers."

"I choose it willingly," Annon replied simply. "My mother followed him. So do I."

Skogen had not spoken much, but he did now. "I will not attempt to dissuade you, Tyrus. You have your own mind. But remember that the last group you brought were much older, better equipped. This is a bold force, I'll grant you that. But they are untested."

"Enough words," Tyrus said. "I do not seek your permission. Solve the problems as you see best. We are going. Lukias?"

Annon noticed that the Rike had not closed the circle with them. His eyes were shifting back and forth, from the Thirteen and back to Tyrus, as if trying to decide something.

Something passed between their eyes.

An explosion ripped through the pavilion.

To Phae, it felt like daggers had jammed inside her ears. The noise was so loud and so close, she felt excruciating pain from both her ears. Shards of glass sliced through her skin and clothes, stinging sharply, but it was insignificant compared to the thrumming ache in her ears. For several moments, she was too stunned to even think. In her mind, she was back in Stonehollow, her ear ripped by a thorn after Shion had chased her down. Panic and fear rose inside of her and she felt herself buried alive. She fought and kicked, trying to free herself from the smothering cocoon only to realize it was Shion, his body pressed on top of hers, shielding her from the worst damage of the explosion.

He rose, staring into her face in concern, his eyes searching hers for signs of life. He touched her throat, feeling her heart pounding, then dropped his head in relief. Then he rose and whirled, daggers in his hands, and went after Lukias.

Only it was no longer Lukias.

The man standing amidst the debris of the tattered pavilion was no man she had ever seen before. His stubbly hair was ash gray, but he was not old. His eyes were so pale they were nearly white, except for the piercing black pupils. He stood triumphantly, holding a Tay al-Ard in his own hand, mirroring the one in Tyrus's, his expression full of delight.

"Please, Kishion," he muttered. "I will be gone before you can touch me. I have an offer to make all of you. You must decide now whether to accept it."

Phae tried to push herself up, but her limbs were quivering from the immensity of the blast. Annon was limp, his face ashen, Nizeera snuffling against his cheek. Was he dead? The Bhikhu were already on their feet, but each of them had sustained terrible wounds, of gashes and burn marks. Khiara ran to Annon, touching his head with her hand and summoning her magic to save him. His eyes flashed open, blinking rapidly.

"I knew you were somewhere in the room," Tyrus said menacingly, grimacing in pain. "I felt . . . your voice coming from many mouths, Band-Imas." He looked around the debris of the room, the shattered furniture. The lumps of ash. Phae's stomach sickened. "You . . . you killed them. All of them!"

"And you will suffer the blame of it," the Arch-Rike replied evenly. "Those exploding orbs you invented are so useful, aren't they? This is my final offer, Tyrus. There will be no safe haven for you after this. No kingdom will ever trust you again. Assume you survive the Scourgelands. Assume you prevail. Who will you tell? You see, Tyrus, I know your heart. You crave the glory of defeating the Plague. That is your deepest desire. Only I can give it to you now. I will not unleash it this generation. We will invent a sickness, a pox maybe, and you will cure it. Everyone will know it was you who stopped the pox from spreading. It will even be written in the Archives. Why, I'll have Possidius scribe it himself. There—you will have it. Everything you have desired. Another generation from now and no one will remember what was done. Nor will they care. But you will have what you have always craved most. The *glory* of it." His mouth spread into a sickening smile. "This is my final offer, Tyrus. You will have a chance to live out your life."

His attention turned to Phae and she shrank, recoiling from his gaze. "You have a daughter. She can remain with you. If she does not bond with a Dryad tree soon, she won't be able to. The magic will pass and she will be just an ordinary girl." He looked at her with that same lurid smile. "Or perhaps she would prefer to go back to Stonehollow. Would you like that lass? With Trasen, hmmm?" Then his eyes sought out the others. "One by one, I will restore what you have lost. Think, Annon. After what was done here, you are now a Black Druidecht. You murdered the Thirteen of Canton Vaud! All of you did!" He smiled savagely. "You thought you could outmaneuver me. Many have tried over the years. All have failed. There is no place you will find refuge. There is no place that will be your home. But I can protect you from even this in Kenatos."

Tyrus was on his feet now, swaying slightly, a rivulet of blood going down from a cut in his temple. His voice was raw with emotion. "We must be very close to success if you would risk such a scene as this. Kishion, take him!"

Phae's heart lurched as she watched the Kishion fly at the Arch-Rike, dagger poised. There was a look of unbridled fear in the Arch-Rike's eyes just before he vanished.

The Kishion landed in the emptiness, his face contorted with rage. He stalked back to Phae, standing over her protectively. He looked savage as a beast, his expression showing a welling of absolute hatred.

"Gather round me. Quickly!" Tyrus snapped. He held out the Tay al-Ard, holding it in front of him as if it were a rod of iron that would steady him. They all had injuries, but Khiara was healing them. One by one, they clasped an arm to his. Phae looked into her father's eyes, seeing the torment there. His mouth was transforming into a snarl of rage.

Spirits began to swirl around inside the pavilion, coming in streamers from all directions.

"Quickly!" Tyrus barked again.

Phae touched his arm, looking pleadingly into his eyes. Shion rested his hand on top of hers, his face grim and determined, his mouth twitching.

Were they going into the Scourgelands? Her heart shuddered with fear. How could they? The blast had nearly killed them all. The Arch-Rike had deceived them and destroyed the Thirteen. They would be blamed for it.

Annon's hand covered next, his fingers like talons. His face was shocked, his mouth gaping. "Tyrus, the tree! He's at the tree right now! You must take us there! I must defend her!"

"We are already too late," Tyrus muttered darkly, his countenance hardening.

"No!" Annon begged. "Please!"

Paedrin and the others quickly gathered around, adding their hands to the mix. There was nothing but death all around them. Ash and smoke drifted in the breezes that came through the slashed vents.

Annon began to wail, his eyes going wide with horror.

In some deep part of Phae's blood, she felt two Dryad trees explode.

She squeezed her father's arm, stifling a choking sob. Streamers of magic began to swirl around them. There were cries of warning from outside the tattered pavilion. Phae shut her eyes, not wanting to be seen, not wanting to even feel. Would they all die?

Her stomach felt the familiar unease and suddenly they were swept away, flung from the pockmarked graveyard of Canton Vaud.

"One cannot overestimate the power of persistence. It is persistence that guides a stonemason's hands and causes mighty castles and temples to be built. It is persistence that persuades a Bhikhu to practice his forms to perfection. It is persistence that allows a Paracelsus to discover new and interesting uses of ancient magics. It is persistence that allows the Rikes to cure diseases. It is persistence that provides a sailor the hope of arriving at a destination. In truth, there is no force in this world as enduring as persistence."

—Possidius Adeodat, Archivist of Kenatos

XLI

Annon drowned with grief. He could see through Neodesha's eyes, had watched as the Arch-Rike appeared in the Dryad grove. He deliberately did not look at her tree, his eyes downcast. She stared at him, trying to do anything to meet his gaze, to snatch his memory of where her tree was. He removed a glass bauble from a pouch at his waist and threw it at the tree. As the glass shattered, his connection with Neodesha and all of his reawakened memories were gone.

The Dryad's kiss was broken.

A thick veil began to settle over his mind. The piercing intensity of his memories and his emotions were tamped down, dulled to almost oblivion. Before he had remembered every detail of his past. Now, it was sucked into a black void, impenetrable. Even worse were the feelings that he had let her down, that he had betrayed her to her fate by leading their enemy to her tree.

The young Druidecht knelt in the stiff prairie grass, clutching himself, doubled over, his stomach starting to heave with the pounding remorse. Hettie crouched next to him on one side, the illusion gone, holding him tightly, trying to soothe him. Nizeera's tail lashed fitfully, for she could share his emotions and knew the torment he faced. It was still just after midnight, the darkest hour. How fitting to add to his misery.

His heart had been shattered like the glass orb. Already the intensity of Neodesha's face was beginning to fade. The memories were hollow, like glass vials. The fullness was gone. He did not want that to happen. He wanted to preserve it.

Annon struggled to his feet, tears wet on his cheeks. They were all huddled together in the dark, in some forsaken wilderness somewhere. He did not recognize the land, though it seemed vaguely familiar. Before, he would have recalled it instantly.

"Is she dead?" Annon asked Tyrus hoarsely, his voice croaking. "Tell me."

"I don't know," came the brooding reply. "My mind is dark . . . right now." Tyrus kneaded his temples with his fingertips.

"Where did you bring us?" Kiranrao demanded coldly. "Where are we?" He was pacing restlessly, his expression toward them full of contempt. "Is this the Scourgelands? Where are the trees?"

Tyrus held up his hand warningly. "This was always a risk," he muttered. "One cannot play such stakes as these without risking everything you hold dear." He winced with pain. "I knew Band-Imas might do this."

"How did he?" Paedrin asked, stepping forward. Khiara had healed his injuries already and he gave Annon a look of sadness. "I recognized the Arch-Rike the moment he arrived. I know the magic he used, for Hettie has the same charm that provides the disguise. How did he slip in amongst us?"

Annon looked at him, his heart melting with pain. Pain was a teacher. What a terrible lesson to learn. "It is my fault," Annon said miserably. "We revived Lukias after the battle in Silvandom. He was a corpse. I saw him revived with my own eyes. But when Erasmus tied him up, we left him and went into Basilides." He shook his head with self-loathing. "Then he appeared to rescue us. It was Band-Imas, of course."

"Ah," Paedrin said sympathetically. "He can speak in your mind. Yes, that makes it clear. He helped you escape Basilides. Because he wanted to see where you would take him."

"And the Tay al-Ard," Tyrus continued, "can only take you to a place you have been before. He knew about the Dryad tree in the Paracelsus Towers. He knew about Annon's tree but did not know exactly where it was."

The pain was unbearable. "I failed her. It's my fault."

Hettie squeezed his hand.

"Yes, you did," Kiranrao said derisively. "Look at them, Tyrus. Look at the heroes you've summoned." He scanned the group with contempt. "Send the striplings away. They will only hinder us. I would fight alongside the Kishion. A Shaliah is always helpful. But really, we don't need any of the others. Leave them behind."

Paedrin bristled at that. "And where would we return to, I ask you? Where would we find shelter from the Arch-Rike now? Tyrus, I know you desire to end the Plague, but we must end the Arch-Rike's rule as well. He murders the innocent. Silvandom must be told of his treachery. The Bhikhu shield him unwittingly."

Tyrus frowned and shook his head. "No one will believe us. But I will not be distracted, not even by such a loss as this." He approached Annon and put a heavy hand on his shoulder. "I feel your hurt, lad. Believe me that I do. But we must go on. We must face the Scourgelands. All of us." The last comment was said with a sidelong look at the Romani.

"Where are we, Tyrus?" Kiranrao asked again, an edge in his voice. "Answer me."

Annon saw the big man swallow, his eyes glittering in the dark. "Where not even the Arch-Rike will dare follow us. We are on the borders of Boeotia."

The small fire crackled, providing a cone of warmth to those sitting nearby. Paedrin and Hettie were hidden in the shadows beneath a giant shade tree, their backs against its trunk, their shoulders touching. Their camp was being guarded by spirits, it was said, but Paedrin was more concerned about some of the people inside the camp than by the threats lurking outside it.

"Poor Annon," Hettie whispered, leaning her head against his shoulder.

Paedrin saw the Druidecht sitting by the fire, his hands playing with the flames—unburned. It was eerie how he could do that. But probably no more eerie than a Vaettir being able to float.

"Yes, he is a poor man. I pity him."

"Love develops differently for different people. For some, love comes softly. But the Romani people have a saying. Whilst kicking and biting, love develops."

"Ah, how very true," Paedrin said with a chuckle. "Though I would prefer another kiss to a bite. I recall Master Shivu having a different sentiment. He said"—using his best imitation of Shivu's voice—" 'Marriages are all happy; it's having breakfast together that causes all the trouble.' "

Hettie shook her head and offered a silver-threaded laugh. She was quiet for several long moments. "What I see between Prince Aran and Khiara is painful too, though in a different way. She loves him. You can see it in her eyes. But he loves no one. He rejects her with his very politeness. I pity her too."

"It is strange to watch," Paedrin agreed. "But I know why it is."

"You do?"

He nodded vigorously. "He expects to die in the Scourgelands. He is preparing himself for it. He is preparing her for it. He will make no emotional attachments until the Plagues are banished forever. He is simple that way."

"Do you think we will survive this quest?"

"I plan to."

"I'm trying to be serious, Paedrin."

"What odds do you think Erasmus would give us? I miss that strange bird. Of all the Preachán I've known, I will miss him the most. I am sure he would have offered a prediction by now. It would have been wrong."

She butted him with her elbow. "I said be serious."

"Whatever for?" he asked. "This is about as hopeless a situation as one can be in. I may as well find some humor if I can."

Their banter was interrupted by Kiranrao marching toward them, his face a mask of anger.

"I hate that man," Paedrin said softly, his eyes narrowing.

"Shhh," Hettie warned.

The Romani reached them, his expression curling into a sneer seeing them so close to each other. He felt Hettie ease away from him, just slightly enough that it caused a prickle of resentment.

"Come, Finder," Kiranrao said, looking down at Hettie. "I would speak with you."

"Is she yours to command?" Paedrin said in a warning tone.

He saw Hettie tense, but he did not care. He looked up at the man, feeling the magic seeping from the blade at his waist. The Iddawc was no longer seeking someone to master it. It had found someone it could master.

"I do not wish to waste many words arguing with you, Bhikhu," Kiranrao said in a flat voice. "Tyrus promised her asylum in Silvandom in return for aiding in his quest. When the dawn chases away the shadows, it will chase away any hope of that safe hold. We are renegades, all of us. But while the Arch-Rike insists that no one will shelter us, I can assure you that we Romani will shelter each other. Come, girl."

Paedrin felt Hettie start to rise and he grabbed her arm. "You do not have to go with him."

She looked in Paedrin's eyes and he saw the conflicting loyalties. "I know I don't," she said, cupping his cheek with her hand. But she stood anyway.

Kiranrao smirked with satisfaction. The look he gave Paedrin was full of enmity. "Come, girl. The stars make no noise."

Paedrin watched them walk off together, his heart turning blacker with each step they took.

"Must you provoke him?" Hettie sighed wearily.

Kiranrao glanced at her. "Yes."

She sighed again. "What do you want?"

"To understand your loyalties. You are Romani."

"I am a Bhikhu now. You got the blade you wanted. You used me to get it. Our bargain is complete. I owe you nothing."

He looked at her approvingly. "I like a girl with fire in her blood."

"You already have a vial of it with you. The price was paid, Kiranrao."

He shook his head slowly. "There is always a debt, girl. You know that. Your talents are wasted as a Bhikhu. You will grow bored of it eventually. And I am patient. I wanted to speak with you because I have a sense that Tyrus is going to fail again."

She stiffened and cursed herself for the involuntary reaction.

"You sense it too, good."

Hettie shook her head. "You mistook me."

"No, girl. I did not. You think like a Romani still. You sniff out the weakness. The Druidecht is weak. The Shaliah is weak. The Dryad-born is weak. Even your Bhikhu is weak. Only the strong will survive the Scourgelands. Only the most ruthless. That is how

Tyrus survived last time. It is how I intend to survive."

Hettie snorted. "You will abandon him already?"

He shook his head. "The dice are cast but they are still rolling. They will settle soon. Very soon. When they do, we must be prepared to flee. Do you know how to work his magic? The one that makes him come and go? I want you to steal it from him."

She stared at him. "You think he might not notice it missing?"

"Don't be a fool, Hettie. When his plan crumbles to dust, you will steal it. And we will flee together. Just the two of us. Remember that. The Sword of Winds you carry . . . it will help us to escape. So will my blade."

She bit her lip. "But if we succeed?"

A crooked smile twisted on his mouth. "Then the Arch-Rike of Kenatos is a dead man."

Trasen plodded up the road listlessly, seeing the home at the end of the rise amidst the grape trellises and the fluttering green leaves. His journey was now at an end. As he saw the trellises, there was a nagging, empty feeling in his mind. A memory about greeting someone amidst them, yet he could not recall when it had happened or who he had seen. There was something just beyond his reach, a recollection that teased and hinted. The sandy dirt was familiar. The looming barn was familiar. Just seeing the vineyard brought back a flood of pleasant memories that warmed his heart, but something was missing. He stared at it, feeling some jagged, gaping hole in his soul.

It was dark and only a thin bit of light came from the home. The barn looked abandoned. He shook his head, feeling uncomfortable and a little nauseous. As he reached the porch, he knocked firmly. He would have expected to hear laughter ringing out from the house. Why was it so silent? It was too early for the family to go up to the cabin, for the grapes had not been harvested yet. No one could leave until after the harvest and the trampling of the grapes. He could not wait to tell them all about his adventures, how he had gotten lost in the woods in Silvandom and finally directed back to Stonehollow by some fellow travelers.

Trasen massaged his cheeks and felt the rough, bristling whiskers. He needed a bath and a shave. His clothes were fit to be burned. So many empty pockets in his memory. So many things he could not recall. He must have hit his head while lost. That must be it.

"Is that you, Trasen?"

Trasen whirled and saw Uncle Carlsruhe come from around the house, axe in one hand as if expecting an enemy. The man was strong and rugged, with streaks of silver in his mustache and hair. He was Dame Winemiller's younger brother.

"Uncle?" Trasen asked, perplexed. "Where is everyone? Why are you here?"

Carlsruhe approached him warily, his face beginning to grimace. "Where is she, lad? Devin and Tate said you'd gone after her."

"Who?" Trasen asked, his mind turning into gnats that flittered every direction at once.

"Where is Phae?" Carlsruhe demanded. "You said you wouldn't come back without her."

Trasen stared at him, completely befuddled. There was a panicky feeling in his stomach, as if he should know the name. But he did not. "Who are you talking about, Uncle?" He could not explain it, but that nervous feeling felt as if it were covering a painful, sleeping wound.

He had never heard that name in his life.

Phae sat right at the edge of the fire, rubbing the warmth into her arms. She watched Annon play with the flames and her heart grieved for him. His face was sunken, bereft, his eyes haunted.

"I know a little of how you feel," she said tenderly, almost shyly.

Annon glanced up at her, blinking as though he had awoken from a dream. "Do you?" he replied but not unkindly.

"Not long ago, I was staying at the Winemillers in Stonehollow. It's an orphanage, you see. It was my home. My best friend was a young man named Trasen."

"The one the Arch-Rike threatened you with," Annon said softly.

She nodded. "Trasen doesn't remember me anymore. I stole his memories." She gazed down at the fire, her heart aching with the loss. "It was grown so subtly, I did not understand how I truly felt about him until after I stole his memories away. It was on a night, not long ago, that I wept as you did. Shion comforted me, strangely." She glanced over at him, watching him conferring in low tones with Tyrus and Prince Aran, the three men standing nearby.

Annon drew a quavering breath. "Even though you have the power to take away memories, Phae, I do not wish it. I've heard Dryads are immortal. Perhaps the blast did not kill them."

Phae nodded hopefully. "I would like to meet her someday. My mother, that is. I did meet the Dryad of your tree. She was very helpful. She gave me what I needed most—the knowledge of how to become like her. If I can cross into Mirrowen, Annon, I will see if they are there. After hearing about Mirrowen, I would like to see it for myself. It gives me something . . . to look forward to. Crossing the Scourgelands will be difficult. As long as there is something to hope for, I think I can bear it."

"You are the key to solving the riddle," Annon said, reaching out and putting his hand on hers. "The fate of us all is in your hands."

Phae felt a thrill at his words, but also a sense of great responsibility and helplessness. "I am the weakest among you. I have the fireblood too, but I don't want to use it. You are a Druidecht with great power. Everyone is going to be so much more useful along the way. But I will do what little part I can." She swiped a strand of hair behind her ear. "If the worst sacrifice I must make is being trapped in a tree in the Scourgelands that no one can visit . . . I suppose that will be my sacrifice."

He shook his head. "Every forest must be reborn eventually." He sighed deeply. "It hurts, doesn't it?"

Phae sighed and then cocked her head as Shion approached them. He sat down next to her. She noticed the look Annon gave him.

"What is it?" Phae asked the Druidecht.

"I'm sorry, but you look so different now." Annon leaned forward, gazing at Shion. "When we first met, in a grove of trees outside the Alkire, he tried to kill us all. I see the face, see the same scars, but it is a different countenance now. You were in chains before. I see that now you are free. How did it happen?"

"I can tell you that story," Phae said, looking over at Shion and smiling at him. "It is a scary story, Annon. I must warn you."

"I should like to hear it," Annon said.

"Before I tell it, there is something else you should hear first. Shion?" She held out her hand.

Her protector reached into his pocket and withdrew the golden locket. The firelight glimmered off its polished edge as he dangled it in front of him. A harmless piece of Paracelsus magic. Harmless, perhaps, but it was the magic that had begun to unravel the coils binding him to the Arch-Rike's service. He handed it to her.

Annon stared at it with great curiosity. Phae held the locket between her fingers, feeling the warmth of the metal. The shock of the dead Druidecht in Canton Vaud flashed inside her mind. The air was full of misery and suffering. Slowly, she opened the locket.

The haunting melody began to drift in the air. Almost in unison, all eyes turned to Phae, drawn in by the spell of the mourning anthem that somehow, in that moment, captured how each of them was feeling.

AUTHOR'S NOTE

One of the causes (or consequences) of being a history major in college is an innate curiosity of how traditions come to be. As I studied ancient and medieval history, the more I learned about an era, the more I came to realize how insufficient the historical records are at divulging all the nuances of the past. Historical witnesses often contradict each other, obscuring the trail of what really happened. Truths we cling to as historical facts start to squeal like rusty hinges as you open the doors of the past. There is so much we do not know about the world we live in. Even looking back five hundred years is seeing through a glass darkly.

The loss of memory (history) is one of the themes of *Dryad-Born*. I'm sure by now you realize that while Possidius Adeodat is an interesting historian, he is clueless about the depths of the Arch-Rike's machinations and often attributes the wrong motives to the people he is writing about. You have to take his biases into account as you read his words. So it is with history. We often take at face value a truth we have learned from someone else, but when we dig a little deeper, our understanding changes.

I have always been fascinated by the lore of Dryads, which come from Greek mythology, and based the Mirrowen series on a new interpretation of them. As always, I weave together elements to try to breathe new life into an older idea. Dryads in history are always associated with oak trees, for example. Mistletoe grows on oak trees as well. In many parts of the world, it is a tradition for couples to kiss under a sprig of mistletoe during Christmas holidays. Hence, the creation of the Dryad's Kiss ties together several traditions and ideas into something new and a possible origin of how the tradition came to be.

I apologize again for another cliffhanger ending. As I've said before, I tend to tell stories in a three-book arc. All will be revealed in book three. One of my all-time favorite reactions to the ending of *Fireblood* came from a friend of mine in Rocklin. I got several distraught texts from him while I was traveling across Nevada because of how things ended with Tyrus. He was especially upset because he has a hard time remembering plot points after finishing a book and waiting for the next would cause him to forget everything. He consoled himself with this concluding line, which cracked me up: *Perhaps I'll go around kissing trees in hopes of improving my memory.*

Until we meet again in Book 3.

GLOSSARY

Aeduan: A race from the southern kingdoms of Wayland and Stonehollow. They are primarily fair-skinned with dominant and recessive traits for hair color, eye color, and complexion. Many consider the Aeduan as mongrels because of the variety of their physical characteristics (hair color, eye color, skin tone). However, they have proven to be very adaptable and most resilient to the Plague. The Aeduan were the principal founders of Kenatos.

Boeotian: A race of tribes from the northern territories known as Boeotia. They have no central government, though purportedly revere an individual known as the Empress. They are nomads with no permanent cities and live off the land. They are strong and typically have brown or black hair and are prone to fight amongst themselves, pitting tribe against tribe. Their skin is heavily veined and tattooed, giving them an almost purple cast. They have sworn to destroy the city of Kenatos and occasionally unify for the purpose of attacking the island kingdom. Silvandom is the primary defense against Boeotia, for they have conflicting ideologies.

Bhikhu: A class primarily found in Silvandom and Kenatos. These are highly trained warriors that specialize in all forms of armed and unarmed combat and are trusted to preserve the peace and dispense justice. They cannot own treasure or items of value and treat life with the greatest respect. They are often mistaken as being cruel for they will punish and deliberately injure as a way of teaching their morality of painful consequences. The Bhikhu are typically orphans and nobility who have abandoned worldly wealth.

Canton Vaud: The seat of the Druidecht hierarchy, known as the Thirteen. These are the wisest of the Druidecht and they travel throughout the kingdoms to solve social and political problems and to represent nature in disputes over land. When one of the Thirteen dies, the remaining vote to replace that person from a promising Druidecht who will join Canton Vaud and travel to kingdoms solving problems.

Carnotha: A small marked coin denoting the rank of thief. Showing it to another ensures cooperation in an activity as well as access to information and illegal items. There are purportedly only five hundred such coins in existence and so in order to acquire a carnotha, one must steal it from another thief. They are carefully safeguarded and hidden from authorities. There is one carnotha that identifies the location of all the others and can determine whether one is a fake. The bearer of this one is known as the master thief.

Chin-Na: A lesser-known class found in Silvandom and only taught amongst the Vaettir and usually only to nobility. In addition to the martial aspects of the Bhikhu, the Chin-Na train their bodies to exist on very little air and have learned to harden their bodies and focus their internal energy to the point where even weapons cannot pierce their skin. As such, they do not float but their attacks are so focused and powerful that they can strike down an enemy with a single blow that damages internal organs. Only the most trusted and dedicated to Vaettir ideals are allowed to learn the secrets of the Chin-Na.

Cruithne: A race from the eastern mountains of Alkire. They have grayish-black skin, ranging in tones, with hair varied from pale blond to coarse gray. They are easily the largest of men, in terms of weight, not size, but not slow or ponderous. The Cruithne are known for their inquisitiveness and deep understanding of natural laws and spirit laws. They founded the Paracelsus order in their ancient homeland and transferred its knowledge to Kenatos.

Druidecht: A class found in every kingdom except Kenatos. Those in Kenatos consider them superstitious pagans, though harmless. The knowledge of the Druidecht is only transmitted verbally from mentor to disciple. It teaches that the world coexists with a spirit realm known as Mirrowen and that the spirits of that realm can be communed with and enlisted for help. A Druidecht cannot heal innately, but it can enlist a spirit creature that can. When a disciple has memorized the unwritten lore and demonstrated sufficient harmony with nature and Mirrowen, he or she will be presented with a talisman that will enable them to hear the thoughts of spirit creatures and to be able to communicate back. The variety of spirit creatures is diverse and so Druidecht often only stay in one place for a few years and then move to another place to learn about the denizens there. The Druidecht are the only outsiders trusted by the Boeotians to enter their lands unharmed.

Fear Liath: A spirit creature of great power known to inhabit high mountain country. Their presence causes fog and fear to disorient and terrify their prey. There are no recorded descriptions of a Fear Liath. They cannot tolerate sunlight.

Finder: A class found in nearly every kingdom, trained to search for lost items or people. They can track prints, discern clues, and are often hired as bounty hunters or guides. Finders trained in the city usually do not associate with those trained in the wild.

Fireblood: An innate magical ability possessed by a lost race. The race purportedly is the predecessor of the inhabitants of Stonehollow and is much persecuted. They appear to be a mix of Aeduan with some physical resemblance to Preachán for most have red or copper-colored hair. Their race is impervious to the Plague and for this reason they are distrusted and hunted during outbreaks and their blood dabbed on door lintels, which is commonly believed to ward off infection to the household. The real name of the race is unknown, but it is said they can conjure fire with their hands and that overuse of such innate ability renders them permanently insane.

Keramat: A Vaettir word for the innate ability to produce miracles, such as healing, raising the dead, traveling vast distances in moments, and calming storms. The secrets of the *keramat* are zealously guarded by the Vaettir and have not been disclosed to the Archivists of Kenatos.

Kishion: A class originating in the island kingdom of Kenatos. These are the Arch-Rike's personal bodyguards and administer the city's justice on those convicted of heinous crimes, such as murder, rape, and treason. Only Bhikhu and Finders are chosen to be Kishion and are given extensive training in survival, diplomacy, and poison. They are unswervingly loyal to the Arch-Rike and to the ideals of Kenatos.

Mirrowen: A concept and possibly a location. The Druidecht teach that the world coexists with a spirit realm called Mirrowen and that the inhabitants of each can communicate with one another. The realm of Mirrowen is said to be inhabited by immortal beings, called spirits, with vast powers. There is little belief in this dogma in the larger cities and they consider the belief in such a place trite and superstitious, a way of coping with the regular horrors of the Plague by imagining a state of existence where there is no death. The Druidecht suggest there is ample evidence of Mirrowen's existence and roam the lands teaching people to be harmonious with nature.

Paracelsus: A class from Kenatos and Alkire. Enigmatic and reclusive, these practitioners of arcane arts study the records of the past to tame vast sources of power. Some Paracelsus excel at forging weapons of power to sell for profit in Havenrook. Others experiment with new sources of energy that they harness into powerful gems to be used by the ruling class. Most Paracelsus specialize in specific forces and phenomena and document their findings in great tomes that they contribute to the Archive of Kenatos. The Paracelsus Towers in Kenatos is the hub of their order though many travel to distant kingdoms to continue unraveling clues from the past.

Plague: A terrible disease that strikes the kingdoms at least once every generation, destroying entire cities and dwindling the population. There is no documented record of the origins of the Plague and over the millennia the kingdoms have drawn closer and closer together for the preservation of their races. Documents discovered in abandoned towns and fortresses reveal that there are complete civilizations that have been wiped out by the Plague and races that used to exist that no longer do. The island kingdom of Kenatos was founded to be a last bastion for civilization and to preserve all knowledge and a remnant of each surviving race.

Preachán: A race from the trading city of Havenrook. They tend to be short, brown or red haired, and have an amazing capacity for deductive reasoning and complex arithmetic. They also have a deep-rooted desire for wealth and the thrill of gambling. They employ the Romani to execute their trading system and are generally devoid of morals. The Preachán take pride that there are no laws or rules in Havenrook. Those who rule are the ones who have accumulated the most wealth and prestige.

Rike: A class who leads the island kingdom of Kenatos. They are often mistaken as a priesthood of Seithrall, but in reality they are more like academics, physicians, and lawyers. While many believe them to possess magical powers, their power comes from the artifacts created by the Paracelsus order. With such, they can heal injuries and cure Plague victims. They are frequently dressed in a black cassock, but the most telltale sign is the ring that they wear. It is a black stone that purportedly gives them the ability to detect a lie spoken in their presence as well as to compel a weak-willed person to speak the truth.

Romani: A class that has no country or kingdom. Romani can be of any race. They control the caravan routes and deliver goods between kingdoms with the strongest allegiance to the Preachán city of Havenrook. They are forbidden to enter or to operate within Silvandom. Romani are known for kidnapping and organized crime. Starting at age eight, they are sold into service at ten-year increments. Their value increases in age and training and usually diminishes with age and disability. Each decade of servitude corresponds with an earring that they cannot remove under pain of death. Their freedom may be purchased for a single, usually large, lump sum.

Seithrall: A quasi-religion existing in the island kingdom of Kenatos. The term is a transliteration of the Vaettir words for "fate" or "faith," as one being under the *thrall* of one or the other. While the Rikes of Kenatos do not suggest that the term connotes a specific religion, the populace of the city has given it a mystical quality as it is not possible to lie to a Rike who wears the black ring.

Shaliah: A class of Silvandom known for the *keramat* of healing. This ability is innate and comes from their closeness to nature and the ability to share their life force with others.

Sylph: A spirit creature of Mirrowen that is tiny and can travel great distances and provide healing and warnings of danger.

Talisman: A Druidecht charm, fixed to a necklace, which is presented to them by the spirits of Mirrowen upon achieving a sufficient level of respect usually achieved by the age of adulthood. The emblem is a woven-knot pattern, intricately done, and it purportedly allows a Druidecht to commune with unseen spirits.

Tay al-Ard: Spirit beings of great power who possess the gift of moving people and objects great distances in mere moments. It is considered a *keramat* to be able to induce such spirits to perform this feat.

Uddhava: A Bhikhu philosophy and way of life. It centers around the observation and discernment of the motives of others, and then acting in a way that validates or rejects the observation. Life is a series of intricate moves and countermoves between people and a Bhikhu who can make the observations and reactions faster than an opponent will win a confrontation.

Vaettir: A race from Silvandom that values life above all. They are generally tall and slender, dark-skinned, with black hair. They do not eat meat and seek to preserve life in all its various forms. Their magic is innate and the wise use and practice of it is known as *keramat*. When they inhale deeply, their bodies become buoyant and can float. When they exhale deeply, their bodies become more dense and solid and they sink.

ACKNOWLEDGMENTS

Many thanks to all the staff at 47North for their hard work and expert advice. I gratefully dedicate this book to my wife, Gina, for supporting my writing these many years and for all the editing sessions at Panera for date night where she provided many great insights into Phae's character and personality. Also thanks to my early readers for their feedback and encouragement: Karen, Robin, Steve, and Emily. I also would like to thank the fabulous Chris Cerasi whose input and guidance once again improved the story. And finally, to all my wonderful readers who have waited patiently (and not so patiently) for this sequel.

ABOUT THE AUTHOR

Jeff Wheeler is a writer from 7 p.m. to 10 p.m. on Wednesday nights. The rest of the time, he works for Intel Corporation, is a husband and the father of five kids, and a leader in his local church. He lives in Rocklin, California. When he isn't listening to books during his commute, he is dreaming up new stories to write. His website is: www.jeff-wheeler.com